The Buying Curve

Shirley,
Thank you for always
believing in me "mm"
you're the best!
Love always
Karen

The Buying Curve

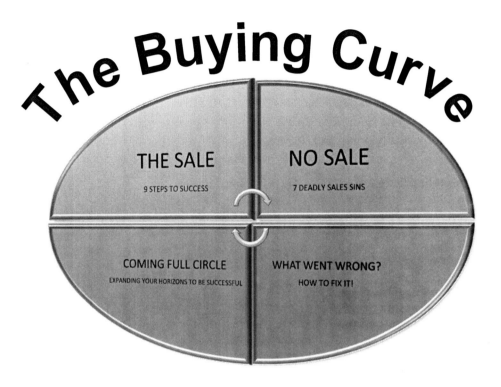

THE SALE

9 STEPS TO SUCCESS

NO SALE

7 DEADLY SALES SINS

COMING FULL CIRCLE

EXPANDING YOUR HORIZONS TO BE SUCCESSFUL

WHAT WENT WRONG?

HOW TO FIX IT!

HOW TO TRULY MASTER THE COMPLETE SALES PROCESS

David Fitzgerald and Karen Holden

authorHOUSE®

AuthorHouse™ LLC
1663 Liberty Drive
Bloomington, IN 47403
www.authorhouse.com
Phone: 1-800-839-8640

Published by AuthorHouse   01/30/2014

ISBN: 978-1-4918-4143-3 (sc)
ISBN: 978-1-4918-4297-3 (hc)
ISBN: 978-1-4918-4144-0 (e)

Library of Congress Control Number: 2013922391

Table of Contents

Dealing with Different Behaviors
Asking Basic Questions

SECTION 2—NO SALE

SECTION 3—WHAT WENT WRONG??

SECTION 4— COMING FULL CIRCLE

This book is dedicated to Eddy and Lori who left the presentation way too soon. R.I.P

Acknowledgements

Over the last 25 years there have been numerous influences that lead to the writing of this book, but throughout the 15 years it took to write this book, I must firstly recognize Karen Holden for her patience, professionalism, and friendship because without her this book would not exist. Big thanks to Robert Kistner and the Villa Group, Shari Levitin and her staff, Ivan Kurtz (his 20 years of partnership, friendship and inspiration) all the sales people and managers I have had the pleasure to work with throughout the years (sorry I was a tad intense sometimes). Thank you to my family in England for their support, Maru for motivating me to finish the book.

To Lori who passed away during the writing of this book. To my children, Liam, Sofia and Dominique, a very special thank you and my sincere apologies as I should have spent more time with each of you instead of being in the sales room.

Lastly to the Thousands of Prospects that I toured and allowed the experiences we shared to the understanding of the Buying Curve.

If we ALL knew everything . . . . no one would ever write a book

The Buying Curve

What exactly is a Buying Curve?

Through the years we know that schools have bell curves to evaluate students, we all have experienced learning curves, business schools teach S curves, supply and demand curves all to ensure success and profits for businesses—all types of businesses, but if you web search "buying curves" or even "business buying curves", you actually get pages of websites regarding women's fitness options. We hear the words "buying curve" used all the time, but if you cannot find it on a web search . . . , what exactly is a buying curve?

A buying curve is the process by which everyone, conscious or otherwise, follows in order to purchase something. Buyers go through a buying curve when they buy and sales people follow a variation of that specific process to get the buyers to buy their product.

A successful salesperson understands that the Buying Curve is designed to walk the prospective buyer through the necessary steps in purchasing their product. Each step of the buying curve, or sales process, is essential to overcoming people's fear of being sold, creating interest and desire with the end result of a purchase.

The Buying Curve is made of two important aspects—the most important, The Sale and the most frustrating, No Sale. As you can see by the curve chart below, each aspect contains various steps that will either gain you a sale or lose your sale.

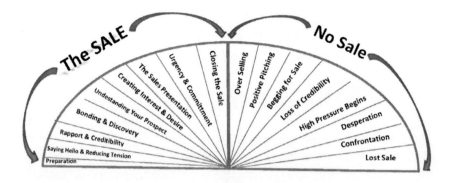

No matter what you are trying to sell—from a clunker to a castle and everything in between—there's a buyer out there for it. Somewhere, in fact, there are likely lots of buyers out there for it. The trick is—as the seller—to unconsciously use the Buying Curve and understand what will motivate the buyer to buy and, more importantly, for you not get in the way of the sale.

For a good long while . . . more than 25 years, I have been selling timeshare and been very good at it—generating almost 1 Billion dollars in sales. Having spent decades observing what works and what doesn't work in every sales situation possible. I have also seen the industry morph from a basic buy a week a year program into a multi-faceted, multi-option, socially aware product which can meet the needs of any potential buyer. In this book, I share it all with you.

This is not a sales motivation book, as there are thousands of them already out there. This is the real deal. After years of providing sales training workshops around the world on understanding the steps of the Buying Curve, I have now given in to the many requests of writing this book as a guide to helping all types of sales personnel. Whether you are a rookie wanting to learn the right sales habits, or you're lost and need a new style, or you're very successful in your field and need a reminder of what made you great.

In the chapters that follow I will break down all of the steps of the Buying Curve, both the Sale and No Sale, but I will also include chapters on how to fix what went wrong and expand your horizons to be successful and be a leader in your field by coming full circle back to being prepared for your next sale.

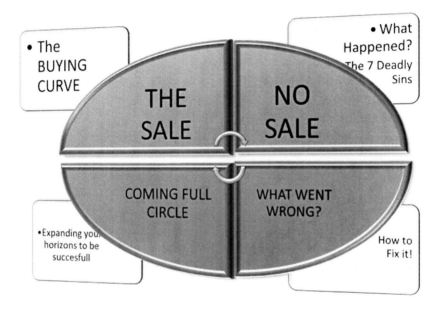

SECTION 1

- The BUYING CURVE

THE SALE

1

Preparation

"Chance favors the prepared mind." This famous philosopher's line is quoted time and time again but it still rings true each and every day. The process of preparing the mind must include attitude, aptitude, people and selling skills, as well as product knowledge. If you are not properly prepared, you are not selling from a position of strength—you'll be on the defensive from the start. To achieve this, the first step to a successful sale is to be prepared . . . for everything and anything.

Would you agree . . . or does it sound a tad dramatic? Do you believe that YOU are prepared to close a sale? In my years as Sales Director, I have seen and still see salespeople who do not understand the importance of preparation. Without a solid foundation of preparation combined with the right attitude, you will crack under the weight and pressure of a sales career. A prospect or client's first impression of you can make or break the sale. Your body language, enthusiasm and mental state all create the foundation on which a sale will be built. Preparing an effective image will enhance communications with your prospect. Think of it as getting ready for a first date.

Preparation is doing everything necessary to completely focus on the task of making a sale. All other obstacles must be eliminated. All successful salespeople prepare themselves mentally and physically every day. Good preparation gives you an unfair advantage over your competition and your prospect. Believe me when I tell you that your prospects prepared themselves before they met you, so why not be prepared to be in front of them? Preparation leaves nothing to chance. Only you, your prospect and your knowledge of the buying curve to close a sale should be factors.

Monitoring how you look, eat, sleep, dream and think will create an air about you that encourages positive things to happen. If you have a poor attitude or are not groomed professionally, your prospect will form a negative opinion of you. Why would you subject yourself to having to change that impression and then do your sales presentation?

Do you have a routine for preparing yourself every day? Establishing one will do wonders for you confidence. In the next few pages I will cover the basics of preparing to make a sale. The way in which you promote yourself is directly proportional to your sales statistics.

There are four types of preparation to consider—physical, mental, common sense and attitude. By understanding these fundamentals, you can gain a huge advantage over your prospect and your competition.

Let's begin with the easiest . . .

PHYSICAL PREPARATION

Do you look professional? Do you take pride in your appearance? Are you a positive reflection of your working environment? Looking good makes you feel better which gives you one hundred percent more confidence. The personal impact that you make on a prospect is vital to your success as a salesperson. People are comfortable with people who are a reflection of themselves. People are also impressed by neatness, cleanliness and simple, tailored clothing. If your prospects see that you are dressed for success, they are more inclined to believe you are a successful salesperson. Everybody likes to be associated with a winner. Were you aware that positive first impressions can help eliminate objections?

DRESS FOR SUCCESS

1. Clothing should be clean, neat, pressed, dry cleaned and in good repair. In order to avoid a morning scramble, coordinate outfits and iron in advance. Do not wear anything that is unnecessarily

flashy or showy. You should dress appropriately for your business environment.

2. Shoes also make an impression. Make sure that they are clean, shined and in good walking order. Have you ever seen an executive in a $1,000 suit wearing a pair of scuffed, curled-toed loafers? What kind of impression did that leave on you? Women should wear pumps or a moderate heel. If your sales position involves a lot of walking, your shoes should be comfortable.

3. Avoid an abundance of jewelry. It is distracting to the prospect. Successful salespeople normally wear a watch, one or two rings, possibly a necklace and earrings on a woman. If your jewelry is too flashy, your prospect will think you are self-centered and only out for yourself. They want you to have consideration for them.

4. Maintain good oral and dental hygiene. Brush your teeth in the morning before work and during if you are able. If not, use mints or chew gum (not in front of the prospect). If you smoke, use a breath mint before you introduce yourself to your prospect.

5. Maintain good personal hygiene. Bathe or shower daily and use an antiperspirant or equivalent. Make sure that your hands and fingernails are clean and manicured.

6. Your hair should be neatly groomed or styled. Try to avoid radical hair styles or colors as these trends are offensive to most potential buyers unless you are selling in that type of environment.

7. Make-up should be tastefully applied. The days of heavy blue eye shadow and giant red lips are gone. If you use cologne or perfume, be light-handed.

8. Hide the tattoos if you can. There are a considerable number of conservative buyers who will not trust anyone with a tattoo. However, if you have a tattoo-laden client, roll up your shirt sleeves to create commonality.

9. Here are some basic dressing guidelines:

Women: Wear dresses, suits, skirts or pants with a tailored shirt or blouse. In tropical areas more lightweight and colorful clothing may be worn, including sandals.

<u>Men</u>: Wear suits if you feel comfortable in them or if they're an employer requirement. Otherwise, a tailored shirt and pants are appropriate. Remember a belt, socks and sensible shoes. In tropical areas more lightweight polo type shirts and Dockers style pants can be worn. Shoes may be closed sandals or light loafers. Ties are optional depending on your working environment.

STAY FIT

If you eat healthy food, you will be healthy. If you live on junk food, let us hope your metabolism is good to you. I do realize that most sales environments doesn't always encourage a good diet or exercise routine. This is especially true due to the long hours of physical inactivity (sitting on tables or just waiting for a prospect or if you do telephone sales) and eating off the buffet tables, take-out or vending machines. If you take the time to have a nutritious breakfast each morning at home, you and your brain will have the energy needed to do your job. If you do not eat properly in the morning, you will find yourself tiring very quickly and becoming inattentive with your prospects. You may also focus on eating during the discovery process instead of listening for how to sell your prospects.

You should try to do some form of physical exercise. This will give you high energy, and you will be more confident, enthusiastic and effective on tables. Walking around or touring with your prospects is not considered enough exercise to maintain optimal health. Top producers go to the gym, run, swim, play some sort of sports and practice yoga or the martial arts.

This next type of preparation is a little harder for some people rather than others, but again, is necessary to building up a strong foundation for your sales.

MENTAL PREPARATION

1. <u>Sleep well</u>. Confucius once said, "Do not let the sun go down on your anger." This is so very true. Have you ever gotten a good night's sleep with something on your mind? My guess is no. I'll also bet that upon waking the next morning, you were not only tired but still angry or upset. How effective can you be after a poor night's sleep, especially when you find a well-rested prospect in front of you the next day? Ask yourself whether or not your problem is so significant that it would affect you next year or in ten years. If the answer is no, forget it and have a good night's sleep. If the problem is that serious and life altering, you may have to deal with it before you go to sleep. If you do not, it will affect more than your ability to make a sale.

   You need to be at your 100% best in sales. Most successful salespeople go to bed early and rise early. Try going to sleep an hour earlier and see what a difference it makes. It is important that you are not enticed by the, "Wow, I made a sale after only two hours of sleep, and I was hung over." In this situation your awareness of your state of mind stimulated a character conducive to a sale and you got lucky.

2. <u>Dream well</u>. Dream or visualize yourself walking your client out the door with your product or service. If you cannot dream or visualize all the steps of the sale, what chances do you have in getting one? Dreams of selling will also provide you with a good mental attitude. Think of how the sale made you feel? How much money did you make on it? If you repeat this dream often enough, you will rise feeling confident and well on your way to making a sale during waking hours.

3. <u>Think well</u>. The third important aspect of readiness is to mentally prepare. You have to have one hundred percent confidence in your ability to make a sale yourself and in your ability to handle any objections thrown at you by the prospect. *Remember, what you think is what you believe <u>and</u> what you believe stimulates your actions.*

7

Common Sense Preparation

Besides preparing physically and mentally, we need to do some commonsense preparation in order to be successful in sales. Commonsense preparation is similar to building a home. You need a good solid foundation on which to support the structure. The physical and mental preparations are the bricks and mortar of the foundation and common sense is the labor that puts it together. Below are some commonsense ways to prepare:

1. Realize that preparation happens every day. You have to sleep, dream and believe you can succeed at all times. If you can visualize it, you can achieve it.
2. Train yourself by pushing and practicing, learning and creating more skills. Prepare yourself in a fashion of going forwards in your career. To be a success in anything, you need to practice repeatedly. There is not one professional athlete who has made a name for him or herself without much hard work and practice. If you want to be in the top five or even ten percent, you need to be continuously growing.
3. Repetition and practice do go hand in hand. You can practice a particular task until you learn how to do it, but you repeat a skill to perfect it. For example, you can learn a new third party story and practice it until it sounds credible. However, until you can incorporate the story into your sales presentation exactly where you need it in the same way every time takes repetition.
4. Actions speak louder than words. The way in which you promote yourself through appearance and gait speaks volumes over what you say.
5. Know your product. If you are asked a simple product question to which you do not know the answer, it will directly affect your credibility. Learn what you need to know in order to promote your product or service effectively. Read through all of your company's paperwork so that you are not embarrassed or surprised by anything your prospect may say or ask. Knowledge is power. Know when to use it effectively. People buy on feeling, and if you cannot answer a question smoothly, they will not have confidence in you.

6. Be on time for work. Nothing shows a greater lack of respect for your employer, your co-workers or yourself than being late. Always allow yourself enough time to arrive at least fifteen minutes early. Use that time to relax and become mentally focused on making a sale.

7. Focus on your work while you are working. You should try to avoid socializing, especially around people who will negatively influence you. Be available to take tours or assist others in getting deals down. Tell your manager when you are going for lunch, and ask permission to leave at the end of the day if it is a requirement by your company.

8. Read industry magazines, trade publications or other educational material if you are just sitting around waiting for a prospect.

ATTITUDE

This is the biggest part of your sale process and the hardest to achieve. Abraham Lincoln once said, "If you would win a man to your cause, first convince him that you are his sincere friend."

To do this you must project yourself as a caring and sincere person whose only desire is to help your prospects. Sales depend on your daily attitude towards how you approach the job at hand. Your income and success are based directly on the amount of effort and attitude that you exert. This includes the amount of desire and determination you have. Your attitude is *the* one hundred percent governing factor that will determine your sales success. If any one thing will assure you of success in sales, it is your attitude.

Unfortunately, in sales, the hardest thing in the world to keep constant is your attitude. Believe it when I say, *closing is an attitude*. You may look good and feel good, but if you do not have a positive mental attitude you will not make a sale. Sadly, you cannot buy an attitude. It is a lot like the chicken and egg theory—people need the right attitude to make a sale, or do they need a sale to get the right attitude. Which comes first?

Because attitude is the most important and one of the most difficult topics that I will cover, I have strategically broken it into parts and have placed them throughout this book. Right now, I will cover the basic aspects of what makes up an attitude. In other chapters I will examine how your attitude affects your sales, motivation, goals, strengths and weaknesses. From my very first selling experience and from many others that have followed over the years, I know that a sale simply does not occur unless a good attitude is present. Once you have read, understood and applied all of my insights on attitude, you should be empowered with the best opportunity of writing a sale when you go out and work with a prospect.

What is an Attitude?

By definition the word 'attitude' means *"a way of thinking or behaving."* Generally speaking, an attitude is the way you communicate your moods to others. When you are happy and optimistic you transmit a right attitude and people respond favorably. People will go out of their way to avoid you if you act depressed, pessimistic or have a negative attitude. Remember, bad breath and a bad attitude will give you exactly the same results—No one will ever tell you that you have it, but everyone wants to keep away from it, and you.

'Attitude' has also become one of the most popular and overused words on the planet. Just remember that an attitude is the easiest thing to get and even an easier thing to lose. It can be your best friend or your worst enemy. It will destroy you if you let it, or you can learn to manipulate it to earn you more money than you ever imagined. To better help you understand your attitude, take a few minutes and imagine yourself as a manager interviewing potential salespeople. What attitude traits are you looking for in an employee? Once you have determined what they are, ask yourself how many of them you possess.

FIVE ELEMENTS OF A GOOD ATTITUDE

Think of your attitude as your perception and interpretation of the world around you. You can either see situations as opportunities or problems. The same applies to sales. Do you see your prospects as opportunities or do you fear them? By learning to emphasize the positive and discouraging your negative thoughts, you are then better able to deal with all aspects of your life.

The first step to emphasizing the positive is to incorporate the following five elements into your daily life:

1. <u>Positive mental attitude</u> Keep your mind focused on positive matters so that you're better able to deal with difficult challenges and choices. A good Positive Mental Attitude (PMA) triggers electric and contagious enthusiasm from those around you.

2. <u>Belief or Confidence</u> Believe there's a sale on every table. One of the biggest obstacles that salespeople have to face, particularly in the timeshare industry, is that you have to believe that there is a sale on every table. No matter what the prospect says or does, you have to believe it. Belief and confidence are essential in the sales process.

    If you allow yourself the pleasure, and it is a pleasure, of pre-judging your prospect to determine if there is a sale on your table, then you will have a very frustrating career. You have to believe in your prospect, no matter what their personality appears to be. I understand that some people are very difficult to like, but I am sure that there are also some people out there who find it difficult to like you, but for whatever reason they try. So never pre-judge your prospect because it may be <u>your attitude</u> that is determining <u>your *altitude*</u>.

3. <u>Goals or Desires</u> Being goal oriented means that you have a burning reason and desire to succeed whether it be recognition,

monetary, competitive, acceptance, self-satisfaction, ego or achievement. Motivate yourself every day to push for every sale.

4. <u>Enthusiasm</u>: Transmit enthusiasm for your product. Everything about your physiology, from voice to eye contact to body language must display your sincere feelings and belief in yourself and the program you're showing. The key element to selling is your enthusiasm, and it accounts for more than half of your closing ability. By transferring your enthusiasm to your prospect, you are transmitting your own emotional belief in your product. This creates a solid credibility foundation for product performance.

5. <u>Commitment or Focus</u>: Quite simply put, what are your commitments and dedication to your sales career? Do you consider it just a job or are you prepared to settle for nothing less than the best that you can achieve

Having a good PMA (positive mental attitude) by itself is not quite enough to help you excel in a sales environment. To excel to a master level you need to combine a Positive Mental Attitude with Belief (Confidence), Goals (Desire), Enthusiasm and Commitment (Focus). When you do, an unbreakable commitment to achieve your goals is launched by your unquestionable belief that anything is possible. The five elements work together to create a strong and confident attitude.

In summary, preparation is the ability to completely focus on the task at hand which is making a sale. You need to prepare yourself mentally and physically to give yourself a distinct advantage over your prospect, your co-workers and your competition. Use common sense. By living well and thinking positively, you will act like a successful salesperson and BE successful as a salesperson.

The definition of LUCK is PREPARATION meeting OPPORTUNITY.

2

Saying Hello & Reducing Tension

Remember, you never get a second chance to make a first impression." This may be a very old saying, but it is one that remains true to this day. First impressions are potent and cannot be ignored. Yes, your prospect comes to you with a preconceived notion of you and your industry. That is why it is so very important that your greeting leaves the right impact on them. Those initial few seconds when you greet your prospects are where they will not only form their impression of you, but one of your company and the industry that you represent. A prospect decides whether or not to look at buying that car, insurance program, advertising or vacation ownership with an open mind within the first <u>five</u> minutes. The greeting serves to create the correct mindset in the prospects and initiate your credibility.

Prospects or customers want to do business with an industry professional. They notice everything about us from the way we dress, to how we shake their hand, to how we represent ourselves. They see this as a reflection of the company and what they can expect after becoming a buyer or owner. By being a professional, we are showing the professionalism of our company. Do not let your customers wait! This does not reflect how busy you are, but how inconsiderate you are being.

MEETING—FIRST IMPRESSIONS

<u>Why do salespeople have so much trouble saying hello and/or greeting a prospect?</u> I have to say, unfortunately, that salespeople have a tendency to pre-judge the prospect. From that first look their whole demeanor and attitude changes so that by the time they reach the prospect to

introduce themselves, they have quite literally talked themselves out of the sale or vice versa.

Why do salespeople pre-judge their prospect? Fear of the prospect disliking them, not listening to them, not being able to buy based on their appearance and, ultimately, being rejected. Interestingly enough, not only do salespeople fear and hate rejection, so do prospects. So, what then ends up happening during the greeting, is that either or both the salesperson and the prospect have pre-judged each other, and formed a first impression of mutual distrust and dislike.

Many years ago, one of my old managers used to say, it does not matter whether the prospect is eight to eighty, blind crippled or crazy. There is a sale in the making. The more rejected by society their first impression (appearance) creates on you, the easier it is to sell them; why is that, because, no one had ever paid them any attention before.

Never pre-judge a prospect because you need them to form a positive first impression just as you need to form the same impression of you.

How can you mentally form a positive first impression? You can create a positive first impression when you initially meet your prospect by BUYING THEM. Take the time to visualize the prospect—physically, mentally and audibly. This can be done in the first five or ten seconds. It is important that you do this so that you can understand their fear and tension level before you meet or greet them.

Following are four attitudes that you should take into consideration before meeting and greeting a prospect. All it will take is five seconds to say to yourself:

On the POSITIVE	or the NEGATIVE
I TRUST this prospect	I do not Trust this prospect
I UNDERSTAND this prospect	I do not Understand this prospect
I will LISTEN to this prospect	I will not Listen to this prospect
I will ENJOY being with the prospect	I will be WASTING my time

If you do not have ALL four of these statements <u>as a positive,</u> what possible reason would any prospect have to listen to you, or ultimately buy from you? Why would you want to continue if any one of them is negative?

When your prospect meets you what do you think, they are thinking? I will guarantee you it has nothing to do with the business you are talking about. They are preoccupied with their fears, problems, health, job, kids, their world and how to get out of being hooked into being sold a condo, a car or anything that involves participating in the sales presentation.

GREETING—THE ETIQUETTE

<u>A good, strong (not overpowering) greeting should be designed to get your prospect's attention and break their preoccupation.</u> If you fail to get your prospect's attention, they will not listen to you and you will never get past the greeting stage.

Be polite, courteous, respectful, relaxed and light hearted. Show genuine concern and sincere warmth to your prospect and you will have begun the bonding process by establishing communications.

THE APPROACH

Do not run at your prospects when you are approaching them. There is a fine line between bowling them over with enthusiasm and scaring the shit out of them. A respectful, somewhat subdued greeting is best. You will find something that you have in common or a character trait that you love about your client very shortly. That's when your award-winning smile and enthusiasm can come out.

Before meeting your prospect, take a few seconds to clear your mind and focus on making the sale. Visualize yourself as relaxed, calm, positive and in complete control of the sales process. Visualize all steps of the sale. Take a deep breath in, exhale and smile. Walk, head held high, in a confident and self-assured (not cocky) manner. Stop walking when you are approximately one to two feet in front of your prospects, face them directly and extend your hand. This shows respect for their personal space and will not intimidate them. When you extend your hand they will invariably extend theirs so that you can shake. Say, *"Good morning. Welcome to [the name of your resort or company.] My name is [your first name]."* If prospects don't offer their names, you should ask, *"And you are?"* Proceed with a welcoming, *"Follow me please,"* and lead them toward the location where you will present an intent statement.

THE HANDSHAKE

So what makes shaking hands so important? Handshakes create a foundation or basis on which communications are done. For centuries people have greeted others by shaking hands. In more ancient times it meant, "I come with no weapons, in peace and with good intent." As time progressed business was done on a handshake, conveying mutual trust and respect.

So why is it that so many people do not shake hands correctly? Well, historically, fathers taught only their sons to shake hands, not their daughters. Women were not permitted to shake hands because it was considered an inappropriate behavior. Instead, gentlemen would kiss their gloved hand and other women would kiss their cheek. Well, times have changed and handshaking has come into its own psychological realm.

Dominant handshakes are very common amongst men, business people (male or female), and defensive men trying to gain control. Handshakes still are perceived as firm, well-executed, and the palm above the receiver's. Most dominant people use this type of handshake to determine the 'stuff' of their opponent. This type of handshake gives the impression of, "I am in control," or, "I am better than you are." As a salesperson you should not want to make this impression, especially not in the greeting stage of a relationship.

To execute a good, credible handshake, take your client's hand gently, yet firmly, and connect your hand with theirs at the joint between the thumb and forefinger. Hands should be even with palms facing each other. A good quality handshake is done with two or three (at the most) modest pumps.

If you are a man, shake the man's hand first, then the woman's and vice versa. Not only is this the appropriate way to greet a couple, but it shows respect. If one of the group members is very dominant and their hand is thrust at you, shake it first and then go to the others. You should try to shake hands with everyone in the party, including older children. Everyone appreciates being recognized. Do not give a double-clasp handshake. It will make strangers feel very uncomfortable and distrust your intentions. As you can see, shaking hands correctly is very important in any relationship. Practice doing it well and inoffensively and you will earn tremendous respect with your prospects.

Other than shaking the hands of everyone in your party, there should be no personal contact . . . no air kisses, no kisses on cheeks, ruffling of the children's hair, touching arms or other body parts. You do not know these people yet. Do not invade their space. You have to earn the right. Allow a few seconds to let the prospects absorb you and adjust to their surroundings. Do not take this opportunity to fire a bunch of questions at them. Ask simple, unthreatening, general questions to start the warm-up process such as, *"Where are you from? or What do you do for a living?"*

When you have gotten your prospects' attention and reduced their initial fears and stress levels, they will start to like you and, most importantly, listen to you. You have only thirty seconds to make that positive impression. Use your meet and greet time effectively.

REDUCING TENSION

In all sales type environments, but especially the vacation ownership industry, the biggest preoccupation of many prospects is fear. They are either afraid you are going to sell them something they do not want, or worse, lock them into a room or bully them until they buy something. It is this fear and the stress associated with the fear that you need to reduce with the greeting. Therefore, the main purpose of your greeting is to reduce that stress in your prospect, which also reduces stress in you.

Besides the fears of both parties, there is also additional stress when meeting a stranger. This stress can be debilitating. When people are under stress their hearing is one of the first sensory functions which gets blocked. So, if stress can block your prospects hearing capacity, how are they going to listen to you? Since listening is vital to the sales process, this stress must be reduced or eliminated.

Following are Ten Ways for Reducing Prospect Stress:

1. Set the tone or mood of the presentation by SMILING and being RELAXED. If you are stressed out, they will become more stressed out on meeting you.
2. Mirror your prospect. Be a chameleon. You should be sensitive to every prospect character that you meet. If your prospect believes that you are like them, then they believe that you will be able to understand them. Remember that only seven percent of effective communication is through your words. So, you are well on the way to making a solid first impression and ultimately a sale if you can mirror your prospect's body language and speech.
3. Along with being a chameleon you should understand that your prospect has similar needs to yourself. You need to make sure that your prospect sincerely feels:

   - under no threat or danger
   - welcome
   - important that they will be taken seriously
   - made to feel comfortable
   - that they will be listened to and understood
   - that they will get what they want
   - that they will not be wasting their time

4. Praise and compliment your prospect BUT you must be sincere. It is hard to be angry at someone who has just paid you a sincere compliment.

5. Always treat your prospect as though they were special. If you treat all of your prospects like owners you will never go wrong.

6. The first twelve words you speak to your prospect should include some form of the word *thanks*. For example, saying "*Thank you for taking time out of your day/vacation to talk with me.*" It makes them feel that you respect how they spend their time.

7. Do not greet a prospect with the phrase—"How are you today?" Their automatic response will be to say fine. However you do have to determine—did they really hear you, or were they just responding to a stock question? Stock phrases make you sound as if you are an automated parrot who is totally devoid of imagination therefore should not be used in your greeting. A successful salesperson is creative, so what better place to be creative, than in your greeting.

8. Listen to the prospect's name and use it to create a personal relationship. Once or twice, initially is fine, then strategically placed throughout the sales presentation to reaffirm the personal relationship. Anything other than that is considered annoying. If you have trouble remembering a prospect's name, mentally repeat it six times. It only takes a few seconds and will go a long way to cementing the bonding process. Another way to remember their name is to relate it to something or someone that you know.

9. Acknowledge everyone in the group, especially if your prospect is with family or friends. Ignoring family or friends may cause your prospect to become irritated at your lack of respect towards them. Remember that first impression. A second reason for acknowledging everyone is that you do not know which person will influence the buying decision. Never assume that the person doing all the talking is the decision maker, you may be wrong and usually are.

10. Greet people warmly and with a firm handshake while looking them in the eye.

Reducing Fear with an Intent Statement

Before the sales process begins, you need to straighten out the itinerary for the balance of the sales presentation. It is important that you outline all the steps of the presentation and get a commitment from your prospects to allow you to do your job. The last thing that you want is any confusion at the time of closing.

Most sales people know what an agenda or breaking the pact is; however in my experience it should really be called the Intent Statement. This Intent Statement sets the overall tone of the sales presentation. By addressing the different aspects of the sales process up front, you not only will reduce their fear and tension, you will put them at ease and establish control for the balance of the presentation.

The best analogy of what a prospect feels like goes something like this:

> *You meet a stranger and they say to you, "Follow me this way." They then lead you to a room where all the lights are off. They then say to you, "Okay, run to the other end of the room and turn on the light."*

Because you do not know what is in front of you, you take very cautious steps. You do not know if the wall is right in front of you or, if there is a hole in the ground or spiders falling from the ceiling. The fear causes you to walk very carefully and eventually you will locate the light switch. Conversely, if the power went out in your home, you can always find your way around. Why, because you have no fear of what may, or may not, be in front of you.

This is what your prospect is concerned about—their preconceived idea or fear of what is going to happen to them. They come into a sales environment feeling that there is going to be a surprise or high pressure and come anticipating it. Because they are anticipating discomfort, they are braced to fight (confront) or flee the scene (bolt). The last thing they're interested in doing is listening to you. Unless you can get them to relax you will be unable do your job. This is why it is very important to give them an idea, itinerary and your intent statement or intent of what is going to happen.

In the dark room analogy, when prospects do not know what is going to happen to them, fear becomes the forefront emotion. The greatest fear, shared by everyone, is the fear of the unknown. It is that fear of what is next that hinders your prospect's ability to go along with you. They will definitely resist moving forward. Therefore the intent statement is very much like giving someone directions. Now let's go back to our dark room analogy and consider the directions for turning on the light as an intent statement, we have no fear.

> *You are told that the room is ten feet long or that the switch is ten paces in front of you. The light switch is at arm's height when you get there. You will then count off one, two, three . . . nine, ten, reach for the switch and, wow, on come the lights. You are now comfortable in your surroundings as there are no surprises in your way.*

TAKING CONTROL

Your intent statement should also be designed to establish and take control of your presentation. Ask your prospects what they expect. Agree with them and let them know exactly what will happen. Expelling their anxiety is a great way of depleting resistance.

The intent statement should take more pressure off and defuse more of their tension and anxiety. <u>Do not let your prospect take control</u> at this point, as you will have a very hard time regaining it later. If you let them start dominating the presentation at this point you might as well just skip to the NO SALE section of this book because you will start justifying your presence, begging them to listen and most, definitely, start positive pitching your product or service. You never want to beg your prospects for anything. You should be taking control by taking the sale away from them. If you act as if you are begging, whether for their time or attention, they will assume control. Therefore the intent statement, designed to take away the pressure, helps you gain and maintain control. Much later in the sales process it helps to disarm the decision.

A secondary reason for doing an intent statement and establishing control is to create a solid foundation for the sales presentation. Unless you have a solid foundation you are just blowing smoke. If you waffle around the intent statement, or make half-hearted mention that they might, maybe, or possibly will have to do something today, they will take control away from you.

The intent statement is designed to map out the journey for your prospect. We all well know that without a map to follow, getting to our destination can prove extremely difficult. So we tell our prospect, "This is where we are going, this is how we are going to get there. Then at the end of it we give them their gifts, prize, tickets, deposit or 'pot of gold,' fair enough?"

THE FIRST YES

The intent statement is also designed to gain your very first YES commitment from your prospect. You need to get a verbal commitment from each prospect after outlining the steps of the presentation. The commitment you want is to allow you to continue with the sales presentation. At the end of your intent statement you should be saying, ". . . here we are right now. All I am asking from you is to let me get to there, is that fair enough?" Get a YES commitment. Do not move on with your sales presentation until you get a verbal OK. It is this first yes that should motivate and spark you with energy and enthusiasm to go forward with your presentation.

WHEN SHOULD YOU DO AN INTENT STATEMENT?

Is there a specific point at which you should do your intent statement? No, not as long as it's done <u>before</u> you begin your sales presentation. When you do it is entirely up to you, but I strongly advise within the first ten minutes. The most important thing is that you do one. Some salespeople do it immediately after the greeting whereas others will combine it with the warm-up. Whenever or wherever you do it, your intent statement should flow smoothly. It is very important that your intent statement be presented in a professional, confident and concise manner. You should have it memorized and it should only vary if extreme personality types require a change of wording.

THE SUBSTANCE OF AN INTENT STATEMENT

Keep your intent statement short, simple and sincere. Make it original. Use words that suit your personality. If you choose to use a co-worker's intent statement, rework the words so that they do not sound canned. Your intent statement should consist of the following:

1. A statement that makes your presentation sound fun and exciting. Grab their attention. Include a teaser statement such as how a part of the presentation will benefit them without telling them what it is. It is important that you neutralize any preconceptions that they may have by being up-front and sincere in your intentions (diffuse any apprehension).

2. Use statements that contain superlatives. Superlatives are words like most, the greatest, biggest, etc. For example, you can say to them, *"I am going to share with you the greatest way to enjoy your vacations."*

3. You should explain each step of the presentation and tell your prospects what will happen during that step. For example, *"When we tour the resort, I will show you . . ."* (Intent statement).

4. Use some form of empathy statement. Appreciate their objections but step over them at this point. Put yourself in your prospect's shoes. This shows them that you are sensitive to their needs. For example, *"I can appreciate how you feel . . ."*

5. Take the pressure off your prospect. Say a small takeaway statement such as, *"We understand that vacation ownership is not for everyone. However . . ."*

6. Tell them that you will be asking questions about their needs and wants so that you can tailor-make the presentation to benefit them. This statement will set up the discovery process.

For example, *"I will be asking you a few questions about how you presently vacation [insert or use your industry words] so that I can cater my presentation [product or service] to meet your needs and wants . . ."* (Expectations)

7. Use a statement that will get a verbal commitment from them allowing you to do your presentation.
8. Eliminate their wondering about their gifts or tickets. Tell them when they will get them.
9. Tell them that they will probably have questions about what they have seen or heard. This is a subtle way to plant seeds.
   For example, *"I know that after I have shown you around you will have questions. Everyone does, so hold onto them until . . ."*
10. Keep your intent statement short, simple and sincere. Make it original. Use words that suit your personality. If you choose to use someone else's intent statement rework it so that it does not sound like a canned speech.

By incorporating these ten points into your intent statement, you will reduce their tension and take away their fear of the unknown, set the pace for the presentation, neutralize anxiety and you assume control. Should your prospect, from this point on, try to "bolt" or leave, you can politely remind them of their commitment to you . . . to let you do your entire job.

If you find yourself having trouble remembering how an Intent Statement should flow considers the acronym **EASTER:**

E =	Empathy	"Thank you taking your time to . . . ."
A =	Agenda	"This will only take . . . . and what we will be doing is . . . ."
S =	Set Up	"I will ask you a few questions to get to know . . . ."
T=	Take Away	"We might not have something for you . . ."
E =	Expectations	"This isn't something that you have to decide today, you can still . . ."
R =	Results	"Even if we can't make a deal here today, you will still receive . . . ."

Side Note: If you meet a prospect who is appears overly friendly and excited, does not project any initial fear, skepticism or resistance— consider that they may be a sales "presentation" junkie or a "tire-kicker". A presentation junkie or tire-kicker is someone who likes to attend or listen to sales presentations just for the gifts or discounts <u>and</u> has absolutely no intention of buying anything. Find this out up front otherwise you may be faced with a too pleasant prospect who will give you a very polite—"no thank you" when you ask for the order.

Having now set the tone for your sales presentation you need to take the next step on the buying curve and learn how to create a rapport with your prospects which will lead to them believing in you, and your product—credibility. Without either, the sales process will become frustrating and most likely lead to the prospect leaving without having purchased anything.

3

Rapport and Credibility

As mentioned previously, your prospects arrive with varying levels of fear and they may appear to be quiet and unresponsive. Once you warm them up a little bit and begin to create some commonality and rapport, they will start to open up to you.

The warm-up is your time to make friends. By establishing rapport and credibility, preconceived notions and fears will be diffused. Once a foundation of trust is established, you will move on with the presentation process. During the warm-up you are not looking for any buying commitments. At this point you want to put your prospects in a receptive state of mind so that they'll let you do your job. The easiest way to make a friend is by discovering commonality. Find a non-threatening topic that you can both discuss.

Follow these tips to establish rapport and credibility as quickly as possible:

- Encourage your prospects to discuss something important to them. Find out what is important to them. ***Take the spotlight off of you***. People like people who are interested in them and who listen to them. (Salespeople have a tendency to talk too much about themselves. Rapport is better built through listening.)
- Find a commonality—through location (where they live or travel), contact, profession, and mutual interests.
- Find something to genuinely like about your prospects—no matter how difficult that may be. If your prospects believe that you genuinely like them, they will like you back. It is very difficult to dislike someone who likes you.

- <u>Talk about anything</u> but your product or service. People like and trust others who like the same things they do. Discuss the weather, sports, current events, etc.
- Mentally file away all the information you are hearing. You will use it later to assist you in making the sale. ***Listen for hot buttons***.
- Determine your prospects' character types. It will be essential that you cater your vocabulary to them. This will be explained in detail in a later chapter.
- Mirror your client subtly in mannerisms or behavior

RAPPORT—THE WARM UP

The purpose of the warm up is to establish rapport and reduce tension. The warm up is as simple as it sounds. It is your opportunity to build rapport with the client and to create a relationship. The Warm Up is critical in that this is we need to begin and build the trust and rapport necessary to engage the customer in a good honest discovery.

<u>Building Rapport is not Discovery</u>. Often when salespeople are in a slump and desperate for sales, they begin asking Discovery Questions and even begin to interrogate their clients to "see if they have anything". This will only raise the tension. In a Warm Up, your goal is to make a friend, not to qualify them! After all, how can you successfully answer questions before you have discovered what is important to the client?

During your general conversation you should find a subject that makes your prospects comfortable and relax. In most cases this is as easy as asking where they're from. Once they tell you, ask them something simple about that area. It might have to do with a sports team, recreational activities, hobbies or family. Your job is also to create some curiosity while building a foundation of a relationship. Give your prospects a sense of security so that they feel comfortable. When people are enjoying themselves, they will start opening up to you and even begin asking you questions about yourself.

Even though the main objective is to get them to talk about themselves, you must not remain a mystery to them either. Tell them a little about yourself—something that will make you as human as they are. Do this without letting the conversation stay on you for very long. Shift the focus back on them in any way you can. Express admiration for their achievements (good skiers or bright kids or job or anything that will let them brag about themselves). By boosting your prospect's ego, you are subconsciously making them feel important. They will believe that you genuinely like them. You as the salesperson should never brag about yourself or blow your horn with a prospect as it takes away any credibility that you may have started to build.

Remember, we all like to speak with someone who is really interested in us no matter how boring our lives may be. What you will find is that once you have found some common ground, prospects will keep talking and talking and talking. While they are doing all of that talking they are creating a very comfortable atmosphere for themselves. Even though you are not talking very much, they like you. The more you listen, the more that you look as if you care about them and the more they like you. You can only learn things about your prospect when you listen. When you talk, you repeat the things that you already know.

Finding common ground is a lot like taking turns—your turn, my turn. Each time it is their turn, make them feel as if they are the most important people in the world. When it is your turn to talk, they will listen to you. You will be surprised that the more you keep doing this, when it is their turn to talk they will be excited about it. When it is your turn again, they will say, "Yeah, go ahead. No problem," and let you continue. They would rather listen to the sound of their voices than yours, so when you are listening, do so with enthusiasm and sincerity. The more you listen to them, the more you are going to learn about them. This will give you more hot buttons to use in the back end. When they talk, you are learning. You are being empowered to move forward by doing absolutely nothing. **One of the hardest things to do in sales is to keep your mouth shut!**

This brings us back again to the reason that your prospects will not allow you to do your sales presentation. They fear being sold. They think that you are going to try to manipulate them into an embarrassing position and they will lie to get out of it. By doing this you are not creating a comfortable atmosphere. Initiating the sales presentation is the art of bringing your prospects gently to a point where they have enough momentum to trust you to forge ahead with the sales presentation. This is why letting your customers talk about what is important to them is so important.

Remember earlier I mentioned that everyone has a buying curve and part of that curve is how we feel. Well, just like you your prospects have feelings about you or your product. If they start to feel that they are not listened to or appreciated, they will become irritated. The more you make a client angry, the less of a friend you will make and the harder it will be to create the relationship that you need to close the sale. If you do not make a friend, your chances of making a sale slide down to zero. Remember, **your prospects buy you long before they buy your product**.

WARM UP TRAPS TO AVOID

1. <u>Do Not Interrogate them</u> At this point in the presentation process you should be using very basic, non-personal questions and sincerely listening to the answers. If you ask personal questions too soon up front, it touches a nerve in your prospect. You have not earned the right to ask them personal questions because they do not know, or trust, you yet.

    Do not confuse the warm-up with the discovery or relationship building process. You are just trying to find a way to communicate with them and warm them up to their environment. When you are communicating with someone you are breaking the ice and bonding. If you delve too deeply, too soon, they will stonewall you. Use general information, or first level questions that are simple, effective and non-threatening to your prospect.

2. <u>Do Not Sell</u> *Remember you are not looking for any commitments*. You have to be very careful here, because if you try to initiate a sales

presentation, or try to manipulate some sort of commitment in the front end, you will get a strong reaction—fear. Then fear will then come out in the basis of a lie, which is a defense strategy on their part. This tension will destroy any rapport or credibility you have built to this point.

> For example, in the timeshare industry when you hear that, say something like, *(Names), I can understand how you feel, and I really do appreciate you sharing that with me. So I guess based on your response I will not be looking at a new owner here today, is that right?"* Their reply will now be, "You are right about that." You continue, *"Well no worries. My job is also to get you to go on tours, attend our fiesta nights, eat in one of our restaurants, use our spa and . . . you see we are a full service resort. Even though you came for a sunset cruise, you might want to spend the day in our spa and eat dinner in our beachside restaurant. What I am going to do is sell you what you came here for, your sunset cruise tickets, and anything else you may want to discuss about our facility. It is up to you. Fair enough?*

Now your prospect is disarmed. What are your prospects going to say to you now, "We still do not vacation and we are not going to do anything while we are here?" No! Immediately go back to talking about something that is important to them. **Prospects will never lie about something that is important to them.**

3. <u>You should Never Give Away ANY Information</u> about your product or service. You give ammunition to your prospect to use for their purposes, not yours when you give information away about your product or service. Be very careful what you say and when you say it. Any opportunity or reason that a prospect can find to avoid the sales process, they will take it.

Here's another example: If your prospects say something like this to you, "So during these ninety minutes you are going to try to sell me one of these condos, right?" What is your immediate response to that statement? If you were to say, "Yes," what would happen? Fifty percent of the prospects would freak out and quit talking. If you said, "No," what would happen? Fifty percent would not believe you. Is there a response to that question? Yes, and it goes something like this: *"Are you looking for a condo?"* Invariably the prospect will say no. Then you continue, "Well, I wish that my job was just that simple, to sell you a condo. My job is to (see above about the tours/ spa/ restaurants . . ."

You must take the pressure off without lying to them. If you avoid the question, you will lose credibility. By dealing with the issue directly, you not only side-stepped a fear (temporarily) but you also avoided firing away any information you might need to tell them later on in the presentation. Do not let your prospect get the best of you.

4. <u>Do Not Pre-Judge</u> In the greeting section, I mentioned that one of the main reasons we pre-judge is to protect our egos. Our fear of the prospect's negativity causes us to regard them as not a suitable candidate so we treat them as such.

    If you pre-judge your prospect, they will shut down and not be the least bit cooperative with you. You then run the risk of them leaving the presentation with a sour taste for you, your company and the industry. Remember, you need to make a positive first impression, not a negative one.

Warming your prospect up is nothing more than putting the spotlight on them by asking them about themselves. By communicating with them you create rapport through commonality. By listening to your prospect, sincerely and with enthusiasm, they will like you.

Once you have the communication based on commonality and rapport, you should also have started building trust and credibility in order to create a good foundation for the relationship you need in order to make the sale.

BUILDING TRUST AND CREDIBILITY

Unfortunately, until your prospect trusts you, a sale will not happen either. If you understand this then you will realize that credibility stems from trust. You will gain your prospect's trust and earn credibility if you are sincere in trying to promote your product or service.

The easiest, and fastest, way to build trust is to listen intently to what your prospects are saying. Conversely there is no better way to lose credibility than to talk too much and listen too little. ***Successful salespeople do not dominate the talking, they dominate the listening.***

ELIMINATING CREDIBILITY ISSUES

- People buy you before they buy your product. Never forget this. Everyone, including your prospect, appreciates family values, manners and imperfections so just be yourself.
- Credibility is the number one reason that people do not buy your product or service. People will not buy anything if it sounds too good to be true. Furthermore, they do not believe that the sales person or company will follow through and deliver on all the promises made during the sales process.
- All prospects have concerns, doubts and misgivings about the any new product, and especially about the vacation ownership industry <u>and</u> your intentions or intent towards them. This is particularly true where prospects have considerable disposable income, are reasonably intelligent, travel a great deal and, in essence, are 'perfect' prospect. Therefore, to insure that you eliminate any credibility issues take away the pressure from your prospect in the front end. This is so important because it establishes primary self-credibility.
- Then later once they have adjusted to their surroundings and trust you, they will begin to trust what you say. Sales people will always have the majority of the self-credibility issues at the beginning. The "how long have you worked here, what exactly is your position with this company, how did you get this job, do you need a license" question. These questions, plus others, lurk

in the minds of your prospects when they initially meet you. They are analyzing you. *They are not even thinking about your product at this point. They will put you under a microscope to test your sincerity, integrity and credibility in your belief of yourself first, then your product.*

ESTABLISHING CREDIBILITY

In years long past, many salespeople started their presentations listing off their credentials, usually to their detriment. The descriptive monologue not only bored the prospect but gave little credence to credibility. It just sounded as if salespeople were blowing their horn and, as a rule, were never very startling or interesting. Keep in mind that your prospect may perceive your credentials as a negative, rather than a positive, so unless they have a direct impact on your product or services do not use them. For example a positive use of your credentials would be you selling educational materials and holding a degree in Education.

In today's world where everything is offered for sale in all types of media, getting the sale is ALL based on establishing credibility. This is essential. Selling in person, on a website or in social media, without gaining the prospect's trust and belief you will just be spinning your wheels.

Following are six ways to establish and maintain your credibility throughout the sales process:

1. <u>First Impressions</u> Remember, that your prospect's first glance at your appearance, attitude and personality leads them to a quick conclusion about your credibility.
2. <u>Let Them Vent THEIR Frustrations</u> Allow your prospects to vent their anger, displeasure or frustrations. Let them tell you how they have been ripped off or why all salespeople are conniving and untrustworthy. Encourage them to know that you, too, are angry at 'these people.' When you do this you will separate yourself from all other salespeople by being sympathetic and

sincere—that then makes your prospect like and trust you because now you are like them (mirroring your prospect).

3. <u>Who are You?</u> You should tell your prospect a little about yourself. A <u>general</u> history of your life, family or background by using third party stories, or a short story that covers the highlights is sufficient. Do not bore them. The purpose of your life story is to get them to feel comfortable and to let them know that you are a feeling, caring person, not an android. Remember, do not recite your credentials unless they will have a direct impact on how you handle that particular prospect. For example, if your prospect has a degree in Education and you do as well, then that becomes a common ground for conversation.

4. <u>Highlighting your strengths</u> as they apply to your prospect without appearing conceited. Your 'story' should be entertaining, interesting, amusing and credible. Do not make up anything to impress your prospect because you will be caught and instantly lose all credibility. The art of self-credibility is giving your prospect the impression that you need them to believe you and your product.

5. Once they have bought into your life, they will begin to share a little of theirs. Trust begins to form. You have trusted them with something important from your life and, in turn, will do the same from theirs. Listen and show interest in what they are saying. Because as you are listening to them you are building self-credibility in their eyes.

6. <u>Roll with the Punches</u> Another way to build self-credibility is to not appear that anything bothers you when they throw out an objection. They will buy into the fact that you feel very confident about yourself and, therefore, must believe in what you are doing, or selling. Each time you confidently let an objection roll off your back you will be gaining credibility with them.

7. <u>Be Consistent</u> Try to avoid contradicting yourself. Prospects feel more comfortable when they can anticipate consistent behavior from others. Concentrate on treating your prospect with honesty and sincerity and they will trust and believe in you.

8. <u>Remember, you are the Expert</u> Be confident and firm in your product knowledge. You are the expert. If you sincerely believe in your product or service, then they will come to believe in it.

Side Note: The product credibility issue comes later once you have created curiosity. If you try, shortly after meeting them, to begin your presentation the prospect is not listening to you. Why? Because they do not yet like you, trust you or believe you they do not believe you have a credible product. Product credibility is assumed after you have formed the relationship and they like, believe and trust in you. Once curiosity about your product becomes more obvious then you can, in appropriate junctures, insert the necessary product or service credibility. Unfortunately, I suspect, this scenario above, occurs more often than not, with a large percentage of sales people.

Remember, there has to be credibility in everything you say or do. Making one mistake, no matter how small, can prove fatal to your credibility. If you do make a mistake, admit to it and move on with the presentation. By showing a human failing you can regain any credibility that may have been lost.

"Get them Real, Get a Deal" and Keeping Credibility

For years I have said to my salespeople, 'Get them real, get a deal.' How can you expect to sell anything if your prospects are not being honest and forthright with you?

Fear is so commonplace in sales. Salespeople fear rejection and prospects fear the unknown. If you learned anything in the last section it is that prospects will do, or say, almost anything to avoid giving you honest information in order to prevent these fears.

Because they believe that this information will be used against them, they find it easier to make something up about themselves or their lives. I call it the 'custom lie.' While this is a natural defense mechanism for them, if you feed on it, then the lie gets bigger and out of control. Once the lie is out of control, even if a sale was possible, the prospect will not buy. Why? Because, they cannot extricate themselves from the web of compounded lies they have created. Even if they wanted your product or service, to protect their ego, they cannot admit their dishonesty.

So, to get them 'real' and avoid the 'custom lie' you should ensure that you do the following four things each time you start building rapport and credibility.

- Do not come on too forcefully when you meet and greet them. It scares them and puts them on the defensive immediately.
- Do not get too personal too soon. In other words, do not start asking personal questions until you have earned the right.
- Tell them how you became involved with your product or service. This is a follow up to your credibility story. If you own or use the product or service, then the prospect feels more willing to learn more about it.
- Reduce the pressure to buy anything through a take away. Cut them a deal. Tell them that you will not sell them anything if they do not want to buy anything. This alleviates a tremendous amount of fear and anxiety and will allow your prospects to drop their guard and relax.

Remember, you have to get your prospects 'real' because you need honest information from them to custom design your product or service to suit their needs, or dominant buying motives.

THE LENGTH

A typical Warm Up will last anywhere from five to fifteen minutes, depending on the client. As you become more competent, you will know intuitively when to move on to the next phase of the presentation. However, observing their body language can be tremendously helpful in determining when it's time to transition to the next phase. Also, if you keep answering objections every time one comes up in the warm up and cut off the dialogue, you will condition your clients to give you less information and shorter answers. You want all the information that you can get.

There might come a time during this process when a prospect may not allow you to proceed with your presentation. The most common, understandable, and true reason is that they are afraid of being sold something. Anything! Even if it's something they want! They think that you are going to try to manipulate them into an embarrassing position. And, remember, if they're in an embarrassing position, they will lie to get out of it. It's a very uncomfortable atmosphere for all concerned. You can only move ahead with your sales presentation when trust is in place.

Just listen, listen and listen. Let them talk. Gather information that will be helpful you as you begin to design your presentation around your client's needs and interests and eliminate their fear of being sold.

Remember get to know your potential customers by putting the spotlight on them. Ask them about themselves. Create a rapport through commonality. Do it warmly. By listening to your potential clients, sincerely and with enthusiasm, they'll most likely feel friendly toward you and you will begin to earn credibility. This is relationship building—a crucial step on your path to a successful sale and is covered in the next chapter—Bonding and Discovery.

4

Bonding and Discovery

Building relationships is not just an important aspect of making sales, it is a necessity. In any sales environments, such as car sales, insurance, retail or advertising and even vacation ownership, where everything offered is similar and competition continuously exists, salespeople must find a way to set themselves apart. Therefore, the salesperson must do everything they possibly can to form a relationship with their prospects from the very beginning of the sales process. This relationship must then develop throughout the buying curve and sales process, and hopefully continue throughout ownership of the product or service.

In the last chapter we talked of finding commonality, building rapport, of making a friend and ultimately, making a sale. So, therefore, in order to sell, <u>we must bond and form a relationship</u>. We learned that to find commonality and build rapport we needed to do four critical things. Those were to put the spotlight on your prospect, genuinely like your prospect, talk about anything other than your product or service and, most importantly, listen to your prospect. This is the next crucial step on the buying curve and without it, No Sale.

The discovery process is, without a doubt, the single most important aspect of the sales presentation but, amazingly, the most unappreciated by salespeople. When done correctly, the process reveals the dominant emotion that you will need to be triggered before prospects will logically justify the purchase of your product. Without the discovery, it is nearly impossible to know how to move prospects from their survival instinct state of mind to the emotional state that will excite them to buy.

BONDING—FOCUS ON THE PROSPECT AND FINDING COMMON GROUND

The building blocks of the relationship sale are found in conversation which leads to discovery. You will not, and cannot, find any common ground if you do not talk with your prospect. Your conversation not only helps build rapport and trust, it also establishes credibility in both you and your product.

The easiest way to initiate a relationship is by finding some common ground of communication. We do this by focusing on the prospect. It is important to always remember that <u>the prospect is the center of the buying process</u>. If you, as a salesperson, do not focus one hundred percent of your energy on the prospect, then there is, more often than not, mistrust, misunderstanding, miscommunication and, perhaps even conflict or confrontation.

Just as you must focus all of your energy on your prospect, you must form this at this stage of the buying curve. If you make no attempt to bond, or develop a relationship, your prospect will then think that you do not care and you will never earn their trust. If your prospect does not trust you, then they will never 'get real' or discuss their inner most feelings, desire or wishes with you. It is imperative that you understand that emotion and feelings close sales, not logic. Remember, you will always win logical battles using emotions.

How do you discover common ground? Ask questions. Find anything that appeals to them. Subjects that they just brush off or pay no attention to, do not talk about, or focus on them. In order to bond, you need to discover what is important to your prospects. I call this part of the buying curve the discovery process or FORM—Family, Occupation, Recreation and Motivation. This is where you extract information about their family, occupation, recreation and motivation. As they are talking you are listening for an emotion and thinking to yourself—how strong is this desire or what puts them into the emotional state they justify to buy. These are called a hot buttons, or dominant buying motives and motivation.

How can you determine what your prospect's dominant buying motives are? Well, what motivates you? By better understanding what your dominant buying motives are, will help you to understand what motivates your prospect.

WHAT IS A HOT BUTTON?

A hot button is the key to their heart. Hot buttons are emotional information. You, however, can also extract cold buttons. Analyzing your prospects hot or cold buttons, then storing them away in your memory, will allow you to determine which direction you will take in your presentation. Whatever the hot button is you have to <u>design or find a benefit</u>, not a feature that will be consistent with that hot button. When you know <u>what</u> moves them, then you understand <u>how</u> to move them.

Watch every subject that excites them. While they are talking, watch how their voice inflections change, their energy level, their enthusiasm, their animation and their body language. Whether they are talking about their family, their job, their favorite sport or anything that is enjoyable to them, you should be listening. Anything, and everything, that they respond to, either positively and negatively, you should hone in on automatically. 'Hey, that is a hot button, or that is a cold button.' These are subjects, areas, attitudes or emotions that your prospects hold close.

The greatest benefit of listening is that people will always volunteer additional information. What this does is opens up the opportunity to ask more questions and learn more about them. In the next chapter we will specifically learn how to further explore your prospects' emotions by using the art of relationship selling.

Remember, their hot buttons or dominant buying motives are emotions. **Without an emotion**, without this discovery process, without bonding, **without building a relationship**, without some sort of trust, rapport and communication between you and your prospect—**you will never make a sale**.

As we learned earlier, most prospects arrive for any type of sales presentation with natural sales resistance. They use defense mechanisms to put you off the scent. They exhibit rude, quiet, pleasant or aggressive behaviors. In an attempt to derail you, they may misinform you about their lives and habits. They may exaggerate or mislead you about the number or quality of vacations they have taken. We have all heard the stock phrases: "We are just looking", "We are thinking its' time to change 'something", "We like to stay with the locals," "This is a special vacation for us, and we will not be doing this again," "This is a once in a lifetime trip." They may relay all kinds of personal stuff such as how a job was lost or a divorce is pending. They'll say anything to justify this incredible defense strategy they have adopted. Relax. This is natural.

The main reason for defense tactics is that you have put your prospects into a position where you are asking them to consider or become involved with, something for which they have absolutely no desire or need. Their pact and mistruths are meant to diffuse or dampen your enthusiasm for them to buy your product or service. They want you to think there is no sale to be had. You either close your prospects or they close you. That is a fact of sales.

Without your enthusiasm for them to buy, or without your belief that there is a sale there, you promote your presence and your presentation without any "oomph!" If you believed that you had a deal with every prospect you met you would act in a completely different manner. It may be the same presentation, but your voice tone, physiology or your mannerisms would convey a different message. If you deliver your presentation with passion and sincerity, it will be a lot more intense and effective. This is the difference between making a sale now and again, or reaching or exceeding forty percent sales consistency and becoming a master closer.

There are also a percentage of salespeople who approach the sale with—I hope I find a hot button, I hope that they see some benefit and I hope they can make a decision. I hope this and I hope that. Hope in sales is for the hopeless.

A prospect can also deteriorate your energy level, enthusiasm and belief when they start lying. The discovery process is designed to prevent this from happening. How many times have you heard the phrase, "Stop right there, do not go any further we do not want to waste your time." Then it continues with, "We are not the sort of people who . . . do not get me wrong, we love what you have here (they have not seen anything yet) but we have other plans." Then you wanting to listen to their life story will become secondary. You have believed their lie and now do not want to listen to them because you do not believe there is a sale there. <u>When FORM and the Discovery are forgotten, then there is no sale</u>. To quote from the previous chapter, "Get them real, get a deal."

DISCOVERY USING FORM—FAMILY, OCCUPATION, RECREATION AND MOTIVATION

In that earlier chapter I mentioned FORM is the best method of discovery and by concentrating on these four areas. It is here you will discover an incredible amount of information about your prospect's character or personality. You will find out what makes them happy and sad. What drives them crazy and keeps them sane. You will find out how important family is to them, what they like or dislike about their job, what they do in their free time and what motivates them to get up in the morning. You are deciphering their attitude towards life and dominant buying emotions.

You work from the commonality that you have created up to this point to go into Family, Occupation, Recreation and Motivation. Without this information you cannot begin your presentation successfully. You need this information to give you the road map or GPS guide necessary to close the sale. Because without knowing what your prospect likes or dislikes, you cannot possibly start tailor making your presentation to suit them.

It is amazing how many salespeople may immediately say, "Yeah, well I know how to talk to people." Just by the sheer title of this chapter, some may have chosen not to bother reading it. You would rather me teach you a 'closing' technique. All of those so called 'closing' techniques are just tricks to manipulate prospects into certain buying situations. Unfortunately, most salespeople have been led to believe that those constitute the art of closing. Those are not necessary when the discovery process, using FORM, is done correctly.

So how, or why, does FORM work?

The process works not only uncovers hot buttons and reveals emotional angles to use later to close the sale, it also establishes a mode for your prospect to tell the truth. You want them to be honest with you before they are asked to offer information on their credit and money. You are probing for general information. You are establishing a rhythm.

When you ask them, ¨do you have a mother or a father and do they live near them¨ they will honestly respond. There is absolutely no reason for them to provide you with anything less than the truth when they are talking about family. In a very short time you can find that one has a mother who lives in another state and her father died. This is good, reliable information and, quite possibly, there is some heavy emotion there. In a later chapter I will cover how to uncover that emotion with good second and third level questions. You will get a lot farther by asking easy, relaxed open-ended questions such as, "Why are winter vacations important to you?"

For example, in the timeshare industry, if you had asked the question another way—"So, do you go somewhere warm each winter?" You will get short, non-information bearing responses. Answers such as, "No, this is our first trip ever or we won the trip" appear. What happens is that you have now blown yourself out of the water—not only are they lying to you, but they are also lying to themselves and devaluing their vacations. You have gone from one lie about their not vacationing, to them lying that they no longer even pay for them. What you have now done is set yourself on a destructive path. Your rhythm or pace then changes because you start thinking, 'that so and so is lying to me.' The more they lie to you, the less intense, the less enthusiastic and the less belief you have in your ability to close them so you give up trying.

The outcome is that using this type of Discovery process is designed to put your prospect in a mode to tell the truth. Much of what you see in your prospect on the outside is just superficial. Think of it as their life with make-up on: what is underneath is a different story and the key to the sale. Remember it is normally the last key on the ring that opens the lock.

<u>The next, important component on why FORM works is the gain of information that you can put in your memory bank to use against them later</u>. The more you learn about your prospect the better prepared you are at predicting possible objections.

COMMUNICATING WITH COMMONALITY BUILDS RAPPORT CREATING TRUST THAT RESULTS IN FRIENDSHIP AND COMFORT.

Technically, the discovery process is an extension of the warm-up process which we covered in the previous chapter. By using FORM, you have found some commonality with your prospect that has started a conversation. That conversation has now created rapport that grows into trust. With commonality, rapport and trust you will have now built a friendship with your prospect. Were you aware, just by being a friend is the highest pressure you can use on anyone? Imagine that. For example, try liking someone who does not like you, or better yet, try disliking someone who likes you. Both are difficult to do, and maintain for any length of time.

FAMILY The highest pressure that you can use is family. If you use this approach correctly your prospects can overcome many of their objections by agreeing with any proposal which betters the "family" unit. What will happen is that money will no longer become an issue. If you do hear the objection, "Well, I do not know if we could afford it," go into a third party story outlining another similar family situation. Alternatively, you can take that objection and pursue closing on it.

The first thing that we are trying to do with FORM is look for commonality. Right away you have something in common—just like you, your prospect has a family. Asking your prospect about his or her family is always a good place to start. If they are old enough, ask about grandchildren and see if they have any pictures with them. Remember, however, if there is a considerable amount of tension there, do not explore it further, move on to something else. I will put in a reminder here that not everyone responds to family emotions favorably. If there are no children involved, ask a about siblings or even the family pet which, in a lot of homes, are the 'children'.

What you are doing is really creating commonality by showing them that you are just like them—a caring, feeling person who has put themselves into his or her channel, so you can now communicate.

<u>With commonality you build rapport</u>. Commonality can be as simple as the siblings you have in common. You have not yet spoken about anything else—mom, dad, aunts, uncles, grandparents. We are bonding with the commonality we share. They no longer see you as this 'salesperson.' Generally, salespeople are normally thought of as androids—you are programmed to go out there, make a sale in a canned fashion and not care. When you show that this is not the case, they look at you as now being similar to them. You can show them, for example, that in Mexico restaurants love to accept kids, whereas in England most restaurants do not allow children. Then, when this guy says to you "hey, I would never go anywhere that would not let my kids in," you have learned some motivation about them.

There is an attitude here—if they cannot get his kids or family involved they are not interested. So later when you are presenting a benefit—you present topics that will involve his children. Show baby-sitting facilities, Disney World, children's programs, etc.

<u>OCCUPATION</u> You can immediately validate the information from survey sheets or questionnaires by asking them the question, "How is it that you make your living?" Never respond to an occupation with a statement such as, "oh, you're a librarian!?" It will come across almost on the verge of an insult and will kill any chances of a sale. Everyone, including you is very proud, or pretends to be, of what they do for a living or else they would not be doing it. Ask them if they work too hard. You

will most likely hear the response, "My boss just does not understand how hard I work." (Emotion)

We all work too hard. There is not one person out there who is being treated fairly, not getting enough recognition, support, opportunity, training or salary. Do you think that anyone else in this world thinks differently than you? We all do not make enough money, and there is always some "snot nosed young, university grad" who ends up being our boss because he or she kissed ass. I have heard many clients, over the years say, "Just because I was not the boss's favorite I did not get the job. I worked for that company for twenty years. It was not fair to give the job to some young kid fresh out of college." If you want to get a prospect emotional, ask them about their job.

From a recent survey of working Americans, it was found that ninety-two percent of workers disliked their bosses. This is an amazing statistic considering that they are the ones who promote them and pay them. Not to mention that they also hire them, train them, are in control of their destiny, will co-sign credit paperwork, you name it. Is it envy or unfairness that controls those emotions? Humans are never content and always want more.

RECREATION How does your prospect spend their free time? Recreation is a very positive thing. It is their fun time and, in many cases, their passion.

If they water-ski, ask them how to water-ski. You will be surprised when your prospect gets up from the table then scrunch down to demonstrate. "You see, the real secret to skiing is you have to kick back and keep your arms straight and . . . off you go." Do you ever get your prospects to actively participate in telling you how they do something? If you suggested to them, that on your day off, you would borrow a ski boat and you want them to teach you how to water-ski, this guy would think he had struck gold. "Wow, I have come on vacation and am going out on a boat, with a local, free and get to teach them how to water-ski, what a great vacation!"

What are you doing now? You are stroking their ego AND bonding with them. You are sticking even tighter to them and making it even harder for them to say no.

MOTIVATION This is the one that you are listening to, but your prospect is not going to be aware of it. You are not going to say, "Okay, tell me about your family, occupation, recreation and motivation!" You have to listen for it. You must find a way to stimulate and discover how ingrained the motivation is and how important it is to them.

Simply put, prospects primary motivation is any one the seven reasons listed below:

1. Gain or Profit—to make or save money or to get a good deal on something
2. Peace of Mind—family bonding
3. Pride of Ownership—the need to possess
4. Adventure—to enjoy life more
5. Fear of Failure or Loss
6. Desire for Approval
7. Love or Hate—which relates indirectly to number 3

Most people are motivated by number 1, gain or profit, more commonly greed, which is why get rich quick schemes are so successful. For examples, in timeshare, the main reason that your prospect is attending a presentation is a free meal, free stay, gift or discounted tickets. It may not sound like much incentive, but look at how many people enter contests or play the lottery—why? Gain or profit. Does it make sense? Not really, but it is a real motivation and comes to light under many different circumstances which is why salespeople find this as the primary motivation for buying their product or service. The balance of your prospects may not be there for greed but they are motivated by one of the other six reasons. The smallest percentage of your prospects will be motivated by love or hate. All prospects are motivated by something and it is your job to determine what motivates them.

Just by talking about a restaurant and the way they are served or the way a taxi driver drove. Any little thing that irritates or annoys them,

"You mean that you just got up and walked out of that restaurant?" "You bet your ass we did. I do not, and will not tolerate bad service from anyone." Your response, "thank you, I appreciate your being up front with me," will gain you more 'discovery' than you expected. To reinforce your 'service,' you can then tell them a third party story on how well your service personnel look after their members/owners.

What happens is that your third party story sells more value than your sales presentation. Watch the impact that your third party story had on your prospects and if it was positive you will use the same format repeatedly and again to enhance the idea of great service.

Finding some form of commonality does not have anything to do with a back end, high pressure sales presentation. All we are doing is letting our prospect feel that we care. While we are defusing the pressure of the sales environment, we are gathering information for value and emotional shticks and benefits that we can apply to their life.

Why does FORM work? It is the salvation for a closer. What eventually happens is you get to a point in your presentation where your prospect will say to you, "Enough about us—tell us about you?" or "How do these things work?" What happens is that your prospect will start the sales presentation for you. All you need to do is sit back and listen.

FORM is the foundation of the sales presentation. Use it—it is your friend AND will always create the relationship you need to make the sale. You uncover needs, desires and feelings by questioning skillfully and listening carefully. Your job is to identify the basic and secondary needs that your product or service can satisfy, only then you can demonstrate this fact to the customer. You can identify these needs by further breaking down each type of question into three levels.

First, Second and Third Level questions are designed in such a way as to elicit information from your prospect gradually. Whichever types of question you ask, you need to ask in all three levels. Through each level of question you earn more credibility and trust with your prospect, as well as gain more personal information. The three levels of questions are:

1. <u>First Level Question</u>: This is a fact question. The response will not have much emotion, but will be honest. For example, ask them, "Where is your favorite vacation spot?" "What is your favorite car/commercial/etc.?"
2. <u>Second Level Question</u>: These are based on the response to the first level question BUT there is some feeling behind them. For example, ask, "What was it about Bali (the car, the ad) that you liked best?"
3. <u>Third Level Question</u>: This is the emotional reason behind the second level response. The example here would be, "Why did that vacation in Bali mean so much to you?"

If you do not reach the third level, you will never identify the needs and emotions necessary to make a sale. The third level is always emotional <u>and</u> the buying motive. The emotional reasons now break down to either the Fear of Loss or the Desire for Gain.

Remember, as long as you are focusing all of your attention on the prospect they will answer your questions and become curious. Remember, closing can come from any angle. Ask enough of the right questions and listen carefully enough eventually you will find the emotion you need to explore.

Speaking of Listening

Throughout this chapter I have stressed that listening to your prospect is the key to making a sale. Listening is such a simple idea and the hardest one to grasp. There is no one who cannot do it. Information, incredible amounts of information can be gained by just listening and asking the right questions.

People love people to listen to them and prospects are no different. There is no one who has ever taken the time and sat down and listened to them. Remember, put the spotlight onto them. Really listen to them. When you are listening you are learning. By listening to all of their wants, needs, problems, fears, weaknesses and self-esteem issues, they come to trust you and consider you a friend. Now you are fully armed to sell them your product or service.

What makes listening so vital to the discovery process? By not listening to your prospect, one or all the following five things will happen.

1. You will end up presenting your product and confusing your prospect with everything that you know. Too much information can confuse your client that may cause them to be unable to make a decision. People would rather make no decision than the wrong decision. This is sometimes called information overload.
2. If you do not listen to them to find out what their problem is you will 'present' the wrong benefits or solutions to their 'problem.'
3. You will talk about so much 'stuff' that you will virtually create objections where there were none before.
4. If your prospect sits still and does not talk, they will not buy.
5. Your prospect will want to listen to you if you listen sincerely to them. This is important because they must want to listen to retain the information you tell them to become interested and ask questions.

Let your prospects do all the talking. Become a spellbound listener. Your prospects are not so rude that they will stop you, if you are doing all the talking. Your continual talking has absolutely no relevance to making the sale. Also, there is no reason for you to throw your two cents worth into their conversation. It is not important to either the prospect or to the mode of your presentation. When you talk you repeat things you already know. When you listen you learn things other people know. When you listen, you are in control.

Whatever turns on your client should turn you on, even if it bores you to death. Listen to them and take an interest, because sincere listening gains trust. Then later when you start asking insightful questions they will feel comfortable enough to answer them. You are looking for how your prospect reacts. What emotion or emotions tie them up in knots and will lead them to making a decision. Only then can you can determine how to mold your product to best suit their needs.

<u>TIP</u>: If you find yourself having a problem controlling your prospect, quit talking. Silence can be a powerful sales tool. Try not talking and see what happens. Besides, how can you not have control over a prospect when you know everything there is to know about them?

THE DEAL STARTS WITH YOU

Using FORM is something that you cannot learn from a book—its takes ATTITUDE! Sales are about having desire, dedication, focus and caring about serving your prospects with your product or service. This includes the burning desire to close them. How many salespeople out there really care about their prospects or clients? We all have prospects that we really like, but you need to make a point of liking every couple because then your chances of making a sale improve tenfold.

By the way, if you do FORM properly and still are unable to make a sale, just remember the secondary goal of the sales presentation. *Have your prospect leave your premises with a better impression of you, your product and the industry than they did when they arrived.*

WHEN SHOULD YOU START BONDING AND DOING YOUR DISCOVERY?

You start in your warm-up and continue throughout your entire presentation. Once you start, you can never stop learning about your prospect until they leave with their paperwork.

The discovery process involves probing. It involves getting people to talk about themselves. You need to interact with your prospects in such a way that they will emotionally open up and tell you all about themselves and their families. **You have to make sure that the questions you are asking them cover all three levels of questions—fact, fact/feeling and emotional.**

Before we can gain the trust and friendship of our prospects you must develop a relationship with your prospects by understanding the rules of a good discovery.

THE TEN RULES OF A GOOD DISCOVERY

Rule No. 1 <u>You must be Agreeable</u>

One of the biggest mistakes which salespeople make is they come off as disagreeable. Your number one priority is that you must be agreeable. You might not like that your prospects because they are motivated by completely different things than you. Never contest or confront your prospect by saying something such as, "You are a Lakers fan—give me a break—they are nothing but a shit team!" This guy may be the president of the Lakers fan club. He may have his house covered in their wallpaper or he might have left all his money to the team. You do not know that. So, unless you can be agreeable it is better to say nothing.

Rule No. 2 <u>Never Argue with a Prospect</u>

What purpose would it service to argue with a prospect? You will never sell to anyone with whom you are arguing nor, I will bet that you would buy anything from anyone who is arguing with you.

Rule No. 3 <u>Practice Acceptance</u>

Probably the hardest thing for a closer to do is to accept the way someone is. Accept your prospects for whatever or whoever they are. They might not like you either. By opening up and accepting them you will be surprised at how far you get.

Rule No. 4 <u>Smile!</u>

Smile all the time you are with a prospect. You can make the most high pressure, off the wall statements when you are smiling. Try this, the next time your prospect throws out an objection—smile at them and ask if it is real. They will more than likely say, "No, not . . . I said that because . . . (real objection)."

No matter what goes on around you or how rough it gets—SMILE. When you are laughing and smiling it is magnetic. Your prospects will also start to laugh and smile and have a good time. Surprisingly, so will most of the people around you. Why? Your positive physiology will cause your prospect to mirror image you. So, just by smiling you can out close your competition. Unfortunately, the second you quit smiling, the sale is finished. It takes considerable practice to get your smile imbedded in your character without looking phony.

Fact It only takes thirteen muscles to smile and one hundred and twelve to frown. Most salespeople exercise their face way too much.

Here is a little test: Turn around, or go up to, one of your friends or colleagues and look them in the face. Then, with a big smile, tell them that you do not like them. Repeat it three or four times. Do you think that person believes you? No, because you were smiling the actual content of your words has no bearing on the motive behind them. The reverse is also true. Try to stroke up someone wearing a frown on your face. They will not believe that either.

Rule No. 5 Attitude of Gratitude

One of the deepest cravings, urges and desires of humans is to be accepted. Every person in the world wants to be accepted as a vital part of their community. Every salesperson wants to be accepted as a vital part of their sales organization. When you do a good job and are recognized for it, you appreciate the recognition more than being paid on the sale. You get more stimulation from being told you did a good job and hearing the congratulations. You crave it. The deepest, most important thing missing from the world right now is recognition and appreciation.

Watch the reaction of a friend or coworker when you say to them, "Thank you I really appreciated what you did." They will smile and their whole physiology will change. If your prospect feels that their contribution to the presentation is being appreciated they will visibly relax and respond in kind. For example, when they complete the survey sheet, answer questions or give you objections, they will do it honestly.

Rule No. 6 Using FORM to uncover Objections

By asking the right questions you can also uncover any or all possible objections that will interfere with you making a sale. By doing this early in the buying curve process you still have the time to deal with, or eliminate, them.

As a salesperson you should want objections. You should bathe in them, love them. Appreciate all objections because without them you are nowhere near making a sale. You have to get all the objections and appreciate them with a smile. Tell them, "I appreciate you telling me that and I understand what you are saying so please, tell me more." Get the objection totally out and on the table so that you can determine the strength of it.

When you get the objection, "look, do not waste your time we are not buying anything here today," respond with, "that is okay, I appreciate your being honest with me, thank you very much." You will then get a more manageable objection in return. "Well, it is not because you have a bad place here or anything like that . . . it is just that we are in the process of building a house." Later on they may tell you, "Well, in the future we would probably do something like this, wouldn't we honey?"

Because you have appreciated the objection you then get them into a rhythm where they think you appreciate all their objections and will more freely offer them. If, however, every time your prospect offers up an objection, condition or an attitude you slam them with a, "Yeah, I know but we hear that all the time." They will clam up and you will not get another objection or any cooperation.

Rule No. 7 Use FORM to Uncover Buying Motives

In addition to listening effectively, you must be able to ask multi-level questions in such a way as to learn the motivation behind their behavior as well as why things are important to them. More specifics on asking questions are covered in the next chapter.

In addition, you must invent new ways to create or uncover problems with their present method of use or vacationing etc. so you can provide a solution.

Rule No. 8 Earn your Prospect's Trust

"Do you mind me asking?" Ask permission to ask initial personal questions. You have not yet earned the right to ask anything else. Once you have received permission to ask questions, listen to them sincerely. When a complete stranger tells you their hopes, dreams, fears and fantasies it is an indication that they now trust you.

What FORM is trying to do is open the door, to let all this information out and when it does we can compute, analyze, digest it and absorb it. In the back of your mind, consider the phrase used by police, "Anything you say, can and will be used against you . . . ."

Rule No. 9 Earn the Right to Advance

Even though we will cover this in more depth in a later chapter, the basic premise can be applied during the discovery process. By repeating back your prospects buying motives at regular intervals, it lets the prospect know that you understand what his motives are, thereby allowing you to continue forward with the presentation.

Rule No. 10 Persuade through Involvement

Get the prospect involved in answering questions and participating in the presentation process. How can you possibly find out what will best serve your prospects needs if they are not helping you to discover them. Determine this by asking a series of skillful questions, designed to find out what your prospect is particularly looking for and it will shorten your presentation time considerably.

Do you know that half of the time your prospects do not even understand what they are saying? Their fear and their ignorance about what is going to happen during the presentation cause them to blurt out plenty of useful information. That stuff is just put there to defend them and to stall you. Thank them, appreciate them, accept them, agree with them and you will be surprised at what happens.

FORM done properly can close a deal in fifteen to thirty minutes. Bold Statement, possibly, has it been done—most definitely, I have done it personally and seen it done by many successful sales people. If your prospect believes that you sincerely care and that you are agreeable and accepting of all their resistance, then you will get all this negativity out in the front end. Then, they will end up believing, "I like this guy, I trust this guy, I believe in this guy. He is so sincere. If he asks me to buy, I will." Because they have come to trust you, because they believe you are their friend and have their best interests at heart, they will now listen to you for the duration of the presentation.

If you want to consistently write sales, know everything there is to know about your prospect. By empowering them at the beginning of the presentation to do all the talking, later they will ask the majority of the questions (interest and curiosity). As you continue to build the relationship you also begin to take control and the prospect will start losing their resistance and become curious. The more curious they become, the more problems they will uncover with what they are presently doing. Once that occurs they will search for any solution, which then creates interest and desire in your product or service which is covered in Chapter 6.

However, before you skip over to chapter 6, you should first understand what makes your prospect tick. In the next chapter, we learn how to get a better understanding of your prospect. This next step on the buying curve is important in that if you know who they are, what is behind their attitude and behavior, it can lead you to triumph, or failure, depending on how you meet, greet and build a relationship with them.

5

Understanding your prospect

So far we have examined three main ingredients needed to close a sale. The first one we covered is your attitude (preparation) that includes your confidence, your desires, your persistence, your goal setting and the way you project yourself. The second was creating rapport, the third and most important sales technique was bonding and the discovery process. However, the fourth step is the most difficult—understanding and exploring our prospect. How? We learn to how to communicate effectively through observing, listening and interpreting body language and the prospects state of mind and unless you can do this step seamlessly, the next step—creating interest and desire will be all that more difficult to master.

In this chapter we will learn how to interpret and understand ALL your prospects behavior so that you can ask more probing questions that will stimulate deeper conversation to create interest and desire. I know that some of you might have skipped over the last chapter or saying to yourselves, "Yeah, that FORM stuff is B.S.—I know how to get someone to talk." The question is—do you <u>really know how</u> to get people to talk about themselves? Do you really know how to create interest? What do you do, or say, to create desire in someone?

So before to examine the aspects of creating interest and desire in the next chapter, I am going to get back to the basics of helping you understand the different types of prospects that you will meet.

Why Listening is your greatest asset

First, it all comes back to listening and asking the right questions. You cannot create interest or desire unless you know what motivates your prospect. What will compel them to want to buy your product or service? What differentiates a mediocre sales person from a master closer? Learning to read and understand the prospect and work with what you learn to move towards the sale. It is their ability to listen and watch carefully and take every product benefit, and turn it into the right question to ask your prospect. At the very least, they listen so that they can find an emotion and immediately ask an appropriate question that will require a response. Unfortunately, one of the biggest mistakes that mediocre or beginner salespeople make is that they fail to ask the right questions. If, by chance they do ask the right questions, they then fail to listen to the responses.

In chapter 4 we discovered that listening to your prospect was the key to making a sale. Listening skills are vital for persuading your prospect. However, there is more to listening than just listening intently. You must also <u>show</u> people that what you are hearing is being understood and empathized. A successful salesperson will <u>listen</u> themselves into more sales than they will ever talk themselves into.

How Good a Listener are you?

Do you really hear what your prospects are saying to you or are you just waiting for them to finish talking so that you can take your turn? The following is a little quiz for you to take to find out how good a listener you really are.

Answer yes or no to each question and <u>be honest</u> with yourself.

1. Are you easily distracted while your prospect is talking?
   ☐ Yes   ☐ No
2. Do you find it hard to maintain eye contact while your prospects are talking?   ☐ Yes   ☐ No

3. Do you find yourself looking at your watch while they are talking? ☐ Yes ☐ No
4. Do you patiently wait for your turn to talk? ☐ Yes ☐ No
5. Do you interrupt your prospect while they are talking? ☐ Yes ☐ No
6. Do you think to yourself, "I have heard all of this before?" ☐ Yes ☐ No
7. Are you thinking of a response while your prospect is talking? ☐ Yes ☐ No
8. Do you honestly encourage your prospect to talk? ☐ Yes ☐ No
9. Do you find yourself realizing you do not know what your prospect just said? ☐ Yes ☐ No
10. Do you really believe that you know what your prospects true needs are before you begin your presentation? ☐ Yes ☐ No

If you answered 'Yes' to more than half of these questions then you are about normal. You are not right or wrong, just normal. Unfortunately everybody, including salespeople, are guilty of bad listening habits. If you fail to give someone your undivided attention it can often result in mistrust, misunderstanding, miscommunication and perhaps even lead to conflict or confrontation or No Sale.

Think about how much time you spend listening to your prospect and how much time you spend talking. You should establish a 60/40 talk ratio with your prospects. That means you listen sixty percent of the time and talk forty percent. As a rule, you should never talk more than 30 seconds anyway and then ask the question(s), "How do you feel about that or what do you think about that?" Perhaps you would prefer the adage "God gave us two ears and one mouth . . . use them in that ratio."

Remember, you cannot possibly learn anything new about them if you are doing all the talking. Besides, people are not bored when they are talking about themselves, only when you are talking.

WHY WE NEED TO LISTEN

We have covered the importance of building a relationship with our prospects and that the foundation for that relationship is communication. Because you need information from your prospect to find hot buttons or dominant buying motives, <u>your prospect needs to talk and you need to listen</u>. By allowing your prospects the time to express themselves the more likely they are to talk and if they are allowed to talk, the more likely they are to buy. Because you listen to their opinions they will like you and if they like you, they will buy from you.

Listening is critical to the sales process. You need to listen carefully to what your prospects are saying to customize your presentation to suit their needs and desires. Listening helps gain rapport and build trust. Listening to someone is the greatest validation that you care about them.

TEN WAYS TO DEVELOP GOOD LISTENING HABITS

To listen to people effectively and especially to your prospect, you should develop good listening habits. Remember, listening skills are vital for persuasion. Some of these habits will require practice and patience as listening runs counter to our natural instincts.

1. <u>Look at your prospect directly</u>. You should always lean forward and listen intently. Successful salespeople listen calmly and patiently as if they have all the time in the world. If your prospect wants to talk for six hours, let them.
2. <u>Focus all of your attention on the prospect</u>. Back in chapter 2, we covered the importance of remembering your prospects name. If you cannot remember names, it is because you are not listening or paying attention. If you want to impress your prospect, remember their names, listen to them and show then that you are more interested in a relationship than in 'making a sale.'

3. <u>Do not interrupt your prospect while they are talking</u>. Do not make the mistake of trying to jump into the conversation while they are talking with something that may just have popped into your mind.

4. <u>Encourage your prospect to talk</u>. You can do this by saying, "Tell me more, go on please, then what happened or I see." In sales, they call these phrase conversation extensions, and they show your prospect that you are listening to them and therefore encouraging them to continue the conversation.

5. <u>Develop good questions to stimulate conversation</u>. Instead of creating a canned pitch or presentation, develop a repertoire of good open-ended questions that will stimulate conversation.

6. <u>Develop good response habits</u>. These may be the phrases already mentioned in number 4 above or they could be projected through your expressions and physiology. If your body language reassures your prospect that you are interested, attentive, relaxed and calm, then they will be encouraged to share more with you

7. <u>Use silence to encourage your prospect to talk</u>. When your prospect finishes talking, wait 3 to 5 seconds before replying because they may be thinking of something to say. Sometimes just sitting quietly will encourage your prospect to start talking again. If they do, keep nodding, smiling and listening intently. If they stop talking, use the time to respond with another open-ended question.

8. <u>Listen for your prospects' feelings</u>.' Encourage your prospect to talk about their feelings. Focus on the way they feel tells them that you are interested in the motivation behind the feeling, (in other words, why they feel as they do) not just the words. Even though you need real information to complete the sales process, your prospects "feelings" are the key to the sale. Remember, sales are emotional not logical.

9. <u>Clarify what you hear</u>. Request clarification if you do not understand what your prospect is saying or asking. When you do this, your prospect will gladly clarify their statement because it shows that you have been paying attention to what they were saying. Clarifying or confirming statements can save you many hours of lost time and lost sales.

10. <u>Practice listening with empathy</u>. This is the hardest listening habit to learn. Learning how to identify with your prospects' needs and feelings can be extremely difficult. Try to put yourself "in their shoes" as you listen to what they are saying. Always be looking to establish empathy and understanding with your prospects. Once you develop the habit of listening with empathy, you will quickly discover how shallow your old listening habits were.

You cannot talk people into buying something, but you can 'listen' them into buying anything. Effective listening is the most important and powerful tool a salesperson can have. The old days of talking a prospect to death are long past. People no longer want to be sold. Today's salesperson is an advisor or a consultant. Listening to prospects closely enough and asking them intuitive questions will eventually provide you with everything that you need to be able to sell them. The best salespeople in the world are those that are low key, very good questioners and are excellent listeners.

Remember you are the professional and should be the one listening to them talk, not the other way around. You will not gain anything if you are doing all the talking. All you are doing is giving them time to think up more logical reasons why not to buy now. If you feel you are talking too much, ask a question about how they feel and go back to listening.

Understanding your Prospect

If you learn and apply the buying curve steps outlined in this book, you are likely to achieve success. However, for those individuals who wish to move towards becoming master closers you need to reach to a higher level of human interaction and understanding. By learning how to identify and understand your prospect better, you are maximizing your abilities for creating the perfect environment needed for creating interest, desire and ultimately making a sale.

When you know what <u>moves</u> your prospect (INTEREST), you will know <u>how</u> to move them (DESIRE). You need to be able to show your prospect how they can get what they want by doing what you want them to do. The only way to do this is to reiterate what I mentioned frequently— understand that <u>all prospects have one thing in common</u>: Fear—whether it is the fear of being sold or the fear of the unknown.

From those first few seconds of the greeting when you read your prospects personality and later throughout the sales process, you need to recognize that their behavior is affected, and in many cases motivated by fear. Once you understand this you can mold your presentation to suit their personality and behavior. Think of your prospect as a raw material. Iron ore needs to be melted, refined, processed, hammered and molded into shape for it to be transformed into a graceful statue. So it is with any sales prospect.

UNDERSTANDING PROSPECTS WITHOUT PRE-JUDGING

There is an incredible variety of people in our world today. That variety means there are countless differences between people from gender, marital status, sexual orientation, religion and ethnic origin to physical attributes—size, shape, weight, age, hair and eye color. These differences extend to their occupations—students, retirees, homemakers, doctors, construction workers, attorneys, salespeople . . . the list is endless! There will also be differences in their financial situations. However, in spite of all this variety, everyone at some time or another, looks at somebody and makes an assumption about them based on a generalization. In other words, everyone PRE-JUDGES.

Unfortunately, in sales you do not have the luxury of pre-prejudging the prospect you meet. If you ever want to become a master closer you must learn to greet your prospect and see right through them. There has to be no pre-judging. No, "oh no, I have gotten a . . ."

One of the basic principles of closing is realizing that you are the 'sale,' not your prospect. You are the one who sets up the sales process and puts yourself in the driver's seat. As such, you have to learn to eliminate any thoughts that would prevent you from making a friend and writing a sale. The hardest thing for a salesperson to do is to REMOVE THEIR feelings, their values, their impressions and their assumptions from the sales process. Until you can train yourself to take your feelings and thoughts off the table and replace them with the feelings and thoughts of your prospect, you will never become a master closer.

I am always amazed at how many salespeople over the years have said to me, "I do not talk to people from . . . certain ethnic backgrounds. No, I do not talk to newlyweds, I do not talk to large groups, I do not like, I do not talk to . . ." Do you know what these statements project to your manager? "That I have an attitude against people and that I cannot close them." What your manager realistically sees, on the other hand, is that you cannot put your personal feelings aside and concentrate on your prospect. Of course, if humans did not pre-judge and could speak to everyone, companies would only need one salesperson or a completely automated sales department.

Because you have no control over the type of prospect that is offered to you, you must treat everyone equally. Never pre-judge a prospect because you never know <u>which one</u> is the sale.

Understanding Prospect Physiology

You cannot close a sale unless you are using your eyes and ears. Body language and physiology are telltale signs for evaluating your prospects state of mind. Granted there are an over-abundance of books written on the subject; however, here we will look at some of the basics.

Reading body language and physiology is important for determining where you are in the sales process and what effect you are having on the prospect. Their physiology will tell you more about how they are feeling more accurately than the words that are coming out of their mouths.

The most common method of discerning your prospects state of mind is by looking into their face and especially their eyes. Eyes are the windows to the soul. If you cannot see what is in their eyes, you cannot see the impact or reaction of what you are saying to them. Keep looking briefly at them—this is far more non-threatening than staring at them for long periods of time. Do not listen to what they say, but how they say it. There are times when the words spoken and the tones in which they are delivered do not match. Listen to your prospects voice tone and volume as this reflects their 'feelings' more accurately than the words they are speaking.

If you see that your prospect is becoming aggressive, confrontational or bored it is because they are not listening to you. Quit talking and go back to your life raft. Get them back into their comfort zone and your life raft. More on the life raft in chapter 6. Later on you can then go back to the point you were at and resume your presentation. By doing this you accomplish three things. First, they will notice that you were aware that they were not paying attention and went back to something that made them feel comfortable. Second, by changing the conversation's topic you show that you care about them and, third, when you do resume your presentation they will be ready to listen.

BASIC BODY LANGUAGE

Before we move forward with recognizing your prospects personality type, here are a few physiological gestures that are easy to spot and read. Use common sense in these situations as they may not be absolutes.

- Eyes looking UP to the left—they are making stuff up as they go along
- Eyes looking UP to the right—they are trying to recall a real memory
- Eyes moving side to side or up and down—they are thinking of making an answer up
- Hand in front of mouth—prospect is uncomfortable or ill at ease
- Hands on hips—prospect is getting aggressive or combatant
- Arms folded across the chest—prospect is very defensive and resistant
- Leaning back on chair—prospect is not paying attention, they are bored

Watch, listen and learn to understand what your prospects body language is telling you. It could make a big difference between making a sale or not.

UNDERSTANDING BUYING PERSONALITIES

What type of buyer are they? Do they buy only on the recommendation of others or are they capable of independent decision? There are many people who will not buy anything until they have the opinions and recommendation of someone they trust. If you find this out early in the presentation you can then modify your 'pitch' to compensate. Maybe they are impulse buyers. Five to ten percent of prospects are impulse buyers easily swayed by the fact that your product or service is new to them.

Prospects have changed tremendously over the past ten years. They are now more sophisticated and no longer influenced by a salesperson's charm. They have done Google searches, gone on Facebook sites for information and to ask their friends, and have seen your product at least twice (and more likely half a dozen times) before meeting you. Prospects literally expect more from salespeople than ever before and are more influenced by a salesperson's professionalism than 'cheap tricks.'

To better understand what today's prospects are looking for you should consider the following consumer expectations:

- Prospects want solid, honest information about how your product or service can improve their lives. Providing valid information tells your prospect that you respect their ability to make a sound decision
- Prospects resist and resent any type of high pressure selling tactics.
- Prospects expect options. They will respond much better to having choices on which to base their decision.
- Prospects expect flexibility. Designing a program exclusively for your prospect that allows for flexibility is very important to them.

- Prospects expect to enter into a long term relationship with their salesperson.
- Prospects expect you to be a consultant or an advisor. They expect you to provide them with whatever information they may require about your product or service.
- Prospects want to hear something new. With so many more products and services available to your prospects your presentation must be new and refreshing, not a canned spiel.

Nobody will buy your product or service because it is as good as anybody else's. They will buy because there is something unique that will enhance their lives and satisfy a buying motive. People buy for their reasons, not yours.

Remember from the last chapter, the motivations that stimulate people to buy are:

1. Gain or Profit—to make or save money or to get a good deal on something
2. Peace of Mind—family bonding, to be healthy, security, comfort and companionship
3. Pride of Ownership—the need to possess
4. Adventure—to enjoy life more
5. Fear of Failure or Loss—not missing out on anything in their lives
6. Desire for Approval—recognition, respect and prestige, influence, popularity and power
7. Love or Hate—to be admired and liked

So far I have looked at what motivates your prospects buying personality. Now we will examine the five buying types themselves. Watch, listen, pay attention and learn to read between the lines to determine your prospects buying personality so that you can tailor make your presentation to them.

1. Analytical Buyers: These types of buyers represent about 30% of the market. Most analytical buyers are classified as Thinker personality types. These buyers want to know about every

feature and/or benefit of your product. They want to read every piece of paper and are not in a hurry to make a decision.

The best approach is to give them every detail about how the product works, how it performs and how much it costs. Let them study every graph and chart that relates to your product or service. This will keep them in their comfort zone.

2. Relationship Buyer: These types of buyers also make up about 30% of the market and all they are concerned about is how other people think and feel. These buyers would be classified as Relater personality types. These buyers are hyper-sensitive about the opinions of others. They want to know what affect your product or service will have on other people.

   The best approach is let them talk because they like to do all the talking. These buyers want to build a relationship and feel very comfortable before making a decision.

3. Practical Buyer: These buyers are very direct and want you to get to the point. They are professional and businesslike and have no time for indulging in small talk. These buyers would be classified as Director Personality types.

   The best approach with these buyers is to relate the facts quickly and in detail. They will want to read, analyze and confirm the facts before making a decision.

4. Lay Down Buyer: These buyers know exactly what they want or can't say no and know exactly how much they are willing to pay for it. You will find yourself talking to a lay down buyer every so often, about 1 in 20 or 30.

   The best approach is to sell these buyers exactly what they want. Do not try to talk them into anything else because you will lose the sale.

5. <u>Indifferent Buyer</u>: Indifferent buyers represent about 5% of the market. They are notably apathetic, cynical and have no intention of buying anything. These buyers have made so many buying mistakes throughout their lives that they just do not care about what you may have to offer them.

The best approach to sell them—**Get a magic wand!**

The fastest and simplest method of determining which type of buyer you have is to ASK them. Have them tell you about when or how they bought their last iPad, Smartphone, car, house, etc.—this will give you a fairly realistic picture.

RECOGNIZING PERSONALITY TYPES

Throughout time, salespeople have tried to use any method that was available to give them the advantage in a selling situation. Renowned Psychologist Carl Jung fostered the idea of categorizing personality types and narrowed it down to sixteen definite ones. Over the years, psychologists, psychiatrists and sociologists have spent many years renaming and analyzing these personality types and again and there are many books written on the subject.

Basically, the theory of personality types claims that each of us has a natural inclination that falls into one type or the other. The theory also states that our innate personality type indicates how we are likely to deal with different situations that life presents us. It also acts to keep us in the environments that we feel the most comfortable. Simply put, people are people the world over and they act and react differently to stay within their comfort zones.

The truth however is that everyone, including your prospects, all have the same needs, wants, desires, thought patterns, questions, fears and goals. The only difference is the manner in which they are projected. So, to give salespeople an advantage over the prospect, we categorize them into personality types. Your ability to recognize your prospects personality type aids you in determining how you will present your product or service.

I have boiled down the prospects into the four most common personality types because they are the easiest to understand, using the type categories that were defined by Dr. Tony Alessandra in 1996 when he described them in his book, The Platinum Rule. From these common personality types and, based on my and other master closers sales experience, I have provided brief descriptions of each and then, over the next four pages, will highlight their characteristics. With each type I will endeavor to show the common traits and how to handle that particular personality type in a sales situation.

RELATER

Relaters will account for a quarter of the prospects that you will meet. Support their feelings and show personal interest by asking them about themselves and their families. The phrase, "tell me more," works extremely well.

Behavior Patterns:	Open and direct. Dreamers, Creative.
Physical Appearance:	Casual, informational and friendly
Pace of Thought Process and Conversation:	Slow and steady. They like to relate everything to something in their life.
Fear:	Confrontation
Behavior Under Pressure:	Submissive. If you pressure them they will give in to your demands.
Seeking:	Attention and Approval.
Emotional State:	Empathetic, Emotional. Support their feelings. Relaters want to be liked.
Benefits they Need to Know About:	How it will affect their personal lives.
Decision Temperament:	Considered
What they want the Salesperson to be:	Pleasant and non-threatening

What specifically Irritates them:	Impatience and insensitivity
Buying Habits:	Relaters are Relationship Buyers. They enjoy buying as it makes them feel good.
Primary Motivation:	Buy to prove accomplishment in life. They want recognition from others and will work hard at achieving it.
Occupational Position:	Professional. Relaters are normally not senior executives, nor owners of companies. They are supervisors, overseers or middle managers.
Examples of Relaters:	Teachers, nurses, social workers, counselors as well as some lawyers and doctors.
General Sales Strategy:	• Support their feelings • Show personal interest in them • Directly point out benefits • Tell emotional third party stories • Talk about personal feelings and family • Actively listen to them • Use 'pressure on, pressure off' technique • Use assumptive closes • Ensure decision involves minimum risk

When it comes down to the wire you need to accurately explain the benefits to them and tell them what they are going to do. As an example, say to them, "My suggestion is that you should do . . . , or if I was you this is what I would do . . ." will make the decision easier for them and less overwhelming.

SOCIALIZER

Socializers account for majority of the prospects that you will meet. Socializers like to make friends and want to be a part of anything that will enhance their ego, and social status. Directly point out the loss of prestige if they do buy your product or service. This in itself may generate a spontaneous buying decision.

Behavior Patterns:	Open and direct. Perceptive. Poor Listeners.
Physical Appearance:	Trendy. They always want to be involved with anything that appears to be 'stylish.'
Pace of Thought Process and Conversation:	Very fast and spontaneous. Easily excitable
Fear:	Loss of prestige or social status
Behavior Under Pressure:	They become sarcastic and confrontational and take offense to your attacking their ego.
Seeking:	Recognition, Approval. Stroke their ego.
Emotional State:	They evaluate themselves how their friends and associates regard them.
Benefits they Need to Know About:	How it will enhance their social status. The "Lifestyle of the Rich and Famous" approach
Decision Temperament:	Spontaneous
What they want the Salesperson to be:	Admiring
What specifically Irritates them:	Boredom—salespeople who do all the talking.
Buying Habits:	Socializers are Spontaneous Buyers because they just like to spend.
Primary Motivation:	They are typically motivated by travel, entertainment and fun.
Occupational Position:	Blue collar, construction and manual labor positions. Adults between 18-30
Examples of Socializers:	Students, hospitality industry workers, first level supervisors and managers.

General Sales Strategy:	• Support their dreams and ideas • Show great personal interest in them • Do not confront or argue with them. • Use third party stories to reinforce dreams • Intent Statement/Breaking the pact must be spelled out to avoid misunderstandings • Use K.I.S.S. approach • Be entertaining, energetic, full of smiles • Talk mainly about of recreational subjects • Use plenty of tie downs • Decisions made with incentives

THINKER

Thinkers account for 15% of the prospects that you will meet. Thinkers are probably the number one prospect that will box you on money, product use, terms etc. Initially however you will get no commitments from them until you have provided justified proof that what you are offering is in their best interests. When they believe you have justified enough they will then make a decision.

Behavior Patterns:	Self-contained and indirect. Detail oriented.
Physical Appearance:	Appear formal and very conservative with a tendency to lean towards "nerd" appearance. They carry backpacks, fanny packs or over stuffed briefcases.
Pace of Thought Process and Conversation:	Slow and very systematic. Need to carefully think out or analyze information offered.

Fear:	Embarrassment. This fear makes them be prepared for every eventuality.
Behavior Under Pressure:	They will withdraw into themselves. They will never get aggressive or confrontational. They will avoid eye contact and become very polite.
Seeking:	Justification
Emotional State:	Stable and private. Will not reveal feelings.
Benefits they Need to Know About:	How they can justify the purchase. Show all the benefits and perks where they can save money.
Decision Temperament:	Deliberate. Once the decision is made they will stand by it.
What they want the Salesperson to be:	Honest, detailed, precise and supportive
What specifically Irritates them:	Surprises and unpredictability. Anything that they are not aware of scares them.
Buying Habits:	Thinkers are Analytical Buyers. They buy to maintain a greater feeling of security.
Primary Motivation:	Thinkers would rather put their money into high yield savings account or pay debts.
Occupational Position:	They are professional, technical and mainly white collar workers.
Examples of Thinkers:	Middle managers, engineers, scientists, accountants and other technical type positions.

General Sales Strategy:	<ul><li>Support their need to be thoughtful and organized</li><li>Show testimonials, magazines, membership lists, everything for visual credibility</li><li>Provide factual evidence of what you are saying is accurate— Appeal to their need to be accurate and logical</li><li>List advantages and disadvantages</li><li>Let them take notes and think about each benefit that you have shown them</li><li>Show how they can justify their purchase</li><li>Avoid gimmicks and tricks to close them.</li><li>No surprises in the back end</li><li>They will not make a decision until they have examined ALL the aspects. Ensure decision involves justification.</li></ul>

DIRECTOR

Directors will make up 10% or fewer of the prospects that you will meet. Director personalities measure almost every product or service for its ability to contribute to the financial strength of their position. They are very deliberate in their effort to figure people out and then move forward to achieve that goal. Do not beat around the bush or try to 'back door' the sale because you will instantly lose credibility and never regain it or the sale.

Behavior Patterns:	Self-contained, direct, organized
Physical Appearance:	Businesslike. They have an intuitive sense for dressing well, if not somewhat conservatively.
Pace of Thought Process and Conversation:	Logical, Fast and Decisive. They want you to hurry and get to the point. They cannot be told anything.
Fear:	Loss of control
Behavior Under Pressure:	Confrontational and dictatorial
Seeking:	Power, control, respect and productivity.
Emotional State:	Non-emotional. They use charm, timing, compliments and incentives to get things done. They know the difference between thinking and emotion.
Benefits they Need to Know About:	They only want to know the truth. Specifically—what the product does, what it costs and for how long.
Decision Temperament:	Quick, Decisive. Once they make the decision they want to move on to something else immediately.
What they want the Salesperson to be:	Accurate, Efficient.
What specifically Irritates them:	Indecision, inefficiency and people being ill-prepared to provide information.
Buying Habits:	Directors are Practical Buyers and are generally more interested in accumulating rather than spending.
Primary Motivation:	Return on investment. They are calculated in their efforts to achieve their goals.
Occupational Position:	Chairmen of Board, Senior Managers, Politicians, Entrepreneurs

Examples of Directors:	Senior level executives, high ranking Military personnel and successful sales personnel.
General Sales Strategy:	• Support their goals and objectives • Maintain a businesslike relationship • Disagree only on fact not feelings Directors deal in 'black and white.' • Give recognition only to their ideas, not to the person • Use Choice or Alternative Closes • Find the benefit that will provide a financial solution to their most pressing problem.

Once you learn to identify these personality characteristics you will be able to interact with them better. By creating an environment that 'mirror' images their personality type, you will find that their resistance level will reduce significantly. Once you have created rapport and made a friend they will then empower you with their trust. This in turn increases your chances of making a sale.

*****Generally, most of the prospects you will be meeting are working class people. The wonderful thing about them is that they are just like you are when confronted with the same situations. It is how you handle the situation that determines your abilities as a salesperson.

EXERCISE: Write down ALL the features and benefits of **YOUR** product or service that you show your prospects. Then create four different third party stories for each part of your presentation. Create one story for a Director, one for a Thinker, one for a Relater and finally, one for a Socializer. By doing this you will then then be able to manage without any difficulty the differing personality types.

Director: They will want to TELL YOU what they will do with your product. You can lay the "perk" out in a very simple manner and then pause at the end of your statement. For example, pausing after, "You know these Getaways have the ability to . . ." By pausing a moment Directors will take over the statement with, "Do what? Let me tell you I would use it for . . ." They will tell you HOW it will work for him and HOW they are going to use it.

Thinker: Thinkers want to know WHY they can get your "perk" for so little or nothing as it appears to be too good to be true. They wonder where they come from and what the catch is. Remember Thinkers want to know every little thing about your product or service.

Socializer: For the Socializer it is WHAT it looks like, WHERE it will benefit him and WHO would they might meet in that location. The prestige of having access to this type of "perk" would make them very popular with their friends and acquaintances.

Relater: Relaters are full blown combinations of all the above personality types. You have to tell them WHERE the "perks" come from, HOW they would work, WHAT benefit it would be to them. Relaters want to know and see everything. Who, When, Why, Where and How. The most important is the 'What is in it for me?'

Remember, if you use the wrong type of close or third party story on the wrong character the results will be DEVASTATING.

RELIGIOUS OR CULTURAL DIFFERENCES

Do religious and cultural differences have an effect on personality types? Yes. There are two questions that you should consider when confronted with a prospect with strong cultural or religious beliefs.

1. What is the cultural or religious background that maybe driving the behavior?
2. How does this cultural or religious background affect the prospects behavior?

Rather than get into long winded religious and cultural differences just consider the two questions mentioned above when you meet your prospect. If religious and/or cultural beliefs are deeply rooted, then the behaviors will reflect it. Use a commonsense approach and, along with respect, you will go a long way towards making a sale.

Taking your Prospect's Temperature

In chapter 2 we examined the importance of an Intent Statement and how it can help relieve that initial tension and stress in order to begin establishing rapport with your prospect. This Intent Statement set the overall tone of the sales presentation. By addressing the different aspects of the sales process up front, you not only reduced their fear and tension, you put them at ease and established control for the balance of the presentation.

Remember, the art of closing a sale is not about showing a ton of features and benefits and hoping your prospect buys. It is about getting your prospect to listen to you. However, to get them to listen to you, you have to eliminate or at the very least get them to put aside their fear. You must find a way to get your client to trust you, believe that you are sincere in your intent and are only looking out for their best interests. This is especially true with today's more educated consumers

There are times however, where an intent statement doesn't completely relieve your prospects fear and they are still exhibiting an unwillingness to participate in the sales presentation. It is important to remember that ALL prospects that come to a sales presentation have a pre-conceived idea of what will happen and to defend themselves they formulate a plan of attack (or Pact).

This RESISTANCE creates FEAR that creates a PRE-CONCEIVED NOTION that leads to a PLAN OF ATTACK or a PACT that stimulates a specific behavior.

Their pact, or plan of attack, is formulated on <u>what they believe</u> they know will happen to them during the sales process. This plan or pact helps them eliminate their fear of the unknown. It will evolve into their unwillingness to participate, in any manner, with the process of buying anything, and in allowing you to show your product to them. You need to make your prospect aware that some action, or involvement, is expected from them during, and at the end, of the sales presentation.

In the past, salespeople would use a very strong break the pact to get the prospect to keep an open mind. In today's world of the internet, social media and the ability to access information from anywhere including the smartphone in their hand, prospects are no longer naive, that stupid or uneducated. They know that there will be some selling involved and they will be required to make a decision, yes or no, to buy your product that day. It is, however, their natural defense against being sold that makes breaking the pact, or a very strong intent statement, necessary. It is up to you, and your prospect's frame of mind, how strong you choose to do it.

How, and when, you break the prospect's pact depends entirely on you. Just as you need to develop a good Intent Statement, you need to develop a good Pact Break for all the different types of prospects that you will meet. You need to evaluate your prospect and determine which method of breaking their pact you will use. Once they have agreed to either keeping an open mind, or giving you a yes or no decision, you are then on your way to creating more real rapport, commonality, trust and belief.

Following are a few tips on breaking the pact which can also be applied to the intent statement:

1. Do not attempt to break the pact until you have the full attention of your prospect(s).
2. Look at your prospect directly and maintain good eye contact.
3. Do not expect to get a yes or no commitment at this point because it will not be real one.
4. Always get a verbal commitment and shake hands to seal the commitment.
5. Do not be intimidated by your prospect's attempts to resist you breaking their pact. It is their natural sales resistance. Take the pressure off them and try a different approach.

I continually stress the importance of having the prospect listen to you and how fear prevents listening. Well, by breaking the pact, you are now looking for the prospect to open their mind, as well as their ears, to you so that they will not start resisting the sale. This is the next, most important, decision you are looking for from your prospect—to keep an open mind throughout the presentation. So, yes, it is necessary to break their pact and you can do this by determining your prospects state of mind, or temperature.

While you are talking with your prospect you <u>should</u> be testing out their temperature. You have already evaluated what type of buyer they are, what their character type is and now you need to determine their state of mind. Are they aggressive or easy going? Are they scared and resisting you or are they calm and open-minded?

Any type of sales can be a very frustrating business and I have learned that the vacation ownership industry is no exception. People traditionally fear salespeople as being high pressure, slick, smooth-talking, rude, dominant and having an answer for everything. Because of this fear most timeshare prospects that you meet tend to be negative, miserable, aggressive, defensive or resistant. All of these demeanors come from natural sales resistance.

Overall prospects will come to any sales environment in one of three ways:

1. Very Aggressive (RED)—"Look we are not doing anything here today . . ."
2. Cordial yet Cool (AMBER)—Reserved and aware of their surroundings
3. Very Friendly, Chatty and Happy (GREEN)—Enjoying themselves and willingly wanting to give you any information that you need

Yes, prospects are exactly like traffic lights. Red light—stop the aggressive, confrontational behavior. Amber light—use caution when dealing with this reserved prospect. Green light—the fast moving, very cheery prospect—I call them the 'The Brady Bunch.'

Whether they are Red, Amber or Green, prospects all have a common denominator in that they fear the sales process. They are ALL skeptical about you and what you are doing. Once you understand that FEAR of the sale is the underlying state of mind in your prospect you can find different ways of reducing the anxiety behind the behavior. It is their pact or plan of attack that is reflected in the Red, Green or Amber state of mind. However, before you can do this, we will examine these three behaviors in more detail. [First, consider which 'color' prospect you would like to have?]

GREEN—"The Brady Bunch"—TRAITS

- Very confident
- Positive, Agreeable
- Believe they are secure in their ability to say NO
- Nothing bad to say about anything
- Will never give you the opportunity to break down any barriers

These prospects are so polite, friendly and secure in what they are doing and agree with everything that is said. They appear very confident in their ability NOT to be sold. They have formulated a plan of attack that resembles a Marine SEAL operation. This type of prospect is prepared to use whatever tactic or methods they need to so that they can get out of the sales presentation. Typically, Green prospects think they 'know you.' They possess egos so large that the outpouring of love and affection that they show towards their families is, in most cases, a show. They use this appearance to strengthen their ego.

It is this ego size that creates the mask of total control. Nothing will bother them and you will not get them to talk about themselves. They will never give you the opportunity to make inroads with them. They will always agree with your best choice. By doing this they never have to go through any barriers to make statements or decisions. Green prospects are so secure within their surroundings that they believe they are NOT going to buy anything. As such they will become very polite, say no thank you, we appreciate your time, but we will take the information home and think about it.

<u>What can you do to get them involved in the presentation?</u> Find something that will get them FRUSTRATED or UNBALANCE them. In other words throw a wrench into the works. You want to find the real emotions behind their behavior. Do not insult them or their family. However make a questioning statement like, "Did the person who invited you fully explain what is going to happen here today and tell you about the qualification process we have?"

A statement such as this creates momentary confusion and will unbalance them. When they are caught unaware it offends their ego. They will most likely respond with something similar to, "hang on a minute. I was not aware of that or he did not tell us that or let me tell you what he told us." They are now out of their comfort zone and moving towards scared, confused, skeptical and nervous and are definitely becoming aware of their surroundings.

Your aim is to move this prospect to AMBER. Moving them to Amber will create a more open mind. By the way, in many cases, the wife of a Green prospect will more than likely admit that they did make a pact before they came to the presentation if you ask.

AMBER—Cordial and Reserved—TRAITS

- Slightly reserved or self-contained initially
- Not overtly friendly but cordial
- Skeptical and aware of their surroundings
- They are nervous and overwhelmed in your environment.

Your Amber prospect will be polite, nervous and curious upon meeting you. They will initially give only one or two word responses. This is because they are so overwhelmed by their surroundings they are not in their comfort zone. They are, however, well-mannered enough to be cordial, but not stupid enough to start signing contracts. After the first few minutes they will be up front and scared enough to ask questions, based on fear and curiosity, about what will happen to them and how long it will take.

This Amber prospect will communicate with you. They may ask questions but they really do not want to know the answers. They only do this to satisfy some time requirements they may have and project to you that they are aware of what is going to happen.

Behind their aware, reserved and non-emotional exterior they are withdrawn so they seldom retain any information or become emotionally stimulated. Their physiology reflects that they are comfortable, but not that comfortable, because their fear of the unknown is making them nervous and skeptical.

What can you do to get them involved in the presentation? Your objective with an Amber prospect is to move them MENTALLY into their comfort zone so that they will listen to your presentation. First, give them an agenda so they do not fear what is to come.

Second, you need to create commonality with them so that they know that they are not alone in this experience. By doing this you make them feel as if they are not from another planet. You may not overcome their skepticism for your product or service initially, but they will become more comfortable in their surroundings. Eventually they will say something such as, "Look we have been told not to become involved in timeshare because it does not work, is that true?"

An Amber prospect will only become involved with your presentation when you get them real and emotional. Tell third party stories about situations similar to theirs and how your product or service made them FEEL.

RED—Aggressive, Angry—TRAITS

- Argumentative
- Believe that they are very confident and in total control of themselves and the situation
- Self-Opinionated
- Verbally and animatedly abusive
- They are resistant and negative to your conversation
- Objects to everything you say or do

Red's sound like the prospect from hell and are if not handled carefully. Ninety-nine percent of the initial conversation will be controlled by them. Their resistance, negativity and constant complaints are their way of dealing with their fear of the unknown and being sold. They are being both honest and straight with you and expect no less in return. Of the three colors your Red prospect is the only one exhibiting true feelings and emotions, but appears to be the most difficult prospect.

The truth is that this prospect is weaker than both the Amber and the Green prospect. So they attempt to put forward an incredible force field of logical reasons why you have no right to sell them. They are also going to constantly be on the attack and suspicious of everything that you say or do. Until you can reduce this negativity a Red prospect will not listen to, or trust, you.

<u>What can you do to get them involved in the presentation</u>? When you have a prospect who likes to control the sales process they feel comfortable. If you try to take control away from them they will become more aggressive. Who really has the control if you allow them to take the initial control? You do because you let them have it.

Let them be aggressive and vent all of their anger. They are the epitome of a "Pandora's Box." If you open the box out will come their whole life story of how they have been mistreated, criticized or stepped on by everyone. By listening very carefully, and patiently, you can pick up details that you can use later on to get the sale. This also includes using their initial aggression back against them at the appropriate times.

If you attempt to do an intent statement, or break their pact, you will instantly meet with aggression and hostility. The more they are allowed to dictate the sales process the more relaxed they will become in the environment. Wait until they have finished releasing all of their negativity and hostility. Then say something similar to, "I realize that you are not going to buy anything right now, and I would most likely react exactly the same as you in this situation." Then create a third party story relating a similar situation to create commonality.

When you use this type of approach, you will find that your prospect will sincerely apologize for their behavior and then move themselves to Amber. In some instances they feel guilty enough about their behavior that they will buy. "Look, we are not mad at you. It is just that last time we went to one of these they wanted a decision on the same day and we are not like that do you understand?"

You cannot have your prospect in the same mental state during the presentation that they were in when they walked through the door. If they were Red, make them Amber or Green. If they are Green, make them Red or Amber. If your prospects are Amber, provoke an emotion to turn them slightly Red. Whether you do it mentally or emotionally, you must unbalance them. Your ultimate goal is to get ALL of your prospects to the point where they are giving you very honest fears and feelings. You can ONLY do that by moving them from one color to another carefully and reveal the real them. Remember get them real make a deal.

It is more advantageous to have an emotional, aggressive, reluctant prospect than a nodding, agreeable one. An important point to remember, very few people can be rude, or unpleasant for hours. Rudeness can only last so long and if you give into their rudeness, they will have won and taken control of your presentation. They won because they intimidated you; broke you and now you have no other option than to let them go. People resist with logic and the first weapon against logic is emotion. In this case, back off breaking their pact and move back into talking about something that they like to do, go back to your life raft.

Whether they are Red, Green or Amber they all have a common denominator—they all fear the sales process and have their levels of resistance. A big killer in selling is pre-judging the Red prospect in the front end and giving up so that you do not have to listen to their tantrums. Which prospect would you rather have now?

DEALING WITH DIFFERENT BEHAVIORS

Learning how to deal with a variety of behaviors can assist you in overcoming many of the obstacles smoothly and professionally. The most important thing to remember is <u>do not focus on the behaviors</u> themselves as it will magnify them and they will end up controlling the presentation, not you.

Below are some examples of specific behaviors that may arise during your presentation and some examples of how to deal with them.

1. <u>Intimidating Behavior</u>: Intimidation is a sign of insecurity. They use intimidation to appear dominant. They want to be heard. They use this type of behavior to protect a fear within themselves that they cannot express.

   If you try to prevent this prospect from talking and tell them what you are going to do, you will only light the fuse to more intimidating behavior later on in the presentation. The best way to deal with it is to just IGNORE IT. Bite your tongue and let them continue. If they see that it is not working they will either stop on their own or TELL YOU how to write their deal. These are probably one of the easiest sales you will write but one of the most difficult prospects on your ego. "Listen here young man, the only way we would join your club is if we were assured the exchange works, understand?"

2. <u>Tough or Stubborn Behavior</u>: This is a prospect who digs their heels in and pronounces that they will not do or buy anything. If you have a stubborn or tough prospect it is important that you do not miss a single step in the sales process. Make certain that you ask specific first level questions before you move to second and third level ones. You must earn the right to advance with them.

   Tough prospects are also a perfect candidate for the Take-Away closing technique. That, combined with sincere compliments and ego stroking will break down even the most stubborn of prospects. "I appreciate and accept your decision not to buy anything today but I have a job to do and I am sure you can appreciate that. So if it is okay, I will do my presentation anyway, fair enough?"

3. <u>Unethical Behavior</u>: This type of behavior appears as outright lying to avoid participating or buying anything. Typically you should ignore this type of behavior. Your prospect is trying to distract you, get you angry or goad you into a confrontation.

    If you detect unethical behavior, or anticipate it, simply tell them that you are aware of their behavior. Do it without confrontation. Be firm in making it clear that you consider the behaviors unacceptable or misleading and that it will affect the relationship you have built to that point. You can usually diffuse the behavior by using a good solid agenda and pact break.

    "Mr. And Mrs. Prospect I am a highly trained vacation consultant and it is obvious that you do not want me to sell you anything. Not everyone I speak to joins the club, but you do not have to go through all of this to make me aware of that. So, let us enjoy the rest of the presentation so that I can finish without you having to fight with me and I will be as quick as I can, fair enough? I mean it is almost as though you were treating me as if your daughter's first date, so relax okay?"

4. <u>Rude and Obnoxious Behavior</u>: This behavior, much like a Red prospect, should be welcomed. If you can patiently wait out the negativity in the front end they will frequently become good listeners and big deals.

    Do not let yourself get upset or defensive at the behavior. Try using this strategy to establish rapport with them. Say, "You must have had a very bad experience, why don't you tell me about it," and then sincerely listen to the response. Let them know that you, too, would be angry at anyone who would do that to you. Remember commonality builds rapport.

5. <u>Bored, Non Attentive Behavior</u>: This behavior is indicative of someone who is not paying attention. They may be staring out the window, looking into their bag or looking around the room. It is because you are not making any impact on them with your presentation.

Entertain them with the things that they like. This prospect is only interested in them self and as such go back to your life raft. Get them talking because people will never become bored with the sound of their voice. Listen carefully for little morsels of information that you can use to show benefits later on in the presentation. It may take some time, but eventually you will find the dominant buying motive.

6. Chatterboxes: These are prospects that are there only to visit and not participate in the sales presentation. Normally they are lonely people who want company and presentations are a great way to meet new people. There are also those people who truly like to hear the sound of their voices.

    Just as the salesperson's biggest weakness is their mouth so is it the prospects. If you find yourself with a chatterbox, kick back and let them talk. Prospects are under an immense amount of stress and pressure coming to a presentation because they feel as if they are going to be sold so they will defend themselves by talking and talking. They feel that if they are talking then the salesperson cannot and, if the salesperson cannot talk then they cannot sell them anything. So just bite your tongue and listen because eventually they will tell you how to sell them. Remember when you talk, you repeat things you already know. When you listen you learn things you do not already know.

7. Hurried Behavior: These are the prospects that are always in a hurry to get to the bottom line. The best way to handle this behavior is to tell them that you know they are in a hurry so you will speed up the presentation for them. However, you then do your normal presentation. All you really do is speed up your speech. This gives the impression that you are hurrying along for them.

    An important aspect is that you do not skip the discovery process. Explain to them that you will need to ask questions. This is because your product or service has so many benefits, you do not want to bore them with features that would not be of benefit to them.

In addition give them as many choices as you can. Because hurried behavior is indicative of controlling personality type, choice closes give them a feeling that they are still in control. Once your prospect becomes interested in your product or service, they will slow the presentation process down themselves. "So, what you are saying is . . ."

8. Interrupting Behavior: Prospects that are constantly interrupting you while you are doing your presentation are trying to distract you from your momentum. Do not tell them to stop interrupting you because you will insult them and this the last thing you want to do.

    Instead thank them for the interruption. Say something along the lines of, "Excuse me, but my manager is pretty strict on this particular point in our presentation. Since your family's vacations are important, will you allow me just five more minutes to finish this and then we are done, okay?" They will agree and allow you to continue believing that they are almost done.

    Interrupting behavior usually signifies boredom, so swim back to your conversational life raft and look for another angle to stimulate interest.

9. Pink Elephant Behavior: This is my favorite prospect behavior. A pink elephant is something that is distracting your prospect but they are not acknowledging it. The best way to deal with it is **do not ignore it**. If you see that your prospect has their arms crossed and is constantly looking at their watch **deal with it**, because in this case, your pink elephant is time.

    Deal with it respectfully. Understand that your prospect is apprehensive and nervous about being in a sales presentation and your empathy towards them will help to dissolve the distraction. **Never let a pink elephant get in the way of developing a relationship.**

You constantly have to be aware of the physiology and body language that is going on with your prospect. When you have a prospect that has an unusual behavior pattern it does not mean there is no sale there. It just means that you need to find something else to stimulate their interest or emotion. Know your prospect. Every prospect shares dreams, wants, needs and fears. Work smart and you will pave the way to more sales, better relationships and a greater sense of personal satisfaction.

While I do appreciate that putting labels on personalities and behaviors is risky, it is important to understand what type of personality is sitting across from you. If you take the time to watch their behavior, listen to what they have to say and evaluate what you hear; then you can provide the solution to what they need. Remember if your prospects like you they will listen to you and if they trust you, they will allow you to show them alternatives.

Has the above information changed your perspective on how you say Hello to your next prospect? I realize that it may be slightly overwhelming to try and remember all the personality types, nuances, and expressions but as long as you have a basic understanding of what makes your prospect tick, you are 1000% ahead of the salesperson who thinks that none of this is important and skipped this chapter hoping to find out some "cool" closing techniques.

Before we do move on to the next chapter on creating interest and desire, I would be at fault if I did not cover how to ask basic questions that will help you build your relationship and explore your prospect, or why they are important.

ASKING BASIC QUESTIONS

Questions are so very important in discovering what motivates your prospect. One of the biggest mistakes that most salespeople make is that they do not ask questions. Of those that do ask questions, they do not ask the right questions. Then, unfortunately, they do not listen to the answers.

The second problem is that most salespeople are trained to look for an objection. Car salespeople are the most notable, but it also occurs within the vacation ownership industry. Many salespeople are trained so hard to look for the objections they completely ignore the buying signals or questions. So, why do so many salespeople automatically discount questions by assuming they are objections? The main reason—salespeople do not know how to tell the difference between an objection and a question.

One of the toughest things that you are going to have to deal with in sales, and specifically timeshare sales, is defining the questions a prospect asks you and the objections they give you. You will have to discern the relevance to them buying or whether it is an objection disguising an emotion.

By definition a question is a request for information. You need to ask questions of your prospect to determine their needs and wants. Good questions give you the keys to your prospect's needs, their problems and objections, and provide a map to the solution. In return, your prospect asks questions to better understand what you are offering them.

Why do we ask questions? The reasons vary from the basic request for information to asking for the order. To help you better understand why we ask questions study the following list:

1. To Gain Information: Using the Warm-Up and discovery process as an example, you are asking questions to gain information about your prospects. If you do not ask questions, how will you discover what their likes, dislikes, wants, needs, motivations, dreams, desires and what they are afraid of. All this information is needed to help you find out what makes your prospect tick.
2. To Show Interest: Remember, people love to talk about themselves. In the last chapter we discussed putting the spotlight on your prospect. By doing this you are showing that you are interested in them and their opinions. Ask them simple,

basic open-ended questions. For example, ask them, "so what are your plans while you are here on vacation?

3. Pinpoint Areas of Similarity: Prospects like and trust someone who is like them. Ask questions to develop a greater sense of similarity that creates commonality and bonding. For example, say to them, "Wow, you guys sound like great skiers. I would probably need lessons to be as good as you."

4. To Focus a Prospects Attention: You are, in reality, competing with everything that is going on around you, at any given time. By asking your prospect a question you are gaining their full attention. If, at any time, during your presentation you see their attention wander, stop and ask a question. It will immediately re-focus them on you.

5. To Get Feedback: This is the basis of communication. If your prospect does not respond to anything you ask, you cannot build any rapport. This also goes hand in hand with observing their body language.

6. To Elicit Trust in You: People do not buy anything from people they do not trust. By asking questions and showing genuine interest and sincerity, you will build trust. Building trust is also based on your voice tones when asking questions.

7. To Clear Away the Cobwebs: More simply put, to help the prospect better understand how your product or service will help them. People will not make a decision if they do not fully understand what they are buying. Good, specific questions can help eliminate the cobwebs.

8. To Pace your Presentation: Sometimes salespeople get lazy in their presentations and try to skip over things. If you ask questions at specific intervals it will help you stay on track.

9. To Buy You More Time: This is for all the salespeople who have had a prospect ask a question that you cannot answer then and need a few seconds to think about your response. To maintain your credibility, ask your prospect another question to give yourself the time to properly formulate a response to their previous question. This will also make your prospect elaborate on the question so that you may better understand it.

10. Showing Your Expertise: By asking enough detailed questions about your prospects potential use of your product or service,

you can usually demonstrate your knowledge of it. Remember, people do like to buy from smart people.

11. <u>Show your Prospects Expertise</u>: Put the spotlight on your prospect. Ask about his or her company, product or service. Again, by putting the spotlight on them it shows you are interested in what they are saying. This then makes them feel important by showing you how much they know which then stimulates a more conducive mental state towards buying your product or service.

12. <u>To Move Towards the Close</u>: This reasoning is very similar to offering your prospect a choice close. For example, ask them, "Would you rather have a one bedroom unit or a two bedroom?"

13. <u>To Ask for the Order</u>: This reason is self-explanatory <u>but</u> the question asked the least by salespeople.

Creating trust, bonding or fusing with your prospect is a high percentage of the sales process. You need to understand the reasoning behind the questions you are asking. What information exactly is it that you really searching for and why?

TYPES OF QUESTIONS

<u>Open-ended questions</u> are questions that require your prospect to answer with other than a yes or no response. An example would be, "Jay, how is the weather back in Denver these days?" They must respond with something other than a yes or no.

You never want to ask a prospect a question that will give you either a yes or a no response. Why? These are <u>close-ended questions</u> and a yes can mean either:

a) Yes, we are just being well mannered and agreeing with you to get out of here, or
b) Yes, we are really want to know more, or
c) Yes, we are a lay down, let us do the paperwork.

Close-ended questions will give your prospect a reason to say no and you will hear no more often than you will hear yes. Instead, ask them an open-ended question about how they FEEL about something. Remember you are selling on emotion. "How do you feel about what you have heard so far?"

Along with open or close-ended questions, there are fourteen other types of questions that we will cover in more detail in a later chapter.

You uncover needs by questioning skillfully and listening carefully. Your job is to identify the basic and secondary needs that your product or service can satisfy and then demonstrate this fact to the customer. You can identify these needs by further breaking down each type of question into three levels.

In Chapter 4 we briefly covered first, second and third level questions. These three types of questions are designed in such a way as to elicit information from your prospect gradually. Whichever type of question you ask, you need to ask in all three levels.

A quick reminder what the three levels of questions are:

1. First Level Question: This is a fact question. The response will not have much emotion, but will be honest.
2. Second Level Question: These are based on the response to the first level question BUT there is some feeling behind them.
3. Third Level Question: This is the emotional reason behind the second level response.

If you do not reach the third level, you will never identify the needs and emotions necessary to make a sale. The third level is always emotional and the buying motive.

Through each level of question you earn more credibility and trust with your prospect, as well as gain more personal information. Only by asking the right questions can you put all the pieces of your prospect puzzle together and if you can smoothly incorporate these levels of questions with your prospect's personality, you are well on your way to a Sale. In the next chapter, we will be examining in more detail how to get the best result from your questions by creating interest and desire and answering your prospect's buying questions?

6

Creating Interest and Desire

In the last chapter you hopefully learned how to interpret your prospects behavior as well as how to start asking more probing questions that will stimulate deeper conversation to create interest and desire. We learned that sales are emotional, not logical and that personal feelings persuade.

Yes, I do keep repeating these phrases but only because it is so important to remember that people buy for emotional reasons, not logical ones. It is the feeling that your prospect experiences, when they imagine themselves in a particular situation that really persuades them to make a decision. They would rather make a choice, or decision, now to avoid what they consider to be a potential embarrassing or dangerous situation later. This fear of loss creates a much stronger motivation for your prospect than the thought of gaining a pleasurable situation.

How do we stimulate these emotional feelings in our prospects? We need to create mental and emotional pictures. Mental pictures create the dream. Emotional pictures create their dream. Stories bring out a multiple dimension view of what you are talking about without stating it as a cold hard fact. Experts have shown that people think in the terms of pictures, not statistics, so we need to create these pictures using third party stories.

Each step of the sales process is designed to maximize your prospects involvement, retention and enthusiasm. Your challenge is to create pictures and scenes that will have the most impact on your prospect in the most memorable, exciting and efficient manner. Third party stories are vivid, colorful pictures to which your prospect can relate. A master story teller can make a sale without ever having put a pen to paper.

WHAT IS A THIRD PARTY STORY?

A third party story is a story told through the eyes of someone else. By transferring the experience to an 'imaginary' third party sitting with you, you will get more of an objective ear from your prospect. A master story teller can tell a third party story so convincingly that your prospect will believe that 'this person' was indeed real and had shared their experiences with them.

To create this effect the story must be told in an entertaining and credible format that highlights certain aspects of your product or service. The story must also be told to them in their channel, realm or thinking or mental state. In addition, it must include their concerns and hot buttons to create the mental or emotional pictures necessary to show the benefits that they are going to derive from your product or service. Your 'imaginary' third party can be a family member, a friend, an acquaintance, or even yourself, providing it is relevant to a similar experience to the one in question. Always give your prospects' analogies that relate specifically to their lives and their circumstances.

WHY WE TELL THIRD PARTY STORIES

The main objective of a third party story is to create a dialogue, as opposed to a monologue. Getting your prospect to open up and share their story with you is one of the essentials for a good presentation. As such, you need to initiate this dialogue by telling a third party story.

Watch your prospects reactions while you are telling that first third party story. See what kind of listener they are. Are they attentive? Do they make eye contact with you? Are they responsive? Do they appear to want to become involved with your story? Anything that you can learn while telling the story will dictate how you continue with your sales presentation. If they are sincerely listening to you then they will begin want to share a story with you. Once they start telling you a story from their lives, you have created a dialogue.

While your prospect is telling you their 'third party' story, be a sincere and attentive listener. You will be amazed at how your prospect will transform from being unresponsive to feeling comfortable within their surroundings. Part of becoming a master story teller is becoming a master listener.

Besides removing that initial sales resistance we also tell third party stories to:

- ease your prospects apprehension and fears
- excite your prospect
- gain information about their family, occupation, recreation and motivation
- create commonality and rapport
- get your prospect participating and involved in the sales process
- show benefits
- ease financial concerns
- overcome any and all objections

Yes, third party stories will also overcome any objection or obstacle. Should your prospect throw you an objection that you do not think you can overcome, respond with a simple third party story. It is much easier than stumbling over words, tripping over your tongue or trying to 'lie' your way out of it. For example, starting your story with, "You know, it is so strange that you should ask that, let me tell you about the time . . ."

Third party stories are the most effective when done <u>before</u> you show benefits. If you try to show a benefit first your prospect may tell you that they have "heard it all before," and not listen to you. Always tell a third party story first then show the benefit. If you do this I will guarantee that your prospect will listen and appreciate the benefits more.

WHY THIRD PARTY STORES ARE SO EFFECTIVE

People buy when they are in an emotional state of mind. As such, a good third party story should contain as much emotion as possible, focused on the benefit or the objection that you are trying to show or overcome.

The three reasons why third party stories are so effective:

1. It is much easier, and less threatening, for your prospects to listen to you tell a good story than to high pressure sell them.
2. Telling a story that directly relates to your prospect makes them feel comfortable and secure. Remember, people readily accept people who are like themselves and are more likely to buy from them.
3. They get and keep your prospects attention. Your prospect is more likely to want to listen to you if the story is entertaining and relates directly to their lives.

You should also toss out two or three curiosity 'seeds' when telling a third party story. These may be potential benefits or features that you wish to cover later on in your presentation, but by casually mentioning them now you are 'testing the waters' so to speak. Your prospect may not hear you specifically, however subconsciously they will remember what was said. Over the course of a sales presentation you may toss out twenty or thirty curiosity 'seeds' which some, or possibly all, may generate buying questions from your prospect. The more seeds you are able to throw out, the greater chance you have of discovering what motivates, and stimulates, your prospect.

Five Rules of a Great Third Party Story

1. <u>Always be consistent</u>. You have to tell the same third party story every time you tell it.
2. <u>Use animation when telling a story</u>. The more involved you are with the story, the more your prospects will become involved with it. The very dramatic part comes in how you tell the story. How you can captivate your prospect with the intensity of your voice, your body movements and your gestures. You should be able to dramatically illustrate your point and mentally draw your prospect away from the dullness of the presentation all while entertaining them.
3. <u>It must be based on the truth</u>. Never lie to make the sale. You can combine stories, alter occupations or change names to make the story relevant, but it must be based on the truth.

4. <u>The story must be relevant and serve a purpose</u>. It must be directly related to your prospects situation by either handling an objection, using a dominant buying motive or benefit.

5. <u>It must include detail</u>. Use as many specific details as you can in the story to make it more believable. Use names, dates, locations, colors, smell and noises. Anything that will create, and stimulate, mental and emotional pictures in your prospect. Without the entire build up the story can lose about fifty percent of its impact.

Though not a rule specifically, you should have, at the very least, fifty to seventy-five third party stories in your repertoire. Essentially you need to have a minimum of five stories for each type of prospect personality and objection situation that you may meet.

Do not overload your prospects with information. Remember to keep your stories entertaining. A good third party story will keep your prospect captivated throughout the presentation as well as giving their mind a chance to rest from thinking of potential objections. What effect can compelling third party stories have on your prospects? Watch them. By using all of your senses and dramatic superlatives you will start creating and stimulating your prospects imagination—so much so that all of a sudden they start seeing and visualizing them self-owning your product or using your service. Once you start to stimulate emotion you will soon begin to hear objections, so a little later in this chapter we will learn how to create interest and desire using those objections.

Establishing need, interest and desire are a major part of the sales process. Your prospects, however, will not permit you to expose a possible need (or their desire) for your product until they really start to like it. This chapter will also start giving you some techniques in how to ask the right questions which will uncover problems which will lead to objections. It is the way in which you ask a question that directly affects the answer you receive. By asking questions effectively, you can then learn to create problems and stimulate the objections you can control throughout your presentation.

You, by this point, have hopefully established trust between yourself and your prospect by asking good, non-threatening questions and having performed a thorough discovery, your prospects will begin to open up and relax. So how can you help solve their problems when they do not believe they have any? For those you in the timeshare industry, remember, these people are on vacation and do not have a care in the world (now). Regardless of the sales situation, **you must create a problem and objections**.

Problems are created by focusing on third level motivations—the Fear of Loss and the Desire of Gain. You must let your prospects know that they are missing out on something by not having your product or service. This is why it is important to create a problem, listen to the objection in order to stimulate interest and curiosity in your product or service. Only by doing this can you then establish their dominant buying motive or need. **Prospects will not buy anything they think they do not need.**

To create interest and curiosity, as well as establish a need in your product or service you need to do the following:

1. Answer their questions as generally as you can. **Create curiosity responses**. Do not be specific in your answers otherwise they will thank you for the "information" and want to leave. For example, you might say, "That was a great question and I am going to answer it for you. However can I do it a little later on in my presentation, because right now I just want to hear more about how you . . ."

2. It is imperative that you find out what they know about your industry (or the product). You should have done this when completing the survey sheet or questionnaires. If you do not find out what their opinion is of the industry, you will never move forward with your presentation.

3. Empathize with whatever they feel about the industry (or your product). Use it to your advantage. For example, say "Jay, I can understand how you feel about the [car, insurance, vacation ownership, etc.] industry and we have come a long way from those days of high pressure and locked room tactics."

4. "Box" their future use of your product or service. For example, find out how important vacations are to them. You must find out if they are going to continue vacationing on a regular basis.
5. Find out how they feel about their present method of service, product, vacationing. Ask about anything that may not have been "perfect." For example, ask them, "Oh, you did not have a problem at the reception desk when you checked into your hotel, did you?"
6. Ask them how they feel about their use of your product or membership, if they are existing users or timeshare owners. Use the information from the survey sheet for reference. For example, ask your prospect, "What made you decide to buy?" This will get you an emotional motive <u>but</u> a logical reason. Do not worry if the response is positive or negative, you want the feeling.
7. In the timeshare industry, we ask them if location is important to them on vacation. This is critical information because if you discover that your prospects would only come back to your location every fifth year, you had better show exchange as the dominant logical vacation benefit. This would eliminate their objection, "We would never come here so why would be buy here."
8. <u>Do not start your presentation until your prospect asks you a buying question</u>. You cannot solve their problems by giving out too much information, too early. This is because you have not yet discovered the need or found the problem therefore there is no need of a solution.

Creating problems, establishing needs and revealing their objections are a major part of the sales process. Your prospect will not permit you to expose a possible need for your product so they offer you objections.

STIMULATING OBJECTIONS

Before the discovery process their primary objection was to being in front of you. Once you enter the discovery process other objections begin to come forth. Do not respond to them at this point. Never sell or answer any objections in the discovery process because your prospect will soon realize that you are using all of their information against them.

WHAT IS AN OBJECTION?

Again, by definition, an 'objection' is the *opposition, or protest, of something that is unpleasant*. Guess what? Your prospects primary objection may be in front of you, or on the telephone, because it is an unpleasant experience for them. This is why, when you get an objection from your prospect you should always acknowledge it, clarify it and then step over it. They will use any excuse, real or imagined, to distract you, throw you off track, create a smoke screen or mislead you.

However, if the same objection comes up during the sales presentation it now becomes a buying concern. They are interested in your product or service but do not fully understand how it can benefit them. Should you get the same objection a third time, it is now a condition of the sale. In most instances, you can use the second objection to create an angle for the third objection. In a later chapter, I will explain how to deal with second and third level objections.

WHAT MOTIVATES OBJECTIONS?

Fear is the number one reason behind an objection. The fear of being sold something they do not want and/or their fear of appearing ignorant. In the timeshare industry, when a prospect comes to a presentation there is a chance that someone has told them that timeshare is a rip off and a scam. They may have been told by the media, restaurant owner, some guy on the street, another hotel guest, an airline employee, neighbor, relative to avoid timeshare. This is so burned into their brain it gives them a pre-conceived notion that triggers off the fear. This fear is their natural defense mechanism that triggers off an objection that is their only way to disguise the fear and protect themselves. If you are in another sales environment, think about whether fear or feeling ignorant maybe stimulating the objections.

Basically, an objection is a camouflaged emotion that has been put into a logical form and presented to you as a justifiable, logical reason for not doing (or buying) anything. An objection can also be used to test your intent and sincerity towards them and your belief in your product.

If your prospect wants to test your belief and integrity they will throw out objections that, in reality, are nothing other than excuses. If you do not deal with them properly in the front end you will not get a commitment in the back end.

HOW DO YOU UNCOVER OBJECTIONS?

The most effective method to uncover an objection is to ASK your prospect a buying question. You will be surprised at what will happen when you ask a buying question. Be careful that you ask the right buying questions so that you uncover the right buying objections.

DEALING WITH OBJECTIONS

The great thing about whatever industry you may be in is that the objections are always the same. Oh, the wording may be different depending on your industry but I still get the same basic objections as I did over twenty-five years ago, when I started in this business. The world has evolved to offer so many more options, features and choices that may confuse your prospect and you in your analysis of it. All objections stem from a basic fear or misunderstanding. Remember, prospects are no longer naive and uneducated, so how do you handle these objections?

First, when you get an objection early in your sales presentation, let them play with it for a little while so they can become used to it. Why? Because if they are concentrating on that objection, they will not think be thinking up another one. Prospects will then adopt this objection as their anchor objection so that it becomes the only major one you will eventually have to overcome.

Later on when you get another objection from your prospect you should do the following five things <u>before</u> you deal with it.

1. **<u>Echo It</u>**: Just repeat back what the prospect says to you. Example: "How do <u>you</u> know that it might not work?"
2. **<u>Understand It</u>**: Let them know that you understand how they feel. Example, "Jay, I understand how you feel about the . . ."
3. **<u>Appreciate It</u>**: Always, always thank them for it. Example: "Jay, thank you for telling me that."
4. **<u>Agree with It</u>**: Example: "Jay, I agree with you. You obviously are not going to join the club today if this program does not exchange to the destinations you want, are you?"
5. **<u>Clarify It</u>**: This will reveal the emotion, and the real concern, behind the objection. Example, "Jay, could you please clarify for me exactly what you are looking for in an exchange?"

To put the points together, here is an example:

Jay: "How do I know that I will get an exchange?"
Salesperson: "How do you know that you will get an exchange?"
Jay :   "Yes, how do I know that I will get an exchange, to Hawaii, at Christmas time?"

Now you have located the real concern as well as found out information to help tailor your presentation to their needs.

ANALYZING THE OBJECTION

Besides Echoing, Understanding, Appreciating, Agreeing and Clarifying the objection, you should also be asking yourself the following questions about the objection. Your analysis of the objection determines how you should handle it.

For example, what is the <u>problem</u>?

- Is it a fear?
- Is it a desire?

- Is it a condition?
- Is it a diversionary tactic?
- Is it to test my sincerity or integrity?
- Is it real?
- Is it worth expending time and energy?
- Is it a problem and can I use it to my advantage?

The next thing you need to determine—what is the <u>need</u>?

- What is the prospect looking for?
- Is this objection a legitimate buying concern or condition?
- Is he really worried about this objection or is it a smoke screen?
- Does he really want me to respond to this objection now or can it wait?
- Are they giving me this objection just to make me angry or rattle my cage?
- If I answer or deal with this objection right now, will it get me closer to discovering the dominant buying motive?

After you have considered these choices, you now must decide how to handle the objection. It is important to remember that you cannot handle the objection, until you have determined in which direction you want to go. In other words, what is <u>your goal</u> in handling this objection?

- What is the goal of the objection? (This relates to the first one above—what is prospect looking for?)
- What is your reaction to their objection?
- Can you identify the objection? Should you to try to dig deeper to find out if there is any hidden emotion or attitude prompting this objection?
- Should you step over this objection and see if they bring it up again as a buying concern?

By the way, an objection is thrown up as a smoke screen to distract you. Just ignore it, because just like water, it will eventually evaporate.

WHAT ARE THE MOST COMMON OBJECTIONS?

In a later chapter of this book I will give examples on how to respond to each type of objection using the six techniques listed above. For now I will just list them for your reference. Even though I have listed these objections specifically towards the vacation ownership industry, just substitute your product or service and see if these are ones you have heard before in sales career.

1. We (I) need to think about it.
2. We (I) do not vacation this way or We do not use your product or service.
3. Vacations are not a priority or we do not see a use for this product or service.
4. We are (I am) buying a home OR some other tangible priority.
5. We are saving to put our kids through college.
6. We (I) need to talk to our (my) attorney, accountant, father, brother-in-law, etc.
7. We (I) just were married (divorced).
8. We (I) need to shop around.
9. I want it, but my spouse does not OR we need to discuss it privately.
10. We (I) cannot afford it.

<u>Whatever industry you are in—fifty percent (50%) of all the objections you hear will be "I/we have to think about it."</u> The truth is that "think about it" is not an objection. It is camouflage for, we do not trust you, we have no desire, we are totally confused and we have not been listening to you. The only way to overcome "think about it" is to go back and find the dominant buying motive, create desire and link it to your product. Create a high level of emotional desire, ask for the order in as many ways as you can and close all the "doors." **There is no magic shtick for "think about it", just a magic presentation.**

The way in which you handle objections must be conducive to testing out the validity, or the weight, of it. If you handle the objections in the manner that I have shown above you will be amazed at how quickly the objections disappear and the questions appear. **It is your perception of**

the objection that causes the problems on a table, not the objection itself.

In the last chapter we learned how and why we ask questions. We found out that by asking good, open-ended questions in the discovery you earned the right to ask more personal questions later. So, by listening carefully to their responses you found their third level or emotional buying motives. Then, because your prospect truly believes that you sincerely care about them and not your bank account, they have allowed (or empowered) you with everything you need to make a sale. They will now begin to ask questions <u>and</u> let you start your sales presentation or presentation.

PROSPECT QUESTIONS

Initially prospects ask questions purely to test your reactions, sincerity and integrity or to put you off your balance in what you are doing. Unfortunately salespeople feel that they need to answer all the questions with too much information or have the exact answer immediately and then try to close the sale against the question. Instead of realizing the question may have been asked only to test your knowledge about your product or service or as a defensive strategy.

When your prospect asks you a question you have to determine whether it has any bearing on your going forward. You can do this by either one of two ways:

1. <u>Clarify the question</u>: Have your prospect repeat the question two or three times. You need to understand what is being asked of you. Ask them to repeat the question you can then make the assumption that they want to know why or how something works. Their chance of listening increases tenfold if they give you a definite "yes" because they have empowered themselves to really want to know the answer.
2. <u>Postpone the question</u>: If you truly believe that the question is being asked to derail your presentation you may postpone the question by deferring it to later. Say something like, "Wow,

that was a great question and I will get back to that in a minute. Because right now I am on page two of my presentation and you are on page eight, fair enough?"

If the question was just a smoke screen then you have not insulted them by refusing to answer and/or they will forget it when the time comes. Postponement also does a "take away" of the answer that now creates curiosity in your product or service.

As you progress further up the buying curve your prospect will begin to ask questions because they are now sincerely interested in your product. Once this occurs you must then anticipate what your prospects are thinking.

In the minds of all prospects, there are three basic questions that must be answered before they will make a choice. The biggest problem is that the prospect will not verbalize them. However, they can turn up as objections that should be overcome.

Prospects have three questions that they will rarely ask, yet you have to answer before you make a sale. They are:

1. Will your product or service work?
2. Is it the best one available for my needs?
3. Will it continue to be the best in the future?

If you remember their questions when you ask your questions, you will not only alleviate your prospects fear and tension, you can accurately pinpoint hot buttons and buying motives. For example, ask, "Valerie, were you aware that you and your family, can now, and in the future, use all the vacation ownership benefits?"

CREATING INTEREST AND DESIRE

Once you have developed a good rapport with your prospect and they now trust you, you have developed the correct relationship, found the dominant buying motive, linked it to a problem and funneled down to the real objections it is time to move on to the next step in the sales process which is creating interest and desire.

The purpose of the presentation is to further qualify your prospect by going over the key benefits, or reasons, of why they should own your product or service. Because you have created a problem by redefining their emotional need you now must create value in the solution. Your prospect must see value in why your product or service is better than any of the alternatives that may be available to them because creating value sparks interest.

From this point forward you will have to show your prospect, from the 'information' you have gathered, one benefit, or feature, at a time <u>until</u> you can pinpoint the <u>very</u> hot button. Then, once you have found that hot button you create value and need (desire) around it. You should be focusing only on what is a benefit to them. Once, you have created enough value or desire for your product, emotionally, logically or a combination of both, you can then go for the close. Desire and decisions are the cornerstones to a sale. If you want to write a sale, get the desire because it will always prompt the decision.

The secret to your presentation is to create emotion. Your presentation should show your prospect an emotional problem and then provide them with an emotional solution. A secret of selling is listening and letting your prospect believe that they are in control. There is no better feeling than taking a raw prospect and getting them to design their membership based on all the information they have heard or volunteered.

CREATING INTEREST THROUGH VALUE

One of the easiest ways to sell your product or service is to build value. If people do not see value in something, then price is irrelevant. You must build <u>the value</u> of your product or service in the eyes of your prospect to the point that it <u>exceeds</u> the value of the money they have in their pockets. If the value exceeds the price then a prospect will make a choice that day.

<u>How do you create interest</u>? You focus on the emotional keys using the benefits of your product. You want your prospect to respond emotionally to everything that they hear about the benefit you are showing them. People buy with emotion and justify with logic later. By doing a logical, yet emotional sales presentation you <u>must</u> get your prospect's to <u>feel</u> an emotional benefit, which in turn they see <u>value</u> that stimulates a logical buying decision.

Behind every person, no matter who they are, or what they do for a living, is an emotion. This is why I believe that there 'is a deal on every table.' People do things and act upon them when they are in their dominant emotional state. When people are complacent and in control of their emotions, they will not do anything that is not logical. When they become emotional and unstable they begin to do things that they would otherwise not do, logically.

As you begin to build value you will find that your prospect will begin to build <u>their</u> value in your product. A successful salesperson is one who can let their prospect's build their value because they have empowered them with the ability to close themselves. For example, prospect's would much rather design their own vacation programs than have you show them the chemical formula for rocket fuel. By keeping your presentation simple (K.I.S.S. theory) and creating value, the emotional impact will overwhelm any of the objections or logical reasons they may have been thinking.

Value Schticks

What exactly is a shtick? Shticks are short stories, examples or comparisons that <u>relate directly</u> to the mental channel of your prospect. Shticks focus on creating value in your prospects emotional or mental state of mind <u>and</u> their hot buttons or buying motives. Your shticks should always cause an emotional reaction in your prospect's mind. Without the emotional reaction to create value and desire you will never get a decision. It is important that you understand that the majority of the value you will create will be done through using some form of emotional shtick.

For example, within the vacation ownership industry, you can use a money shtick to show value with your product.

> "You will probably continue to go on vacation every year without this membership; however it will have to be places like Mexico, where it is relatively inexpensive. If you had to make a choice between a $1,500 package deal to Mexico and a $4,500 one to Australia, which would you choose? You would choose Mexico more than likely because of the lower cost. On the other hand, if you could vacation in Australia for that same $1,500, would you consider that to be better value for your money?"

The second way to create value is to simply be direct. Ask your prospect what they would need to see in your product or service for it to be of value to them. You will find that extremely successful salespeople will just ask their prospect what they want specifically and build value around that.

USING BENEFITS TO CREATE DESIRE

You cannot give out information and expect to get a decision. The same theory applies in that you cannot talk all the time and expect your prospect to be listening to you. You need a relationship or a bond before you can expect a decision. The sales process is not an information-relationship sale, it is a relationship sale. If you expend your energy on talking at the beginning of the presentation, then you will be burnt out by this point in the sales process. This is where you need your energy and enthusiasm the most. It takes energy to be creative in building value and interest. By using the hot buttons and buying motives of your prospect you show them the benefits of your product or service.

Using benefits to create desire is done by translating those benefits into a course of action. Prospects want benefits that they can relate to feelings or things that can be used directly to acquire something they want or to avoid something they do not want. Fear of loss or desire to gain.

FEATURE OR BENEFIT?

Quality features should always be explained to the prospect by <u>how it will benefit them</u>. However, it is never a benefit until it solves the needs of the prospect. Prospects never buy features, only benefits.

Think of it as selling a Rolls Royce. You want the prospect to buy the whole car so you show them how ALL the features will benefit them by owning it. However most salespeople sell only one or two features such as the stereo system or heated seats and should something ultimately go wrong, they no longer want the car. If they have purchased the whole car and the stereo quits working, they have the iPod station to use while the stereo gets fixed.

Discerning between features and benefits requires some thought. You have to mentally sift through all the information you gathered during the discovery process and decide—is this something they might like or something they truly need?

The underlying concern here for the prospect is—what is in it for me? Every prospect that you meet will ask themselves this question with every statement that you make. In addition, they are also saying 'so what' to everything else you are saying. Make sure that everything that you say has a very definite benefit for them and you will never go wrong.

Remember, the product or service must always be the most suitable for their needs before a decision enters into the equation. Just as people will not buy if they see no value, quality is not a determining factor until after the benefit has been shown.

If you choose to show a feature to a prospect, you <u>must</u> show a corresponding benefit and why it is important to them. Theoretically, a sale depends upon three things:

1. The benefits that your prospect is willing to pay for
2. A product or service that has these benefits
3. Your ability to tell the prospect why it is important to them

If you cannot communicate a corresponding benefit to a feature, do not mention it because it has no value to your prospect. You have to be showing beneficial value to stimulate interest and desire, all the time, to get your prospect committed to your product or service.

Little Test: <u>Which is a feature, which is a benefit</u>?

1. Make a list of all the benefits and/or features that are applicable to your product or service.
2. Read through the list and choose what you think is a feature (F), benefit (B) or a dominant buying motive (DBM). Use as many as you think would apply to each item listed.

How did you do? What you may have listed as a feature can also be molded into a benefit if it can be seen as a dominant buying motive for your prospect. If you were listening carefully enough to them in the discovery process, then <u>your</u> only problem is deciding which benefit to show them first. Remember you have to go through each feature or benefit you have uncovered until you find the one that stimulates the dominant emotional buying motive.

Once you find the third level buying motives, stop 'selling the feature' and create dreams and emotions on the benefit. Let your prospects 'see' and 'feel' the benefits whenever possible. Get them to 'see' sunsets in Bali and the beaches in Hawaii or 'feel' the wind in their hair as they drive the spectacular Monterey coast with the top down (if you are selling a convertible).

You are not there to educate them (information-relationship); you are there to make your prospect's dreams come true. Keep showing benefits that they respond to emotionally. Be creative. Intertwine the benefit with a good third party story.

Prospect's buy three things in a sales presentation:

1. Your constrained enthusiasm
2. Your sincere personality
3. The emotions they will receive by owning your product or service.

Oh, by the way—without a prospect, there is no benefit to you!

Now that you have uncovered objections and started to create interest and desire, your prospect will begin asking real questions. They are now ready to hear about your product or service. Only then, should you start your presentation which is the next crucial step in the buying curve.

Side Note: Before I move on to the importance of the sales presentation, I am going to mention **your LIFE RAFT.** Yes, every salesperson needs a life raft. Why? Well, what happens to some salespeople during their presentation is that they all of a sudden will find themselves hitting a brick wall. They believe they are focusing on giving value to the right benefit, but soon realize that they have gone nowhere. So, how can you get back on track? Get back on your life raft.

What is your life raft? This is the conversation topic that makes your prospect <u>feel</u> the most comfortable. This can be anything from family to ecological preservation to their tennis game. Talk about anything that they are passionate about <u>and</u> it will get them emotionally centered again.

The secret, however, is to see the wall coming. When you do, say to yourself—oh god, where is my life raft? Immediately jump back on that life raft to avoid the approaching wall. How? Divert your prospect back to the life raft by saying, "You know what let us not talk about that any more tell me about . . . (their favorite topic)." By pulling them back with you on the lifeline to the raft, it takes the pressure off and gives you the opportunity to try another benefit angle. Remember, all you do is start talking about the most comfortable topic you were talking about during the discovery or FORM.

7

The Sales Presentation

This is where you are planting the seeds of the sale. The seeds are all their benefits, watered with value, interest and desire. If you do your presentation correctly it will <u>create a perception of your product or service in your prospect's mind</u>.

Up to this point you should have been doing trial closes, tie downs and asking for the order through subtle and non-aggressive methods. We will learn more about these techniques in the next chapter, however by the time you start your presentation you should be assuming the sale.

Do not start your sales presentation until you have invested sufficient time in building up your customer's trust and your credibility. Everything that you say, every third party story that you tell, has to tie into your 'story' that you told them when you initially greeted them. Then, you need to build your whole presentation around that to ensure their trust in your credibility. Whatever story you told them in the beginning to gain self-credibility, must be maintained throughout your presentation. If you do not, you will lose your prospect's trust and your credibility and just end up spinning your wheels for the balance of your presentation.

You need to have a defined presentation that will sift out use, need, desire, interest and not go past the buying curve. If you remember back to the chapter on the Preparation, I discussed the importance of a good, well-defined presentation.

Every time you take a prospect you must use the same presentation. You can achieve twenty to thirty percent sales if you are consistent. When you are consistent, you get consistent results. If you do the same presentation, <u>with</u> the same attitude, the same conviction and the same belief every time, you will get the same results (sale). Conversely, if you do the same presentation <u>without</u> the same belief every time you will also get the same results every time (no sale).

With that in mind, which one of the following statements applies to your presentation?

- Great presentation—no attitude—no sales
- Same presentation—great attitude—sales
- Off the cuff presentation—great attitude—no sales

By keeping your presentation short, simple and emotional you will be able to create value, interest and desire in the eyes of your prospect. Remember, the Definition of Insanity is doing the same thing repeatedly and expecting different results.

How Long Should it Be?

Your presentation should be designed to show or explain your product in five to fifteen minute increments. However, be as quick and simple as is needed, or as slow and precise as is needed. Remember, people only have an <u>attention</u> level of twenty minutes and a <u>retention</u> level of about thirty seconds, so make your presentation creative and enthusiastic to use their retention time effectively.

A successful salesperson has high energy, enthusiasm, humor, vitality, intensity, creativity, sincerity, is a great listener and is totally relaxed. The simplest presentation in the world will work when delivered with enthusiasm and sincerity. The most complicated presentation will fail if not done with passion and belief.

Checking your Presentation

You must be able to continuously ask yourself the following questions. Always be moving forward with your presentation. If you feel that you are not moving forward at any time, stop 'presenting' and get back onto your life raft.

- How does it work and how it going to benefit your prospect? This should be the primary objective behind your presentation.
- How entertaining is my presentation or how absorbing is my presentation?
- Is your presentation being accepted in the right fashion or attitude?
- Is my presentation keeping my prospect's attention?
- Are they becoming curious?
- Is my presentation planting seeds?
- Does my presentation have little morsels or tidbits that keep them on the edge of their seat?
- Is my presentation stimulating?
- Is my presentation hindering my relationship with my prospects?
- Is it productive and moving me forward and closer to a decision today?
- Is my presentation so confusing, boring or non—stimulating that I am hindering the closing process?
- Are you moving too fast? Are you going from "gee those are great picture of your kids to, now how would you like to handle the down payment?" Sometimes this does work, but only in rare instances.
- Can I make my presentation better? How many of you out there, honestly believe that your presentation could be better? If you want to make your presentation better take things out, do not add anything more. To ensure that your presentation does what it should, use your smart phone and video yourself or have a colleague listen to see what areas you may be weak on, then fix them.

Every time someone new gets into sales, nine times out of ten they will write business immediately. They are so excited that sales just happen. Then, believing they must learn everything about their product or service they start changing their presentation and soon find themselves in a slump. All of those new shticks, new third party stories and other things they thought would help them, only serve to hinder. They neither get out of their slump nor make more sales.

What happens in reality is that when you start gaining knowledge about your industry so you want to promote every feature in the right or most beneficial way. Even though your intention is good your technique becomes non-conducive to closing sales and you end up with what I call technicalitis.

The definition of **Technicalitis**: The art of adding something technical to a presentation that causes said presentation to work even less effectively.

By adding more 'stuff' that you think will help, you soon have designed that formula for rocket fuel and "technicalitis" begins. You can no longer entertain your prospect because they are so busy thinking about the formula they are no longer listening to you.

As you start becoming successful in this business you <u>will</u> start adding more information to your presentation, guaranteed. All of a sudden your presentation has no beginning or end. You do not know when to start it or have any control over it. I have seen this happen to salespeople a thousand times. The solution, take stuff <u>out </u>of your presentation and end the suffering of "technicalitis".

THE CONTENT OF A SALES PRESENTATION

In order to get your prospect in a buying frame of mind is to make sure that they are totally comfortable, relaxed and are no longer fearful of your intentions. When they get to that stage, your presentation can go into millions of different forms and you can then say almost anything to them.

Some examples are:

> "Let me show you the difference between . . ."
> "Let me show why . . . ."

> "Wow, that is(was) a great question and I think that is number four, or maybe number five, of the most frequently asked questions. [Pause] I bet you are now wondering what questions one through four might be?"

Once your prospects are thinking more about how to get into the deal rather than out of it, they will start thinking about asking buying questions. They are wondering what the most frequently asked questions (FAQ) are. Very similar to the game show Jeopardy—"the most common brand of toothpaste on the market is?"

By the way, if you are confused, your client is most definitely confused. Remember your client does not know anything, so only tell them what they need to know, not everything that you know.

I am willing to bet that most people reading this book will know more statistical information about their industry or the timeshare business that I do. However, I believe that it is my style of closing that comes across better to the prospect. Prospects can feel my sincerity, my belief and my intensity behind each statement or question. My presentation consists of my just asking questions because I want to know the answers. I do not tell them anything until they ask me specifically.

You must provide your prospect with enough information about your product or service so that they become curious and interested enough to start asking questions.

As to the content of your presentation, consider the following ten suggestions:

1. Keep it simple, individual and unique to your personality.
2. Provide your prospects with a piece of paper and a pen to write down questions or make notes for themselves.
3. Be animated, have fun, and use THIRD PARTY STORIES to illustrate the benefits to them and make your point.
4. Use VALUE shticks throughout the presentation on why it is more advantages for them to buy your product or service than their present method.

5. Use TIE DOWNS and TRIAL CLOSES to get commitments from your prospect. (These will be covered in more detail in the next chapter)

6. Briefly explain the difference between your product and the alternatives. For example, timeshare versus package vacations.

7. Show your membership benefits to build value by putting them into the picture.

8. Maintain steady eye contact to convey your sincerity and rapt attention to what they are saying and maintain control.

9. Talk loudly. It is presumed that if you are whispering to your prospect then you must be lying to them. Conversely, if you are talking in a loud and animated manner then what you are saying must be the truth.

10. Do not positive presentation. Maintain the attitude that you have a product that would greatly benefit them and they need to persuade you to sell it to them.

You must use the same, simple presentation with each prospect to achieve consistent results.

Over the past thirty years I have heard and seen many different variations of the same presentation. I would also hazard a guess to say that there are as many variations as there are salespeople presenting them. Specifically, they are all a variation of the same presentation—however it is the manner in which they are offered that makes them individual and unique.

T-PRESENTATIONS

These types of presentations are applicable in certain sales environments but not all, however as an exercise you can try to see if your product or service can be explained in this manner.

If you are in the timeshare industry a <u>Rent versus Own or T-Presentation</u> can be used quite effectively. This logical presentation is probably <u>the</u> most important step in using logic as a justifier. It is a simple, yet powerful, presentation comparing the benefits of renting versus owning.

It is a <u>choice</u> that you are offering your prospect that has a logical base, yet an emotional response. You logically <u>compare</u> what your prospect is current doing to what you are offering, providing that you make the comparison using their emotional reasons. Third, you use your prospects numbers (under hotel cost per night) when you are comparing what they are currently doing against what you are <u>offering</u> them.

A sample of a Rent vs. Own or T-Presentation may be as follows:

RENTER	OWNER
Hotel Room (2 people)	Room (2, 4, 6 or more people)
$100.00/night x 14 nights (No inflation)	Condominium, Kitchen facilities
= $1,400.00	Personal Vacation Use
	Loan it out as Gift
	Will it as part of your estate
x 30 years	Rent it = $$
	Resell it = $$
	Exchange (4500 Worldwide locations)
$ 42,000.00 LOST	**$ 21,000 EQUITY GAINED**

Note: This will vary based upon your product offering.

The most important point to remember in a T or rent versus own presentation is that the prospect is always right. We learned in earlier chapters never argue with a prospect because you cannot win with logic. Remember, prospects buy for third level emotional reasons, not logical ones.

PRODUCT PRESENTATIONS OR DEMONSTRATIONS

In sales environments where you need to show your prospect a physical product you can do this in pretty much the same manner as you did showing a benefit to them. If you can demonstrate your product in person, you should make sure to highlight your products benefits to suit your prospects needs. If possible, have them touch it or see how it ¨feels against their skin¨, if selling cosmetics, how much younger or healthier it will be for them. If you are working through some form of social media, you can combine the webcam, webinars, tweets or Facebook options to get your prospect to interact with you. Remember, fear of loss or gain.

If you are selling by telephone, try to get your prospect to see themselves using your product, again using the 'see and feel' techniques on how it will benefit them. The secret to your presentation is to create value, using emotional benefits. Your presentation should show your prospect an emotional problem and then provide them with an emotional solution.

THE TOUR

Not all sales environments require a physical tour, however if they do, the tour portion should occur after you have given them your product presentation. By taking your prospect on a tour of your resort or property you can relate things said to what they are now seeing. Visual confirmation of a benefit reinforces their emotional buying motive.

The second reason to tour is that your prospect has now been sitting for a considerable time and is becoming bored and tired. If you see them getting fidgety or their attention span is getting shorter, get up and go on tour. Take them out to sit in the car and feel the leather upholstery, tour your resort and highlight the views, show the model suites. Changing the environment is vital to maintaining your prospect's attention.

Third, do your tour as late in your presentation as you can. Psychologically, taking the tour first puts your prospect on the defensive. They are quite aware that when they enter the showroom or salesroom you will begin your presentation and 'closing' them. By doing the tour later on in the presentation you also maintain the control you acquired during the agenda.

WARNING:

ALWAYS DO A TOUR BEFORE YOU CLOSE. If you wait to do your tours after you begin the closing process your prospects may not like the property, or the accommodations or what they see. They can lose their emotional 'ether', change their mind and say no. Use the tour as one of your closing tools.

TIPS ON TOURING

1. Take control of the tour. Ask your prospect to follow you so they do not become lost or left behind.
2. Refresh their memory. Remind them that you told them during the Agenda, that you would be taking them on a tour of the property.
3. Familiarize or point out to your prospects the features or amenities for which they have shown interest. Do not point out any potential negatives while on tour.
4. Use Tie Downs and Trial Closes while on tour. The tour provides a perfect opportunity to seal your deal.
5. Put them into the picture or that "Rolls Royce" or . . . Get them to visualize themselves as an owner.
6. Greet other owners if you can by name. This lets your prospects know that they would be appreciated as members.
7. Take the opportunity to do further discovery or reinforce their emotional buying motives.
8. Ask them to think of any questions they might have for when you return to the salesroom.
9. When you get back from touring, ask if they would like a soda, juice, water or something else. This will make them feel

comfortable back in the sales environment and get them back into the habit of making choices.

10. Have fun, be animated and tell little third party stories about something that relates directly to your product, service or resort or current clients. This must be done in relation to their circumstances of course.

If you follow these tips, your tour will result in positive reinforcement of all the steps you have done to this point. From here on out, you will begin to close the sale.

One last note before we move towards creating urgency and getting a commitment. Even though I keep reminding you to keep your presentation simple, I can almost guarantee that everyone reading this chapter has way too much 'stuff' in their presentation. To further elaborate the need for simplicity in your presentation or presentation, I will share a personal note. The only things that I use to close sales are:

- a picture of my resort during pre-construction
- a photo album of my family and our vacations
- a price list
- three calculators
- A solid gold Montblanc pen I called 'Big Bertha'[1]

When I started in sales I was told I should have an expensive pen, because it would reflect my status as a successful salesperson. However, over the years I have learned that selling materialistically is akin to positive pitching, so from 'big Bertha' I went to a regular Montblanc. From the Montblanc I went to a BIC pen and then I started to borrow pens from my closers, now I use a pencil with a missing rubber thing (okay, the eraser). Soon I will start breaking the pencils in half or going to crayons. One day I will just close a sale with just my finger.

---

[1] I retired 'big Bertha' fifteen years ago after she had written about $250,000,000 worth of business. I had a glass box made for her and she now hangs proudly in my house. Although, she is all dented, twisted out of shape with the tip almost falling off, she was worth every cent of the $2000 she originally cost.

The point that I am making here is that the secret to closing a sale is not putting stuff in, but TAKING THINGS OUT. The more sales I do, the more I know it is _me_ the prospect buys. Remember to keep it simple because there is less chance of your confusing yourself and your prospect. Oh, one last thing, you really should use an expensive pen for them to sign the contract!

8

Creating Urgency and Gaining Commitment

A successful salesperson recognizes when their prospect has sold themselves on their product or service, has no more objections and their physiology is transmitting—I want to buy now—so ask me to buy. However, recognizing these signals and asking for the order is not always that simple. At some point in every presentation you, as the salesperson, have to take hold and ask for the order. The most difficult part of the sales process is crossing the line between the friendship you have now forged and asking for the order.

This is why I have continually stressed the importance of the discovery process of your presentation. Because the art of relationship closing is not showing many features and benefits and hoping that they will buy, it is about getting your prospect to listen to what you now have to say.

Up to this point we have gotten our prospect's attention by <u>completely focusing on them</u>. We asked simple, open-ended questions to gain acceptance into their lives. We then <u>earned the right to advance</u> by asking more personal questions to locate their dominant buying emotions. Because every prospect you speak to has different emotions you need to carefully listen to their responses, both spoken and those that remained unsaid. You need to learn to read 'between the lines' as it was and see the sales process from their side of the fence. If you do not empathize with your prospect you will never be able to understand what their dominant buying emotions are.

Then, finally, we <u>persuaded through involvement</u>. You gathered support for your asking for the sale by involving the prospect throughout the sales process. By asking specific questions you have guided your prospect to a realization that they can get what they want by doing what you would like them to do. They have now empowered you to get them to make the decision. You have also provided enough information to encourage your prospect to ask questions. By doing so, the prospect will expect the close and is conditioned to accept it. All through the presentation you should be aware of what your prospect is thinking and allows them to participate. Remember, they would much rather design their membership than have you do it for them.

How do you know when you need to quit selling benefits and start creating urgency to close the sale? There is a point in every sales presentation when your prospect is ready to make a decision about your product or service. Every prospect eventually reaches a point of actual persuasion and it is at this point that they will begin to transmit buying signals. Over the years, I have seen many salespeople miss the various signs of interest that prospects transmit either orally or through their body language. These signals come in a variety of forms—through active participation, speech patterns or obvious conversational pace. The first signal is when your prospect begins to ask buying questions. **When you hear the first buying question, stop selling and start closing the sale**.

To assist you in determining when to close, this chapter will help you to recognize buying signals, encourage prospect participation (urgency) and tie down your prospect with trial closes (commitment).

ENCOURAGING PROSPECT PARTICIPATION TO CREATE URGENCY

Being successful in sales has less to do with your 'brilliant sales presentation' and everything to do with leading your prospect to understand what they want and need. The only way to do this is through encouraging prospect participation throughout the sales process.

There is a quotation that states, "Keeping the prospect interested increases the success of any sales presentation. There is a basic psychological principle that states 'disinterest is more likely to occur when there is a lack of physical involvement.' Therefore good salespeople make concerted efforts to keep prospects physically active during the sales presentation."

Persuade through involvement. Many a master closer knows that when your prospect is fully involved in the presentation they are more easily persuaded to buy. *Remember that people love to buy but they do not like to be sold.*

Give your prospect's activity tasks during the presentation. Have them use calculators, give them things to play with and look through as well as things to complete. Tell them what to do—sit closer, turn that page, jot this down and add up these numbers—anything that will keep them actively involved. By the way, this also includes taking your prospect on a tour of your property.

You will be surprised at how little work you have to do by giving your prospect a calculator. Prospects will believe their numbers far more readily than yours. Believe it or not, when your prospect is using that calculator they know that you are going to ask for the order at some point. They expect you to try to close them and are conditioned to accept it happening.

The point here is that you have to do something in your presentation to initiate active involvement by your prospect so that you can move closer to asking for the order. Your chances of making the sale decrease immensely if you allow your prospect to sit passively while you talk. No active involvement relates directly to having no interest in your product.

Once your prospect is actively involved in the sales presentation they will begin to transmit buying signals.

RECOGNIZING BUYING SIGNALS

Buying signals are easy to spot once you are sensitized to recognizing them. However, in the heat of a sales presentation it may be easy to miss the many signs of interest that your prospect may transmit. How do we go about learning to recognize these buying signals? We watch and listen to our prospect.

Buying signals appear in five forms. You should be able to recognize most of them.

1. <u>Prospects go from a speaking to a listening mode</u>. You most likely noticed that when you greeted your prospect they were not in a speaking frame of mind. The only time they did speak was to warn you that they were not going to buy anything today. They stayed quiet at the beginning of the presentation, but as you moved into the discovery process they began talking to you. As you approach the close using your 'benefit hooks,' they will change to a listening mode.

2. This listening mode can also indicate that they are thinking things over, may be still apprehensive, need more information or are ready to buy. Whichever the case, the prospect is waiting for you to take the lead.

3. The best tactic here is to review the last words spoken by your prospect. It was these words that triggered the silence and should be your focal point. Clarify whatever information is necessary for them to feel comfortable enough to move forward in the sales process.

4. <u>Prospects change the pace of their conversation</u>. Prospects literally talk faster when they become excited about what they can or could do with your product or service. They will start sentences with, "You mean we could do this or this or . . . ?"

5. Their voice tones and speech will fluctuate in tempo and volume. The more excited they are about your product the faster they will talk. The more thoughtful they are, the more they will slow down and talk slower, as if they were formulating their answers. They will, however, slow down to ask for clarification if they are a little confused about something.

6. When your prospects find something that they really like about your product or service, they will want to go over and over it. Use this situation to move into trial closes or tie downs.

7. <u>Prospects begin using ownership phrases.</u> This is very similar to the 'puppy dog' close that we cover in a later chapter. In their

minds they have already taken ownership of your product. An example of this might be, "Let us suppose that we did buy this, am I right in assuming that we could . . . with it?" It is amazing how many salespeople disregard these buying signals and phrases because they are too busy talking instead of listening.

8. <u>Prospects start to complete your sentences</u>. This buying signal is overlooked by most salespeople. When your prospect finishes your statements or sentences, they are excited about your product and are actively closing themselves. Remember, persuade through involvement. Nothing reflects a prospect's involvement more than them finishing your sentences.

9. <u>Prospects ask buying questions</u>. When a prospect begins to ask buying questions they are revealing their true emotions or feelings about your product or service. The questions have no bearing on how well they understand your product, <u>only on how it will affect them</u>.

Examples of common buying questions are:

"Can we use this to travel to . . . ?"
"How far in advance do we have to make our exchanges?"
"Can I pay cash for this now or do I have to finance it?"
"When did you say that my maintenance fee would be due?"

<u>When you hear the first buying question, stop selling and start closing</u>. You can do this by using more selective trial closes.

TRIAL CLOSES AND USING THEM EFFECTIVELY

Throughout your presentation you should be using trial closes or tie downs. They are an effective way to test your prospect's temperature. In other words, you are asking for your prospect's opinion so that you can discover what their buying state of mind is at any given point. Remember, all that you are trying to do is to find out if the benefits you are showing are important to them. Use trial closes at any time you feel that there is a good chance that your prospect is near a buying point.

The real secret to using trial closes is that they must be disguised. Because this is a relationship type sale and your presentation must flow, your trial closes must be part of that flow. You need to have a set plan of action (which is part of preparation) that includes knowing when to use trial closes.

When a salesperson earns the right to advance at *every* step of the sales process, they have earned the right to ask for the sale. Remember it is not important where the salesperson is in the sales process, it is where the prospect is in the sales process? You must match your sales presentation to the prospect's buying steps.

All closing really is, is a bunch of little yes's. Those little yeses came from all of the disguised trial closes you have done throughout your presentation. By getting those little commitments along the way you have broken down any resistance that your prospect would have had and they are in the mood to say yes which makes a decision easier.

If you have eliminated all the obstacles during the presentation that make your prospect nervous about making a decision, then there will be no nervousness in making the decision. As closing is a relationship sale, your presentation must be the same every time and flow smoothly, therefore your trial closes must be a part of that flow _and_ be done in your closing style.

Trial closes are one of the most effective ways to make the close easier in your presentation. A trial close tests your prospect's temperature by asking for their opinion. Trial closes can be done at any point in the presentation.

Trial closes are also a great way to keep yourself from talking beyond the point that your prospect is ready to buy. Remember, use a trial close at any time you feel that there is a good chance that your prospect is near a purchasing point.

When Should you use a Trial Close?

1. <u>Use a trial close after overcoming an objection.</u> After you have provided a response to the objection you can use a trial close such as, "Now can you see why so many people want . . ."
2. <u>Use a trial close after a strong point in your presentation</u>. If you have been talking about the exchange programs, use a trial close to reinforce your point. For example you could ask your prospects, "What you do think about taking unlimited vacation weeks for as little as $149 per week?"
3. <u>After every buying signal that comes your way</u>. When a prospect gives you a buying signal you <u>must</u> use a trial close.
4. If they say to you "you mean we could start using this membership right away?" A trial close would be "Are you telling me that if you could start using this membership tomorrow you would want to become a member with us today?"
5. <u>Use a trial close at the end of any important segment in your presentation</u>. Whether it is after the tour of the resort, showing a major benefit to them or any other major step in the presentation you must use a trial close.

Trial closes work much in the same way as training an animal, except in this instance you are training your prospect. You have to start off with the basics. Simple things like taking a breath—keep breathing—here's a biscuit. Okay, sit down here. Have a biscuit. Now, follow me—here is another biscuit. Like your prospect, or any animals that you train you have to start off with simple tasks and commands. When they see that they are answering your questions correctly, and that you agree with their responses, they are encouraged to keep on going.

> For example, "Hey you guys are picking this stuff up very quickly" or "that is the most popular reason why people do this."

Stimulate and appreciate their opinions. This type of positive reinforcement moves you forward towards the close.

Every time you, or your prospect, achieve a new level in your relationship—you feel good. Therefore you need to encourage your prospect every time they provide the correct answer or behavior. By encouraging their positive responses you are empowering them to continue. Because they feel so good about what is going on, they know when they answer any questions they will not get an electric shock, just their 'treat.' By the time you get to boxing them on use and money, they will answer honestly and positively. You have to train your prospect to participate in your presentation.

Along with the four points that I mentioned, there are three specific types of trial closes that are used to gain commitments from your prospect. These are:

1. <u>Opinion Oriented Closes</u>. These are always open-ended questions. You are asking your prospect's opinion about how they feel about your product or service. You should use questions that contain the words why, how, where, when and what. For example ask them, "How do you feel about what you have heard so far?"
2. <u>"Yes" Momentum Closes</u>. Every time you present a strong selling point or benefit, you should always ask a question where the only answer will contains a YES. By accumulating "yes" commitments, you will condition your prospect to say YES when you go to close. A sample of a YES momentum close would be, "In your opinion, do you feel that participating in an ownership program has more advantages than renting your vacations?"
3. <u>Involvement Oriented Closes</u>. This type of trial close directly relates to the prospect taking ownership of your product or service. As an example, ask them, "Would you use the benefits yourself or let your family and friends use them?"

Before we move on to tie downs, I would like to repeat a warning—continued use of trial closes can irritate your prospects, so use them carefully and selectively to gain the most impact. Your prospect has to feel that what they are offering up as information and commitments will make a better program for them. If they believe that the information will help you, they will freely and honestly respond to your trial closes.

Trial Close Tips

1. Too many can irritate your prospects. Be careful not to abuse trial closes.
2. Practice making trial closes a natural, meaningful part of your presentation.
3. The prospect has to feel that what you are asking for is information to design a better ¨mousetrap¨ for them. Your prospects must believe that the information they are giving, and the questions that they are answering, will enable you to design a better, more flexible program for them. Only then will they feel that you are tailor making it for them and freely offer the information.

Whichever types of trial close you use—use them effectively. By having your prospect commit to a point you can then use that point as the foundation for your next one. Remember, everyone has a dominant buying emotion. You just need to keep getting enough commitments on minor benefits until you locate the primary buying motive. Remember, you have to be systematic in your presentation which must start at A and go to Z, in order.

Tying your Prospect Down—Gaining Commitment

Tie Downs are simple statements or comments made to create positive responses. They are designed to get your prospect into the habit of saying YES and to confirm that they are listening to the most significant parts of your presentation. They are very helpful when trying to get commitments from your prospect. "Wouldn't it be great if all of your prospects were as easy to tie down as you are?" This is an example of a tie down.

Tie downs can also help your prospects realize the value of what you are saying. If you are explaining something to your prospect and you do not think they are paying attention, a quick tie down will alleviate the situation. Remember, the attention span of the average prospect is not that long so if they were not paying attention it will re-focus them. As well, if they did not understand what you have been saying it gives you a chance to repeat it in another way. For example you could say, "You folks do understand how that benefit would work for you, don't you?"

The four objectives of a good tie down are:

1. Tie downs are simple statements or comments made to create positive responses.
2. Tie downs are designed to get your prospect into the habit of saying YES.
3. Tie downs allow you to confirm whether your prospect is listening to your presentation.
4. Tie downs assist in helping your prospects realize the value of what you are saying.

By using tie downs at the end of sentences, you will gather thousands of minor yes's. None of these little yes's have any bearing on them giving you a full down payment, but it does create a mode, rhythm or tempo to have them move in your direction. It also creates a mind-set and putting them into a certain mental state by having them come your way. Every time they say YES to something that benefits them, you are moving closer to a sale. Selling is a simple function. The final sale is nothing other than the sum of all those minor yes's, isn't it?

TIE DOWN TECHNIQUES

1. Like a lawyer, never ask a question you do not already know the answer to. It is the same with sales, never ask question with the intention of getting a tie down if you do not already know the answer. Use COMMON SENSE. That is so important.
2. For example, you are touring a prospect and say, "Great unit / view/car isn't it?" Normally this would be a quick tie down, however if your prospect has already got that great unit, view or owned the car, would you use the same one? It is not very likely. Think about how your prospect is going to respond to your tie down before you use it.

3. Pose the question in such a way that the only way your prospect can answer is positively. How you ask a question, determines the answer.

For example, say, "Don't you agree that you need to take time away with your family every year?" The only response here is a positive one.

Examples of Tie Downs

Wouldn't you agree . . .	Isn't it . . .	. . . wouldn't it?
Couldn't you . . . . ? . . .	aren't they?	. . . don't you?
Doesn't this . . . . ? . . .	couldn't you?	. . . . won't you?
Don't you agree . . . ? . . .	isn't that right?	. . . isn't it?

You can either start or finish the question with a tie down.

- "Wouldn't you agree that we vacation more now than our parents did?"
- "Wouldn't you enjoy seeing the world with your family?"
- "Couldn't you see yourself benefiting from owning this product or service?"
- "Doesn't this make sense for you and your family?"
- "Traveling is a vacation experience in itself, isn't it?"
- "More people, it seems, are trying to find ways to save money these days, aren't they?"
- "This would be an excellent gift for your parents and/or children, wouldn't it?"
- "Your family deserves the best, don't they?"
- "Isn't this easy? There are others, of course.

Following are twenty more examples of tie downs for you to use.

Could you	Shouldn't you	Haven't you
Won't they	Should you	Didn't it
Wasn't it	Won't it	Can't you
Aren't you	Isn't that right	Hasn't he (she)
Shouldn't it	Won't you	Haven't they

Don't you agree   Doesn't it   Don't we
If I could would you

Remember, you can use tie downs at either the beginning or the end
of a question or statement. Find a way to incorporate these and the
previous twelve into your presentation and you will be amazed how easy
it becomes to recognize when to close.

Selling is a simple function, and the final sale is nothing more than the
sum of all your yes's, isn't that right?

So, BEFORE CLOSING THE SALE . . .

Remember, you will never close a sale if you do not have the following
four elements on your table. All of those little yeses mean nothing if you
do not have the following:

1. Get the desire before you ask for a decision. **DESIRE before
    DECISION**
2. Wait until the prospect is ready to buy before closing (buying
    signals).
3. Make it comfortable for them to make a decision. Take the
    pressure off the decision to gain the commitment (tie downs and
    trial closes)
4. Do not force a close before the prospect has high interest and is
    committed to make a positive decision.

To close a sale is easy, but to justify why they should own is the hard
part. I have seen too many good salespeople who have put the
justification before the close, when it should be the other way around.
Close your prospect first then justify the sale afterwards.

WHEN SHOULD YOU ASK FOR THE ORDER?

Timing all depends on where your prospect is in the sales process. If all
the buying signals are present, ask for the order. One of two things will

happen. One, your prospect says yes and agrees to buy your product or service. Two, they will say no and give you another objection.

If your prospect gives you another objection, relish in it. Appreciate it, because all it means is that you have not yet found the <u>real</u> buying motive. So, take the pressure off, go back to your life raft and think about where you are going. If you have to, go back and do more FORM, trial closes, tie downs or work on a different angle for their perceived benefits. After doing more FORM, ask for the order using a different tack. You will find that if you ask for the order often enough, in a variety of ways, you will either wear them down (persistence overcomes resistance) or the real objection will surface. Should you get another objection when you ask for the order, handle it and then ask for the order again! There is no limit on how long, or how often, you may have go back and forth, but you do need to create the urgency along with the commitment.

Closing is getting the decision. They buy you. You are the deal. You have to empower yourself to have the right attitude.

If you are presently in sales and not writing any business, go home tonight and take the engine out and throw it away. Take all the unnecessary stuff out of your presentation. Focus on your communication and relationship skills, not on your shticks or the features of your product. Look in a mirror, not in any sales book. Ask yourself—would you buy off this person?

Remember, you are the presentation. If they like and trust you, truly believe that you are sincere in your intentions towards them, they will offer any, and all, information freely. They will, however, expect you to use the information to provide them with a great solution to their problems. If you have eliminated all the obstacles (objections) that made your prospect nervous about making a decision, then there is no nervousness in the decision.

The secret to closing is having fun, because when you are having fun people want to be around you, including your prospect. It is the energy behind what you say and do that creates a sales environment. In return for having fun your prospect will listen. If you have a prospect who will listen, you have a reasonably good shot at closing a sale every time.

So, when it comes time to ask for the order, summarize the benefits to them, be direct, concise, confident and have no fear. If you have found commonality you created rapport, trust, credibility and friendship. All are the building blocks necessary to make the sale. If you just kick back, relax, have fun and take everything thrown at you with a grain of salt, closing will be the easiest job you have ever had in your life.

From here on out, we will go for the close by asking for the order then tying up the loose ends of the sale.

9

Closing the Sale

Okay, you finally have your prospects where you want them, so to speak. You have been successful in building a relationship with your prospect and stimulating their interest by asking good open-ended questions. You have listened, understood and dealt with their objections. You have uncovered and stimulated their dominant buying emotions by telling effective third party stories. Well, now you are down to the wire so where do you go from here? You start closing your prospect. How you close your prospect depends mainly on your closing style. This chapter will focus on using their desire to get a decision, which leads to finding the dollars and then closing the sale.

The most important point to remember is that without their desire for your product or service you will not get a decision. Ninety percent of the buying decision will be based on ten percent of the benefits that your product or service can provide. You should also be aware that ten percent of the decision will more than likely come from just one benefit. If you have not stimulated enough emotional desires for a benefit by this point, do not consider going ahead with closing your prospect.

Before you begin to use any type of closing technique on your prospect you should have fulfilled **ALL** the following **Rules**.

1. Make you prospect like (love) you.
2. Create a relationship or bond with your prospect.
3. Ask your prospect good first, second and third level questions about them.
4. Make your prospect believe that they are special.
5. Earn your prospect's respect and credibility by showing integrity, honesty and sincerity.

6. Show your prospect that you care about their needs. Respect their opinions.
7. Watch and listen carefully to your prospect.
8. Probe, using the discovery process, to locate the dominant buying emotions or motives.
9. Remember to keep your presentation simple (K.I.S.S.) and remember to smile.
10. Earn the right to solve their problems and overcome their objections.
11. Use gentle persistence to overcome resistance.
12. Refuse to accept 'no' for an answer. This should be done without confrontation because they may be saying no to that particular benefit, not your product.

When it comes 'down to the wire' you should ask for the order directly and with confidence.

In addition to the twelve rules above it is important that you also consider using all of the following five closing tips to get you that much closer to your sale.

1. **Summarize the benefits**. Your prospect's need, desires, goals, dreams, and aspirations.
   - Summarize the *Consequences* of not getting what they want and the *Payoffs* when they do. When you summarize, the prospect is reminded of the urgency to take action.
   - Keep summarizing, highlighting and stimulating up the benefits that the prospect would use most. By keeping the summary positive you will keep getting those little yes's.
   - It seems that in this business the prospects are more motivated by fear of loss, rather than the desire of gain.

2. **Close directly**. Ask for the Sale.
   - Be direct. Say, "Okay guys, all things considered I think it is high time that you got your own membership. Let us do this, let's fill this out and see if we . . ."
   - You will come across as incompetent if you waffle around while asking for the order or trip over your words. A

statement such as, "Let us suppose that you sort of, would like to, maybe go ahead . . . ," sounds as if you are drowning in your insecurity and fear of asking for the order.

- If you ask your prospect directly to buy, whether or not they are in the deal, they will give you a direct response. If you are doing a Kentucky side step when asking for the deal, they are going to do a Tennessee back step to avoid answering you. What happens is that the prospect then finds security in your betrayal.

- If you are feeling relaxed and comfortable, are direct and sure of yourself your prospect will mirror image that feeling and attitude and will most likely buy. However, if your prospect does not feel confident in you, or their ability to purchase, they are not going to buy anything. Because most people fear the unknown and since they do not know what they are facing it is easier to say no than yes.

- Even if it feels good to them, but you are not asking for the order, they will then wonder what is wrong with them, or you. They begin to question if they are normal and start thinking to themselves, "Why isn't he asking us to join his club?" The reason the closer is not asking them to join—he is too scared of the rejection response.

3. **Be concise**. Use economy of language.
   - Don't be unnecessarily talkative as it communicates your nervousness and uncertainty.

4. **Close with confidence**.
   - Use body animation, voice and posture that communicates that you fully expect the prospect to take positive action or make a positive decision.
   - You need to appear confident, have great body language and keep your eyes wide open. By your looking at them and talking loudly they are more inclined to mirror you and buy. Watch you prospect, focus on the prospect. When your prospect's are feeling good and in the deal, ask them to buy. If they are not ready to buy, go back to your life raft and create more desire.

5. **Don't be afraid if they do not respond immediately**. WAIT FOR AN ANSWER.
    - Do not fear the silence. When you remain silent, you encourage the prospect to respond.
    - Have you ever noticed what happens when someone, a teacher for example, walks into a room going to the front but does not say a word? The room will quiet down automatically. The silence has more impact and is considerably more effective than the teacher trying to tell the class to be quiet.

For years there has been a Rule of Thumb for closing a deal. *Ask for the order then quit talking. Maintain the silence because the one who talks first loses.* In the vacation ownership industry this can work to your advantage only if you have the desire and a decision. If you have not yet boxed the money, do not let the silence linger more than three seconds because your prospect will begin to dwell on the money issue and will reverse their decision.

By the way, you can take control of any situation by not saying anything.

GOING FOR THE CLOSE

When you go to close and you will see when your prospects have made a decision. For example, you can use a choice close to complete the decision. "I know, you were thinking that this should be in both names, not just yours Valerie, am I right?" Of course when you say this you better have a pen handy for them to sign. You have to be right on the ball because any little pause will cost you the sale.

If she is down and he is not sure, he may say something such as, "Well, don't look at me, what do you think?" She will invariably say in return, "Well, I don't know, what do you think?" Then the invariable "I think we should think about it" will rear its ugly head. Bang, you are back into another objection.

You should know when your prospects have reached a decision or choice. The response you will get will be much more positive and similar to "well, it will be in both our names . . ." She is looking for someone to tell her to do it. A considerable number of closers do not see this. They are hoping that the negative element on the table will all of a sudden turn into a super master closer and tell the other to do it.

You have to understand there is always going to be one person at the table in the deal and one who is not. The one who is positive will be giving their spouse the, 'can I have it please' look. When you are just about to get a bout of negativity, dive in at that instant and say "Valerie, you want his support on this, don't you?" Now you and she are asking him because she just wants to make sure that it is all right with Jay. Then you can say, "Of course it is okay with him." You call the shots you have the control. The one who is in the sale needs your support.

Remember to use FORM to get yourself out of a sticky situation. Go back to your life raft when you need to chill them out or relax them. Something has happened to make them uneasy, such as asking for a credit card or checking their credit—get back to your life raft. Go back to your life raft whenever you sense that they are chilling out on you, to warm them back up and have them participate. I cannot repeat this enough—FORM is your life raft. This is something that they know everything about, they are very emotional about and they like to talk about because no one else ever listens to them and shows interest.

Remember, there are two things necessary in closing a sale—the DECISION <u>then</u> the MONEY. The money issue will look after itself once your prospect makes the decision to buy your product or service. If you focus on getting the money before you have a decision, you will lose the sale.

CLOSING TECHNIQUES

How do you go about asking for the order? Which closing technique is the most effective? Unfortunately, I cannot answer that for anyone other than myself. Your choice of closing techniques is as individual as your personality.

Successful salespeople have various techniques that they use which are modified to the personality type of prospect they are with. Choosing the technique that works best for you is a matter of trial and error.

Following are some basic closing techniques that are fairly standard in sales. In the Help sections I will be covering more advanced techniques for those who would like to add to or modify what they are presently using.

To achieve optimum sales statistics you should, like your presentation, stick to the same closes every time. Find three or four that you think suit your style and personality and adapt them to your presentation. Once you have become more experienced in sales, you can then adapt any or all of these pretty standard closing techniques to the different types of personalities that you will come across in your career.

SIX BASIC CLOSING TECHNIQUES

1. Puppy Dog or Adoption Close: This is where you allow your prospect to take mental possession of your product or service. Let them adopt your product. Let them assume its' ownership by playing with it for some time while you show how it benefits them. Then, mentally ask for it back and watch their reaction. They will say no to you, and then offer you the real objection that is standing in the way of them making a decision.

   For example, say to them, "Let us suppose that you folks were already members, how would you use it?"

2. Take Away Close: This close practically tells your prospect they cannot have it. It is very similar to telling a small child they cannot have, or do something. By saying no they now want it more.

   For example, say, "Guys, do not get too excited, this is only an application process and we find that six out of ten applicants will qualify."

3. <u>Assumptive Close</u>: This close you can do from when you pick your prospect up—it just assumes that they are going to buy.

    > For example, put them into the picture. Say, "You guys are going to love having this membership. For instance, you are on a mini-vacation to Puerto Vallarta, sipping margaritas on your patio while watching the sunset. You just happen to strike up a casual conversation with the people on the next patio and soon are asking where they are from and what brought them to Puerto Vallarta. They tell you they are from Wisconsin and are on a $2500 package deal. You chuckle to yourself because as members your little mini-vacation only cost you $299. Think about all the money you saved. What do you think you would buy with all that extra money?"

4. <u>Demonstration Close</u>: This reinforces to the rent versus own presentation. You are showing your client how much they are spending and how much they would benefit by owning your product. Successful salespeople also use this close to break their prospect's pact. The other benefit to the demonstration close is that you can also create curiosity along with credibility in the same sentence.

    > For example, say something such as, "I am going to show you how you can take the money you are presently spending on vacation and take a higher quality vacations. In addition I will show you how you can save thousands of dollars and eliminate inflation, okay?"

Using this close as an example to break their pact you could say, "Well, since you folks are on vacation, spending thousands of dollars, I am going to show you a way in which you cut that cost considerably. However, before I start the presentation I would ask that you please pay attention to what I am going to show you. Remember that you are under no cost or obligation and all I am going to do is talk about the money you are spending anyway, fair enough?"

5. Power of Suggestion Close: If you work in a salesroom that does a tremendous volume of business, either on a daily or weekly basis, you will benefit more from this close. Why? Excitement is contagious. This close can overcome any objection if your energy level, intensity and excitement are so contagious that your client is more interested in following your presentation than focusing on their objection.

    > For example, tell them, "If you were a member of our club, you would be able to travel the world at a fraction of the cost." (Or, "wow, that is the best question you have asked so far and I will answer that in a minute.") First, I want to tell you that I do my presentation in a certain way to cover every question and concern that you could possibly have. So, please hold onto that question so you do not forget. Better yet, write it down in case I get so excited about our membership that you forget to ask me again. Okay, fair enough?"

    Remember, your prospect relies on you to suggest and help design a program just for them. This close empowers you to pack some punch behind your words to get the sale.

6. Trial Close: This close is very similar to the little trial closes you have been doing all along except this deals directly with asking for the order.

    > For example, say to them, "Can I ask you a question." [Okay] "Let us suppose that you submitted a membership application today and could be qualified, if the money and qualifications are there, do you see any reason for not doing this today?"

To become a great closer you have to work hard and have determination, patience and perseverance. Finding the right closing technique requires practice and, in many cases, trial and error learning with prospects. Use every opportunity you are presented with to practice your closing techniques.

SECONDARY CLOSING TECHNIQUES

Above we covered six common and basic closes, but following are six additional closes you should consider adding as part of your repertoire. Just as I mentioned earlier find three or four closes that you think suit your style and personality and adapt them to your presentation.

1. Minor Point Close: Similar to trial closes, minor point closes get your prospect to agree to minor points thus making the big decision easier. Think in terms of the least important benefit you can ask your prospect that they will agree with. By having your prospects agree to minor points they imply consent to your entire product or service. Using a minor point close usually slips by the normal defense mechanism and allows your prospect to unconsciously start closing themselves.

    An example of a minor point close would be, "Would this be the address where we would send your membership information?"

2. Ascending Close: These are also similar to minor point closes. With an ascending close, you start right from the beginning of your presentation by asking YES questions. You then create such a foundation of yes's that the no's virtually evaporate.

3. Alternative Choice Close: This close offers your prospect a choice between two products or services. This type of close NEVER gives your prospect an option to say no. This close will also get your prospect to step over the line into a decision so smoothly that they may not realize it. A master closer has the ability to 'alternative choice' close their prospect all the way down to completing the paperwork.

    An example of this type of close would be, "Let me ask you folks this, would you be more interested in a one, or two bedroom unit?"

4. Hot Button Close: This can be one of the most powerful types of closes if used correctly. The success of this close is based on the salesperson's ability to discover the MOST important

reason for buying and REPEATING IT constantly throughout the presentation. By concentrating on selling on this one main point, the point then becomes imperative to the buying decision.

5. Third Party Story Close: This one goes hand in hand with hot button closes. When you keep pushing a hot button you can increase the emotional impact by relating a similar third party story.

    Another aspect to third party closes is that they MUST be entertaining and FOCUSED on the prospect. They also have to contain urgency, credibility, value and EMOTION.

6. Summary Close: Summary closes are just what they appear to be: a summary of benefits covered during the presentation. In some instances, you can show how a feature benefits them. However, you must be careful not to focus specifically on features. Remember, prospects buy benefits, not features. A summary close will also ensure that your prospect focuses on the correct benefits as they were probably not paying one hundred percent attention to you earlier in the presentation.

    An example of a summary close would be, "So, based on what you have told me, the things that we have covered here today . . . [summarize the benefits] we know that these would be a benefit to your lifestyle, so all we need to do now is make sure that we can get you qualified."

Remember, all buying decisions are emotional, so you must assure that whichever closing technique(s) you choose stimulates their emotions.

TAKING THE SALE AWAY—SAYING NO!

The biggest problem in any sales situation and specifically in the vacation ownership industry is getting your prospect to make decision. Everything else is irrelevant. One of the most effective ways to get your prospect to make a YES decision is to tell them NO.

The strongest word in closing is "NO." By taking away the sale, one, or all the following situations will occur:

1. The take away is used to psychologically force your prospect to admit that they are the only ones responsible to make the decision. Simply put, it attacks your prospect's ego and forces them to come to a decision. This technique will make them feel that if they do not go ahead and buy, they are making a major mistake. It also implies that they are not bright enough to see the value of your product or service.
2. The take away immediately puts any lost credibility back into your product or service. People tend to believe that your product must be credible if you are willing to walk away from a sale.

By taking the sale away from the prospect early on in the presentation, most obstacles and objections that can impede you later in the sales process are removed. Prospects naturally resist when asked to provide information. By the salesperson saying NO first, it significantly reduces resistance later, especially during the discovery process.

THE FOUR D'S—DESIRE, DECISION, DOLLARS, DEAL

The art of closing is getting your prospect to make the decision that you want them to make. So make the decision an easy one. Find the desire first because without that you will never get a decision.

DESIRE—You cannot buy desire; you create it. You can create and build desire by showing value, but you cannot get them to buy desire.

DECISION—The hardest thing to achieve in any sales process is the decision. You have to empower your prospect to make a decision by creating enough desire that they cannot see themselves living without your product or service.

There is an old quote I like, "The biggest DECISIONS are made on the IMPULSE of the MOMENT." Sales are made because people feel good at a particular moment. Capitalize on that moment.

DOLLARS—Once you have created enough desire to stimulate a decision ONLY THEN will you find the money. It is imperative that you keep these two steps separate. **Get the decision first then use the decision to get the money.** If you try to close your sale on a money angle before you have a decision, your prospect will feel that you are "high pressuring" them and they will say NO.

DEAL—DESIRE + DECISION = DOLLARS + DEAL

If you follow this FOUR D closing method you will increase your closing percentage substantially.

FINALLY—ASKING FOR THE ORDER

You should now be able to determine if your prospects are in a decision making mode based on their body language, their eye contact and their voice inflections. There has to be the right feeling present. Watch your prospect's reaction when you ask for the order. This reaction tells you how well your trial closes and tie down's worked along the way.

When you are asking for the order, you have to put on a face as if you have just discovered the cure for old age. You have to believe that they are going to say YES. Guess what? If you do not believe you have a sale then your prospect won't either. No sale!

After you have asked for the order, quit talking. Allow a second or two of silence to aid in the decision making process. There is another adage that states, 'He who talks first loses.' As a Sales Director I have altered that adage to state, "If after two seconds they have not replied to your questions jump in and save them. Anything more than a few seconds and you are about to create a pre-buyer's remorse situation because they are not ready to make a decision." So, go ahead and volunteer an objection that makes them feel comfortable. For example, say to them, "Let me guess, you folks are hesitating because you are not sure what credit card you will use for the down payment?"

Two things will happen—they will say YES or give you another OBJECTION. If they say YES, congratulations, you made a sale. If they give you another objection, relish it. Ask more questions to uncover the motivation behind the objection and handle it like any other objection. Then ask for the order again. Repeat this step as often as necessary until you hear YES.

When you get down to the wire, just remember the secret to closing is having fun. Ask for the order with confidence, be direct, concise and have no fear. If you have found commonality, created emotional desire and have the decision, then you have all the building blocks that make the sale. Relax, have fun and reap the rewards.

FINDING THE MONEY

So now you know that there are two parts to closing the sale—**the decision first, then the money**. You should never show prices or talk money before you have a decision. By showing the price too soon you are giving your prospect a reason not to become involved. Only show or talk about money when your prospects are in the deal and want your product or service.

If you want to test this, watch what happens when a prospect asks the price before adopting your product or service. You will usually hear a response that goes something like this, "Well, thank you for your time. We will knock it around for a while and get back to you. Oh, by the way, do you have a business card?"

I cannot say this enough, "Get them real, get the desire, get the decision **then** find the money." Concern for price is usually reduced during the close when trust, confidence and rapport are established up front. When no trust or rapport is established in the front end then price very much becomes the issue in the back end.

Everything relates to the front end including ensuring you get the money. If you did not create DESIRE during your presentation, you will waste a considerable amount of time trying to close your deal in the back end. This also includes putting yourself into a position to ask for money. The desire that your prospect has for your product or service is directly related to the desire they have to want to be with you.

Prospects view the value of your product or service through you. This desire sets up the final stage of negotiations. Now is the time to **Qualify, Verify and Certify** that they can pay for what you are selling and they are buying.

WHY WE QUALIFY OUR PROSPECT

Initial qualifications are based on taking away the product and creating a negative sale. We want our prospect to step up and participate in the sales process. By using a take-away and a choice close in the same question you are letting your prospect know that they have to qualify and expose their level of desire. *"If you were to qualify for our membership, which one of these benefits is the most important to you?"*

You will gain more ground in your closing process if you use the statement, *"If you were to qualify . . ."* more often during your presentation. The reason for this is that their response will usually be somewhere between an objection and a statement that will ultimately turn into a question. Consider the following two scenarios:

Scenario 1: You have three single guys in their middle twenties who appear to not have much money, are sporting scars, tattoos and have chains hanging off their clothing. Rather than tell them that they need twenty years of good credit history and a Ph.D., tell them they need three people, not family members, to provide references to qualify to buy. You may wish to be a little more creative in how you approach them as not to alienate them from being part of your club. By using this shtick they will step up with something like, "Hey, what do we need references for? We all have good jobs and have never needed references before to buy anything else we wanted. What is the deal?" You can respond with, *"Well, it is just the stuffy qualification process. You just relax, and I will help you through it."*

<u>Scenario 2</u>: If you have a wealthy prospect, and you know that getting the money is not an issue, you should tell them that they will need personal references to qualify. You may also tell them that you will also be checking their attitude towards paying their bills. Rather than a credit check per se you want to know if they have a good credit history. You may say something similar to, "*We do not care how much money you may have. We are only concerned with your attitude toward paying your bills.*" Wealthy prospects will appreciate the fact they have to qualify and have their credit checked because they do the same in their business dealings. It adds to your overall credibility and clarifies the fact that the other members are also in good standing because of their status.

Qualifications are important to the credibility of your business and its customers. Again, in the timeshare and even real estate industry, it is normally the mistake that some new developers or marketing companies make—they will let just anyone buy. This is why projects go belly up or into bankruptcy. Remember, people buy when they are emotional. When salespeople are encouraged to sell without checking qualifications, there is an inherent risk—risk that the mortgage or maintenance payments will not be made, thereby potentially causing the resort serious financial problems. People expect you to check their credit and their qualifications because it is required in most every other aspect of their lives. The process of qualifying is a normal request that creates a comfort zone for your prospect and eliminates the fear.

WHY DO YOU QUALIFY YOUR PROSPECT?

In many sales environments your prospects may be pre-qualified. In others, they may be walk-in's or responding to social media or advertisements. Others may be cold calling to prospects. Whichever type they are, they all need to be qualified sufficiently so that they can actually purchase your product. You can create all the desire and urgency you need in a prospect, but if they have no money to purchase your product or service and because of this you should make sure to qualify them.

A good example of the need to qualify is that the majority of timeshare prospects who attend a presentation are promised something in return for their time and, as such, it is greed or attention that usually gets them in the door. They then are told they need to qualify to buy your product or service as this creates a need to be accepted. Using that take away close I mentioned above, *"If you were to qualify for our membership, which one of these benefits is the most important to you?"* This further sets up the greed or acceptance stimulus that we need in a prospect.

These greedy, or needing to be accepted clients, are the perfect prospects for the timeshare industry. Unfortunately over the years I have seen too many salespeople tell their prospects with they arrive for a presentation, "Today I am going to show you something fantastic and I hope that you will like it. Why? Because the (product or service) that I am going to show you will save you thousands of dollars and help you take better vacations". This statement has now empowered your prospect with the ability to make the decision or not to buy. When you give them the decision, then you give them the feeling that 'this cannot be very special because we did not have to work very hard for it.' It will also deprive you of the opportunity to create urgency.

By creating an atmosphere of 'greed' and desire to be accepted you then set clients up to want to become involved. People always want something they cannot have. Remember, all special clubs around the world require people to qualify. Whether it is a private club, health club, golf club, airline club, credit cards, bridge clubs or professional associations they all require, or have, some form of qualification process. There are also some restaurants that require men to wear a jacket and tie. Whatever the qualifications are, people must meet them to gain entrance. Include qualifying for your product or service as well. <u>It also is a great technique to gauge how much desire or value you have built into your presentation</u>.

How Do You Qualify Your Prospect

Before you actually began your presentation you should have developed rapport and trust with your clients. You should also have done a good discovery so you know who is sitting in front of you and what they can qualify for (bankruptcy, divorced, criminal records, and income?).

Asking what your prospects do for a living can help you determine what their buying habits are, how they handle their money, and what their attitude is towards credit and purchasing on credit. You may have a lumberjack with no credit cards because he has been in the bush for six months and pays cash for everything. Maybe you have an accountant or CEO who pays bills the second they arrive in their email. Once you have determined these things you can estimate how much money they may have, how successful they are and what their buying habits are.

Consumer Agencies report that the average American has eight major credit cards and owes between US $8,000 and $10,000 on them. There is enough plastic in your prospect's pocket to do a full down payment at least ninety percent of the time. Do not be fooled between desire and the money objection.

Salespeople in every industry, country and language have heard their prospects say, "Hey, do not worry about qualifying me! If I wanted to do this I would just pay cash." It is not the purchase price that you should be worrying about. It is the after purchase costs that you also need to take into consideration. For example, you may have the $10,000,000 to buy a yacht but can you afford the $500,000 in yearly maintenance fees? You want to make sure that your prospect does not default on his membership after he buys it because you want to be paid your commission. You also want to ensure that you enroll a member who will be in good standing.

The first thing to consider when financially qualifying your clients is what personality characteristics they portray.

- What sort of qualification shtick will you use? Will it be based on money, credit, vacation lifestyle or attitude?
- Second, when you qualify them you should also let them 'win' a couple of points in the process by qualifying them on minor points. For example, the survey sheet says that they vacation eight weeks a year. Tell them they need a minimum of four weeks to qualify. They will usually respond with, "Is that all it takes to qualify?" You can then say, *"Well, there are a couple of other points and . . .* (Then tell them what you will expect of them)."

Later on when you go to further qualify them, they are expecting to have already met the qualification. Preparation is the secret to selling without surprises. Third, focus on the prestige of qualifying for membership benefits. Use the American Express motto, *"Membership has its privileges."* The promise of status is akin to the greed factor or acceptance. Last and certainly not least, do not prejudge your prospect's ability to pay. I have had a college student wearing jeans and a torn Grateful Dead T-shirt pay $65,000 cash to buy four weeks. I have also seen a well-dressed, successful looking banker of fifty-five who could not put $1,000 together using six credit cards. Never allow yourself to prejudge your prospect's ability to pay.

The following are some examples of qualification shticks that can be used in any sales environment:

> *"Just sit back, relax and take it easy because we do not even know if this is something that you would qualify for or even want."*

> *"We talk to about 100 people/couples a day, every day, and we can appreciate that not all of them will qualify for what we have."*

> *"This time of year our problem is not finding people to talk to but finding people who qualify."*

Prospects will not buy anything that is made easy for them without going through buyers or sales resistance. You have to make people jump over the hurdles to create perceived value. Your prospects should see the value of your product or service at its gross price and should go through various money objections before they (or you) give in to a specific price. They have to assume ownership and then you have to take it away from them until they see true value in your product or service. If you do not, verifying and getting the money will become difficult. We call this the adoption of product or puppy dog close.

VERIFYING AND BOXING THE MONEY

You should have, from your discovery and continual questioning throughout your presentation, a rough estimate of how much your prospect can or cannot afford. If you have closed your sale properly, finding the money will become a breeze. You may even find that once the decision has been made, your prospect will offer the money solution for you. If you have been asking throughout your presentation for little, inconsequential things (tie downs), then asking for the money becomes easy. By the time you get into the paperwork you can ask, without hesitation,

> *"For the down payment—will that be cash, traveler's checks, on-line bank transfer, regular bank transfer or credit card?"* If you have a very good rapport with them, you can lighten the tone, *"We stopped taking children because of the human rights laws. However, we now take jewelry or you can do three years' worth of cleaning for us. Perhaps for your down payment you might like to do a combination of all the above?"* **(Your silence)**

By doing this is a light-hearted tone they will offer you a solution. If you had just asked for a credit card, they may not feel comfortable enough yet to tell you that a credit card is not a viable solution for them. Second, if you have been offering them the ability to provide solutions all the way through your presentation, stopping now will derail the momentum.

When you say, *"Charge it,"* it gives the impression that someone else is going to pay for it. People like to use credit cards in this fashion because they do not associate it with real money. Remember, the average American has at least eight of them.

FOUR QUESTIONS TO BOX THE MONEY AND COMMITMENT

If you are not as lucky in having them offer up a monthly payment or a down payment sum, you need to do some work to box the money. To do box the money effectively ask the following four questions, and you will always be able to get money as the objection:

1. **Like it and Use it**: *"Would you like to have something like this?"* *"If you had something such as this you could obviously use it, yes!"* (You should have already boxed **use** at the beginning of the sales presentation and are using this as a statement of fact rather than a question.)

2. **Understanding**: *"From what you have seen so far do you understand how the membership works?"* *"Do you have any questions that have not been answered or any gray areas that require further explanation from me?"* Prospects will very rarely disclose that they didn't understand or that they may have not been paying attention to you.

3. **Self-Credibility**: *"Before you answer this next question, and please, do not be afraid to answer it because you think you may hurt my feelings, do you think that I am trying to rip you off?"* *"If you were considering becoming a member with us, would you feel comfortable in dealing with me?"* "Oh, it is not you. You were great. However, we just are the sort of people who . . . (Objection)." Take this as an opportunity to close.

4. **Affordability**: *"Okay, so you like it and you will use it and you feel comfortable dealing with me. Is this membership 100% affordable? My job is to make sure that you do not get involved in a program that is over your head or is not 100% comfortable. Honestly, is this (product or service) 100% affordable for you?"* Welcome the NO you will hear! You can also phrase it, *"Okay, so you like it and you will use it and you feel comfortable dealing with me. Is this membership 100% affordable? Please be honest with me. Is this 100% affordable? My job is not to increase your vacation budget but to increase your vacation lifestyle."* If they have answered yes to the first three, the fourth question will stimulate them to tell you what may be affordable. If they answer no to any of the first three, go back and tell another third party story to create more value or credibility. Then go back and ask the four questions. There is a direct correlation between desire and finding the money. Concentrate on getting the desire and the money will appear.

CERTIFYING THE MONEY

Certifying the money essentially means collecting the money. For larger purchases most resorts, real estate projects, car/boat etc. dealerships do have either lending personnel or some other financial person who assists in the final stages of the sale. If your product or service only takes credit cards, make sure you have enough ¨credit¨ to accept the purchase. You should always follow the established procedures and guidelines of your company for collecting the money (either full or down payments).

For years I have been telling my closers, "Get the decision, get the deal down and let the finance guys find the money." Minimize your energy by focusing on the decision and nothing else. Your job is to close the sale, not to be the financial expert. Closing is one thing. Collecting the money is another. The second is easy. The first is paramount.

Another example of a no-no I keep hearing from sales people—¨my prospect was said they were so broke so they could not possibly do this." I do not know of one tourist who would fly three, four, six or more hours to another country with the family or friends if they're broke and penniless. They would not be so financially strapped that when they got home they could not feed themselves or their animals, put gas in their car or pay their mortgage or rent. Do not let your prospects bully you into focusing on the money. If you cannot get desire you will never get the decision or the money.

To test this theory I once told a salesperson that by pre-judging the quality of my prospect's ability to buy just because of 'low season' or that they were honeymooners was foolish. I told him to tell them that the membership is free and that there will be no down payment or monthly payments. In other words, tell them it is free. Well guess what happened? Every one of them bolted from the presentation. They were scared because it was free.

CAN OR SHOULD YOU DROP THE PRICE?

When you make the issue money, the sale becomes contingent upon the numbers. You have forgotten to get the desire when you keep dropping or chopping the price. Why are you working so hard to get the sale like that? Never think that it is the money. It is not. It is the decision to purchase or the perceived value. <u>Justify your prices with value</u>. Do not cheapen what you're offering. Unfortunately most salespeople want to justify the value in their heads, so they cheapen the price. Once you give your clients what they want, they are now in control and will most likely say no. Cheapen your price and they no longer see any value in owning your product or service. Say, *"Jay, Valerie, we made a commitment that we would never cheapen our product to get your business here. Otherwise I would have to apologize every year for the maintenance increases. We would rather justify our price today than apologize for it tomorrow."*

Do not give away a better price. Lowering the price is not an option. It does not exist. If they really want to buy your product they will pay your gross price or negotiate a reasonable discount based on 'conditions' of the sale. When you move off your gross price, your prospect immediately expects there to be something even better. On the other hand, when they want to negotiate they are in a buying frame of mind. Do not lose sight of the sale. Always move them along in a positive direction.

The second that you start discounting a product, your prospect waits for the landslide to appear. What happens when you let them out of a 'high price' ether environment and drop your price? They want to 'think about it.' Remember you want them to forget all of their other objections and focus on, "Your price is too high." Do not give them an excuse to 'think about it." Discounting your price also leaves you little price flexibility or room to negotiate. You can obtain the required urgency or decision, including the method of payment when they want a better price.

GETTING YOUR PROSPECTS TO ASK FOR A DISCOUNT

No, I am not contradicting from my earlier statement of 'do not give away a better price.' What I am referring to is getting your prospect to

ask for a better price. When you offer a lower price you are cheapening your product. If they ask, it means they wish to negotiate a better price. Do not telegraph a better price. Always get them to ask for one. It makes a big difference in the outcome of the sale. Think of it as haggling in a marketplace in Marrakech or a Mexican beach for a better price on a souvenir trinket.

Many salespeople have had prospects say to them, "Don't you have a better price than this?" What separates the average salesperson from the master closer is the response.

If you believe this is truly a buying question, you will immediately focus on the money and say, "If there were a better price, would you buy it?" You may as well shoot yourself in the foot. In almost every case their response will be, "Well, that depends on the price." Welcome to a fishing expedition.

The last statement shows that your clients still do not perceive enough value in your product. They are waiting to see if YOU will make the first move in the negotiation step. Do not allow yourself to fall into this trap. If you are a highly successful closer, you will respond with, *"So what you are telling me is that if you could get a discount today, you would do it?"* Even though this response sounds similar to the above statement, it includes a right angle close. You will find that your prospect will respond in one of the following manners:

1. "Well, it's not so much the discount. It is just that we cannot afford XX dollars today."
2. "Well, no, it's not that we do not see the value. We do. We just cannot afford it today."
3. "No, not at all, it's just that we cannot afford the $1,500 a month. A $500 monthly payment would be much better for us."
4. "Well, no, it is just we know you can do better than this, so just give us your 'bottom line' and we will either give you a yes or no!"

In the first three, they still see value in your product. Now it is the price that they wish to negotiate. From here you can say, *"So what you guys are telling me is that you see the value. However, you would do this today if* *the payments were $500 a month instead of $1,500 and we could get you qualified?"* At this point they will probably say, "Yes" and you have gotten yourself a buying commitment and sale. Unfortunately, salespeople tend to fall for number 4 thinking that their prospects have seen value, but really they are still unconvinced and just want a price so that they can "give you a yes or no."

However, be careful in how you give it away. **Never say yes to their first offer.** This is another important rule of closing a sale. You must always be in control of your prospect, especially during the closing process. In the front end you gave up 'control' because you wanted them to vent all of their frustrations and negativity so that they would relax. When they relaxed they became curious and started asking questions. At this point you started taking back control by using shticks, trial closes and tie downs. By the time you are here, looking for the money, you are back in control. Never throw it back to them by agreeing to their first offer. Make them jump over some hurdles. Things that are obtained easily in life have little value. People tend to cherish things when they perceive more value. You have to work hard at negotiating for things that you really want.

You now know that they can comfortably afford $500 a month. Why not push them a little and see if you can get more. You have to understand that people will counter your offer with something lower than they can afford. Therefore, you can continue the above statement with, *"Unfortunately, a $500 a month is not doable at this time. I am afraid that the price for this membership package is more than you can afford at this time. However, we might be able to find you something of less quality, if you are interested, for less than the $1,500 a month."* What you are trying to do here is get them to step up further with another money offer or come back with a demand. "Look, we want this program, not something cheaper, but we want it at the $500 a month payment." Once your clients start demanding their price, it becomes a done deal.

Qualifying, verifying and boxing money can be fun, simple and easy. Just let your prospects step up and become involved in the process. Price and the money are directly proportional to the discretionary income of your clients, the amount of value they perceive, and the amount you have created in your product. Remember, the DESIRE gets the DECISION that finds the DOLLARS and the DEAL.

Note: The only difference between an owner of your product or service and a prospect is the payment.

TYING UP THE LOOSE ENDS

You believe that you have done everything right up to now. You have made a friend and found out their primary buying motive. You created a problem, offered a solution and they said yes. You closed the sale and all you need to complete the sale is tying up the loose ends.

Earlier in this chapter I said there are two parts to closing the sale—the decision first, then the money. It is very important that you keep these two steps SEPARATE. When we try to combine the steps, we cause anxiety. Your prospects are not ready for the sale if you find yourself searching for the decision and the money at the same time. If you moved too fast your prospect will think that you are pushing and will find another objection. So by the time you get to the paperwork you must ensure that you have both the decision and the money. Why? Because from this point forward there may be quite a bit of discussion or details to work out from the time your prospect made their decision, and when the money is collected. I cannot stress this enough—always get the decision first. If the sale has gone down at the right time, everything from that point on will go with the flow. A good closer can get the decision so smoothly that the prospect may not even realize what has happened.

AFTER THE DECISION

The most important thing to remember is that it is easier to get a choice than a decision. The first thing that you should do after they have made a positive choice or decision is affirm that choice or decision to purchase. Help them to feel comfortable. When the decision goes down, congratulate them. Say something to them such as, "Great! You are going to love having this membership or car" or "Congratulations, you have made a wise choice on this particular insurance policy." After sincere congratulations any technicality or detail that may come up later will go right out the window.

Show your excitement for them. Keep it simple. Keep it fun. Keep it personal. Let the conversation be about them. Your prospects need to feel comfortable. If possible and you are able, ask if they would like a drink. If they have already asked for one, humorously say to them, "Well, I think it is about time you guys bought me a drink, don't you?" By responding this way it leads the prospect to feel as if they owe you something for all of your help and friendship during the sales process.

The second thing you should do once the decision is down—**do not go past the close**. Rule number two in closing is when the sale goes down, STOP CLOSING. Now is the support time. Now is the time for holding their hands. Now you are there as their counselor, their friend and their ally. You are the person who is going to help them through this after-sale maze. You are going to be someone who is just as excited as they are, if not more.

If you carry on selling or justify what they are doing right then you will overload them with information. So, do not start throwing out all the extra things or perks that they can do with your product or service until they are ready. Keep them as a surprise for later during the paperwork.

On the other hand, you start giving them the feeling that you are trying to justify what you have just sold them, you are no longer in control of the sale when you start back pedaling or justifying every little thing. If you promote this feeling all you are doing is creating a confidence and credibility problem. They might begin to believe that they could have gotten a better deal, or maybe, they are the first ones to buy this product, ever. Doubt creates all sorts of weird stuff to start going through their heads. By justifying and doing more selling by calling for more brochures or catalogues again, you are going so far past the close. Remember if you confuse them, you will lose them. You go from The Sale to No Sale!

When someone has made an emotional decision to go with what you have been projecting, the sale is good. They want to have that sparkle in their eyes so then when they think, 'now we have done it, but what the hell did we do? They feel exactly as you do. Excited, happy, animated and pleased they made a good decision. Because once the sale does go down, and they have signed the worksheet, reality begins to dawn and two things occur. One, they realize that they have bought something and two, the most important of all—you realize that you have just closed the sale.

The first thing that you need to do, after realization hits home, is to turn the conversation into something light and non-threatening. The tone of the conversation must to go back to what you were doing when you were starting to get to know them and what built your relationship, in other words get back to that Life Raft. Say something such as, "So, you guys said you like . . . ? Maybe you can take me (help me, teach me) with you! Ha, Ha, I was just kidding." Totally distract them from the sale. Take all the pressure off their decision by going back to your conversational life raft.

By doing this, when it comes time to collect the money and do the paperwork, they are again relaxed and comfortable. This is quite important because when they start getting into the paperwork they should be in a positive frame of mind. Talk about kids, family, work, sports or whatever it was that they loved. You have to put them into their comfort zone. While they are filling in paperwork, to which they are not knowledgeable of, put them into something where they are knowledgeable. Then they are talking and thinking about something that they can relate to and feel more comfortable about what they are doing with their hands.

DOING THE PAPERWORK

By the time that you get to the paperwork it should be as easy as opening Christmas presents. You can now start showing little hidden benefits of their membership that you were 'saving' for this moment. It makes your prospect feel special.

"Now take this bit here. This one is for whenever you want to split your weeks. You can use four days now and then three days some other time. Did I happen to mention that our members consider this to be one of the best benefits to them?"

If you have closed your sale properly then the paperwork is a breeze. If you sold the sale on features rather than benefits, the features will come back to haunt you in the paperwork. Remember, features are technical and benefits are emotional. Close with emotion and justify with logic.

If you have dictated and controlled the tempo and pace of the sale so far, do the same when you complete the paperwork. The most important thing is that they need your support. If your prospect sees that the paperwork is no big deal to you, then they will feel the same way.

Keep it light and chatty. The same type of conversation you were having when doing the survey sheet. They have to believe that this sale is no big deal to you and you are not acting as if they just signed their life away. By doing this they will begin telling you everything that is important to them. Do not allow any technical conversations to destroy the moment that both you and the prospect are enjoying because right now they are excited.

The other, very important point to remember is that there SHOULD BE NO silence after the sale is actually closed and especially not during the paperwork. So many times I have watched Closers leave the table to go to the washroom and come back to hear the prospect say, "Oh, while you were away we were talking . . ." Cancel! You will be surprised, but a pause or a gap that you have allowed to take place can turn their realization into reality. Then, the "oh, my, we did not realize that we really are doing this, we are not sure we are doing the right thing"—fear sets in and they panic. You should never leave them alone once you have gotten a decision because you may lose the sale.

One last thing, if the sale is wobbly you will have to be very careful when doing the paperwork because the decision has not yet been made. Your sale would have been more solid if you had done an hour more work, or possibly created more value. If you were weak in asking for the order, boxing the money or explaining a certain benefit to them, you will be weak in filling in the paperwork.

What should you do, just go back to doing FORM. Take what looks like dynamite or a mine field and turn it into a bed of roses. It will be whatever you allow it to be. Put yourself in your prospect's shoes. If they think that they got a good deal, have taken advantage of you, screwed you out of a commission, they will feel great.

Completing the Paperwork

Start with your simplest, easiest paperwork first. By doing the little things first, by the time that the actual contracts and loan documents come out they have signed and completed so many forms and papers that one more is easy.

An another important point to mention is that your name, as well as your prospects, goes on the paperwork so step up and sign first. Lead by example. Remember, you are supporting them through the paperwork. If you initial or sign something first, they will initial or sign more easily.

On any other application forms fill in the pertinent company information, then sign and have your clients complete the owner or member portion.

Knowing Your Paperwork

You should read through ALL the paperwork that your company gives the buyer at the time of closing. A buyer cannot take you by surprise when they ask a question if you have read through the contracts or legal documents beforehand. You should have sufficient understanding to answer simple, basic questions. Leave the legalese to your financial or legal personnel.

Even their asking something as simple as "This paragraph says that we have the right to cancel within five working days is that correct?" This question only requires the response, "Yes, the contract does say that you have the right to cancel within five days." You have now eased whatever concern was in their head just by answering them with confidence. You do not need to get into a lengthy, legal response when all they sometimes want to hear is that you know what it says.

If you see a pause coming, or doing the paperwork becomes a little sticky, stop what you are doing. Divert their attention. Ask where they think they will be going on the first vacation. Ask them to send you a risqué postcard. Put some humor into it to take the edge off the tension.

DEALING WITH FEES

When you close the sale and you are in the paperwork, the monetary items or fees that come up should be covered with a self-assured confidence. Every sales contract or financing document has fees. Outline fees as a benefit to them, rather than making it come across as an 'extra payment' that they will have to make. You can say, "Remember, if you cannot use the week(s) this year, you can accumulate them and double the usage next year for a small fee." Whatever the charge is <u>show it as a benefit, not a cost</u>. If you start elaborating on all the little extra charges that are involved with the memberships, you will never get a sale completed.

Throughout your presentation you should have lain in the charges, indirectly or even directly, through third party stories. In most cases the prospect heard you but it did not register with them. When you get to that item in the paperwork, just say, "Remember I mentioned that earlier when I told you about so and so . . ." Then the prospect will say they remember because they are too embarrassed to admit they were not listening to you. They will not worry about it because it was not a 'hidden item' they were not aware of. However, there are some items that you may not need to lay in during your presentation because they can be handled easily if they are portrayed as a benefit, not a cost.

Using a $.99 Pen

Always have enough pens with you. I suggest at least three that work. If your company or resort has logo pens, buy a box of them and give them to your prospects to use and take home. It is a small price to pay against a commission check.

You should own a good quality pen or pen and pencil set. If you want to be successful you have to look successful. Nothing looks worse, or can deteriorate your credibility faster than writing a $50,000 sale and doing the paperwork with a $.99 pen.

Use your good quality pen for completing and signing the paperwork. Hand them your expensive pen to complete the paperwork, but remind them that they can take the logo pen as a souvenir.

Be Prepared

Have everything ready at your table or desk. You should know when you are very close to making the sale or going to call for managerial assistance, so clean off your space of those dirty cups and glasses. Get rid of all the negative things and make the area presentable and professional looking. Only keep what you need to complete the sale.

Many professional Closers will have complete paperwork packages in their briefcases or desks to use when they need it to keep the tempo going. If you have a paperwork package in your possession, you are assuming the sale. You are prepared and ready for anything.

Always have extra copies of the paperwork handy. Agreements, application forms, floor plans, charts, brochures, etc . . . whatever you need to smoothly finish the sale. It looks unprofessional to start having to rely on someone else to bring you something and not do it promptly. Why would you rely on someone else to play potential havoc with your income?

READING THROUGH THE PAPERWORK

A successful closer will always tell their 'members' to complete the paperwork while they give them the necessary information to fill in the blanks.

When you go through the paperwork with your prospect, go through it. Summarize the points of the document that you are reading, just as you did when you summarized the benefits for them.

Always read a paragraph to them when you are going through the paperwork and then initial next to the paragraphs (if you can). Tell them that it is their turn to initial after you have read through all the paperwork and contracts. By seeing you sign or initial first will make them feel more comfortable about signing.

Again, when you go through it, point out the things that relate to their benefits and get them to understand how it will benefit them after they have become a member. Remember, once they believe that they are buying, they have an attitude about it and it will not matter what you say to them now. They have now adopted their puppy and you are not going to take it away from them. Remember people buy on emotion and then justify with logic.

There are many locations, and companies, where the final paperwork, or the equivalent, is done by the salesperson. If this is the case, stay with your people throughout the whole process. Do not leave them to fend on their own during the paperwork. Especially do not leave them alone with the paperwork so that they can read it and find a way to get out of doing the sale. If paperwork is done by someone else, stay close by just in case any questions arise that may require answers.

This business is an attitude. The way that you do your paperwork is a direct reflection on what is going on, on your table.

FOLLOWING UP ON YOUR SALE

Even though this is covered in more detail in the last section—What does this mean? Primarily it means doing or giving something with your prospect turned client after the sale to seal the deal and say thank you. It could be taking them out to eat, buying a few drinks in a sports bar, taking them golfing or fishing or maybe even buying them a small gift.

SEVEN REASONS FOR FOLLOW UP YOUR SALE

1. It makes your clients feel secure in the fact that you care about them and not the commission.
2. You really do like your clients and want to spend time with them. By spending time with them they will feel comfortable in their decision and not be looking for a way to cancel.
3. It gives your 'new clients' the opportunity to voice any concerns they may have or ask additional questions about what they have just bought. You need to make sure that your sale is solid and a button up does this.
4. Should another salesperson or project try to entice your 'new client,' they will immediately come back to tell you. You want the relationship to be so strong between you and your prospect that they have no desire to speak with anyone other than you.
5. You can ask them to upgrade or buy more weeks. This usually eliminates most post-sale concerns immediately.
6. Ask for referrals. If they provide you with names, or think about it, this also eliminates concerns. If they feel comfortable enough referring someone else to you, your sale is solid.
7. You want to be paid.

If your new client wishes to cancel the sale because of buyer's remorse, accept it. Buyer's remorse is a fact of life in every sales industry. Do not be afraid of it and not only learn to live with it, learn from it.

Should your new client have a couple of questions, there is usually no problem. If they come back with a sheet full of questions for you to answer, answer some of them and then remind them that their membership package, or informational/instructional video, should answer most of their other general questions.

If your response does not seem to satisfy or appease them, take the list of questions and go down it ticking off who, besides you, should answer them. Ask them if they have any more questions other than the ones listed. They will say "no, that is about it" to which you can reply, "So which question would you like me to answer first for you?" Usually the wife will say to the husband, "Well it was the one about . . . oh, which one was it that you did not like honey?" Let them explain themselves completely. Let them tell you which one is the most important question and where these questions are coming from, just as you did with their objections.

Discover, explore, look for the reason, look for the emotion and then deal with it. The person who justifies all the questions with logic, or starts back pedaling is usually the one that wants out of sale. Do not make the mistake of jumping in immediately to respond to the questions, because you may say something that is not related to their concern and may raise another problem or objection.

Also, do not make up answers to their questions, because they will most likely be untrue and you will be caught. The prospect is just waiting for you to lie about something to provide them with an excuse to cancel the sale. Remember they are internet savvy, linked into social media and can get the truth at the touch of a finger.

Remember, if you sell on logic, they will cancel on logic. Your prospect may have been up all night reading through paperwork and contracts, working on questions for you to answer the next morning. They may have questions such as, "How do I go about verifying that airfare discount information you gave me yesterday? Well, Article 16 says that should there be an assessment . . . the Homeowners Association will sit down and increase the fees. How will that increase relate in a dollar loss to me?" If they cannot verify a piece of information, they will cancel. They came prepared for your meeting the next day, did you? Were you up all night working on the buttoning up your sale? I would guarantee that you were doing something else. To avoid these situations from occurring sell on emotion, not features.

A skilled salesperson can also counter paperwork or contract concerns by encouraging them to read the paperwork in their own time. I once had a salesperson who would encourage their buyers to read all of the paperwork that night and the next day come back with at least 20 questions or they would have to buy breakfast or lunch. What would happen? The next day, the salesperson would meet with their buyers, ask for their questions and invariably the response was "since you wanted us to read through the paperwork we figure you have nothing to hide and if we have any questions in the future we will let you know." This approach works similarly to saying no and taking away the sale, it has validated and secured credibility in you and your company. What salesperson in their right mind tells their buyers to read ALL the paperwork? A successful and confident one! This technique does come with a warning—make sure that your sale was rock solid because should they actually read the paperwork, they will find nothing new in the paperwork that will jeopardize your sale.

Like the example above, the best way to solidify your sale during a follow up meeting is to go on the offensive. The best defense is a good offense! Try to sell them another week or something else that compliments what they bought. Be creative in finding a way in which to that. What do you think their response will be? No, we just had a couple of questions. We are quite happy with the one week we just bought but thanks anyway. If you get very creative you might just double your income. If you do decide to sell them another week, remember you already have sold them a week, so there is no need to do a second warm up, agenda, breaking the pact, etc. Eight of ten will tell you that they are happy with the one they own, the other two will buy another week.

A good closer in this business should be able to do thirty percent of their business through referrals or upgrades. Every sale that you make can generate you more income if you just ask your new clients to upgrade or for referrals. I will go more into generating referrals in the last section expanding your horizons.

By being prepared and having great attitude you can greet a new prospect with self-assured confidence and sincerity. From there you can warm them up, find some commonality and build rapport. Once you have gained rapport you will make a friend. With friendship you earn the right to ask questions. Then, having discovered the prospect's dominant buying motives you can better explain the emotional benefits to owning your product by creating desire in it. The decision to own comes from their desire for your product or service.

In summary, closing is nothing more than a transmission of your emotions to theirs. It is the most incredible feeling to have that kind of power over other people. We capture people. We capture their emotions and we can keep them riveted to their seats or bore the pants off them. They either stay tuned to the channel or they change it with a remote control. The prospect buys you. Let them buy you first before you start. It is so important that your prospect feel as if they are making the sale. They need to feel as if they are buying it and not being sold.

The Chinese Philosopher Sun Tzu once said, "Compel others, and do not be compelled by them." People buy the interpretation of you. Let your emotions compel your prospects. Whatever you feel, whatever you believe is going to happen on that table, will happen.

What I have covered so far will work on any prospect that walks in the door, no matter who they are or what industry you may work in. Whether your prospect is an attorney, construction worker, doctor, secretary, executive, truck driver or an Indian chief, if you just greet them with a great attitude, be relaxed and sincere you will make The Sale.

Well, that is the Buying Curve and the Sale. Stick to the basics as outlined and you will write sales. From this point forward I will review what happened and there is NO Sale. In the third section, we will review how to fix what went wrong and to come full circle, the last section is all about expanding your horizons using today's tools and technology to increase your sales potential.

One last thing before moving on, if you approach every day with the attitude that it is your first sale, you will never go wrong.

SECTION 2

10

NO SALE

Sales are made or lost by a single determining factor—what you do. Everything that you do moves you either closer to a sale or farther away. Prospects buy because of the attitude, competence, credibility and personality the salesperson portrays. Your prospect may not be able to sort out all the different benefits you have shown but they do trust their personal judgment regarding you. You can then use all techniques I have shown you to this point to close the sale but only after your prospects trust you. Successful salespeople orchestrate all aspects of their sales presentation to guarantee their prospects trust, especially the close. So, if you want to become an exceptional or master closer it is imperative that you learn how to manage the close to reduce the number of No Sales. Realistically no one sells 100% of their prospects, master closers close between 40-50% but if you can achieve a closure rate of 30% and 40% (3 or 4 out of every 10 prospects) then you will be successful. Less than that percentage you need to understand what is holding you back from becoming exceptional.

In the last section we learned that before you 'go for the close' there were a few things that you needed to understand about the psychology of closing. It is *the* most stressful part of a sales presentation and is the part that your prospect hates the most. Second, there is a buying curve. Third, people do not like to be sold, anything.

First you hopefully learned that managing the tension and anxiety in your prospect can be a very effective tool in increasing your ability to make the sale. When you meet your prospect the tension and fear levels are high and as you start to build rapport and trust the levels will ease off thereby becoming more manageable. A successful salesperson understands that the way in which your prospects communicate with you is the same way they will hear your words. What this means is that if your prospect is open and direct, be open and direct in return. You need to soften your approach if they are vague and less direct.

Prospects are not naive, they know when the closing point is coming but it still creates tension, reluctance and fear. As you approach the close your prospects anxiety levels increase. Their heart rate increases, they will begin to feel a tightness in their chest and may even experience a dry throat. All of these sensations are caused by a fear of the unknown and of being sold. We all fear making a mistake but it is your prospect who realizes that the decision they are about to make may be irrevocable. Due to this anxiety created by the closing process it becomes your job to make this transition as smooth and painless as possible.

The second part of the psychology of closing to understand that there is a buying curve. Anyone who has ever bought anything has gone through a buying curve. The buyers buying curve consists of a path of resistance that is lessened by desire and need until enough urgency has been created to force a decision. The salesperson's buying curve is a series of steps which need to be followed in order to create the desire and urgency in order to force the decision.

We all understand that there is no set time limit for a buying curve—either for buyer or seller. It may take fifteen minutes, three hours or two weeks. The timing is based on the amount of resistance that a prospect has towards the product and perceived value. Everyone possesses a natural sales resistance. The sale will only be made when the salesperson has provided sufficient information and value to overshadow the objections and the prospect is at their maximum attention, retention, enthusiasm and desire for the product.

The only thing that prospects can savor is the experience of purchasing and a master closer will know exactly when their pitch complements the benefits creating sufficient desire and urgency for their prospect to buy. Once that prospect has reached their peak buying point on the curve you must ask for the order. If you wait, which many amateur salespeople do, for the prospect to ask to buy—you will keep waiting because it will never happen. After that peak point the prospect will start to lose their enthusiasm, intensity and desire and the presentation will end and you will have No Sale.

The third part of the psychology of closing really understands that people do not like to be sold. Everyone likes to buy, but they do not like to be sold. Being sold and buying are two separate activities. Buying is fun, being sold is? Well, I will let you fill in the blank. The theory behind this is that we all like to have control over our decisions. When we buy we believe we have control of the sales process. Only then do we believe we are confident enough to make a buying decision. You must lead your prospects to believe that they are making a buying decision while in reality you control their decision making throughout the sales process.

Think of the last person you spoke with who was unhappy with a product or service. "Oh, that S.O.B. sold me a . . . never again!" Possibly they were excited, "We bought a beautiful three bedroom condo or great new sports car and we just love it." **Remember, people like to buy, not to be sold.**

You have an obligation to your prospects to make the sale go smoothly. By understanding the psychology of the close you are better able to manage the close and support them through it. Should they do not buy, hopefully it is for a "real or valid reason" such as the complete lack of money available to purchase. This should be the only reason you realistically lose the sale if you have done everything else right, however this is not usually the reason there was No Sale.

As I stated in the first line above—Sales are made or lost by a single determining factor—what you do. In reality, it does not matter what type of sales that you are involved in, each step of the buying curve covered in the previous section is important in ensuring that the building blocks are in place so that you can manage and close your prospect on your product or service.

Can you remember Rule number two in closing? Maybe I should change it to Rule number one—when the sale goes down—STOP CLOSING. Once the decision is down—**do not go past the close** because as soon as you do—there is **No Sale**. It is amazing how many salespeople go past this point, which is why this section will examine the seven deadly sales sins on why, or how, salespeople end up going past the close and what happens to all salespeople, even those exceptional ones, from time to time. Additionally, this chapter or section will show you ways in which you can manage the close and hopefully avoid not getting the sale.

THE 7 DEADLY "SINS"

I am pretty confident that almost everyone reading this book has heard of the 7 Deadly Sins. According to Christian beliefs, they consist of human vices or frailty that supposedly lead to personal downfall—these sins are greed, lust, pride, envy, gluttony, sloth and anger. Well, guess what, in sales, we also have seven deadly sins which can also lead to personal (sales) downfall—they are:

1. Over Selling
2. Positive Pitching
3. Begging for the Sale
4. Loss of Credibility
5. High Pressure Tactics
6. Desperation
7. Confrontation

The above seven sins account for the majority of the lost sales. Although the order may vary depending on the salesperson, these "sins' tend to build upon each other culminating in the lost sale. Strangely enough, if you compare the list against the Christian list, there are extraordinary similarities between the "sins." Think about it!

Each of the following sins is a direct result of your losing control of your sales presentation at the most critical time of the buying curve—the decision. Once salespeople realize that they have gone past the point of no return, any, or all, of the following sins rear their "ugly" heads. As we break down the seven deadly sins into what causes them, what effect they have and a solution, you will find that all are caused by that single determining factor—what you did or did not do during your sales presentation. I realize that this sounds harsh, but you cannot put blame on your prospect because technically you were in "control" of the process. If you gave over control to your prospect, you failed to manage the closing process—so shame on you and you should go back and reread the earlier chapters.

1. Over Selling

Cause: Over Selling involves being too eager and continuing to sell the prospect(s) even after they have already decided to purchase your product or service. This is a frequent mistake made by unseasoned or poor salespeople who did not listen to the decision carefully enough and continue to sell features or benefits.

Effect: The buyer may hear something that they do not like or want and suddenly wish to "think about it" and you may ultimately lose the sale if you cannot bring them back into the "sales ether."

Solution: After they have agreed to purchase—stop selling and congratulate your prospect on making a smart decision that will benefit them. Let your buyer (s) enjoy the moment of purchasing and help them through the paperwork process. As stated in the last chapter, you are now their advisor, not the sales person. If you want to tell them about other benefits, do it selectively during the paperwork as "reminders".

2. Positive Pitching

Cause: While similar to Over Selling, positive pitching is just throwing out anything and everything about your product or service in the hopes that one thing will grab your prospects attention enough that they will buy.

Effect: Your buyer sees absolutely no value or benefit to anything you are telling them and will ultimately give you the "we need to think about it" excuse for not purchasing.

Solution: Take the time to do a proper warm up and discovery so you can manage the close on what you learned about what is important to them. You should have been listening to your prospect instead of talking at your prospect.

3. Begging for the Sale

<u>Cause</u>: The salesperson believes that the prospect needs their product or service and makes comments such as "are you sure that this product or service is not something you need?" or, "what else can I show or explain to you that you will change your mind about buying this?" Tone of the voice changes to almost sound like a child begging for something.

<u>Effect</u>: Your prospect has absolutely zero interest in your product, or service and have said no repeatedly to you, but are too polite to get up and walk out (or hang up) on you.

<u>Solution</u>: As with number 2 above, take the time to do a proper warm up and discovery so you can manage the close on what you learned about what is important to them. You should have been listening to your prospect instead of talking at your prospect.

4. Loss of Credibility

<u>Cause</u>: Overstating a benefit or even a feature to the point of "too good to be true" status, not providing enough background to create credibility in you or your company, lack of trust in you, your company and/or your product or service due to social media, internet and/or personal experience.

<u>Effect</u>: Unfortunately, until your prospect likes and trusts you, a sale will not happen. In addition, they will never tell you that you have lost their respect, which ultimately leads to a "thanks but we do not think this will work for us" response and you may never find out unless you hear about it from someone else.

<u>Solution</u>: If you understand that credibility stems from trust. People buy you before they buy your product. Never forget this. Everyone, including your prospect, appreciates family values, manners and imperfections so just be yourself. Additionally, you will gain your prospect's trust and earn credibility if you are sincere in trying to promote your product or service. Reread chapter 3 if you feel you are having credibility issues.

5. High Pressure Tactics

<u>Cause</u>: High pressure tactics usually start after the you realize that positive pitching and begging for the sale have not gotten you anywhere, or any closer to a sale, but you believe that maybe a little more pressure will convince them to buy.

<u>Effect</u>: Prospects will leave your sales presentation with a very negative impression of you, your company and your product or service. This impression will be spread amongst friends, family, Facebook pages, Twitter and other social media warning others to stay away due to the "high pressure tactics at such and such company."

<u>Solution</u>: Stop using high pressure to sell your product or service. If people like you and trust you, they will buy from you without the pressure. Ask yourself, do you like to be pressured into making a decision and if you have, did you really like what you were sold??

6. Desperation

<u>Cause</u>: Feeling that you need to do anything to get the sale. This sin follows begging for the sale because you have lost credibility which led to high pressure tactics and now you are desperate.

<u>Effect</u>: Desperation can be smelled by prospects and they may "play" with you by saying that they have changed their mind but in the end, still say no.

<u>Solution</u>: Thank your prospects for their time then wish them a good day and say—Next!

7. Confrontation

<u>Cause</u>: You will not accept that your prospect is saying no and you do not recognize that the tension level has increased to the point of confrontation.

<u>Effect</u>: Confrontation is the culmination of all of the previous six sins and once it reaches this point—it can become ugly. Over the years I have seen instances where both salespeople and prospects have resorted to verbal abuse and actually start throwing punches. This definitely leaves your prospect with a negative impression of you, your company and most definitely your product and may ultimately end up being viewed on YouTube, Facebook or any number of social media sites because guaranteed, someone has used their smart phone to video the confrontation!

<u>Solution</u>: Apologize for your behavior and walk away or hang up. If necessary, have someone else escort them out (or call back) with apologies and offer some form of compensation—dinner coupon, free sample or something which can regain some sort of positive impression instead of the negative one.

So, how many of the above sins have you been guilty of in your sales career? Be honest. I am sure that the vast majority have experienced at least the first two or three and some of you maybe more . . . maybe all seven at one time or another. The solutions to most can be found in following the steps of the buying curve, more specifically doing a good warm up, creating good rapport which leads to credibility, then asking good questions and LISTENING to the answers to help you control and manage closing the sale.

How to Manage your Close to reduce your "No Sales"

People traditionally do not like to make decisions and will surprisingly allow you to take the decision making process over if they trust you. You want your prospect to believe that they are making the decision without specifically handing it over to them per se. Remember your prospect will take control of the sales presentation when they have the decision whether or not to buy. Therefore, you must create an environment that takes the decision away from them without their being aware of it—in other words you are in control and managing the direction. You do this by using the rapport, communication, credibility, trust and desire you have created <u>and</u> stimulated throughout the closing process.

The first hurdle that you need to address is whether or not your prospect is fearful of making a decision—any decision. All decisions are stressful and below are five ways in which you can manage their fear, tension and anxiety levels to avoid losing the sale and possibly becoming confrontational:

1. Increase your awareness of the varying tension levels throughout the sales presentation. By recognizing them you will be able to deal with them before they become a negative influence on your sale.
2. Develop a variety of ways to handle different prospect or personality types.
3. Use third party stories and testimonials to establish additional rapport and credibility.
4. Adjust your communication style to help your prospects feel more comfortable.
5. Communicate with your prospect in the same manner that they communicate with you. By mirror imaging them initially they will start to mirror image you later on in the sales presentation and when you are ready for them to make the decision.

MANAGING THE CLOSE

Managing a sale involves knowing what you are doing before you ask for the order. You need to be prepared emotionally and mentally. This also includes arming yourself with the confidence that you are going to need to dodge the barrage of negativity and objections you will hear during your presentation.

The following are a selection of strategies for managing the close **before** you ask for the order.

1. Plan your close in advance. The first step to managing the close is to plan it well in advance. Know exactly where in your sales presentation you are going to use your closing techniques so that they are the most effective in creating desire and need.

Planning does not mean overkill it involves whatever time is necessary to plan your presentation.

2. All successful salespeople plan out every step of their sales presentation, word for word. Amateur salespeople fly by the seat of their pants and hope that the prospect buys in the end. When you plan your close in advance you have confidence, energy and enthusiasm which make you more relaxed to deal with any situations or objections that arise.

3. <u>You must have a positive mental attitude</u>. This also includes being enthusiastic, energetic and creative. Successful salespeople will always find new ways to rework old ideas or methods to offer a viable solution.

4. <u>You must be open-minded and have clearly defined objectives</u>. If you are open-minded then you are capable of offering small concessions on the road to reaching your objectives. Successful Closers know exactly where to give up concessions before they ask for the order.

5. <u>Do not offer these concessions too early</u>. You will teach your prospects bad habits if you start offering concessions too early in the sales presentation. Wait until they start giving you a buying signal before you offer a concession. Before then, use trade-off suggestions.

6. <u>You must negotiate with yourself first</u>. This one takes considerable discipline. There are many salespeople who will give in to prospects demands because they fear losing a sale. You have to decide if you are willing to sacrifice your credibility for the sake of a deal.

7. <u>You must be willing to take risks</u>. This involves the discipline of not feeling compelled to answer every demand or statement that your prospect makes. Successful salespeople also know when to walk away (or take away) from a sale if the situation arises.

8. <u>Taking all the time necessary to learn what your prospects' requirements are</u>. You must listen and understand all of your prospects needs and desires before you even attempt to close the sale.

9. <u>Your prospect must understand what you are offering them</u>. Many salespeople assume their prospects always understand

what they are offering. This is not true. They must understand what value your product has for them and you can only do that by asking questions. It is your responsibility to clarify all assumptions and define the loose-ends before you ask for the order.

10. Your credibility must be unquestioned. If you do not have trust, rapport or a relationship there is no credibility in you, your company or your product. If there is no trust there is no sale.

11. Manage your Ego. If you let your ego determine the outcome of the sale rather than the prospect, the outcome will be dangerous. Learn to bite your tongue and never argue with a prospect.

12. Learn to put yourself in your prospects shoes. This is a very big part of managing the close. When you look at the sale from their perspective you can better understand how they are feeling about themselves and the 'deal,' how much value they see and what they fear. If you are sincere and your prospect can feel your empathy they will trust you, and ultimately your product.

13. Use reminders to plant seeds. This trick is to suggestively re-educate your prospect about your product while focusing on value. You must continue to stimulate desire throughout the sales presentation because without it there is no sale.

14. Use as many tie downs or trial closes as necessary. A significant part of managing the close is by effectively asking as many "yes" questions as you can. A successful closer knows how and when to use them to create the most impact without overdoing it.

15. Know how your product best suits your prospect. This one can be tough on an amateur salesperson that will frequently end up 'selling or telling.' It is important to remember that you are not there to sell ideas you are there to close sales. Successful salespeople know that it requires your listening to your prospect to know how your product will best suit them.

16. Recognizing the Buying signals and Questions. Successful salespeople can almost smell a buying signal or question coming. They have planned their presentation to the point they know exactly when, or where, their prospect will begin to show interest in their product.

17. Any positive change in your prospects attitude, posture, voice, behavior at this point is a sure sign that they are considering your product. A master closer will go ahead and ask for the order. Their answer will direct you from there and determine if you were right or not.

18. <u>Look for all the reasons they would want to buy</u>. Never consider the reasons why they should not buy. Remember, you close them or they close you.

19. <u>Find something that excites and stimulates you</u>. When you find something about your prospect that excites or stimulates you, stick with it. Eventually you will find the angle that you can use to close them if you keep on communicating.

20. <u>Become a chameleon</u>. Turn yourself into them so that you can understand their dominant buying character. Remember, people will only buy from people they can relate to.

Managing the sale is defining what you are doing *before* you ask for the order. It is amazing how many salespeople do not even expend the energy to plan. Being unprepared affects your credibility and professionalism. Being unprepared increases the chances that you will lose your prospects attention because they see that you are not prepared to work with them.

A Little Test: Take a few minutes and go back and review each suggestion again comparing them against the seven deadly sins and see how the suggestions will help you overcome your particular "sin(s)."

EARNING THE RIGHT TO ASK FOR THE ORDER

Another reason that sales are lost is that during the process of managing your close you did not earn the right to advance in the sales presentation. What this means is that if you do not have the right to pass the point in your presentation where your prospect was comfortable. Simplified, until you have created enough desire you should not ask for the order.

A successful closer realizes that a prospects mild interest in not sufficient reason to ask for the order. They know that you cannot close a sale until the prospect has reached a high level of interest and desire <u>and</u> is ready to make a positive decision.

The biggest problem in sales, however, is recognizing that you have earned the right to ask for the order. To help distinguish this point, ask yourself, "Where is my prospect in this sales presentation?" "Have I done a good job of getting them into the deal, creating enough motivation, stimulating desire and do I have the right emotions present to ask." If you sincerely believe that you do, then you have earned the right to ask for the order.

In anticipation of earning the right to ask for the order you must make sure that you have done all the following five things:

1. You have gotten basic commitments.
2. Determined that all issues, concerns, questions have been answered to the complete satisfaction of your prospect.
3. You have solved their problem by showing the value to them of owning your product.
4. You have stimulated whichever emotion or motivation you need—greed, love, fear, etc. The decision is usually based on one of these three emotions.
5. They are asking buying questions or their physiology has changes to indicate that a buying decision is near.

Okay, so you have gotten them into the deal, created enough motivation, stimulated their desire and have all the right emotions, now what?

WERE THEY READY TO MAKE A DECISION?

Did you know when you had the sale? Asking for the order is a timing issue. If you focused on your prospect and involved them in the sales presentation then you did earn the right to ask for the order. When your prospect has shown the desire and made a subconscious decision, can they now make a verbal decision? This is where we go back to the beginning of the chapter and examine the third aspect in the psychology of closing—the agony of making a decision.

The hardest part of the sale for your prospect is stepping up and making a decision. Yes, people do like to buy but getting to the point where they buy consciously again becomes a fearful proposition. The onset of making a verbal commitment frightens people although you have eliminated the fear through rapport, communication, credibility and trust.

This is where you take away the agony of making the decision from them. If you ignore the verbal decision by assuming the sale then your prospect will also assume the sale by ignoring the decision. When you have progressively advanced through all the appropriate tie downs and trial closes the natural assumption of the sale is accepted by both parties. This already assumes that their objections and concerns have been handled.

By further stimulating their emotional, rather than logical needs, you then make the decision easy for them. When you focus on something that is very emotional to them it stimulates that emotion, which then overtakes the logical objection. Remember, we are all dreamers. We all dream of something. We all have desires or goals and these things dominate our ability to make a decision. Find something that stimulates and excites your prospect and the decision will become easy.

Unfortunately one of the biggest mistakes I see is salespeople giving the decision to their prospect. This is particularly true in the case of an amateur salesperson positive pitching his or her product (sin #2). You will always get a no decision if you positive pitch, especially if you give your prospect the right to decide. Never give your prospect the decision, assume you have a sale.

DID YOU ASK FOR THE ORDER AND WAIT?

Your prospect is now peaked at the top of the buying curve. They do not want to hear any more information and if you do not ask for the order immediately, you will never get the sale. If you do not ask at this point you are ultimately doing more damage to yourself than if you had asked and they were not ready. If you do not ask your prospect for the order when you have all the appropriate signals, you are showing a lack of confidence in your ability to close the sale.

What do you do after you ask for the order? You should have quit talking, closed your mouth and waited about 5-10 seconds. I am sure that you are familiar with the adage which states, "He who talks first, loses." It is believed that if you talk first then you are buying their reasons for not buying. Your prospects are stepping up to make a decision when they talk first.

These few seconds are called the "Golden moment of silence." Do not be self-deceived regarding its effectiveness. Try it. Quit talking for thirty seconds and see how long it really feels. The stress put on you not to talk is staggering. The vacuum created by the silence is overpowering to the mind and eventually someone is forced to break the silence. Yes, the prospect should be the first one who talks so possibly the adage should be changed to, "he who talks first, wins," because you want them to feel good about owning your product. Silence is probably the most effective closing technique that you can possess however it is seldom used effectively.

The only exception to this rule is when you are dealing with money as the last objection. If you give your prospect too much silence they will decide no, it is better for you to step up after five seconds and offer a solution. For example, tell them, "You know what, I bet it is because you are having a hard time with this payment, what would a more affordable payment?" This makes the prospect feel that you are not pressuring them but assuming a viable alternative decision. By obtaining a yes you will continue to move forward in the closing process.

One of two things will happen after the silence. One is they will ask for your business card and tell you they will call you later and thanks for the information. Two, they will confess their last condition or objection. It does not matter how ridiculous you may think the objection or condition is, once you have one, you have a commitment to buy. Everything else becomes irrelevant from this point forward.

When you ask for the order you are at a point of no return. If they take option one and tell you that they will call you, just admit the defeat and say, "you know what, I am done. I have never spent this long with anyone this must be a record. I will have to ask my manager to see if there is a plaque for this." You are using humor to take the onus off the sales presentation that gives you the right to go into a related third party story and then ask for the order again, using another angle.

Each time that you ask for the order and they do not respond or you are rebuffed with an excuse or objection, use another third party story with their hot button and ask again. Eventually you will either get their real objection or they will fill in the paperwork. When you have earned the right to ask for the order you can ask and ask and ask.

The law of persistence overcomes resistance is the difference between writing sales or biting amateur salespeople in the ass. In chapter 9 we covered why salespeople are afraid of closing or asking for the order— fear of failure and rejection. However, we are back to why you lost the sale and to the number one reason that your prospect did not buy—they did not trust you.

Once you ask for the order, stop selling. You will overload them with information if you carry on selling or justifying, and they will say no. When you start justifying things you have said you are no longer in control of the sales presentation or the decision. You are promoting a no through your physiology. Your confidence and credibility decline and then prospect will no longer trust you. Remember those sins we covered above. If you find yourself falling into this position, go back to your life raft and quit talking. Remember, listening is so easy. Besides what else are your ears good for? Use your ears and mouth in the ratio that God gave them to you.

All right, you assumed they are going to buy, asked for the order and the only thing left was your final negotiation tool—money. You should always leave yourself something as a final negotiation tool and it should <u>always</u> be the money. At this point do not let your prospect try and sidetrack you with a problem or objection to the money by asking more questions, just continue to answer their concerns [taking back control] and funneling the objections back to the money.

Even though the following four questions should have been asked *before* you ask for the order I have included them here because they will always funnel you to the money objection. To show their effectiveness I have included them in a shtick that I have used very successfully over the years.

> "Valerie and Jay we have found through our extensive market studies that there are really only four things from holding people back from joining our club today; so before we move on I am going to ask you four questions to see where you are—okay?. <u>Note</u>: These eliminate use, product knowledge, credibility or trust. [Take a clean sheet of paper]

1. [Pick up the survey sheet as your <u>write "Vacation"</u>] The number one reason that people do not join the club [look at survey sheet] is that they don't vacation. Well, since I notice you have listed a number of destinations [list them out loud] it is obvious that you vacation so that can't be it. [Make this a statement of fact]
2. Now, please don't be embarrassed but I want you to be honest with me here—I can start over again if there are some things that you don't fully understand, or more if necessary! [<u>Write "Understand"</u>] Do you understand or would you like me to start over? [They will always agree with you and say yes they understand.]
3. Next, I don't want you to be scared of hurting my feelings so are you one hundred percent comfortable in the way I have promoted [your product], this company and the industry? [<u>Write "Credibility"</u>] Do you trust me and the company? [Again they

will usually say yes] Thank you. [Shake their hand to seal the commitment]

4. So, ninety-five percent [pick any number] of the people who walk in here become stuck on this one. Correct me if I am wrong but the only reason that you the only thing stopping you today would be making this justifiably affordable. Would I be correct?" [Yes] You could also finish with, "In other words, it is the money isn't it?"

You have now funneled the whole sale down to the money. All the objections that they have given you were just blown away with number four. If they balked at any point then you are grateful for the real objection. You should not care if they object here. You would rather have them say, "You know, we could use a little verification on . . . or how are we sure that our money is safe with you." You would rather have it come out now before you ask for the order.

Whatever sales industry you are in, find a way to create similar shtick s like those above to summarize the main issues and bring it all down to the money objection.

I once heard that a major university participated in a marketing study that revealed 80% of salespeople fail to ask for the order 90% of the time. Although I cannot verify this statement, my thirty plus years of experience reflects it fairly closely. Do not let yourself fall into this statistic, take every opportunity to ask for the order. It is a lot like winning the lottery. If you do not have a ticket you cannot win, so if you do not ask for the order, you will never know if you have a sale or not.

DID YOU SET UP THE MONEY OBJECTION?

You should have narrowed all of their objections down and the only thing left is to ask for the order at your gross price. This is where you require nerves of steel because you will always hear the words, "Your price is too high." There is always an objection to the price. There is a natural resistance to price because nobody can ever afford the price the first time it is mentioned. It is your job to insure that the benefits far outweigh the price.

Following are eleven ways to properly handle the price objection issue.

1. Always be focusing on the value of your product, then benefits. Price is always last.
2. Never mention the price until the prospect brings it up first. When it is the right time they will mention it.
3. Never talk about the price without mentioning value and benefits to your prospect.
4. Never talk about the price unless you cannot avoid it. Always talk about benefits.
5. Always restate value and benefits when talking about the price.
6. Stimulate their desire because it reduces the price issue diametrically.
7. Only justify the price with valid reasons that include their benefits.
8. Only compare your price with a comparable product. You cannot compare an apple to an orange, no matter how hard you try.
9. Use the lowest common denominator approach if necessary. In other words show the price over the lifetime of your product or service.
10. Never argue over the price because you will always lose.
11. Tell them that you would rather justify the price today than apologize for it tomorrow.

After you show them the prices they more than likely would have 'freaked out' because they do not see enough value. Immediately take the money away and tell a third party story focusing on more value. Every time you get a money objection, take it away and tell another third party story to add more value. Keep doing this until you have created enough value to overcome the money objection. Prospects buy only after they resist, so you must appreciate the subtleness of the buying curve. Prospects have to expel all of their resistance before they will see any value in what you are showing them. Remember, when there is NO fight for the NO items, then there is NO sale. People who do not see any value or relate any value will view your product as cheap and not worth the investment.

It is important to also realize that price and cost is not the same. Prospects perceive value to include price and cost. If the price remains constant and the cost is perceived to be too high then you must build up value to lower the cost. Always justify the value of your product and never allow the cost to supersede value.

Other points to remember when you hear the objection, "the price is too high" may be related to one, or all, of the following five points.

1. <u>All buyers fear cheap products or services</u>. Your prospect wants to believe that your product or service has value to them therefore you must maintain value throughout the money gathering process.
2. <u>Prospects expect to negotiate</u>. Prospects will automatically compare their perceived value to your price in an effort to determine the cost to them. When they have done this they will begin negotiating with you.
3. <u>The Greed factor</u> Use the value you have created to justify the high purchase cost. Never drop the price to justify value. Prospects, like everyone else, want to feel that they have gotten a great deal.
4. <u>Self-credibility</u> Remember that product credibility stems from your credibility. If you believe in the value of your product at that price then they will believe it too.
5. <u>It may be a buying signal</u>. If your prospect believes in you, they will believe in your product. They will see its value and want to negotiate a price to acquire the best deal. Use this objection as an opportunity to close your sale.

Remember, when you have created the desire to own your product, your prospect will assume ownership of it. Once ownership has been assumed then, and only then, depending on your company price structure, should you show a price (or incentive) that is about thirty percent higher than you know they can afford. By showing an incentive or price twenty-five to thirty percent higher will eliminate all the other objections and focus your prospect on the money objection. "Well, if it was XX dollars we would do it but we cannot afford that much." "So what you are telling me is that if it were XX dollars you would do this?"

Note: It is important you do not show money that is so far out of their depth they could not possibly afford it even if they wanted it. Keep the money within a range that you realistically know they can afford.

What if your prospect says yes to your product at gross do you sell it to them? Only you can answer that. If you believe in your price at its' gross price, sell it at gross. As long as your prospect believes that they are getting value you will never need to reduce your price.

Additionally, did your physiology reflect that you know there is a better price that you are signaling, which will ultimately drop your price to that 'bottom line' because you feel you do not want to cheat your prospect? Unfortunately, if you do this you have now cheapened your product by reducing its' value in the eyes of your prospect. In this instance you will most likely get another objection totally unrelated to money and they have started back pedaling out of the sale. It should not matter whether you are selling a $15, $1,500 or $50,000 product, you are the only one who can make the decision on whether to credibly reduce your price or not.

Finally, when your prospect tells you that, "It is just the money," it is never just the money. It is value, credibility and bonding. All of those things will get you a decision and a decision will always get you the money. This all brings us back to the number one reason why prospects do not buy what you are selling. They do not believe at the point of sale that the product or services presented to them are going to be honored in the years to come. You, as a salesperson should take a good look at what you are doing and how you are managing the sale, including the last hidden objection—money. If you remember at the beginning of this chapter I stated that sales are made or lost by a single determining factor—you. You are as much of the sale as your product (or service) and company. The money (or price) should only and always be the last objection. It is also the last closing technique that you should have in your arsenal. If you eliminate all the objections except for money, your prospect has no alternative but to say yes.

After all of this, what does losing a sale really mean? Some salespeople believe that it is because their prospect cannot make the decision that would have satisfied whatever their need was at that moment in time. There are others who blame their prospect for being "too stupid or ignorant" to understand what they are selling. Others yet, believe the decision was based on no interest or no money. In reality, closing is your perception of how you are acting and feeling—your attitude and your energy towards yourself and your prospect.

Remember, prospects buy you therefore you need to be able to captivate people. You need to capture their emotions and find a way to keep them riveted to their seat. Remember closing a sale is nothing more than the transmission of your energy and enthusiasm to your prospect.

Well, that concludes the No Sale section. It was relatively short compared to the steps of the buying curve, but in reality you lost the sale because you went past the close and found yourself committing one of the seven deadly sins. In the next section—What Went Wrong? We will examine how your attitude affects your sales potential, different techniques to help you throughout your sales presentation and some advance closing techniques to take you from an average salesperson to an exceptional, or master closer.

SECTION 3

WHAT WENT WRONG?

How to Fix it!

11

Let's Go Back to the Beginning

What does closing a sale really mean? Some salespeople believe that it is having the prospect make the decision to buy. There are others who believe that it is empowering your prospect with an emotional feeling that by making a decision will satisfy whatever their need they have at that moment. In reality, closing is your perception of how you are acting and feeling—your attitude and your energy towards yourself and your prospect. Remember, prospects buy you therefore you need to be able to captivate people. You need to capture their emotions and find a way to keep them riveted to their seat. Remember closing a sale is nothing more than the transmission of your energy and enthusiasm to your prospect.

There comes a point in selling where to do the best you can possibly do you will still come across road blocks. No matter how successful you are in sales you will experience periods of reduced sales. Unfortunately, when you are not writing business, or on a roll, you will go home frustrated and snap at loved ones. You will begin to think about why you did not or could not get the sale . . ." You will talk to other colleagues about it trying to figure out why you are not writing business. You may then either get on a computer and start working out some new fancy pitch. Maybe you go to a colleague who is on a roll to ask them what they are doing to write sales. Possibly you may add their pitch or shticks to your presentation that just creates more problems rather than solving them.

In this chapter we are going back to the beginning. I will put you "on the couch" by asking tough questions about what makes you tick and what may have caused you to lose sales. If you cannot be honest with yourself to fix your presentation then you will never become a master closer. If you can become critical of yourself and your presentation then you can pinpoint exactly where you are having trouble and try to rectify it. The absolute and most important thing to remember, whether you are a new or seasoned salesperson, is simplicity; keep it simple and sincere.

If you are closing more than 30% on a consistent basis, this chapter may not have much benefit for you. However, if you want to achieve a better than 30% closing ratio, it could definitely help. For those of you who are under the 30%, or better yet, under 20%, use this chapter as often as you need to help you get over those nasty areas that cause you the most trouble. If you have less than a 15% closing ratio, I would highly recommend that you start reading this book again (ha ha!).

FIRST, ARE YOU IN A SLUMP?

Sales Slumps are normal to every sales person. There are periods of great joy when it seems that everyone you talk to buys from you and you think nothing can go wrong. Then one day, the joy stops when the sales dwindle down and become fewer and fewer to one every now and then. Going a few days or even a week without writing a sale is not a slump, it is most likely your normal sales percentage catching up with you.

Salespeople usually fall into a slump when they stop writing business for periods of weeks or months. Why? The first symptom of slumping sales is a change in your attitude. Your energy level depletes, you become stressed out and you begin to look at your prospect as a "monster." Once this happens your presentation suffers which creates more resistance from your prospect causing you to lose even more confidence in your closing ability. Your confidence level then goes down and you start analyzing what you did wrong and look for some technical reasons why you are not writing business. Therefore, in order to maintain consistency you should not change anything before you take a good look at your attitude.

The first thing is do not mess with your presentation. Do not add anything to it or take anything out of it. All you may need to do is take out all the logic and put in YOU. Remember, prospects buy you. Prospects buy nothing but you. As a side note, every sales organization I have worked with, after the sales process is completed the new owner/

members were asked what was their main reason for purchasing—I have never heard the color of the paint on the wall or the swimming pool, 99% of the time it is the name of the salesperson—try it. Look back at your past sales and see the reasons your clients purchased. If you look at, and sell this product logically, prospects will not buy it. So you should not be talking logically, talk emotionally. I will cover more about understanding and managing your attitude in the next chapters.

Next, what problems are you having with your presentation that is driving you to the point of frustration? What is it that you cannot overcome? Well, this chapter and section will provide you with some exercises, suggestions and tips on how to how to troubleshoot your presentation so you can resume writing consistent sales.

I am always amazed what salespeople will say to prospects when they have lost their rhythm. When they lose their confidence or cannot find the niches that they want, they begin to change everything that they do and say. You start doing 'off the cuff' sales pitches and you begin to lose faith in your presentation, then you begin to lose faith in the system, your prospect and ultimately, yourself. Many salespeople feel as if they have no control over their destiny when they get into a slump. It is as if you are living your worst nightmare and the longer it goes on and the harder it becomes to shake the feeling that you will never write another sale. Well, there is good news you will write another sale.

In the meantime, to help you determine what other factors are contributing to your sales slump I suggest that you go through the following list and check off the ones that apply. If you are honest with yourself throughout this troubleshooting section you will soon discover what areas you need to improve on so you can prevent future slumps.

Some common factors that cause sales slumps are:

- Lack of recognition for your efforts
- Your lack of confidence in your closing ability
- Your lack of clearly defined goals and motivation
- Your poor attitude management

- Your focus has shifted from 'what is good for the prospect' to 'what is in it for me.'
- Your lack of product knowledge
- Lack of good sales training, coaching and feedback
- Lack of management support

There are other administrative or management factors that can contribute to sales slumps however these are the ones that <u>you</u> can deal with directly. It is your organization's responsibility to provide you with good opportunities to make sales, adequate rewards or compensation and an environment that encourages honest communication.

What Type of Slump are You In?

Now that you have an idea of what prompted your sales slump, let us examine which area specifically you are having the most difficulty. You may experience any, or all, of the following areas at one time or another during your sales career.

1. <u>Attitude Slump:</u> If you are not writing any sales it absolutely drains your energy. Frustration then sets in when you cannot see why you did not write a sale so you start to lose control of your attitude. From this point you begin to blame everyone and everything else for your attitude.

    Attitude slumps are recognized by your feeling tired and stressed out all the time. You have lost your enthusiasm for your product, your prospect and your company. Rather than go to work you would prefer to a take day off, go on vacation or see a movie. In other words, you would rather be any place but at work.

2. <u>Client Slump:</u> You will find that when your attitude is screwed up you then find yourself dreading the prospect of speaking to prospects. Your prospects appear to be 'not qualified' and you begin looking at them differently.

Prospect slumps are triggered by your indifferent attitude towards your prospect. You care less about what they have to say and spend more time thinking about how to escape from the situation, than by listening to them.

3. Presentation Slump: Now, because your attitude is screwed up and you are looking at your prospects differently, your presentation becomes an informational session. Since you are not emotionally caught up with your prospect you are not enthusiastic that allows little things to distract you. During your presentation you either welcome or do things to interrupt your presentation that then allows your prospect to take control, and ultimately say no.

    Presentation slumps can be recognized by your spending more time talking than listening. You sell features not benefits and continually repeat yourself because you are not focusing on your prospects needs. You will start showing the price before you have shown any value.

4. Sales Resistance Slump: You cannot pinpoint objections and resistance is coming from all angles. Because you cannot pinpoint the objections it adds to your existing frustration creating a domino effect. Frustration affects your attitude that affects your perception of your prospect.

    Sales resistance slumps are most easily detected when prospects appear to be not listening to you or bring up too many trivial objections. Your prospects will ask for the price early, and often in your presentation. When you try to use trial closes your prospect will react very defensively.

5. Closing Slump: You have no confidence in your ability to close the sale. You are in fear of asking for the order and will rely on your 'bottom line price' to close the sale for you. Most of all you are afraid to ask questions for fear of rejection.

A closing slump is the ultimate bad attitude. You take the stance that you had zero opportunity to write a sale, therefore did not.

UNDERSTANDING YOUR STRENGTHS AND WEAKNESSES

What is the best method for snapping out of a slump? <u>Honest self-evaluation</u> of your strengths and weaknesses is the best way. If you do honest, consistent self-evaluations you then will become an asset to yourself, your colleagues, your manager and your company. Even the best salespeople in the world find themselves going off the track occasionally. However, the sign of an exceptional salesperson is someone who realizes they have derailed or fallen off, will pick themselves up and then motivate themselves to get back on track. Unfortunately, the rest of us find ourselves in a slump and need help to get out of it.

Back in the last section I covered first, second and third level questions and why each level is important in determine your prospects dominant buying motive. Well, in order to give you a better understanding of why you may have fallen off the track, derailed a little, or hit a slump following is a series of first, second and third level questions for you to answer. Go through them and **answer honestly**. When you have finished you should see a pattern develop of what your strengths are, or quite possibly where your weaknesses lie.

First Level Questions   **Answer YES**   **or NO**

1. Do you like yourself? _____
2. Do others like to be around you? _____
3. Do you like sales? _____
4. Do you understand that enthusiasm breeds enthusiasm? _____
5. Are you affected by the ups and downs of your sales? _____
6. Is your personal integrity what you feel it should be? _____
7. Do you keep the customer's personal and emotional needs foremost in your mind at all times during the presentation? _____

8. Do you believe that the customer is always right, even when he/she is unreasonable? _____

9. Are you assertive enough to ask for the order when the time is right? _____

10. Do you ask for help when you need it? _____

11. Do you understand the law of averages: the more prospects you talk to, the more you sales you will make? _____

12. Do you refrain from embarrassing or confronting prospects or putting them on the spot? _____

13. Do you always make the effort to be personable and friendly? _____

14. Are you well paid? _____

15. Do you feel good when you make a sale? _____

16. Do you take the time to learn when you are not with a prospect? _____

Give yourself one point for each YES and zero for NO answer. Excellent: 13-16 points; Good: 10-13 points; Fair: 7-10 points; if you are below 7 points you should go back and read the first section again to get yourself back on track

SECOND LEVEL QUESTIONS—On a blank sheet of paper complete the following questions.

1. Why do you like yourself?
2. Why did you believe you would be good in sales?
3. What do you believe to be the end result benefit to your prospect?
4. What value and uniqueness do you deliver to your prospect?
5. What excites you the most about your presentation?
6. What is your least favorite part of your presentation?
7. What is it, in your environment that affects your attitude?
8. What specific objectives or goals are you working on?
9. What, if anything, has kept you from reaching your goals?
10. Who do you go to for help, guidance and support? Why?
11. Why do you think that you pre-judge your prospects?
12. What do you think would make you a better closer?

13. What would you be willing to do, if anything, to make yourself a better salesperson?
14. How do you think your attitude affects your sales?
15. What was your greatest sales experience?
16. What specific sales skill would you like to improve?
17. What image would you like to communicate to others?

Third Level Questions

As with your prospect these third level questions deal specifically with feelings and emotions. This next set of questions will hopefully motivate you sufficiently to get you back on the track so that you will be again riding the rails to success. So if you are ready to do a little more hard work, these final questions can help you. Use a separate sheet of paper to write out your answers.

1. Name three salespeople (in any field or anywhere in world) that you consider to be the most successful.
2. What attitudes, beliefs, feelings or emotions do they exhibit that you believe make (made) them a success?
3. Would you say that they are successful because they first **developed** and demonstrated these attitudes, feelings, beliefs and emotions <u>OR</u> do you think these are positive traits as a **result** of their success?
4. What positive thoughts would you like to automatically pop into your mind the moment you wake up each morning?
5. As you plan your daily sales activities, what attitudes or emotions would you like to feel automatically?
6. When you pick up your prospect—what inner feelings or confidence levels would you like to instinctively feel?
7. When you are talking to you prospect, what positive, confident thoughts would you like to have pop into your mind?
8. When asking for a decision, what beliefs or emotional expectations would you like to automatically feel?
9. When encountering rejection, rebuff or negative responses, what would you like to automatically feel or think?
10. When you experience ego clashes with people, how would you like to automatically handle situations?

11. When following up with people, not knowing whether they will be happy or unhappy with your product, what kind of thoughts would you like to automatically feel?

There is a Universal Dynamic Law that states:

> *"We translate into physical reality the dominant thoughts and attitudes that we hold in our minds, no matter what they are. **You can develop the habit** of having positive, confident thoughts flash into your mind in critical selling situations."*

The next two exercises are designed to help you understand what affects your behavior in selling situations.

EXERCISE ONE—HOW DOES IT FEEL?

1. Describe a time when you were <u>sold well</u>. What did the salesperson do, or say, to make it a pleasant experience? What did you like the most about the experience? How did it feel?
2. Describe when you were <u>sold badly</u>. What did the salesperson do or say? What did you like the least about the experience? How did it make you feel?
3. Describe your best sales experience? How did it make you feel? What did you say or do to make your prospect buy?
4. Describe your worst sales experience? What did you learn from it?
5. What attitude do you project in a sales situation, both as a buyer and a seller?

EXERCISE TWO—UNDERSTANDING YOUR BEHAVIOR

Back in Chapter 5 we examined your prospects personality type so that you had a better understanding of them, now we are going to find out what your personality type is. This is a questionnaire that describes your behavior by using pairs of statements. Make a choice, either "A" or "B" depending on how you think or behave. If neither "A" nor "B" typically reflects your behavior, choose the one that would feel would be the most like you. Remember, be honest.

1. A. I am a bottom line person and like to get right to the point.
   B. I take the time to think about the information before I answer.

2. A. I prefer or like finishing what I start.
   B. I would rather deal in abstract thoughts

3. A. I let my emotions guide my actions.
   B. I get all the facts before I make a decision.

4. A. I need to look at the 'big picture."
   B. I am practical and realistic.

5. A. I focus on my immediate needs.
   B. I am sensitive to the feelings of others.

6. A. I like to work with people who are real and sincere.
   B. People think my ideas are 'weird' or strange.

7. A. I only work on today's problems, not tomorrow's.
   B. I constantly daydream about my future.

8. A. I am considered to be level headed.
   B. I can make decisions on a hunch or gut instinct.

9. A. I would rather deal in fact than theory.
   B. I always finish tasks that I start.

10. A. I base my decision on how I feel at that given moment.
    B. I immediately solve problems when they arise.

11. A. I am considered a good problem solver.
    B. I sometimes let my mind wander and become distracted easily.

12. A. I express my emotions when I feel them.
    B. I am considered cold and detached by others.

13. A. I am considered too emotional.
    B. I am considered very creative but cannot act on that creativity.

14. A. I live for today.
    B. I live in the past.

15. A. I love to brainstorm ideas with friends and colleagues.
    B. I dislike listening to people's opinions or ideas.

16. A. I like to make long term plans for my future.
    B. I have to analyze every piece of data before I make a decision.

17. A. I trust my intuition.
    B. I only trust documented information.

18. A. I am considered too intellectual.
    B. I always need to analyze why people do certain things.

19. A. I am sometimes considered to be too emotional.
    B. I am sometimes considered to be "far out in left field."

20. A. I like to initiate projects or stimulate people.
    B. I like people.

21. A. I like to deal with people who are practical.
    B. New concepts or ideas excite me.

22. A. I am a no-nonsense person.
    B. I enjoy having fun while I work.

23. A. I am a logical thinking person.
    B. I like to help people solve their problems.

24.A. I need to make my deadlines at work.
   B. I weigh all the pros and cons before making decision.

25.A. People say that I am stuck in my ways and do not want to change.
   B. I spend considerable time gathering information.

26.A. I envy people who have great social skills.
   B. I envy people who are perfectionists and well organized.

27. A. I tend to consider the past, present and future.
   B. I only think about the future.

28.A. I like to need reports which include considerable data.
   B. I tire very quickly when reading long reports.

Circle the letter that you chose next the corresponding number in the following chart. Now add up the total number of circled answers in each column. The highest number indicates your personality or behavior type.

The following types summarize your dominant behavior characteristic:

SOCIALIZER you are a SENSATION person
THINKER you are a THOUGHT person
DIRECTOR you are INTUITIVE person
RELATER you are a FEELING person

	SOCIALIZER	THINKER	DIRECTOR	RELATER
Question 1	A	B		
Question 2	B		A	
Question 3		B		A
Question 4	A		B	
Question 5	B			A
Question 6			B	A
Question 7	B		A	
Question 8		A	B	

Question 9	B	A		
Question 10	B			A
Question 11			A	B
Question 12		B		A
Question 13			B	A
Question 14	A			B
Question 15		B	A	
Question 16	B	A		
Question 17		B	A	
Question 18			A	B
Question 19			B	A
Question 20	A		B	
Question 21	A		B	
Question 22	A			B
Question 23		A		B
Question 24	A	B		
Question 25		A		B
Question 26		B		A
Question 27		A	B	
Question 28	B	A		
TOTAL²				

ARE YOU PREPARED ENOUGH TO FACE YOUR PROSPECT?

The next step in troubleshooting your presentation is to determine whether you are prepared enough to face a prospect. Each of the following areas represents the entire sales process from goal setting to following up after your sale. As you read through each of these areas, think about how well prepared you are at that point in your sales presentation. I have used this method for years in training to help sales people get back on track. Even though I have not yet covered goal

---

2   The above statement pairs are based on Carl Jung's Theory of Psychological Types.

setting or sales follow up, which is in the last section, you should be able to score your current ability in these areas.

Use the numbers 0 (not prepared) through 10 (very confident) to reflect how prepared you think you are.

The Sales Process	0-10
Goal Setting	_____
Preparation	_____
Your Attitude—Is it right?	_____
Greeting your Prospect	_____
The Warm-Up (Statement of Neutrality)	_____
The Intent Statement (Agenda)	_____
How is my Pact Break?	_____
Am I Credible?	_____
Do I present my Product Credibly?	_____
Recognizing Character Types	_____
Am I projecting the right Image?	_____
Do I do a proper Discovery or F.O.R.M.?	_____
Do I Uncover all the Objections?	_____
Do I Handle Objections well?	_____
Do I do sufficient Tie Downs and Trial Closes	_____
How is my Product Knowledge?	_____
Do I create sufficient Value and Desire?	_____
Closing Strategies and Techniques	_____
Asking for the Order	_____
Paperwork and After Sale follow-up	_____

To help you fully understand where your strengths or weaknesses are, make a conscious effort to do this exercise at the beginning or end of each month. Then go back and review your previous month(s). If you have a good month, go through and find out where your strengths were. If you had a bad month, use it as a way to find out what may be lacking from your last good month. I guarantee that any defects you may notice will be under your attitude. At the end of a year, compare the months and see how your closing percentage is affected by your "sales biorhythm."

By the way, if you have answered 10 to all the questions you should have a 100% closing ratio. If you have too many areas below 5 consider another career choice or spend <u>all</u> your free time learning how to sell.

WHAT ARE YOUR STRENGTHS?

Above you were asked first, second and third level questions so that you could understand what your strengths and weaknesses might be. Now, we will look at your strengths. Strengths are things that are positively displayed in our actions, performance and abilities. If you have a positive attitude you have a positive attitude that is reflected in your actions, performance and abilities. Negative attitudes are reflected by weakness in our actions, performance and abilities.

Now, go through the following traits and decide which of your attitudes would be considered a personal strength or an advantage: (P)ersonal Strength or (Ad)vantage. What you may consider strengths in others may not necessarily be a personal strength for you.

	Ambitious		Animated		Assertive
	Confident		Creative		Desire
	Discipline		Eager to Learn		Easy Going
	Enthusiastic		Focused		Goal Oriented
	Hard Worker		High Energy		Honest
	Integrity		Knowledge		Leader
	Manageable		Motivated		Optimistic
	Organized		Persistent		Personable
	Pessimistic		Reliable		Respectful

| | Self-Starter | | Sense of Humor | | Sincere | |

_____ Team Player _____ Work Experience _____ Trainable

The ability to separate Strength from an Advantage is crucial to determining what your self-concept is. If you cannot separate these two areas then you may find yourself working towards the wrong goal.

For example, let us presume that you are a gifted tennis player and have the opportunity to play professionally. However, along with playing tennis you choose to also attend college and receive a degree in business. Which goal should you be working towards—being a professional tennis player or a professional businessperson? There is nothing in life that says you cannot do both however by doing both, are you doing them both to the best of your ability? There is an advantage to having an education, but your strength lies in your ability to compete professionally.

To help you determine Strength from an Advantage, answer the following fifteen questions by indicating the same letters (P or Ad) next to the question.[3]

	1. Buy a new car or home.
	2. Write a best seller or fly an airplane
	3. Be president of a corporation.
	4. Earn an Ph.D.
	5. Be close to my family.
	6. Have a wonderful imagination.

---

[3] **Answers**: 1. Advantage; 2. Strength; 3. Advantage, 4. Advantage; 5. Advantage; 6. Strength; 7. Advantage; 8. Strength; 9. Strength; 10. Advantage; 11. Strength; 12. Strength; 13. Strength; 14. Strength; 15. Strength.

	7. Belong to a private club.
	8. Run the Boston Marathon.
	9. Be competitive
	10. Have many friends and acquaintances
	11. Have courage
	12. Be organized
	13. Know how to make money.
	14. Have the ability to judge character
	15. Lead and motivate people.

Strengths are driven by motivation and desire. Advantages are gained through pursuing Strengths and you should always use your strengths to their full advantage. The ability to use your strengths wisely can create a very satisfying and successful sales career. One last thing to consider, if it does not feel right you are not working from a Strength.

Remember always focus on your strengths, mange your weaknesses and you will always be on the right track.

LEARNING TO MANAGE YOUR WEAKNESSES

You may feel you that you do not have enough Strength's however it is because you <u>believe</u> you have more weaknesses. A weakness is just <u>something</u> that you do not do well. It does not include everything in your life. Unfortunately, that 'thing' ends up hampering our ability to do <u>anything</u>. This is because society conditions us to focus on the negative or weakness rather than on the positive or our strengths. You should make a point of not listening to what society dictates and focus on positive.

Following are some weakness behavior indicators:

1. <u>You become defensive</u>: This is the primary response to a weakness. When you are using strength you will show little or no defensive behaviors. When you are on the defensive you are protecting your weakness. Think about this in relation to your sales prospect.

2. <u>Suffer from burnout</u>: When you are working from a weakness you resist doing it, therefore ultimately feel 'burned out' and become frustrated.

3. <u>You cannot think positively about the future</u>: Have you ever thought to yourself, "If I can just get through this then I can . . ." If you have then you are working from a weakness and cannot think past what you are doing at that moment.

4. <u>Become obsessive over the weakness</u>: This is in contrast to intensely pursuing Strength when the weakness becomes the obsession. You obsess at trying to master the weakness instead of learning how to manage it.

5. <u>Slow learning curve</u>: Despite repeated training and continuing education you fail to grasp simple basic concepts and information.

6. <u>You suffer an inability to learn from experiences</u>: If you are working from a weakness you will continue to plod along because it is safe. People who work from strengths learn continuously, update and re-evaluate their behavior based on those experiences.

7. <u>Always need to 'follow the directions</u>: It does not matter how often you add contacts to your smart phone, you still need the directions to do it. If you are operating from a strength the 'manual' is thrown out after the first time you use it.

8. <u>Lose confidence in your ability to perform</u>: This is a primary loss of self-concept or self-esteem. When you lose confidence you lose both your energy and motivation.

We have all, at one time or another, experienced one, or all, of the above eight signs of weakness. It is your ability to recognize them that ultimately plays a role in your self-concept. In what areas do you think you have weaknesses? Realistically we all posses' weaknesses and do our best to manage them. Go back to the first table listing the thirty-three traits and add a (W)eakness next to each that apply to you. By doing this you will be taking the first step in determining which weaknesses you need to manage.

In the next chapter I will cover how salespeople believe they fail is because they are not trained enough, or educated enough. In reality, it is a weakness in something that has manifested itself as a fear which prevents salespeople from being successful. Fear is the strongest motivating emotion humans' possess. It keeps people from enhancing their lives, enjoying their lives and being successful in their lives.

To help manage or eliminate the fear is to work from your strengths. If your weakness is something that can be altered then your immediate goal should be to do whatever is necessary to manage it. Yes, I did say manage it. You can never transform Weakness into Strength—all you can do is just manage it so that it becomes less of an influencing factor in your life. It is estimated that for every strength we have we have one thousand non-strengths. In that ratio it would be a huge waste of time, not to mention energy, to try to eliminate them.

There are two quotations that best describe how to manage your weaknesses. The first is the Serenity Prayer:

God grant me the power to accept the things I cannot change, the courage to change the things that I can, and the wisdom to know the difference.

The second is, "Managing our weaknesses allows our strengths to overpower them, ultimately making them irrelevant."

You have now begun the process of changing your sales closing percentage when you learn to identify your strengths and manage your weaknesses. All the above questions and exercises, if answered honestly, will help you determine where your weaknesses or strengths lie. By learning to manage your weaknesses and focusing on your strengths will allow you to write consistent sales and move you towards being a very successful or exceptional salesperson. To be consistent at what we do, consistently use the same techniques that have <u>worked</u> for you in the past. The best way to remain consistent is to KISS (Keep It Simple and Sincere) each prospect you meet.

Remember, the worst prospect is the one you never get. The best prospect is your next one. Once you can brainwash yourself that this is true you will find it so much easier to prepare yourself and create the right sales attitude.

"I am confident, I am powerful and I cannot be denied"

12

Believing you are the Sale

The last chapter involved getting to know yourself through honest self-evaluation as to what your strengths and weakness are in order to lessen the frequency of sales slumps and increase your odds at writing sales. Unfortunately, many salespeople believe that sales are a numbers game but realistically, it is your sales attitude that is a numbers game. It is your attitude and energy with a prospect that will determine whether the sale goes down or not.

This chapter will examine how your attitude is directly proportional to your sales closing percentage. We will look at what affects your sales attitude, understanding how your attitude affects others to tips on how to improve your attitude. Emerson once said, "The ancestor of every action is thought." If that is the case then what you think is what you believe, and what you believe will dictate your attitude, behavior and closing percentage.

I am pretty sure that Emerson was not necessarily talking about a sales attitude. I am sure however, he meant that before you can achieve success you have to first create the thought, or motivation to succeed. It takes a very large sacrifice to succeed in whatever we choose to do. Because the rewards or goals outweigh the rejections, failures and negative parts of it, it is important that we learn to how manage our attitude to achieve our goals and rewards. In this chapter we will explore how your overall attitude, your sales attitude and your motivation which are all inter-related in how successful you are in sales. However, before we can create success you need to ensure that you have a good positive self-concept.

What is Self-Concept?

It is our idea of what type of person we are. It is built upon our belief structure, successes, failures and experiences, good or bad. Each person has a self-concept and performs in a manner consistent with it. All of your thoughts, including subsequent actions, feelings and behaviors are all consistent with the image that you portray.

Self-concept is about self-esteem. Your self-esteem determines how well you will do in life and therefore it is important that you have a driving self-concept. How do we get a driving self-concept? We change our belief system. Yes, you can change your way of thinking because self-concepts are subjective.

If you believe yourself to be a winner, you will be. If you think you are going to fail you will find a way to fail. The same principle applies in sales. If you believe that you will be successful you will be and if you believe you cannot close a sale then you will never close one. You will always sell in the manner of your self-concept.

Determining Your Self-Concept

Even though we covered strength and weaknesses in the last chapter, take a few minutes and think about yourself and what makes up your belief system? Do you believe yourself to be a winner, or a failure? We are going to do redo the little quiz below to help determine what type of self-concept you have by examining the traits that describe: (S)trengths, (Sk)ills or (A)ttitude. Your job is to decide which they are and place the appropriate letter next to each.

	Ambitious		Animated		Assertive
	Confident		Creative		Desire
	Discipline		Eager to Learn		Easy Going
	Enthusiastic		Focused		Goal Oriented

	Hard Worker		High Energy		Honest
	Integrity		Knowledge		Leader
	Manageable		Motivated		Optimistic
	Organized		Persistent		Personable
	Pessimistic		Reliable		Respectful
	Self-Starter		Sense of Humor		Sincere

_____ Team Player   _____ Work Experience _____ Trainable

Now go through them again and indicate whether you possess these traits. Either a (Y)es and a (N)o. **Be honest with yourself**.

ALL the above traits are a reflection of your attitude and self-concept. The only ones that are skills are knowledge earned by education and work experience. Even both of these are not gained unless you have the right attitude in which to learn them. Have you ever noticed those school children with a great attitude are called overachievers and ones that do not pay attention, or are problematic, are called underachievers. Those statements can also apply to sales. How much of a role does attitude play in these definitions? Self-concept is about attitude and your attitude dictates your self-concept.

CHANGING YOUR SELF-CONCEPT

The only way to change your self-concept is to change your belief system and habits. Unfortunately saying it is much easier than doing it. It takes considerable discipline to want to change, make the change and maintain the change. The hardest thing you will ever do in life is to change old habits for new.

There are three ways to change your belief system and they all entail the power of suggestion. Just as we would use the power of suggestion on a prospect to lead them towards the close, you can do the same with yourself. By using the following three techniques you CAN change your belief system and self-concept. Remember create the thought in your mind, then once your emotional belief accepts the change then you will begin to change.

1. <u>Influential Suggestion</u>: This involves the process of using pictures, words or ideas to influence your unconscious thoughts, beliefs, and memory.
2. <u>Self-Suggestion</u>: This involves the process by using influential suggestion of conscious words and commands and putting them into your subconscious to build memory. This is done by the constant repetition of motivations, affirmations and verbal commands. Self-suggestion will then start to have an impact on your actions.
3. <u>Auto Suggestion</u>: The third step in the process is when your subconscious mind sends out commands and messages that are now automatically reflected, and have impact, in your emotions, behavior, actions and speech. By using self-suggestions you are using these repeated suggestions to send messages and commands to your conscious mind, as well as other parts of your body.

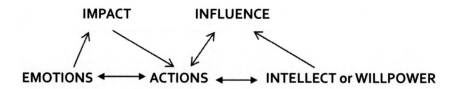

You cannot use just intellect, willpower or influential suggestion to change your self-concept because it generates no long-term influence on your emotions. All three suggestion processes must work together to create change. Just as your original self-concept or esteem was formed by these methods without your awareness, now use that awareness to make the changes you want to make. Who ever said that you "can't teach an old dog, new tricks?"

SUGGESTION TECHNIQUES

The following 'Suggestions' for changing your self-concept have been broken down into two areas. The first list is of power affirmations and the second, asking yourself power questions. Use those that you believe will help you. Better yet, take a few minutes and write out some of your own.

1. Power Affirmations:
    - I am going to see positive results.
    - I will work hard to achieve my goals.
    - I feel good about myself.
    - I believe in my abilities and myself.
    - I am proud of my accomplishments.
    - Today, in every way possible, I will do better.
    - It is my responsibility to change my life.
    - I have the courage to face the truth.
    - When I give more of myself to others, I gain more than I expect.
    - I will do the right thing because it is the right thing to do.
    - I choose to make the best of every situation or opportunity.
    - I will not be brought down by minor problems or setbacks.
    - I will focus on my strengths, rather than my weaknesses.
    - I am a winner.
    - My closing ratio will increase the more sales I make.
    - I am self-confident and relaxed because I am motivated to accomplish any goals.
    - I can focus on the task at hand and will not be distracted by anything negative.
    - I will consider all problems opportunities to be created.
    - I will continuously strive to improve all aspects of my life.
    - I will learn from every experience to become more successful every day.
    - I will make decisions with confidence because I believe in them.
    - I will have complete confidence in all that I think and do.
    - I will learn to accept constructive criticism and suggestions that will make me a better (sales) person.
    - I will learn to be respectful of others' arguments and learn to disagree in a calm and rational manner.

- I will learn to be able to visualize situations before they occur. I will 'see' my goal clearly and know instinctively what steps are necessary to achieve my goal.

2. Power Questions:
    - What do I love about my job?
    - What is my goal for today?
    - How will I feel after I write a sale today?
    - How can I make someone happy or feel good today?
    - I am strongly committed to achieving . . . (what) at this point in my life?
    - Who are the people in my life that I love and why are they important to me?
    - What makes my family proud of me?
    - What do I like about myself?

Learn to repeat as many of these affirmations and questions you need, to yourself, a minimum of fifty times a day for a month. You will find that your subconscious will be reprogrammed with new beliefs and confidence levels. The challenge is—are you willing to do something to change your self-concept, or self-esteem level? Is your attitude so weak that you will not even try to do anything to improve or change it?

Suggestions and *thoughts* that generate *emotions and actions* determine your *attitude* that leads to *success or failure*. What would you rather become—a successful or competent salesperson? Self-concept is our idea of who we are and what we want to become.

MANAGING YOUR TIME

What an interesting concept time is. We never seem to have enough of it and everybody wants more of it. While some people kill time, others believe it to be a competitive advantage. Time is a precious commodity, especially in sales because you are only working when you are face to face with a prospect.

Think about what you do when you are not sitting with a prospect? Are you talking to colleagues, playing with your smart phone, reading a magazine or having a cup of coffee? Is any of these things moving you towards making your next sale? If you are not working you should be using your time to prepare for when you are working.

Besides discipline being the key to successfully maintaining your attitude salespeople also need to be able to manage their time. Let us look at the realities of time and what you can do to better manage yours.

1. Respect and cherish your time: If you do not respect or cherish your time nobody else will either.
2. Schedule your time: Not only is it important to respect your time you need to schedule it appropriately. How many times have you said to yourself, "Wow, I have no idea where my time went today" Use some method of scheduling your time—Smart phones, iPads, Blackberry's, Daytimers, Outlook Calendars, Notepads, even put Sticky Notes everywhere if you have to. By learning to schedule your time you will find that you can easily double your income and enjoy your life more.
3. Work Hard VS. Work Smart: Even though you may work hard to achieve a goal it is not enough. You may end up spinning your wheels rather than completing the task. Working smart is having a plan to achieve a goal and following it.
4. Time is equally divided: Everyone has the same amount of time. It is how you choose to spend the time that determines whether you are successful or not. How do you choose to spend your time—being productive or wasting it?
5. Time should be proactive and positive: You should always consider time a positive. When you get up each morning you should ask yourself, "How productively can I use my time today?" If you view time as a negative you will always be reacting to it, rather than using it.

   For example, compare the following two questions:
   i.   "What do I want to accomplish today?"
   ii. "What do I need to do today?"

The first is pro-active and implies confidence and self-assurance. The second is reactive and defensive. The difference between the two questions is attitude.

6. <u>Never postpone time</u>: Time is your only asset—make every effort not to waste it. If you procrastinate or postpone taking the time to do something you will never regain the opportunity, or time.

7. <u>Take advantage of time</u>: Always think in terms of seconds and minutes, never hours, days or weeks. Make every second and minute of your life count. Never kill time.

   There is quotation that best describes this—"People, who would never think of committing suicide or ending their life, would think nothing of dribbling their life away in useless minutes and hours every day."

8. <u>Use time as a learning tool</u>: Take time to learn about your product, your competition and what you need to do to become successful in sales.

If we have a positive attitude we will use our time effectively and productively. Without a positive attitude we all do things that waste or distract time. We all experience periods where our minds wander and we do not pay attention to whom or what may be around us. Fatigue and illness also make us believe that time stands still. What is it that creates these situations? Is it time or is it attitude? How we spend our time is directly proportional to our attitude. By learning how to manage time you will then be able to manage yourself and your attitude.

MANAGING YOUR ATTITUDE TO ACHIEVE SUCCESS

Selling is a game. It has nothing to do with education, cultural background, physical characteristics or whether you are smart or not. It is what goes on in your mind that makes all the difference. A study done years ago at Harvard University found that it is the human mind or rather, the psychology of the human mind, which is above everything else. It is this psychology that provides the foundation for success and it is success that causes people to want to create a strong foundation. Simply put, what you think is what you believe and what you believe dictates your goals and actions.

Throughout this chapter I have reiterated the importance of managing your attitude. Without a positive self-concept and a positive mental attitude, especially in sales, you cannot possibly achieve success. Managing your attitude is as simple as following the tips below.

Tips to Maintaining Your Attitude

1. Get rid of distress: Since it is almost impossible to eliminate stress from our lives, consider eliminating distress. Distress is the inner turmoil that starts when decision making stops. Distress is negative and allows your natural instincts to become dull.

2. Learn to breathe correctly: This is especially true if you get nervous before meeting a prospect. Being nervous is normal occasionally. If you learn to breathe correctly during times of stress, you will feel better both mentally and physically. If you are breathing quickly and in shallow breaths, stop and take a few deep breaths remembering to exhale completely.

3. Give yourself regular breaks: Working in sales is emotionally demanding work. To stay in a positive frame of mind allow yourself to take short breaks while working. There is no law that says you must sell all the time. Stop talking about your product and talk about something interesting with your prospect for ten or fifteen minutes and you both will benefit. You will find that your sales presentation will also benefit from their renewed interest.

4. Do not let anything distract you from your goal: You become depressed and anxious when you allow someone or something to distract you from your goal.

5. Learn continually: If you make the effort to continually learn new things you will become stronger mentally and have more confidence to pursue your goals. Use the time you drive to work to listen to self-help or motivation tapes, attend more seminars or read more books. Sharpen your skills and you will find that you will close more sales.

6. <u>Maintain your integrity</u>: Shakespeare said, "To thine own self be true." Take whatever steps are necessary to maintain your integrity because it is the most important thing you will ever possess.

7. <u>Avoid deception</u>: Unless you are a sociopath when you lie or cheat someone you experience a sense guilt that creates a negative state of mind. This relates directly to number 6 above.

8. <u>Maintain a sense of humor</u>: It is next too impossible not to be in a positive frame of mind if you maintain a sense of humor. Laughter is definitely the best medicine. Start laughing if you are in doubt about anything, it will make you feel better and negativity will be kept at bay.

9. <u>Focus on your strengths</u>: Be creative. We are all born with some ability to perform at a genius level so think of yourself as a genius. Use whatever god given talents (strengths) you have and use them to become successful.

10. <u>Maintain your energy</u>: Learn to maintain your energy level by eating, sleeping and exercising properly then you will not experience chronic fatigue or depression. Vince Lombardi once said, "Fatigue makes cowards of us all."

11. <u>Learn to keep your cool</u>: Sales are not a perfect science so why let people or things upset you. Handle confrontation calmly and professionally.

12. <u>Develop your style</u>: This comes from your goals and the means that you use to achieve them. If you use someone else's style you will soon tire of it and become bored.

13. <u>Be confident in your abilities</u>: This message lets others know that you have confidence in what you are doing which promotes integrity and credibility.

14. <u>Do what you love to do</u>: If you do not enjoy what you are doing how can you maintain a positive attitude?

15. <u>Be persistent</u>: If you are persistent are determined in attaining your goals you will become successful. Persistence overcomes any obstacle.

16. <u>Never neglect the little things</u>: One of two things will happen. One, they become big things that are more difficult to handle. Two, neglect causes guilt that leads to depression.

17. <u>Never hide behind busywork</u>: The only person you are fooling is yourself when trying to look busy.
18. <u>Never apologize for the way you feel</u>: Your behavior will become defensive and reactive when you start apologizing to others for it. We all experience temporary periods of depression or exhalation, why apologize for them.
19. <u>Learn to give without thought of reward</u>: You will experience a sense of satisfaction and accomplishment when you do more than is expected of you.
20. <u>Enjoy life to the fullest</u>: Instead of living to work, learn to work to live.

By incorporating these with the above twenty tips, you will find that when dealing with prospects you will always have a positive attitude.

Now that I have shown you how to manage your personal attitude and how it can affect your sales, we will now look at how to help you to manage your sales attitude. You need to have both working together to be successful.

YOUR SALES ATTITUDE

If you are in a slump, think of the last time that you were writing many sales. Were you magnetic to your prospects, your co-workers and your managers? Most likely you were. The only difference between then and not writing sales is your attitude and energy.

I keep referring to attitude <u>and</u> energy because closing a sale takes a positive attitude and energy. A positive attitude triggers enthusiasm. It has been proven that when people are upbeat, happy, have positive energy and enthusiasm they tend to have no bounds. In a relationship sales situation it is your enthusiasm, energy <u>and</u> positive attitude that create the sale. It is also that energy and enthusiasm that gets you through any negativity you encounter from your prospect.

If you are confident, you project confidence. If you are laughing and having a good time with your prospects you are "oozing" an attitude of confidence and positive self-esteem. If you believe in yourself and believe that there is a sale sitting in front of you, there will be one. Confidence in yourself and your ability to close a sale is created by having a positive sales attitude.

Whereas, when you begin to doubt yourself, become negative or depressed you lose your energy and enthusiasm. When this happens, most salespeople fall into the "poor old me" self-pity routine just enhancing that they are negative, miserable people and they end up in the proverbial 'slump.'

WHAT AFFECTS YOUR SALES ATTITUDE?

Statistics show that eighty percent of salespeople are willing to accept a ninety percent rejection rate. Why is that? What causes salespeople to accept rejection rather than a sale? The primary reason is that they fail to close the sale when the prospect is ready. In other words they were not listening to the prospect. They are most likely doing a canned presentation so they go right past the buying signals and the close. Salespeople who do not consider the prospect possess what I like to call a self-defeating attitude. They are programming themselves to sabotage the sale.

Yes, sales are a very competitive and very frustrating. They may take place in a cutthroat environment but why sabotage your efforts before you start? There is a tremendous amount of rejection. Sales also require that so many things be asked or done during a presentation. Most prospects that you meet start off aggressive, defensive and negative, so why would you want to put yourself in a situation where you have to defend yourself and your product? Yes, there are a lot more negatives than positives, but why are we focusing on the negative rather than the positive?

It is these negatives that affect your sales attitude. Stop limiting yourself with excuses for not writing a sale. You can write a sale every day. Love the feeling of competing against all the elements that are resisting you so that you can win. Love the rush of closing a sale. If you do not derive self-esteem, gain satisfaction or feel your ego inflate when you a closing a sale then you definitely need to change your sales attitude (or your career choice). Every time you go out to make a sale it should empower you and make you more confident. You should walk straighter and make yourself richer. The only person who can stroke you up and affect your attitude is you.

UNDERSTANDING THE SELF-DEFEATING ATTITUDE

Salespeople that are reluctant to ask for the order do not derive any self-esteem from closing the sale. They do not possess a positive self-concept because the underlying attitude is fear. In the last chapter I went into considerable detail on maintaining a positive attitude but in this chapter I am also examining what prompts salespeople to acquire a self-defeating attitude and ends them in a downward spiral.

There are ten limitations that prompt a self-defeating attitude. At certain points in our sales careers all salespeople suffer from one or more of these limitations. It is your ability, however, to understand what motivates them so that they are no longer any limitations.

1. Your ego: Sales are not a "who is going to win the argument" competition. If you approach sales with the attitude of winning at all costs to protect your ego, then you will always lose. It is self-defeating to take that approach. Remember the seven deadly sins!

2. Your feelings: You focus more on how you are feeling during the sales presentation than on how your prospect is feeling. "They do not seem to like me, they want to leave or they do not want to make a decision." Do these statements sound like familiar excuses?

3. Belief that sales process is manipulative: Salespeople are reluctant to ask for the order because they believe that sales are a self-serving manipulating process. They believe that the sale is something that is done *to the* prospect, rather than *with the* prospect.

4. <u>You feel intimidated</u>: We are all aware that our prospects are intimidated by their surroundings, but why are you intimidated by your prospect? You know more than they do, especially about your product.

5. <u>You feel that your efforts will go not rewarded</u>: There are those salespeople who say, "I never get a good shot so what is the point of trying to close them." They believe that they will not write a sale so why exert the effort.

6. <u>You develop a **strong** bond with your prospect</u>: This self-defeating limitation comes from making such good friends of your prospects that you become embarrassed to close the sale because you do not want to disrupt the relationship.

7. <u>You think you are smarter than your prospect</u>: Not only is that attitude self-defeating it irritates the hell out of your prospect. Trying to think of ways to outsmart your prospect not only burns up valuable energy and enthusiasm, it annoys them.

8. <u>You become complacent and/or frustrated</u>: Both of these attitudes are very self-defeating in that once complacency or frustration set in then your attitude hits rock bottom. Without one hundred percent conviction you will never be able to do your job.

9. <u>You are there *only* for the money</u>: So many salespeople go out every day just for the commission rather than the satisfaction of writing a sale. You have to NOT be doing it for only the money. Worrying about money is all consuming and controls your life. If you put yourself under that kind of pressure you will never write a sale. When you desperately want a sale you are projecting that 'desperation aura' to the prospect, they sense it and will do everything they can to either 'play' or get away from you.

10. <u>Fear</u>: There are two types of fear that are major obstacles to writing a sale. First is the fear of failure the second is the fear of rejection.

The fear of failure is a deep, ingrown, subconscious fear. It can be the fear of making a mistake, buying the wrong product or being criticized.

The fear of rejection is the fear of being told no. A large percentage of your prospects will say no to you, you must learn to develop some sort of resilience or thick elephant hide to deal with this rejection. If you cannot do this you will never become a successful salesperson. All master closers have reached a point where they no longer fear rejection.

Fear itself is the underlying motivation for all the self-defeating limitations but it is the fear of failure and rejection that control the others. Salespeople, and prospects, will do whatever they deem necessary to protect themselves from failure and rejection.

THE FEAR OF FAILURE

Do not ever be afraid of Mr. and Mrs. Real Prospect because they are the best, and only, opportunity to make a sale. The only time you should be experiencing fear is if you do not get a prospect in front of you. If you have no prospect, you have no chance to make a sale.

Fear is a bigger motivator than desire. You should not fear today about your prospect tomorrow. If you see yourself as a failure today, what kind of attitude will that get you for tomorrow? It is easier for salespeople to expect failure than success.

Since we already know that the fear of failure is self-defeating, let us take a closer look at what the fear of failure really is.

1. Destructive: The fear of failure can be considered a self-fulfilling prophecy. In its' destructive nature it can make people waste their lives because they always anticipate failure.
2. Learning life is full of curves: Much like a baby learning how to walk, fear teaches us what will work and what does not. The trick here is to learn from your mistakes.
3. Failure can be beneficial: Yes, there are certain times where failure is beneficial in your life. For example, failure makes you humble. When you have to work hard to achieve something the thought of failure keeps you striving to do your best. Failure can be a motivation when used appropriately.
4. Sales may not be a numbers game but failure is: You can only hear no so many times because eventually you will hear a yes.

Dealing with the fear of failure is as simple as:

1. <u>Change your mind set</u>: In the last section we learned how to visualize the sale—whether by thinking or dreaming about it—you must visualize the sale. You can prepare your attitude by creating the sale in your mind. You can do this anywhere, your car, your house, buying groceries and so on, but the whole idea is that you believe you made a sale. It is not as easy as it sounds. Let us pretend we wrote a sale today. Let us act and think that we were great.

2. <u>Be prepared</u>: Follow the same pre-sale procedures every time. Mentally prepare yourself to meet your prospect. The best way to be prepared is to clear you mind. "The will to win is not nearly as important as the will of preparing to win."

3. <u>Change your expectations</u>: Expect that you are going to be successful. If you expect failure you will not be disappointed.

4. <u>Take a risk</u>: A risk is something that takes you out of your comfort zone. The premise behind this is if you do not take the risk you will not be rewarded for your efforts. If you never take a risk you may never get another opportunity. So, if your prospect does say no when you ask for the order, do not worry, at least you *asked* for it.

Never settle for less than you deserve. Find any means possible to lower your fear of failure and increase your desire for success.

THE FEAR OF REJECTION

In addition to sales being a frustrating business, sales can also be a devastating because of the constant rejection. The hardest thing to deal with in sales is the amount of rejection that you receive.

Remember, unless you are a superstar, you will only write twenty or thirty percent of the prospects that you speak with so you are going to hear no the majority of the time. Unfortunately you never know which of your prospects will be a sale, which makes the anticipation of rejection even worse than the rejection itself. What does the fear of rejection prompt?

1. <u>Fear of failure</u>: If you are afraid of being rejected you are setting yourself up to fail.
2. <u>Fear of asking for the order</u>: If you are afraid your prospects are going to say no they will. The way in which you ask for the order determines the response that you get. If you come across lacking confidence in yourself, you will hear no more than yes.
3. <u>Apathy</u>: This is my personal favorite. I have salespeople that say, "Why should I talk to so and so because they are not going to buy anyway or I knew that they were not going to buy." If you do not care about what you are doing it is reflected in your attitude as apathy.
4. <u>Doubt:</u> When doubt enters any thought process there is an immediate loss of confidence and self-esteem. This is also a self-fulfilling prophecy because doubt is destructive.

Dealing with the fear of rejection is as simple as following these seven steps:

1. <u>Remember, no does not always mean no</u>: No can also mean, "Tell us more about your product or I am not yet convinced this is right for me." Create more value in your product. You will never fear no it if you honestly believe that it is just another objection or the need to create more desire.
2. <u>Change your mind set</u>: Think positively about rejection. Say to yourself, "The next time I hear no I am one step closer to closing a sale."
3. <u>Think of success</u>: Convince yourself that nothing in life comes without hard work. If you know that you are going to have to work hard to achieve your goals then you will not be disappointed with rejection along the way.
4. <u>Think of your goal</u>: Do not allow rejection in the early stages of your sales presentation to hamper your attitude. Think of the goal of writing a sale.
5. <u>Ask your prospect why they rejected you</u>: This takes confidence to ask but you may be surprised at the response. You may find that they were not rejecting you, just your product at this time. Consider it a possible sale for the future.

6. <u>Learn from the rejection</u>: Understand why you were rejected and learn from it.
7. <u>Remind yourself of your accomplishments</u>: Remind yourself of those sales you did write and how they made you feel. This feeling of accomplishment will generally spur you on, despite hearing no.

Another way to overcome the fear is to realize that even if you are an exceptional salesperson, you will fail some of the time. If you did not get a sale today, maybe it was one 'that got away' and tomorrow will be 'the one.' You have to keep coming up with little ways, or thoughts that reassure you that tomorrow will be 'the day.' Optimism eventually becomes habitual.

Fear can be best summed up in the following, often quoted quotes:

"There is nothing to fear but fear itself."
"Courage is easy. You simply overcome the fear, the first time."
"Courage is fear turned into action."
"Do not let failure have its way with you. Life is too short to live in fear."

It is important to understand that the fear of failure and rejection can be overcome. If you look at them both as necessary components of success then they will work positively rather than as a negative.

Your Attitude VS. your Statistics

It is your attitude, energy and physiology that sell you to your prospect. If you believe it, your prospect will believe it. You have to capture your prospect and keep them riveted to their seats. If you are not willing to do this you will not become successful or wealthy.

Your attitude works in direct proportion to your statistics. If you are consistently writing sales then you are working from a confident, positive attitude. Conversely, if you are not writing sales I would hazard a guess that you are experiencing a negative attitude. Here are a few of the reasons that prompt a negative sales attitude:

1. We begin to pre-judge our prospect: When we allow pre-judgment to enter the sales process a pre-judging attitude is formed. It reflects itself not only in the prospect themselves but in the way they were invited. We take that attitude and convince ourselves that we cannot sell them or they will not buy which then stimulates our negative attitude. If you allow yourself to pre-judge a prospect for just one second you have lost the opportunity to make the sale.

2. Listening to your colleagues: Yes, we are all guilty of listening to our colleagues at one time or another. You have probably said to yourself on more than one occasion, "Who do they think they are kidding saying that," whether it is true or not. If you say these things while working with a prospect, guess what, you just blew your credibility in yourself. Do not let your colleague's influence how you talk with your prospects because you do not have the luxury of getting a second chance.

3. Doubting your ability to sell: When you begin to doubt your ability to sell you begin losing your confidence and frustration sets in. Then you begin to analyze your sales presentation, or start adding more ingredients, which only setting you up for more personal doubt.

4. You focus on the wrong statistics: This is a very common problem among salespeople. Instead of focusing on the sales they do write they focus on the percentage they do not write. By continuing to focus on the wrong percentage you lose your confidence because you continue to believe the sales you did get were just luck. Always focus on the right percentage. The definition of luck is preparation meeting opportunity.

5. Your energy level is low: This is a chicken and egg theory again. When you have a negative attitude your energy level is always low. When you have low energy you have a negative attitude. You also lack enthusiasm and the quality of your conversation becomes poor when your energy level is low.

6. You are not prepared: You will experience a sense of inadequacy to deal with people or situations when you are not prepared. It

is easier to fall into a negative state of mind and blame those around you rather than take responsibility for your inaction. As I mentioned in chapter 2, preparation is a sign of a positive attitude.

7. <u>You feel ignorant</u>: Ignorance is not an excuse for having a negative attitude. If you feel you are lacking in sales training go find it. If you wish to pursue sales as a profession, treat it that way and learn everything you can about it.

8. <u>You feel unappreciated</u>: Never complain about how hard you work or how hard things are for you. I will guarantee there is someone else who has probably worked harder or had a tougher time than you.

9. <u>You do not take responsibility for your actions</u>: The weakest salesperson is one who blames the prospect. There is never a prospect you can blame for not writing a sale. If you put out no effort or intensity, do not have the audacity to blame your prospect. If you keep blaming others for your inability to make a sale you will always have a negative attitude.

When you are in a slump you have confidence problems and end up carrying around all the above negativity. Then each time you take a prospect you put all of these negatives on the empty chair next to you where your subconscious mind sifts through the list to find the ones that fit that situation and apply it. You have then stimulated the negative to appear and it usually does.

Over the years I have listened to salespeople say to me, "What am I doing wrong?" "Where am I screwing up?" "Why don't these people buy from me?" Well, I know exactly what they are doing wrong. They are not focusing on what they are doing. **If you do not know what you are doing wrong you are not paying attention to what you are doing.** Focus and grow.

Think of your mind as a long playing video. Play it back and take a good look at what you do with a prospect. For example, go back and think about how you greeted your last few prospects. What was your attitude towards them and towards yourself? By answering these two questions you will more than likely determine the reason behind your inability to write a sale.

Go out with a positive attitude every day and you will never go wrong. Just relax if you are trying everything to write a sale and you still cannot write one. Have fun, be an entertainer, be intense, excited, be enthusiastic and believe you are a winner and you will be.

POSITIVE ATTITUDE = CONSISTENT STATS

There is one telltale sign that there is a sale—you look as if you are into the sale. When you look, feel and act as if the sale has been written, you are ninety percent there. The sale is in your head and your attitude. Remember, prospects buy you. They buy your energy, enthusiasm, intensity and body language. Prospects do not listen to what you say they listen to how you say it so, if your attitude reflects a sale on your table there will be. One of the best lessons my mentor taught me was that my prospect will mirror image me. If I believed they should buy they would.

Closing a sale is most definitely an attitude. Attitude makes the difference between writing a sale or not. To keep a consistent attitude is also the hardest thing in the world to do. This is one of the reasons why salespeople see their statistics take on a roller coaster ride and do not understand why. It is because their attitude is along for the same ride. A consistent attitude leads to consistent sales statistics that ultimately lead to security in your life.

To maintain consistent sales statistics you need to learn how to maintain your attitude. Earlier in this chapter I covered everything you needed to know about maintaining your attitude. Following are some reminders I continually give my salespeople for maintaining a consistent sales attitude and stats.

1.   Build a relationship with your prospect. Make it interactive. Do not use the old fashioned 'sell and tell' method as it uses up enormous amounts of energy. By letting your energy

     level deplete you will find it very difficult to keep up a positive attitude.

2. Your job is to gather information, not give it away. Ask questions and open Pandora's Box. Only ask questions that will get you a yes response, or discover the fear or weakness that can be capitalized.

3. Making sales should be simple, effective, enthusiastic and intensely focused.

4. Closing is as hard or as easy as you make it.

5. If you are professional you will earn your prospect's respect and trust.

6. If you allow your ego to determine what types of presentation you are going to do you are in for a rough ride. Never allow your ego to determine your income.

7. Making a sale is an ongoing process not a singular event.

8. Your prospects first impression of you is just as important as your first impression of them.

9. What you sell is not nearly as important as *how* you sell it.

10. Sales are not just a Monday through Friday job. It is an on-going commitment.

11. Never start a sales presentation without being mentally, physically and emotionally prepared.

12. Unless you make the commitment to prepare yourself you are never going to be successful.

13. Look your prospect straight in the eye, pay attention and block out everything that has no bearing on the task at hand.

14. Avoid arguing with your prospect, even mentally with yourself.

15. Answer your prospects' questions directly. Never beat around the bush or skate around an issue that deserves attention.

16. Do not try to fake a positive attitude with your prospect you will be caught.

17. Take the time to think from the prospect's perspective how many, "if I could, would you . . ." closes you can get out of your sales presentation.

18. It is your responsibility to learn how to do your job.

19. Your energy level is a direct reflection on how many sales you write. I have never seen top producers write consistent sales with low energy levels.

20. Let your personality shine. Be real and human.
21. Learn the names of your prospects. How can you possibly form a relationship with your prospect if you do not take the initiative to learn their name?
22. Develop a non-self-serving attitude.
23. If you do not make a sale, consider that prospect practice for the next one. Better to use the time wisely than not. Learn from it and move on to the next one.
24. Believe in yourself, believe in your product and believe in your prospect and you will never go astray.
25. Find a way to get more stimulation, motivation and satisfaction from making the sale than from being paid on it.
26. Substitute positive thoughts for negative ones.
27. Managers are there only to help you with the sale, not close the sale for you.
28. There is not one prospect that is not a sale—you just need to find the right key to unlock the door. In the majority of the cases, it is the last key that fits the lock which only confirms that persistence overcomes resistance.
29. Do not focus on one area too much. You can create objections where there are none.
30. Remember that your prospect is just like you—they are not from another planet, even if you think they appear to be.
31. Make your talent be to take away the fear on the table. If you can take away your prospects fear then you will become a master closer.

Learn from every experience that you have. Buy a notebook and after you have finished a sales presentation write down pertinent information about that presentation. List all the dominant buying motives, objections, needs, everything or anything that will help you with the next sale. To be more successful than everyone else, find a way to do just a little bit more than the next guy every day. Create an edge over your competition.

It is consistency that makes the difference between a 15% closer and a 30+% closer. You are only as good as your attitude. You must empower yourself with a positive attitude. Attitude plays an essential part in sales.

The minute you let your attitude start cutting corners and not put any effort out, it is reflected in your stats. Hard work will never let you down.

If the slump continues, go home and take the 'engine out' and throw it away. Take all the things out of your presentation that do not promote a positive attitude. Ask yourself, "Would I buy off this person?" The most powerful suggestion that I can make for you to keep your stats consistent is to "*go back to the buying curve.*" Remember, the K.I.S.S philosophy. The prevention of anything is easier to find than the cure.

One last thing to remember, the determining factor between a positive and a negative attitude is a sense of humor. A positive attitude and a sense of humor enjoy a symbiotic relationship. The more positive your attitude the happier you are, and vice versa. Humor and laughter in any form helps resist against negative forces. Humor and laughter also restore your perspective and sense of balance.

How you write a sale is based on your perception of how you are acting and feeling. It is your attitude and your energy towards yourself and your prospect that determines your success as a salesperson.

13

Communication = Rapport

Back in Chapter 2 we learned that those first few minutes of your presentation are crucial to ensuring that you create a positive first impression. It is this impression that creates the atmosphere or tempo of your presentation however it is your attitude that primarily creates that first impression. Later on curiosity and interest created the rapport and communication. In chapters 1, 5 and 12 we learned that your attitude is directly affected by your perception of the outside world and how we communicate these perceptions to others. More specifically, what 'reality' you meet with in your environment plays a crucial role in determining your sales attitude each day.

While we have learned that sales depend primarily on your positive mental attitude, commitment, sincerity and an unerring belief in yourself in addition to building a solid relationship with your prospect, it becomes critical that you do not allow negative thoughts to influence your attitude, especially when entering into a sales situation. By combining those traits with the basics learned in the first section you will have the foundation for a successful sales career. However, for those individuals who wish to move towards becoming master closers you need to reach to a higher level of human interaction and understanding. In this chapter we will explore why good communication is essential to creating rapport, which creates the solid relationship you need to close the sale.

When you know what <u>moves</u> your prospect, you will know <u>how</u> to move them. You need to be able to show your prospect how they can get what they want by doing what you want them to do. What was the first thing we learned in chapter 2, that we needed to understand? <u>All prospects have one thing in common</u>: Fear—whether it is the fear of being sold or the fear of the unknown.

From those first few seconds of the greeting when you read your prospects personality and later throughout the sales process, you needed to recognize how their behavior is affected, and in many cases motivated by fear. Now that you understand this, you can mold your presentation to suit their personality and behavior. You should be thinking of your prospect as a raw material. Iron ore that needs to be melted, refined, processed, hammered and molded into shape for it to be transformed into a graceful statue. So it is with any sales prospect.

We also learned that closing is nothing more than the transference of your emotions to your prospect. It is imperative that you capture people and their emotions. You must find a way to keep them riveted to their seats so that they listen to you. The impact that you make on a prospect is vital to your success as a salesperson. Prospects buy you. Whatever you feel is going to happen on your table will happen. It is **your** ability to communicate that determines whether you develop rapport with your prospect.

Master closers have long understood that to be successful in sales you must have good communication skills. It is the ability to effectively use communication skills that separate salespeople from master closers. Communications skills are broken down into four distinct areas:

- Personality type indicators to understand specific behaviors
- Body language to understand what your prospect is thinking and feeling
- Your body language and what it communicates to your prospect
- Your linguistic skills and the words you use

The first two of these four communication skills were covered in some depth in chapter 5 and the last two will be covered in this chapter.

Back in the Buying Curve section, we learned that we need communication to create rapport. We learned that understanding what your prospect may be thinking and how they are behaving is crucial for establishing rapport. Rapport stems from commonality and leads to trust. Have you ever noticed that you have immediate rapport with some people and not with others? People with whom you have great rapport believe that you really understand them and therefore they trust you implicitly.

THE SECRET TO RAPPORT

Rapport is unconscious. Psychologists and communication experts show that 93% of face-to-face communications is unconscious. Most people do not even think about body language or voice tones when they meet or talk to someone. Those same psychologists and experts tell us that everyone subconsciously follows the 7-38-55 theory. This theory states that[4]:

- 7% of our understanding is derived from the spoken word
- 38% of understanding comes from voice tone
- 55% of understanding comes from body language

It is that 55% that makes or breaks your sale. Prospects sense what you feel and <u>that</u> determines whether they want to do business with you or not.

What is the solution? Well, you could consciously learn how to control your communication skills by studying any one of the thousands of books on body language or Neuro-Linguistic Programming (NLP). However, I will endeavor to condense the reading into something more easily digestible. NLP defines how people create and maintain their experiences and ideas. NLP consists of five parts:

- Voice—Speed, tone and quality
- Sensory Recognition—How it feels, How it sounds or How you visualize it
- Conceptual Chunk Size—Matching how people think against their level of detail
- Breathing—Matching your breathing patterns with your prospects
- Body Language or Physiology—Posture, appearance, movement, animation and gestures

---

4   The 7-38-55 Theory was defined by Professor Albert Mehrabian, who has pioneered the understanding of communications since the 1960s and is currently Professor Emeritus of Psychology, UCLA. Mehrabian's work featured strongly (mid-late 1900s) in establishing early understanding of body language and non-verbal communications.

You, like everyone else, already do most of the 'NLP' elements unconsciously because creating rapport is based on how you interact with someone.

Most people assume that rapport is only created by talking. However, we now learn that words only account for 7% of building rapport. To best develop your rapport skills, focus on one element at a time, gradually increasing your skills to a level that will not disrupt your natural communication style.

In these next pages we will explore how your body language and physiology have an effect on creating rapport. Understanding and influencing your prospect requires self-confidence and this can only be accomplished through how you present yourself.

IMAGE

Back in chapter 1, you learned about preparing yourself mentally and physically for your prospect but are those enough? If you appear professional and your attitude is calm and positive then the only other factor that influences people is how you project yourself. In other words, what IMAGE or IMPRESSION you convey to people.

In many cases, it is very difficult to make up for a bad first impression. Your appearance, attitude and personality have to be credible. If you have something that is against you, change it. If you are young and want to look older, dress to look older. Act professionally if you want to appear professional. It does not take money to iron shirts it takes an attitude. Anything that you can do to make a great first impression should be your primary consideration in your preparation routine.

Take a minute and answer the following questions. After each question you will find a brief analysis to consider. When you have finished think about what type of image you are projecting to your prospect and the people you come in contact with each day.

1. <u>Are you friendly?</u>

    ☐ All the time   ☐ Sometimes   ☐ Not very often
    People like to feel friendly towards others who appear friendly.

2. <u>Do you smile?</u>

    ☐ All the time   ☐ Sometimes   ☐ Not very often
    It only takes 13 muscles to smile and 112 muscles to frown. When you genuinely smile at someone they feel valuable, important and worthwhile. Even if you are not having a good day, force yourself to SMILE genuinely at people you meet and you will immediately begin to feel better. Smiles are contagious, the easiest thing to do and the most effective gesture you can use. It is sad, however, that most of us do not use them.

3. <u>Are you agreeable?</u>

    ☐ All the time   ☐ Sometimes   ☐ Not very often
    When you smile, nod your head and agree with someone, you are showing respect. **There is a quotation that states, "Any fool can disagree with people. It takes a smart, shrewd man to agree with people."**

    Remember these three points:
    - People like people who agree with them
    - People dislike people who disagree with them.
    - People dislike being disagreed with.

4. <u>Do you argue with your prospect?</u>

    ☐ All the time   ☐ Sometimes   ☐ Not very often
    People do not want to be around people who always want to win an argument. It is worth losing the relationship just to win the argument?

5. <u>Do you appreciate people?</u>

    ☐ All the time   ☐ Sometimes   ☐ Not very often
One of human nature's deepest cravings is to be appreciated; it makes people feel important.

6. <u>Do you make people feel important?</u>

    ☐ All the time   ☐ Some of the time   ☐ Not very often
You make people feel important by skillfully listening to them. Additionally, you should use their names often. Using a person's name is one of the most powerful words in your communication skill set. The more important you make someone feel the more they will respond to you.

7. <u>Do you practice acceptance?</u>

    ☐ All the time   ☐ Sometimes   ☐ Not very often
People need to feel accepted. People will only relax when they feel accepted in an environment.

8. <u>Do you compliment people?</u>

    ☐ All the time   ☐ Sometimes   ☐ Not very often
Giving and receiving compliments is a very important skill to learn. A successful salesperson knows how to handle compliments. First, accept all compliments graciously. Do it simply and directly. Second, never stretch the truth to give a compliment. Never lie or exaggerate. Compliments must be honest and sincere. The secret is to notice real things about people and create the compliment so that it appears natural.

9. <u>Can you admit when you are wrong?</u>

    ☐ All the time   ☐ Sometimes   ☐ Not very often

10. <u>Do you admit when you are wrong</u>?

☐ All the time   ☐ Sometimes   ☐ Not very often

People have respect for those who can admit their mistakes. Remember, a weak person will lie, make excuses and create justifications. A confident person will admit their mistakes which will ultimately result in a stronger relationship.

11. <u>Do you encourage people</u>?

☐ All the time   ☐ Sometimes   ☐ Not very often

To keep your prospect involved and participating in your presentation, you should encourage them. Ask questions that require more information or clarification. Listen to them and acknowledge what they are saying to you is important. Empathize with them to let them know that you that you understand how they feel. Give them an affirming nod or a verbal, "Really, go on or tell me more," to encourage them.

12. <u>Are you a sales mugger</u>?

☐ All the time   ☐ Sometimes   ☐ Not very often

These are salespeople who are aggressive, impersonal and in a hurry to get to the next prospect. They do no preparation, dominate the conversation and are only interested in 'what is in it for them' not their prospect.

So what image are you projecting to your prospect? Congratulations on projecting a positive image if you answered a majority of the questions "All the time." "Sometimes" is more normal, as people tend to have an off day occasionally. A majority of "Not very often" answers indicate that you should consider seriously improving your 'people' skills.

Exceptional and Master salespeople are excited about what they are doing. The energy with which they present themselves and the conviction behind their words and actions creates an 'All the time' image. Remember, 93% of your presentations are oral and visual. Use every opportunity that is presented to project a positive image. What your physiology says is as important as what is said by your appearance. First impressions are made up of appearance (clothing) and body language.

Your overall body language, combined with the tone of your voice, the look in your eyes, your gestures and the expression on your face is what tell people who you are. The Japanese have a saying that "it is worth far more to have person to person contact than anything else because you can SEE the person. You can see all the nuances of how they are thinking, feeling and reacting." Body language is the best indicator of how you are reaching your prospect than any question that you could ask of them. Your physiology also creates more credibility than anything else you say or do. Besides your eye contact and voice tones, it is the way you react to things, the way you look and listen to people and how you respect their thoughts that stimulate communication.

EYES—DO THEY LOOK <u>AND</u> SEE?

Eyes really are the window to the soul. Not only do you see how your prospect is reacting to you, but they see how you are reacting to them. There is a difference between looking and seeing—'LOOKING' means using your eyes only to see something. 'SEEING' means becoming aware of what you are looking at. This is why the idiom, 'look and see' is used constantly in society. Do you really see what is happening when you look at something?

To communicate better with your prospect, consider the following five rules regarding good eye contact.

1. Never ever stare. It is rude, threatening and confrontational.
2. Look at your prospects entire face rather than just their eyes.
3. Focus first on one of your prospects eyes and then the other. This shows that you are really listening to them without being rude.
4. Look and watch your prospects lips. By watching or 'reading' their lips you can better hear what they say.

5. To create an atmosphere of relaxation, avert your eyes every so often to look at something in front of you. Take some notes or find a piece of paper you need.

If you fail to make frequent eye contact with your prospect you are just setting yourself up to be a nervous, hesitant and untrustworthy salesperson.

ANIMATION

Animation closes sales. Have you ever listened to motivational speakers, religious leaders, successful business people and heads of state and wondered why their audiences become so entranced? Is it the movement and animation of the speaker or the 10,000 kilowatts of energy, intensity and enthusiasm that they exude that excites, entice and captivate the audience.

So it is with you and your prospect. Even if they are not listening to you with their ears, they are "listening" to your physiology with their eyes and they "hear" your enthusiasm. High energy, intensity, animated physiology, regular eye contact, changes in voice tone and pure intensity are essential in closing sales. I have never met a successful salesperson who is not animated in what they say or do.

VOICE

The ability to use your voice to control your prospect is the sign of the exceptional salesperson. By changing the tone and volume of your voice, you can get your prospect to respond in any way that you choose. It is your voice that controls the presentation and the communication. Remember, those motivational speakers etc. I mentioned above.

Animation, voice tone and volume all work together to communicate to your prospect. The presentation you make to your prospect is vital to there being a sale. Indeed, the way in which you present your product or service makes up 85% of their final decision. Many a salesperson has forgotten that it is not the product or service that closes the sale it is the impact of the delivery. By using your voice tones combined with animation, you should have your prospects laughing, crying, in awe, angry or whichever emotion you want. When they are emotional, they are communicating with you.

Take your voice seriously. People react positively or negatively to different sounds so it is very important to realize that your voice plays a crucial role in sales. If you sound like a child you lose your credibility immediately. Have you ever heard a child whine or complain? Unfortunately, many salespeople raise the tone of their voices when they become frustrated or nervous. This rise in tone creates a child-whine effect that is deadly. No one wants to listen to a child whine, so why would your prospect want to listen to you if you are using that tone? Child-like speech patterns work against a salesperson and usually come out when you start "begging for the sale".

Instead, your voice must possess an authoritative tone conveying confidence, enthusiasm, credibility and warmth. To be persuasive you need to not only sound like another adult, but it must be an adult in a special authority position. A parent or teacher holds a special authority position. Both have kind, loving, firm tones that convey to the listener that they <u>should listen and obey</u>. It is imperative that you use this type of tone when dealing with a prospect.

The best way to determine what you sound like is to listen to yourself. Shut your mouth and then HUM the sentences. You will very quickly hear the intonations in your voice. Learn to speak in varied tones and volumes depending on the point that you are trying to make. By doing this you will not become boring or monotonous. It is important that you maintain a clear voice throughout your sales presentation. Speak clearly and slowly. You should pause at the end of sentences, at the end of particular phrases and especially at natural breath points. It is these natural pauses that are also projected to our prospect.

Here is another exercise to help the intonations in your voice. Stand up straight, relax your neck and throat and then open your mouth and say very slowly, "Ding Dong, King Kong, Ping Pong." Repeat this phrase at least five times and drop your voice down a tone each time. This brings your voice down into your throat making the sound deeper and more resonant. This is why authoritative figures have such deep, mellow voices that sound calm and reassuring.

If you feel that your voice is cracking or becoming tired it is a sign that you are talking too much. Take a rest and let your prospect talk for a while—you should be listening anyway! To avoid hoarseness do not drink very cold liquids or drinks with caffeine as they cause your vocal cords to contract and your voice to become raspy. Drink room temperature liquids to keep vocal cords lubricated and in prime shape. By the way, sucking candy also irritates the vocal cords, so it is better to suck a glycerin lozenge instead.

One last thing I should mention on voice tones and volume. Have you ever heard the adage that states, 'if someone is whispering, they are gossiping or telling a lie?' Well, in sales the same can be said as being true. If you are constantly whispering to your prospect then others around you believe that you do not want to be heard because you are lying. What is the solution? Increase your volume. Remember, the other half of the adage states, 'if you are talking loudly what you are saying must be true because you have nothing to hide.' Which do you do?

WORDS (IMPROVING THEIR EFFECTIVENESS)

All of us use words to which we have attached personal and unique meanings that help us to define our relationships. We use certain words to keep people from getting to close to us and others to bring people nearer to us. These words are a reflection of our inner selves and our values.

It is therefore, true to say that people will hear certain words that they are interested in and drawn to immediately. Certain words have unique meanings to each of us. Why? Because hearing certain words do prompt specific images and memories. These may be positive or negative. If they are negative, the words are filtered out because we have conditioned ourselves not to hear them. In a sales situation this is no different. People hear what they want to hear. So you must use your words persuasively to communicate on more than just a verbal level.

Successful salespeople understand the need to be persuasive and what better way than by using subliminal commands or words. These commands or words go into the subconscious bypassing the logical or conscious part of the brain. We are all aware of how effective subliminal advertising is in the marketplace. Because people buy on emotion rather than logic, it is crucial that the words you use go directly to the emotional subconscious. It is these words that stimulate chemicals in the brain to flow which then stimulate or motivate you. Without motivation you cannot develop rapport.

A good way to initiate this process is to ask your prospect, "For you, what is important about . . . ?" Their response will give you all the words or phrases that you need to sell them. By listening carefully you can then repeat them back to your prospect using subliminal techniques.

The secret to using subliminal or command words is that they grab your prospects attention and they create an urgency to take action. Subliminal commands also stimulate your prospect to react and respond as though they themselves had the idea or suggestion. The tricky part here is the timing. You have to know your prospect well enough to determine when they are ready to subconsciously hear what you want them to hear.

WORDS THAT INFLUENCE

The following is a list of twenty words that evoke powerful emotions in a prospect. Use them throughout your presentation and when closing. I guarantee you will love the results.

You(r)	Money	Save	New	Easy
Love	Discovery	Results	Health	Proven
Guarantee	Free	Important	Because	Together
Benefits	Privileges	Gain	Profit	Loss
Difference				

WORDS AND PHRASES THAT CAN CREATE A WRONG IMPRESSION

The following words are detrimental to any sales presentation and should not be used. If you are using any of them currently you should try to replace them with the words I have listed above.

I	Me	My	Mine
Please	Honestly	Basically	Cost
Sign here	Contract	Pitch	Super or Terrific
Sell	Program	Buy	Commissions
No Problem	I'm Sorry	Excuse me	Pardon me
Very, very	Sir or Madam	Problem	Have a nice day
I'm not sure	I beg your pardon	Let me tell you the truth	
I'm not going to lie to you		Let me be perfectly honest	

MISUSED WORDS

Following is a list of words that are used very commonly in speech however they are not used correctly.

Implement: Simplify by using 'carry out' or 'get started.'

Hopefully: Hopefully is a frame of mind and should not be used if you mean, 'I hope.'

Irregardless: No such word in the English language, use the word regardless instead.

Unique: This really means 'one of a kind.' Nothing can be 'very unique.'

Interface, Interact, Interpersonal: Big words for simple ideas—Use 'meets with, work with and people.'

Utilize, optimize, Prioritize: Again, big words for simple ideas—If you mean 'use,' say use. 'Make the most of and put things in priority.'

Affect and Effect: These words are often interchanged incorrectly. Affect means to influence someone or something. Effect means to execute something.

Ensure that you are using your words effectively. They should be designed to have the maximum emotional impact on your prospects.

PREFIX WORDS

Look and Listen, are words that show consideration, compassion and empathy to your prospect. These words will permit you to use arrogant or cheeky tones without coming across that way.

Examples for using Prefix words are:

- "Look, I realize that this might not be affordable but . . ."
- "Listen, have you ever considered . . ."

Along with using look and listen as part of your verbiage, you should also consider that people can be divided into **Lookers and Listeners**.

Lookers for example are very highly visual. They use their eyes to acquire more than 80% of the information that they process. Lookers also tend to be impulsive buyers so you should preface most of your communications with the word "Look." "Look Jay, the information that I am going to tell you is important so please listen carefully."

Listeners are highly aural. This type of person relies on what you say, rather than what they see. Listeners tend to be older and more thoughtful in decision making. "Listen Val, the information that I am about to share with you is very important so please listen carefully."

TWENTY TIPS TO IMPROVE YOUR WORD EFFECTIVENESS

1. <u>Avoid Exaggeration</u>: As very few things in life are absolute take every opportunity you have to tell the truth. You will have lost your credibility and persuasiveness if you are caught embellishing your product or services' ability.

2. <u>Avoid Unnecessary Words and phrases</u>: All these do is confuse your prospect and make them feel uncomfortable. Remember, confused people do not feel comfortable making a decision.

3. <u>Do not use Cliché's, Slang or Acronyms</u>: When you make a presentation be aware that not everyone you talk to will understand these phrases. For example not everyone knows what ASAP means.

4. <u>Do not beat around the bush</u>: Remember, you want the undivided attention of your prospect so rid yourself of unnecessary words.

5. <u>Simplify your speech</u>: People are more inclined to remember a few short, understandable words than multi-syllabic, multi-meaning words. Numbers 2, 3 and 4 are also included here.

6. <u>Use definitive words</u>: *Always* and *never* are words that inspire trust and confidence.

7. <u>Do not use the word 'Dollars'</u>: By using the word dollars it sounds like a lot of money. Using just the word numbers sounds less expensive. For example, "The price is nine thousand, four hundred dollars OR the price is ninety-four hundred." Which sounds better?

8. <u>Always start with your highest price</u>: Later when you show a lower price it looks like a bargain after what they first heard.

9. <u>Use action words to motivate your prospect</u>: 'Just do it' or 'Let's get started.'

10. <u>Use words that stimulate emotional hot buttons</u>: Refer to the words listed above that influence your prospect.

11. <u>Be animated</u>: Energy, enthusiasm and animation are powerful communication skills.

12. <u>Voice tone and inflection</u>: Use your voice tones and volume to create emotional pictures.

13. <u>Use the word 'feel' not 'think'</u>: Thinking causes stalling or objection's, feeling creates emotions.

14. <u>Use subliminal command words</u>:
    a.   You **have** to consider your future . . .
    b.   You **need** to take a vacation . . .
    c.   You **must** spend time with your family . . .
    d.   You **need** to **buy** this now to **guarantee** you . . .

15. <u>Do not stutter or hesitate when you talk</u>: Stuttering can be nerves, lack of confidence or a natural affliction. People who hesitate can be perceived as having a lack of knowledge, lying, thinking up answers that may affect your credibility. If you hesitate or stutter when you respond to a prospects question you will immediately cause your prospect to become embarrassed and they will quit talking.

16. <u>Do not educate your prospect</u>: Remember, telling is selling. Do not use words that reflect your telling your prospect about your product or service. For example, "Did I tell you that . . ." You are there to search for dominant buying motives and to close the sale so you need to learn, not educate.

17. <u>Eliminate ego words or phrases</u>: These words are self-important. Even if you think you know more than your prospect, do not say or act like it. These words just aggravate and are considered high pressure tactics that went out with the Ark. Examples of some ego words are:
    a.   Obviously you knew that . . .
    b.   Everyone knows that . . .
    c.   Of course you were aware of that . . .
    d.   Anyone who does not understand what I am trying to say is . . .

18. <u>Words to regain control</u>: Prospects are famous for trying to divert a salesperson's attention. However, the following words can be used to get your presentation back on track.
    a.   Tell me more about . . .
    b.   You were saying about how you . . .
    c.   Let us go back to what you said about . . .

19. Talk in sensory words: Use words that appeal to your prospects five senses. Sight, sound, touch, smell and taste.
    a. Tell me what the flowers **smelled** like when you were in Hawaii.
    b. Can you imagine **seeing** our spectacular sunsets from this patio?
    c. Can you **hear** the birds? I wonder what they are saying to each other?
    d. What did it **feel** like to ride on that camel when you were in Egypt?
    e. Tell me what the food **tasted** like in Thailand I have never tasted it.

20. Use 'we' in closing sentences: It creates a feeling of togetherness and confidence in making the right choice. "Based on what you have seen, it is important that we . . ."

Put yourself in your prospects' shoes—are you coming across effectively? Remember, speak slowly, clearly and be concise in words. Get out a dictionary or a thesaurus if you feel that you could use a better word vocabulary. Create a list of emotional and powerful words that you can use in your sales presentation.

How words and subliminal commands are used marks the difference between master closers and competent salespeople. One last thing, the words that you *think* are just as important as the words that you *say*.

BODY LANGUAGE

Words are an essential piece of the communication process puzzle. However it is the non-verbal way in which we communicate that 'backs up' what we say or do. How many of us have grown up hearing the phrase, "Actions speak louder than words?"

Why is understanding body language so important?

1. Life experience has taught us that people tell 'little white lies.' They lie by omission or they simply do not tell the truth. If a person's words are consistent with their body language then we will believe them. If they are different, we tend to believe what we see rather than what we hear.
2. People have a better visual than aural memory. For example, a facial expression will be remembered long after the words said at the time have been forgotten. "Did you see the look on his face when we . . . ?"

Your body language will tell someone how you really feel about them. It will also relay to them the things that you are <u>not</u> saying to them. By telling someone you dislike them, but keeping a broad smile on your face while <u>you</u> tell them; they will not believe you. If you tell someone you love them, but will not look at them while you say it, will they believe you?

Unfortunately, unlike verbal language, body language is inexact. You must use common sense when trying to interpret it. In the next few pages you will find some common positive and negative body language gestures and the generally accepted meanings. These gestures are not just limited to what you may be projecting they also include your interpretation of your prospects behavior. If a gesture appears exaggerated it should be considered more negative than positive.

The first groups of gestures listed are considered **positive**. Positive physiology is an excellent indicator of how the other person feels. It can also indicate interest, openness, enthusiasm and a willingness to listen.

FRIENDLINESS

- Body posture is erect, relaxed and alive
- Body posture also moves towards the other person
- Hands are open and arms are extended
- Eyes are alert, wide and focused on the other person
- Facial expressions appear lively with genuine smile
- Voice is well modulated and animated
- Legs are uncrossed with sitting and slightly spread while standing

- Talk with hands, particularly with the palms open
- Nodding in agreement to other person's words indicating that you are listening
- Reaching out to shake hands

CONFIDENCE

- Consistent eye contact with occasional blinking
- Body posture is erect with chin up and shoulders back
- Leaning back in chair with arms behind head with fingers interlaced
- Fingers put together steeple fashion—the higher the hands, the greater the confidence
- Standing with hands on hips or in pockets with feet slightly spread
- Feet resting up on desk or chair—Use this posture if you are CEO of the company, otherwise it has a negative connotation

INFORMATION ANALYSIS

- Head will tilt to one side
- Eyes will appear to focus
- Body posture will come forward towards table
  o Movement to sit on front portion of chair with upper body leaning forward
  o Moving of ones hand to chin or cheek, with slight stroking motion
  o Will lick or appear to bit lower lip while nodding one's head slightly
- Hands will rest on thighs

In NEED of ASSURANCE or SUPPORT

- Look of pleading in eyes
- Biting of, or chewing on, fingernails
  o Wringing of hands with rubbing of thumbs on fleshy part of hand
- Twisting of rings, watches, necklaces

ACCEPTANCE

- Body posture moves closer to other person
  - o Leaning back in chair with arms behind head or hands spread open across chest
- Consistent eye contact
- Smiling

Negative body language is much harder to interpret and therefore much less reliable in determining your prospects state of mind. This negativity may be stimulated from your prospect being over tired or their mind focusing on something not even related to you or your product. In this case you should watch to see if the physiology changes. If so, interpret the change rather than the initial behavior. It is the transition of body language that is important. If the physiology does not appear to be changing you should use your other communication skills to prompt a behavioral change.

DEFENSIVE

- Body is tense, stiff or rigid
- Arms and /or legs are tightly crossed with fingers clenching upper arms
- Hands are clasped tight together or clenched into fists
- Jaw and mouth are set and lips are pursed
- Facial expression is narrowed, scowling or frowning
- Head may be lowered so chin touches chest
- Leaning away from person, even if handed something

NERVOUS

- Fidgeting with anything and everything
- Constant clearing of the throat (if person is not obviously ill)
- Tapping or drumming fingers and feet
- Facial expressions are twitchy
- Pacing or shifting of weight from one foot to another while standing
- Whistling under one's breath

- While seated and legs are crossed, the cross-over leg foot is moving constantly
- Eyes move rapidly from side to side
- Ears (lobes) are tugged at or hair is played with
- Mouth is covered by hand when person goes to speak

SUSPICIOUS, SECRETIVE or REJECTING INFORMATION

- Body posture is withdrawn
- Failure to make eye contact
- Raising or arching of eyebrows
- Only looking sideways at people, not directly into their face
- Peering or looking over one's eyeglasses or sunglasses
- Touching or rubbing one's nose
- Arms and legs are crossed, but not tightly

ANGER

- Body is rigid
- Fists are clenched or hands are palm flat on table
- Lips are tightly closed in a thin line
- Breath sounds become shallow and rapid
- Maintains diligent eye contact including dilation of pupils
- Face color changes to crimson

FRUSTRATION and IMPATIENCE

- Opening of mouth frequently as if wishing to speak or wanting to interrupt the speaker
- Fists are tightly clenched and are shaking
- Wringing of hands or drumming of fingers on table
- Rubbing the back of one's neck or the bridge of nose
- Running of fingers through hair
- Tapping of foot while standing or sitting
- Breathing becomes short controlled breaths
- Eyes stare straight ahead and do not appear focused on anything or anyone but seem ready to explode

BOREDOM and INDIFFERENCE

- Yawning
- Very relaxed body posture such as slouching
- Leaning one's chin on the elbow (one of two hands)
- Tapping lightly of one's fingers or foot
- Swinging feet under table
- Doodling on paper or napkins
- Eyes are in distant stares or wandering around room
- Fidgeting with one's clothing, purse or packages
- Cracking of knuckles
- Unconscious or continuous bobbing or nodding of the head
- Drooping eyelids or hearing sounds of snoring (asleep)

You may laugh at this last one however I have seen prospects fall asleep during a sales presentation.

When trying to interpret any of the above gestures you should do so in combination with other gestures that is taking place at the same time. A combination of gestures is much more meaningful. For example, if your prospect is leaning forward up onto the table, nodding their head and smiling they are giving you are very strong indication of interest and friendliness. If their words are not confirming the behaviors use their gestures as a guideline.

Your best body language is leaning slightly forward, observing your prospect and listening carefully to what they are saying. Smile and nod you head. It is very difficult to resist a person who is actively listening and appears interested in what they have to say.

CREDIBILITY

Earlier in this chapter I covered how image and impressions affect your prospect. Part of maintaining a good image or impression is by being credible. Whether you gain credibility by the words you speak or your actions it is important that your prospect trust you. I cannot stress enough that credibility is crucial when you are building a relationship with your prospect and later when making your presentation.

There is a difference between self and product credibility but quite often salespeople believe the two are one in the same. This is not true. For example, a recognized hotel chain already has credibility through brand name recognition. However, your prospect may not believe that you are credible enough to sell it because they do not trust you. Which weighs more on a prospects mind—your product or you? If this were so, Hilton would not use professional salespeople.

The impressions you convey, their perception of you, the way you walk, talk and respond to your prospect are more important than the product. Many salespeople lose sales, not so much on their lack of confidence or technique, but lack of credibility. People buy you first, then the product.

Self-credibility is enhanced by your ability to deal with any situation that may arise with your prospect. Prospects will, quite often throw out a 'whopper' to test how well you react to situations. They buy your physiology. It is your reaction to that 'whopper' that will either add or delete from your credibility. If you fumble around or hem and haw you will lose credibility and control of the sales presentation. Your prospect buys you. If your prospects buy you, then whatever product or service you are pitching has credibility. Unfortunately, many salespeople believe it is product or industry knowledge that is vital to writing a sale—it is not. The number one rule in closing—people buy on emotion not logic. You prove yourself with credibility and they will give you a chance to sell them which put you half way there.

In a sales presentation I find that only 15% of what you know about your product or service is required to promote it. In the majority of sales it is after the prospect has made the buying decision that they will say, "Now could you explain how this works to me." If you are already in sales isn't it amazing that after the sale is down and your new member is doing the paperwork, they will then start to ask about your product. "So how do we do an exchange to Hawaii?"

Knowledge is important however when you want to do the paperwork. Know where to look, or whom to ask, in your industry and your company for the knowledge you need to best promote your product or service. After the sale, knowledge about your product is a necessity in promoting good customer service.

Master Closers know every little thing there is to know about their product or service and most importantly, when to use it. When you offer a piece of information you should always tie it down or use a trial close. Master Closers will never offer a piece of information without getting anything back from their prospect.

The five best ways to promote self and industry credibility are as follows:

1. Third party stories or Testimonials: Either of these methods are a perfect opportunity to gain credibility by relating a similar situation as your prospect.
2. Your personal experiences: When you relate how you feel using or experiencing your product or service lends tremendous self and product credibility.
3. Industry publications: By showing a prospect magazine and newspaper articles, surveys, financial reports or anything else that blows your product's horn will provide all the credibility that you need.
4. Corporate image: The bigger your company, the longer they have been in business and the larger their market share the more credible you look. This is why having name recognition is so important.
5. Your product: Tailor your product or services benefits to meet the needs and wants of your prospect.
6. Providing guarantees: Putting your money where your mouth is. This is not necessarily a monetary guarantee it may just be emotional. Prospects will be more inclined to trust you if your product does what you say it will and you prove it.

The last one, providing guarantees, is the number one emotional reason why people do not buy a majority of products, including timeshare. Prospects did not believe that either the company or the salesperson would provide the promised service, or guarantees, once the sale had been completed.

Remember, if you are unable to close the sale ensure that your prospect leaves the presentation with a better impression of you, your company and your industry than when they, or you, first arrived.

CREATING A MIRROR IMAGE

Remember in section one I mentioned you need to become a chameleon, why? because body language is a strong determinant of how a person feels and there is a way in which salespeople can drastically shorten the bonding process. It is called mirror and matching.

Mirror and matching is an extension of understanding physiological behaviors. It states that if behaviors are modeled precisely they can be duplicated in almost any individual. By matching speech patterns and speed, body language, breathing patterns, eye contact, posture, sense of humor (or lack of it), prejudices and opinions of your prospect you can shorten the rapport stage considerably.

At the beginning of the sales presentation your prospect will initially not accept our character. However after a short period of initial defense behaviors your prospect will become accustomed to the image that you are promoting, whether good or bad. Once they begin to feel comfortable in their surroundings then will then begin to assert their personality. Once this occurs then you have to begin to mirror image them. Remember, people are drawn to other people who are similar to themselves. It is this attraction that marks the beginning of the bond between two people.

Therefore, it is important that you adopt the character of your client. **Become a chameleon**. By mirror imaging your prospects' behaviors and attitudes you will understand them better if you look at the sales process through their eyes. Mirror their body language, their voice level and their facial expressions. They only way to capture their interest is to be like them. Keep the tempo set by your prospect at first. If they walk slowly you do the same. If they talk fast, speak faster. Remember prospects will only communicate with you when they are feeling comfortable. How many of you have seen the movie Young Frankenstein with Mel Brooks and Marty Feldman? I am referring to the train platform scene when Marty, playing Igor tells Mel Brooks (Dr. Frankenstein), to "walk this way" as he is alternatively limping and moving his shoulders to create the effect his hump is moving (which it actually does). Dr. Frankenstein followed his lead by walking the same way, although I am sure his original thought was to actually walk straight off the train platform. It is all about mirroring body language.

By mirror imaging your prospect you can then determine how they are going to react to the presentation, the questions you will ask and the closing process. If you know beforehand how they are going to react then you can better steer them in any direction. This process helps you define what lines you can cross over, which ones you cannot step over or where you can go straight ahead. You work out your limits because it is those limits that will help you create the character within you that will best work with your prospect. By doing this you are better able to determine their hot buttons or dominant buying motives.

Your prospect will always mirror image your feelings and attitude if you are feeling comfortable, direct and sure of yourself. Your prospect will accept your body language more readily than the words you are saying to them. Use mirror imaging to your advantage. Understanding your prospect behaviors and body language is an important key to communicating with them, reducing their sales resistance and creating an atmosphere for them to buy. Mirror imaging is complete when prospect and salesperson work together to overcome objections and find solutions to a problem.

It has been proven that 93% of our presentations are based on physiology. Your image, eye contact, animation, voice tones and pattern, use of command words, your body language and your ability to mirror image your prospect. I have discovered over the years that by using these areas effectively you not only grab your prospects attention and create urgency, but you can also subconsciously high pressure them to take action.

TWENTY TIPS FOR BETTER COMMUNICATION SKILLS

1. Smile naturally and often. People get a good feeling from a smile and will associate it with you and your product or service.
2. Make sure that you are properly attired and groomed.
3. Use open body language. Maintain good posture (whether seated or standing) with your hands visible and open.
4. Use facial expressions to show emotions to your prospect.
5. Maintain good eye contact, especially while your prospect is speaking.
6. Focus all of your attention on your prospect by listening to them.
7. Provide spoken and non-verbal signals to encourage your prospect to speak. Nod agreement or say, "tell me more, etc."
8. Match and mirror your prospects physiology to gain a better understanding of them.
9. Show enthusiasm, confidence and conviction in your product or service.
10. When speaking, be clear and concise. Use your words effectively.
11. Speak slowly and clearly. No matter how slowly you are speaking, slowing down even more is beneficial because we tend to believe we are speaking slower than we really are.
12. Avoid gestures that convey a negative impression such as crossing your arms across your chest.
13. Never lean back against your chair when you are talking or listening. Your prospect will mirror your posture and then they are not in a positive position to make a buying decision.
14. Offer a firm handshake. There is an old Polish proverb that roughly translated says, "Stick your hand out in friendship and shun any person who hesitates to return the gesture."
15. Match your words with your body language. If you are honest in both areas it will come across sincerely.
16. Walk briskly and with confidence. This implies that you are confident in your abilities, can be trusted and have a sense of urgency about them.
17. Do not crowd your prospect. People have a comfort zone that needs to be respected. Do not move into their comfort zone until you have been invited. Stand father away to maintain their comfort zone if you are taller than your prospect. This distance

also provides a better line of sight. Once you are seated you can move closer to them if necessary.

18. Change your physiology to change the course of your sales presentation. This will cause your prospect to mirror and match you.

19. Do not fidget, fumble around, drum your fingers, tap your feet, clear your throat constantly or squirm in your chair. You are a professional salesperson, not a child.

20. Be careful when touching your prospect. Firm, brief handshakes are acceptable. Occasional touches between the wrist and elbow are acceptable however it is wise to watch for a negative reaction the first time. Occasional, non-sexual, touching does eliminate barriers, creates a bond of trust and being supportive. You should be aware of which person will react favorably to your touching them. A hug or a high five can be great gestures to aid in your sale.

If you can communicate you can create rapport, which then leads to trust. Remember, people will only buy from people they trust. **People buy your interpretation and physiology. It is not what you say but how you say it.**

One last thing before we move on to the next chapter, following are some additional tips to help you build a solid relationship with your prospect and increase your closing percentage.

1. Listen to your prospect sincerely because eventually they will tell you everything that you need to close the sale.

2. Pay attention to your prospects body language as it speaks louder than the words spoken.

3. Never, ever beg a prospect to listen to you or buy from you.

4. Develop tolerance and patience for your prospect. Find something to like about them.

5. Never disagree with your prospect as it will only lead to confrontation and a lost sale.

6. Get and keep your prospects attention by talking about what is important to them.

7. Ask your prospect first, second and third level questions to uncover emotions and needs.
8. Show your prospect how your product will benefit them, never tell them.
9. Appreciate their objections because without them you will never close a sale.
10. Treat your prospect with sincerity, appreciation, respect and honesty. If you do they will eventually do the same to you.

One last thing, remember never to pre-judge your prospect with your physiology, because it may just cost you a sale.

<u>So, are your communication skills effective?</u>

☐ All the time   ☐ Sometimes   ☐ Not very often   ☐ Need work

Communication begins with you. Be normal, be human, be confident, relax and stick to the basics of these communication skills and you will develop rapport with all of your prospects. Now we will use our improved communication skills to delve deeper into your prospects psyche by learning how to ask more effective questions in order to write more sale.

14

Are you Asking the Right Questions?

As we have seen from that past few chapters, attitude and good communication are the keys to successful sales. Whether it is spoken or non-spoken, you will now see that just by asking your prospect certain types of questions you will see how they react to life and this will tell you how easy or difficult the sale is going to be. Questions help you determine how logical or emotional you need to be and how quickly or slowly they understand what you are asking. From their responses you can tell how little or much information you need to give them. Their responses will also tell you how much you need to listen and how much you need to talk.

I have never seen a sale where the prospect and the salesperson were not interacting or communicating. Even if you are talking about the most negative thing in the world, they are still communicating an emotion. Since the secret to sales is to create emotion, let them talk. Listen to them. You are looking for every opportunity for them to tell you their problems so that you can gain the opportunity to create solutions.

When you listen to your prospects you gain little pieces of information. Think of your presentation in the terms of a jigsaw puzzle. At the beginning of your presentation you are trying to put together the border pieces. By the middle of your presentation you are working your way towards the center, so that by the time you begin your pitch your prospect should be able to see the whole picture. Just as it takes time to put all the pieces together, gathering information, however irrelevant it may appear, will come together the more pieces you have. The only thing that you have to determine from your prospects character is are the pieces big and easy to put together? If not, maybe they are like a seascape, made up of a thousand pieces in varying shades of blue.

Initially you, as the salesperson, are in control of the tempo of the sales process will ask all the questions. After you have asked a question, stop and listen carefully to the responses. The more your prospect talks, the more they begin to believe that they control the tempo of the sales process. When they feel in control, they feel safe and their resistance will lessen. Therefore, we can see how asking questions create a reciprocal relationship. You ask a question and listen to the response; they ask a question and they listen to your response.

Remember, the proper use of questions will give you the keys to your prospect needs, their objections and the map to the solutions. In addition, if questions are asked correctly, your prospect will not feel as if they are on the receiving end of a third degree interrogation.

ARE YOU ASKING THE RIGHT TYPE OF QUESTIONS?

In chapter 5 we learned why we ask questions and that questions are so very important in discovering what motivates your prospect. One of the biggest mistakes that most salespeople make is that they do not ask questions because they do not understand that first, and most important, the reason to ask questions is to gain information. Of those that do ask questions, they do not ask the right questions. Then, unfortunately, they do not listen to the answers.

We learned that first level questions do not elicit much emotion, but do produce honest answers. Second level questions arouse general feelings, while third level questions provoke true emotion. Remember, you need to know every little thing about your prospect. You have to dig deep into their lives to discover their hot buttons and dominant buying motives. Unfortunately, most salespeople prejudge their prospects buying habits on first level responses even though they buy for third level reasons. You should never assume that you understand your prospects needs and desires. People buy for **their** reasons not **yours**.

During any sales presentation there are four types of information that you must elicit from your prospect before you can show any benefits of your product or service. You need to discover the following:

1. <u>What do they know about your Industry or Product</u>: These questions help you to discover what product or service your prospect is using and how they feel about that product or service.

2. <u>Who is the Decision maker</u>: You need to find out who in your party (either directly or indirectly) is the decision maker.

3. <u>What are the Hot Buttons and Dominant Buying Motives</u>: As you progress with different types of questioning techniques you must get clarification as to which are desired benefits and which are features.

4. <u>What is the underlying Fear of Buying</u>: Is it the high pressure they perceive? Is it being ripped off by a salesperson? Is it third party ridicule? Is it the fear of being sold something? Is it ignorance about your product?

Learn to understand what fear or risks your prospect THINKS they will meet with when they do not buy from you. You have to determine if they are going to be motivated by security (fear of loss). Remember, most people will make a decision based on fear of loss rather than hope for gain. They will buy if they perceive the risk will outweigh the cost.

By incorporating the different types of questions that follow, you will gain all the information that you need and stimulate emotions and interest in your product or service. By eliciting emotions from your prospect, you create curiosity about your product. Remember, the number one rule in closing—it is an emotional sale, not a logical sale.

OPENING UP CLOSED ENDED QUESTIONS

In the beginning of your sales presentation you want to ask your prospects as many open-ended questions as you can to get them to tell you <u>how they feel</u>. Open ended questions are ones that elicit something other than a yes or no response.

There is an old saying, "If you always start off with the same canned questions, you will always hear the same canned responses." Close-ended questions are just that, canned questions. To avoid situations where you are asking questions that gain only yes or no responses, you must learn to convert them to open-ended questions.

For example, ask them, "Do you know anything about my product?" Do this when you are trying to discover how much your prospect knows about your industry. You will get one of three responses—yes, no or everything. These three responses will generate one of the following thoughts in a salesperson:

1. Yes—I need to change my presentation because they know all about it
2. No—I now need to tell them everything about it
3. Everything—I do not have to tell them anything because they know everything

None of these responses is going to move you forward in the sale process, so why subject yourself to asking a close-ended question. By changing the tone and order of the question you will get an entirely different response. Open up the question so you now ask, "What exactly do you know about my product or service?" In the example below, I have used the timeshare industry as the product, but try to reconfigure it by inserting your product or service into this type of situation and see what happens.

Jay: "Well, we don't know that much about vacation ownership, except that we had been to several presentations in Florida and then we bought one in Arizona while vacationing there years ago."

David: "Congratulations, are you using it right now?"

Jay: "No, because we got such a good deal for this trip."

David: "Really, do you mind my asking how long you have owned it?"

Jay: "Hum, I think it will be three years now."

David: "Do you mind my asking, what made you buy in Arizona when you like to ski so much?"

Jay: "Well, Val and I went there for our anniversary one year and were suckered into attending a presentation. Initially we were very skeptical, but this very pleasant

> sales guy took his time and explained everything to
> us. We bought a week when he showed us how we
> could benefit and because there was no high pressure
> involved."

David: "Did you buy it mainly for the exchange?"

Val: "Absolutely."

David: "So, I gather it has worked well for you over the years?"

Jay: "Well, yes, generally, except this year we could not get
an exchange; that is why we bought a package deal."

By just rewording the question you have gained more vital information about your prospects. You have found out that they do not like to be pressured and that their emotional state at the point of purchase was exchanging (adventure). You have also found an angle on which to focus enhancing the future exchange benefits associated with your resort. Congratulations, you have found a hot button.

Other examples of close-ended questions that many salespeople are guilty of asking are:

1. Have you heard anything about timeshare ownership (your product or service)? "No, never or cannot say that we have," are all the normal responses to that question. Do you honestly believe that no one, especially your prospect, would come to a sales presentation without having heard one thing about the industry? This is not very likely in today's world of social media, the internet, Facebook, Twitter, television, radio, newspapers and word of mouth.

2. Do you travel much? "Yes, no, not like this, usually in our RV, or we backpack all the time." These are a sampling of responses I have heard when salespeople ask this very question. You would be better off asking, "Since you folks are vacationing here in Mexico this year, which other great places have you been to (or plan to visit) in the future?"

So many salespeople are just putting a gun to their heads by asking close ended questions of their prospects that gain little or no information. One of your goals is to endeavor to discover what makes your prospect tick so that you can map out solutions. You must learn how to adopt the ability of opening up your questions. Ask yourself, "What questions am I asking throughout my presentation that are closing the doors to discovery, angles, knowledge, tools and hot buttons which will produce closure on the back end?" Remember, asking the right questions provide the map to solutions.

Every time you ask an open-ended question you give your prospect a license to talk. By using open ended questions you are doing three important things:

1. <u>You are discovering more about them</u>. You are finding out what motivates them. What they like, dislike and what passions drive them. In essence, what makes them tick.
2. <u>You are turning on the starter button of your prospect</u>. Good, bad or indifferent, it does not matter. When your prospect is communicating with you it makes them feel more comfortable about their surroundings. They begin to feel as if they are in control, that someone cares and that they are being heard.
3. <u>By listening, you are going to empower your prospect with the ability to speak</u>. Everybody, including your prospect, loves to hear the sound of their voice. The longer they talk the more comfortable they feel and the more secrets they will reveal.

When you ask an open ended question correctly, you may find that your prospect will give you a ten, twenty or even a thirty minute dissertation of their traveling history. During this dissertation your prospect will bring up their values, their feelings and their motivations. How hard are you now working now? All you are doing is sitting, listening and thinking of all the angles you will use against them later when you begin closing.

Here is another example of a canned, close-ended question that should be converted to an open-ended one. "Tell me, where did you go on your last vacation?" This is probably the worst question that you can ask a timeshare prospect. You will get a variety of responses ranging from, "Nowhere, we didn't, Hawaii or we just visited the family." None of these responses will give you any information about their vacations and will only ensure that they clam up and become uncooperative. What makes this seemingly simple question so ineffective?

Also, by asking a prospect, "tell me, where or when," you are making a demand request. It is not only rude, but it forces people to stop talking. You will never usually get more than a one word response to a demand question. Remember, questions are designed to get more information and to get your prospect talking not to stop them talking.

Before going on to other types of questions I would like to state that just because you ask a question does not mean necessarily you will get the perfect response. Your prospect is human. You cannot change the way they have been vacationing or using your product or service. Just look for another way to ask open-ended questions. What you are trying to do with the sales process is to create a solid enough foundation so that you can earn the right to ask third level questions later during the presentation.

There are many different types of questions (or closes as some people call them). Questions should be designed to generate and stimulate effective communications, especially during the discovery (or FORM) portion of the sales process. Later I will show you how they can be changed slightly and used to stimulate closes and a decision.

Opinion Oriented Questions

These are questions designed to get your prospects to give you their opinion. By asking someone their opinion you will always discover an emotional hot button. Opinions are something that people feel passionate about, whether positive or negative. For example, ask your prospect, "<u>How do you feel</u> about what you have heard so far?" Their answers will vary; however, you will always get an honest, emotional response. The following is a sample of prospect responses to this question:

- "Well, it sounds pretty good. It is different from what we thought it would be!"

- "Well, it sounds interesting. It is incredible that you can do that. Can you tell us more about that . . . (benefit)."
- "Hey, don't get me wrong but it still sounds too good to be true and we don't need the hassle of having to worry about . . ."

During the sales process you should be asking your prospects as often are you can, "How do you feel about . . . ?" This is the difference between making a sale and selling a condo. You have to be constantly looking and seeking for the way they feel, because feelings create sales.

In most instances if you ask an opinion oriented question the prospect will not only give you their opinion but also ask a question in return. When they do this you can then ask them an active involvement question.

ACTIVE INVOLVEMENT QUESTIONS

These are questions designed to elicit involvement from your prospect so that you can get a subject for a third party story. Active involvement questions usually being with the words Who, What, When, How or Why. The best, non-threatening way to phrase a question using "where," in this type of situation is as follows—"Oh, where was that?"

Examples of active involvement questions are:

- How many presentations have you attended so far?
- How long in advance do you normally plan your vacations?
- What is the most important thing that you look for when planning a vacation?
- What types of things do you normally like to do on vacation?
- What benefits appeal to you the most?
- Who, besides your family, vacations with you?
- What time of year do you normally take your vacations?
- Why are vacations so important to you?

All the above questions empower your prospect to give you more information. Most importantly, they get them actively involved in conversation. This involvement on their part will then allow you to turn their responses into assumptive type close. For example, if you ask your prospect,

> "Would you use this membership yourself or let your family and friends use your benefits?" They *could* answer:

> "Well, we would probably use it and let our friends and families have some weeks as well."

There are situations where, if you do not ask an assumptive question after their response to involvement oriented questions, you lose an opportunity to close your sale. You could wait all day for them to ask, "Can we give this membership to our family to use?" It is unlikely however that they will ever ask you that question specifically. You must move your presentation forward and involvement oriented questions do just that. There are many salespeople who have a very hard time gaining interest and commitments from their prospects because they do not use this type of question.

If your prospect resists your opinion or active involvement questions, change the topic of conversation by using comparative questions.

COMPARATIVE QUESTIONS

These are questions designed to eliminate a topic you do not want to talk about that will enable you to focus on the task at hand. The format for this type of question is as follows: **Isn't it true that . . .** (state something you want to talk about) **is more important than . . .** (something you do not want to discuss)? The following is an example. "Isn't it true, that spending quality time with your family is more important to you than spending money on vacation each year?"

What you are doing is selling an emotional benefit to your prospect because there is nothing more valuable than family, love, and their time together and bonding. Should your prospect respond with, "Yeah, well how much does it cost?" You can ask another comparative question in response. "Can you really put a price on your family time together or maybe, isn't spending time with your family more important than any dollar figure that I could throw at you?"

These responses may sound harsh however I used this particular example to show that within the timeshare industry most prospects will normally choose the second option rather than the first. Because of their fear and ignorance (especially the fear) prospects would rather spend $400 per night or stay in a dump than choose the alternative. They are so afraid because of their ignorance, that they will not even consider a logical alternative. Prospects will cut off their nose to spite their face. If you use enough strategically placed comparative questions focusing on their emotional state, you will eventually break down their fear and ignorance.

CHECKING QUESTIONS

Do you think your prospects have quit listening to you? Did your prospect understand what you just said to them? If you are not sure, ask a checking question. These questions are normally general in content and are designed to check your prospects understanding, reactions, and temperature, at any point in your presentation. You need to know if what you are saying is being understood and retained. It is highly unlikely that your prospect will come to a decision if they have missed even one material fact.

Some examples of checking questions are:

- "Are you with me so far?"
- "Can we agree on that point?"
- "Do you follow me on this?"
- "Does any of this make sense to you?"
- "Does that sound fair enough?"

These may sound like close-ended questions and your prospect might respond with an automatic yes or no. If this occurs, you should follow up their responses with the question, "What part exactly do you (do you not) feel is of benefit to you?" Always follow up closed-ended questions with an open-ended one.

UNDERSTANDING THE QUESTION

Not only is it important that your prospect be listening to you, but it is vital that they understand the questions you ask them. Just like an objection, questions must be clarified if there is the slightest doubt as to the meaning or intent. If your prospect misunderstands your question you may create an objection where none existed before. Remember, prospects will not ask you to clarify your questions, they will just assume they understand because they do not want to appear ignorant to you or their spouse.

This also works in reverse. Do you know how many prospects will ask you a question that you misinterpret? You may think it is an objection rather than a question and make it more difficult than it sounded. To avoid these situations, always clarify your prospects' questions so that you create no objections or misunderstandings with your response.

I use the following little story often in my training sessions as it is the best example I can provide. Even though it has nothing to do with the sales it does make the point.

> One day, little eight-year old Johnny went up to his mother and asked, "Mom, where did I come from?" She knew that someday this question would come up and had prepared herself to answer it. So, setting Johnny down, she carefully and patiently explained where babies came from in terms that she thought he could understand. When finished, she asked, "Johnny, now do you understand where you came from?" "Well, not exactly," he replied, "Carl said he came from Cincinnati and I just wondered where I came from."

You should always make the meaning of your questions clear. There are too many instances where what you are asking and what the prospect is actually hearing may be completely different.

WHAT ARE THE RIGHT TYPE OF QUESTIONS?

Master closers know that the very heart of any sales process is their skill in asking questions. The more skilled you are at asking probing questions the more you will open Pandora's Box. Exceptional salespeople also understand that knowing when to ask certain types of questions will expose many buried issues and will normally provide both the prospect and the salesperson with new insights into their specific situation.

So what makes the right questions so vital to the sales process? They allow you to do the following:

- Gain crucial and necessary information needed to sell them (Discovery/FORM)
- Test your prospects temperature
- Determine if the commitments they have been making are real
- Motivate your prospect to tell you have they FEEL
- Determine your prospects values by asking their opinions
- Lead your prospect to a decision

PROBING QUESTIONS

Probing questions are those that challenge your prospect to do one (or all) of the following four things before they answer your question.

- Become personally involved in the sales process.
- Evaluate or analyze their current method of vacationing.
- Speculate on what their future vacations may be like.
- Express their inner most feelings (good or bad).

Specifically you are asking your prospect questions that will encourage them to think before responding. If you have asked a probing question your prospect will normally respond with, "I never thought about that before" or "That is a very tough question (or tough to answer)."

Earlier in the sales process your prospect may have told you "little white lies" because it was what you wanted to hear. Now, by asking more probing questions you will get honest information because your prospects are required to <u>think about how they feel</u> before they respond. As such it is very difficult for them to think of anything else.

Additionally, due to the nature of these questions you must also encourage your prospects to answer them. Use the phrases, **"Tell me more"** or **"Go on"** to gently persuade them to continue. Be careful in your encouragement as it is very easy to make this type of questioning appear as an interrogation session. So keep the questions and encouragement natural and conversational.

Effective questioning can also help prospects discover needs, wants and desires that they never thought of before. Soon you will begin hearing about all the heartache, happiness or intimate details of their lives. Once they have started telling you something personal you can begin to ask more probing questions to expand on that particular feeling or emotion. The more you probe the more they will tell you.

Along with your questions your total physiology must be focused on creating value. These feelings and motives are communicated to your prospect and, as such, they will then mirror you. The relationship will then strengthen because they now trust you. Remember, people trust people like themselves and want to buy from them. Therefore the more skilled you are at asking questions the more effective your questions will become. Once you help people verbalize a need, want or desire it then becomes easy to create dissatisfaction with their current method or product. From dissatisfaction you can then have them visualize a solution (which is your product or service).

Ask yourself these two questions before you ask any question of your prospect.

1. "If I ask this question what kind of response will I get?"
2. "When I ask this question, what responses do I expect?"

Even though they may sound like the same type of question they really are not. One reflects how your prospect reacts to the question, the other refers to the information that your prospect will give you. Both are probing questions for you to use on yourself first.

APPROACH QUESTIONS

These questions are designed to get your prospects attention. Structure your questions so they are non-threatening and encouraging because you want your prospects to willingly participate in the sales presentation.

Examples of some approach questions are:

- "Tell me about your work (business)?"
- "What made you chose (location) as your vacation destination?"
- "What is it about (your product or service) that you like?"

From your very first question, and their response, you should be able to tell whether they are going to be willing participants or not. Even if their response is negative it will still provide you with information that you can use later on in the sales process. Remember, you are now becoming a detective and every question you ask from that point forward will gain another piece for the informational puzzle.

NEEDS IDENTIFICATION QUESTIONS

Initially you asked your prospect basic, first level questions to identify their needs—"Where is your favorite vacation spot?" "What is your favorite car?" Then you asked them some second level questions to help further identify what they were looking for in a vacation—"What was it that you liked about that spot?"

However, to really identify what it is that your prospect is looking for you need to understand the motivation behind the first two levels of questions. Until you can identify this motivation you will never discover your prospects needs.

Following are some third level probing questions that you should ask:

- "Tell me, why are vacations important to you?"
- "Tell me, how do your vacations make your feel?"
- "If you could improve or change anything about your vacations what would it be?"
- "What makes a memorable vacation for you?"
- "Is there a specific reason why you have never gone on your dream vacation?"

VALUE DETERMINATION QUESTIONS

Aside from creating value when showing benefits, you must also determine if what you are offering has value to your prospect. If the value created is significant enough they will then buy from you. Determining whether something is of value (or not) can be done one of two ways:

1. Value in solving a need or problem
2. The negative value of not solving the need or problem

To give best explain the difference let us examine a situation where you have a hole in the sole of your shoe. The first choice would have your sole repaired so that you feel better when walking and no longer experience painful foot problems. The second involves a projected image of someone "down on their luck" and not being able to fix the sole because of the perceived high cost of repair.

To understand what your prospects perception of value is involves asking questions that probe their beliefs.

- "How would you feel if you could no longer take vacations?"
- "How would your vacations change if you no longer had to worry about the cost?"
- "What would be the effect on your family (or work) be if you were no longer able to afford vacations?"

Listen carefully when you ask value questions because you will usually find a very important hot button mixed in with their response.

HOT BUTTON QUESTIONS

As you have been listening to your prospect tell you about their family, occupation and recreation you should have been hearing key words or phrases. Your prospect will give you all the words or phrases that you need to sell them. Ask hot button questions repeating back to your prospect these words and phrases using the subliminal techniques we learned in chapter 12.

A good way to initiate this process is to ask your prospect:

- "For you, what is important about . . ."
- "What do you mean . . ."
- "So what you are specifically looking for is something that will . . ."

By asking hot button questions to probe for their motivation you will soon discover their third level or emotional buying motive. Remember emotional desire is all you are trying to create in your sales presentation.

The balance of this chapter will deal with more advanced types of probing questions. The ability to determine when, and where, in your presentation to use them separates the average salesperson from the master. Although I am continuing to use example references to the timeshare industry, you should be able to insert your product or service into any of the question types. By reworking all of my timeshare examples to incorporate your product or service, will also help you learn and understand more about what you are selling, as well refine and strengthen your sales presentations.

Feedback Questions

Feedback questions are used when your prospect responds to any question with an aggressive statement. By simply feeding the question back to them you are forcing your prospect to explain what they meant by their statement. You can also rephrase the response and feed it back to them for the same reason.

For example, your question asked about using the exchange program:

Prospect:	"Well, the exchange doesn't work!"
Salesperson:	"You mean that nobody has explained to you how the system works?"
Prospect:	"Well, we did try it once."
Salesperson:	". . . And it didn't work? Did you stop trying, or possibly did you not do it properly?"
Prospect:	"Well, I did fill in something and send it off to somewhere."
Salesperson:	"You filled in something?"
Prospect:	"Yeah, some space deposit . . . bank . . . something or another."
Salesperson:	"Some space deposit . . . something or another?"

What finally happens is that the prospect will break down and say, "Well, I do not know what to do," and the element of doubt is now been planted. Because of the persistent feedback questions you have prodded them until they have reached their level of ignorance and ability to admit it.

Challenging Questions

Challenging questions are designed specifically for tackling a major objection head on and eliminating it as a problem. You may not realize that you use challenging questions each day in your personal life. An example might be, "David, why are you refusing to do your homework when you know that if you don't you will not graduate or get a good education?" All you have to do is apply these challenging questions to your sales process.

There are two methods for asking challenging questions.

1. **"Why is** . . . (state the problem) **more important to you than** . . . (state the benefit)?"
   a. "Why is flexibility more important to you than saving money?"

2. **"Why do you refuse** . . . (your family, yourself) **the enormous benefit of** . . . (state the problem)?"
   "Why do you refuse yourself and your family of the enormous benefit of a guaranteed vacation every year?"

Learn to ask challenging questions without being confrontational and your sales closing ratio will increase. The more often you can repeat your prospects responses back to them, the less important the objection or statement becomes and they then begin to focus on the benefit.

ALTERNATIVE CHOICE QUESTIONS (IN YOUR FAVOR)

These are questions that do not allow for single word responses. You must never give your prospect the opportunity to make a choice between doing, and not doing, **only** between doing it this way or that way. In other words, instead of asking someone if they like steak and getting a "yes" in return, offer them a choice. "Between steak and fish which do you prefer?" Whichever answer you get moves you forward in the sales process. Alternative choice questions may also be used as closing questions. An example of a closing question can be, "What size of suite would work best for you, a studio or a one bedroom?"

SWITCH OFF QUESTIONS

Switch off questions are designed to have your prospect overcome their objection or problem by your providing an alternative to the objection. The two most effective methods of asking switch off questions are:

1. **"May I ignore** . . . (state the problem or objection) **if I can prove** . . . (state the benefit)?"
   "May I ignore that you need your accountant's approval for a minute if I can prove to you that you will save money with this membership in five years?"

What you are doing here is putting their objection aside while at the same time protecting the strength of the objection. In addition you are determining whether to address this objection now so you can move forward or save it until it becomes a condition of the sale.

If you get a negative response it may be a valid buying concern and must be dealt with appropriately. If your prospect does not stop you from "ignoring" something, then the objection or problem was more than likely a smoke screen to derail you.

2. **"While** . . . (state the objection or problem) **seems vital at this moment, in the long run your ability to** . . . (state the benefit) . . . **does dominate your decision, doesn't it?**"
   "While your accountant's approval seems vital to you at this moment, in the long run your ability to vacation at a much lower cost does dominate your decision, doesn't it?"

By using switch off questions effectively you can all but eliminate your prospects objections or 'assumed' problems. Always look for an opportunity to get a tie down or commitment at the end of your response.

MULTIPLE CONCLUSION QUESTIONS

Prospects can overcome their objections with switch off questions however multiple conclusion questions are designed to surround the objection with benefits and bury it.

When you have an objection put to you and try to overcome it, invariably you will get into a confrontation with your prospect. If you pay it any value then you create an anchor for them to hold onto during the closing process. This type of question will surround the objection with so many benefits that it will evaporate.

The format for this type of question is, "**I know that you want** . . . (state the benefit) **so isn't it true that** . . . (state the objection) **is less important than** . . . (restate the benefit)?"

> "I know that you and your family want to get together every year for a vacation. As you still want your family together every year isn't it true that the instability of your job takes away that fact. Isn't that even more reason to secure your families future vacations by submitting your application for membership today, don't you agree?"

By surrounding the objection with benefits that are of value to your prospect you will overcome even the strongest objection. You must <u>always</u> use a benefit, not a feature.

DECISIONAL OR CLOSING QUESTIONS

Decisional questions are only to be used to force a decision from your prospect. Ask one of the following two questions if you believe that your prospect is at a decisional crossroads.

1. "**Am I right in assuming that if** . . . (condition exists, is done or happens) **you will** . . . (take a specific action) **right now**?"
   "Am I right in in assuming that if I can get you the price you want you will join our club today?"

2. "**Don't you agree that** . . . (state the condition you want them to agree to) **is a more important reason for ignoring the fact that** . . . (describe the action you want them to take)?"

Don't you agree that the ten bonus weeks I am offering you is a more important reason for ignoring the fact that you need to join the club today?"

By asking either of these questions two things will happen. One, you will get a YES response and your prospect will buy your product or service. Two, you will get another objection so you can continue moving forward.

Decisional or closing questions are much the same in that you are asking your prospect to make a decision. There should be no trickery or manipulative questions. By asking your prospect to buy in an honest, sincere manner you will make the sale and earn your prospects respect because you have created credibility in both yourself and your product. Anytime you ask your prospect to buy, that in itself is a credible pitch and you are transmitting to them that you believe you have earned the right to ask for the order.

There is one last decisional question that you can ask your prospect. The question is, **"Do you have any other reason why you would not be able to buy this product or service today?"** By asking this your prospect will offer up the last condition to the sale. This question should only be used if you believe that there is only one issue, objection or condition standing in the way of your prospect making a decision. This is also a good technique in smoking out any hidden objections that could hinder the final closing of the sale.

The wonderful thing about sales is that if you learn to ask questions correctly then you can just sit back, relax and listen. It does not matter whether it takes ten seconds or ten minutes for your prospect to answer the question. You can watch your prospect squirm and fidget in resistance but, in the end, they will answer freely and honestly.

Questions should start off very general, get progressively more personal until you are asking questions that probe deep into their inner selves. It is using any of these types of questions that will help you discover the true motives and objections.

The sign of a great salesperson is one who can direct the flow of the sales process by asking good questions. Your intelligence and professionalism are demonstrated more by the type of questions you ask then by anything else. If you are astute enough to ask the right questions, it will pay off handsomely in sales and income.

FIVE TIPS TO REMEMBER ABOUT ASKING QUESTIONS

1. <u>After you ask a question, quit talking</u>. Silence may be all the high pressure you need to make a sale.
2. <u>Have a good repertoire of questions in your sales presentation</u>. Just as there are differing personality types you should know which type of questions you will ask of each type.
3. <u>Have a reason for asking a question</u>. Questions should be asked to gain something, not just to pass the time along.
4. <u>Never phrase a question using the word "why."</u> Instead use "How." Research has shown that you will gain twice the information.
5. <u>Always try to ask questions that will include a feeling response</u>. "How do you feel about . . . ?" "How would this membership affect you?" "Can you tell me more about how you . . . ?"

THE WRONG QUESTIONS TO ASK

Never, ever ask a prospect what they **think** about your product or service. You will always get a response like, "sounds okay or it seems all right." Asking someone what they think creates a conflict or confrontation. In my almost thirty years of sales I have never heard a prospect say, "Sign us up it sounds great." If you are waiting for your prospect to say that, get out of the business and sell ice cream, then you can ask them what they *think* about chocolate chip flavor.

If you must find out what they think, ask for their opinion instead. Opinions relay values and express emotions. Remember, the only way to sell someone is to get them emotional and it is those emotions you are trying to uncover with your probing questions. Any aggression, hostility or negativity that prospects may have towards your product or service will evaporate when they are emotional. It is your job to set them down, ask them questions, listen patiently and carefully then guide them through the sales maze.

One last point to mention is that if your prospect is talking they will not want to leave. Have you ever seen a prospect that is talking trying to bolt out the door? No. The worst thing that will happen when you ask a question is that they answer it and start talking. So get them talking, whether positively or negatively and enjoy the experience of communicating with your prospect.

Should you ask all these questions and your prospect still chooses not to buy your product or services ask them this one last question and see what happens. **"What was the one thing that we could have done that would have made you buy our product or service?"** You may be surprised at the answer.

We now know how to ask the right type of questions to stimulate conversation to build a relationship, which will discover the dominant buying motive, but is that enough? In the next chapter we will learn how to stimulate the right objections and use them to close your sale.

15

Defining, Understanding and Eliminating Objections

As you have learned so far, the primary objective is to develop rapport and build a relationship while your secondary objective is to eliminate the objections by asking the right questions. If you spend the majority of your time concentrating on overcoming objections, you are going to expend much energy focusing on too much 'smoke'. This chapter will help you learn to master the most common objections and overcome the last real objection.

It is important to first understand that resistance manifests itself as objections. There is a natural tendency in all of us to resist. We resist change, we resist against making a decision, we resist against agreeing with someone and resist against anything or everything that is different. Prospects even resist talking to you, being friendly or opening a door for their spouse. In addition, they will resist participating in the presentation, resist giving you information and most of all, resist in allowing you to do your job and listen.

Resistance is the emotion created by fear. Fear is the predominant reason for objections and a natural resistance to the unknown. Whether it is ignorance, a preconceived idea of what will occur, or fear of the sales process specifically prospects find a way to object.

It is important to remember that your prospect is not there to make you look stupid or insult your intelligence they are there to defend themselves. Their objections are not against you personally, or even necessarily against your product or service, they are just fearful and desperate. When desperation becomes a focal issue they will start grasping at whatever objection will keep them from buying.

Remember, objections are nothing more than emotions translated into logical defensive justifications to avoid an unpleasant situation. As such you will meet with them in any sales process no matter how good you are, therefore you need to develop your ability to sense this fear and understand what prompts it. Ask yourself is it really an objection or is it your perception that a problem exists?

ANTICIPATING OBJECTIONS

Exceptional salespeople are able to 'second guess' their prospects by knowing exactly where in their presentation they will get certain objections. In addition, by anticipating these objections you can also begin the process of switching their objections for yours. Later on in this chapter I will cover more on switching objections.

Below are the four main areas that create objections. By understanding and recognizing objections you will find that your ability to anticipate them will help you in uncovering and dealing with them.

FEAR	'NO' PROBLEM	CREDIBILITY	VALUE
Unknown Being sold Ignorance	There is NO Need There is NO Use There is NO DESIRE	Self Product	Emotional Logical
Fear accounts for 30% of ALL objections	If you have no *use* or *need* you have no *desire* and you will get an objections. You have to create an emotional problem. Desire is emotional.	Self-credibility leads to having product and/or service credibility. Without self or product credibility you will get objections. Credibility accounts for 10% of objections.	Create emotional desire and close on emotional value. Justify with logic after the sale. Value accounts for 60% of objections.

Along with those above you should also anticipate objections from the following four areas.

MISCONCEPTION	SKEPTICISM	VALID DRAWBACK	VALID COMPLAINT
You need to clarify the objection by finding out what prompted the misconception and then explain why it occurred.	You need to prove that the product or service will work using examples, testimonials, facts or other hard evidence.	You need to show how the advantages of your product or service can outweigh the disadvantages through third party stories.	You need to provide your prospect with a solution that will make your product or service work for them.

Throughout the sales process your ability to anticipate an objection approaching is directly related to the type of relationship that you have developed with your prospect. The minor objections are eliminated as you near the close if you are asking the right questions and doing enough trial closes or tie downs. This will then only leave you to deal with the real objection.

Unfortunately, many salespeople do not sense, or hear, any objections because they themselves fear them. Fear of loss is a bigger motivator than the desire to gain. They believe that the objections are obstacles that slow down the sales process so they chose to ignore them. It is the fear of uncovering and dealing with the objections that creates a confrontational situation on the table and the ultimate loss of the sale.

Everything that your prospect feels, their pre-conceived ideas and their belief of what you are going to do comes from what you are transmitting. The majority of objections that you will get are because of what your physiology and personae are transmitting and that you are failing to anticipate or recognize these objections before they appear. Prospects sense this and just like a boxer who takes a knockout punch, you are inviting the flurry of objections until you are knocked out.

UNCOVERING THE OBJECTIONS

If your prospect has hidden objections that may potentially undermine your sale it is crucial that you find a way to uncover them. Many times it is the salesperson's perception of the final objection that is the problem and they then become afraid to ask more questions. They are afraid to confront their prospect and would rather ignore the last real objection than deal with it. In the majority of the cases that last real objection may just be a condition of the sale and by failing to uncover it you are setting yourself up to lose the sale. So, always remember to ask for the order. You may be surprised what happens.

Remember back in chapter 6 we learned that the first time you got an objection it was offered to throw you off track, create a smoke screen or mislead you. You acknowledged it, clarified it and stepped over it. The second time it may have been a buying concern or drawback that you then eliminated by telling a related third party story or related value shtick. However, if the objection is repeated a third time it is most likely a condition of the sale. If you do not ask those final questions you will never discover if the last objection is the real one or not.

It therefore becomes important to be able to distinguish an objection from a condition. A condition is something that must be satisfied in order to complete the sale. An objection, on the other hand, generally has to do with the product itself or your portrayal of it and will be specific with each type of prospect that you meet. The best way to determine whether something is a condition or an objection is to ask your prospect.

You have learned that anytime that you ask your prospect a question you let them completely answer before you ask the next question. Well, the same premise applies to an objection. Let your prospect finish expressing their objection before you answer. The whole objection must be allowed to spew forth. If you stop the expulsion of the objection then your prospect will never get the opportunity to rid them self of that thought and it will continue to reappear. Think of uncovering an objection as an expulsion of resistance.

After your prospect has finished, echo the objection back to them for clarification before answering it specifically. They will either expel the rest of the objection or realize how silly it sounded and overcome it themselves. An example follows:

Prospect: "We do not vacation!"
Salesperson: "You do not vacation?"
Prospect: "Well, we do vacation however only every year or so."
Salesperson: "Are vacations not that important to you?"

Use that expulsion to create value in your product. Make it harder for your prospect to buy your product or service if they continue to object. The harder you make it for someone to buy something the more they see value in it. For example, you receive a cashmere sweater as a gift. After you wear it the first time you just toss it on the floor before going to bed. However, if you had bought and paid $250 for that cashmere sweater you will take it off carefully, no matter how tired or drunk you were, and place it folded on a chair. What is the difference? The difference is perceived value.

Think of uncovering objections as creating value and you will soon find that most of the time your prospects will close themselves. While uncovering objections, you should be listening very carefully. Why? Because the last objection that you hear on your table will most probably be the first one you heard when you started your sales presentation.

SWITCHING THEIR OBJECTIONS FOR YOURS

The art of master closing is empowering your prospect to give you the objection that you want. Your ultimate goal during the sales presentation is to replace their objection with yours in their mind. They will adopt your objection if it appears more viable than theirs because if it presented in the right way, your prospect perceives that you are credible. If you have built a solid relationship, created value and shown the benefits correctly, then when they get to 'your objection' they will simply grab hold of it and listen to you.

Your goal is to have your prospect eventually throw their objections away, pick up yours and think it is a better one. You want them to use it as a "we do not give a damn what you say or do now this is our objection, we like it and are going to use it." This is especially the case if you show a big ticket item. "We are not going to be buying anything today at that price!" Now the "think about it" objection they were offering disappeared into outer space and your money objection takes it place.

It is important to remember that every product or service offered on this planet has the same objections. Every prospect that enters into any sales environment has a common denominator—they are all emotional. Not one of them buys the same, has the same job, the same background and so on, but all have the same reasons not to buy. Whatever the reasons may be, they are all the same.

Every time that you can empower your prospect with the option of giving you an objection another one will come up and so forth. However, when you create the objection, their objection (which is not real) is forgotten because yours sounds better than theirs so they then adopt it. Your pitch should be designed to include these objections because you want your prospect to find the catch or the "too good to be true."

Become excited about the objections that you know you can overcome and ignore the ones that you cannot. When you divert your prospects attention to an objection that you know you can overcome they will soon adopt it. By focusing on what you can easily overcome gives your prospect the belief that you cannot overcome it, so they adopt it believing it is their way out of the presentation. Once they have adopted your objection they will have forgotten theirs.

For example, knowing that you can overcome a restricted *use* problem, but not a 'we have to talk to our son-in-law' objection, focus on how *use* is restricted. Tell them when and why leading them to find that it is a "too good to be true" problem. In giving them this objection they will nurture it and believe they have a good reason not to buy and soon forget their son-in-law. Once they have adopted the restricted *use* objection you can close using an "if I could would you" closing approach.

Another way to empower your prospects is to create a trap around the objections that you have the hardest time overcoming. In the front end you bring up the most common objections and deal with them superficially. This is so that later on when your prospect tries to use it they will remember, "Oh yeah, we cannot use that one," so they move on to another objection. It is such a simple technique that unfortunately most salespeople never think about doing it. The majority of salespeople wait until the last minute to bring up objections which by then is too late to offer objections.

To help you learn this technique, take out a piece of paper and write down at least five of the top ten objections that you hear. After you have written them down, then determine the most effective way for you to bring them up during your presentation. You will be surprised to learn that you will always hear the same objections which should now make it easier to find ways to eliminate them early on in your presentation.

Trapping objections can be done during your intent statement or when you break the pact. The idea is to let your prospect know, that you know, what all the 'standard' objections are and hopefully they will not insult your intelligence by trying to use any of them. For example say to them, "Let me tell you about what we are going to be doing here today."

Continue with, "We know that everyone who comes to these presentations has to 'think about it or talk to someone before making a decision. Maybe you are putting a child through school, buying or building a house . . . or cannot afford it. So in an effort to save time and energy my presentation will cover all of these areas. When I am finished if you have any other concerns I will be pleased to deal with them . . . fair enough?" Be careful when using this because if it is not delivered properly you can create the 'think about it' objection. Sell all of your answers with conviction.

The easiest way to close a deal and get rid of their objections is by discovering and probing in the front end to find out what really ticks them off or excites them. Throughout this book I have been relentless in my reminding you that it is emotion that closes sales. Therefore, as a salesperson you must find a way to encourage your prospect to tell you their innermost feelings, needs and wants. It is your ability to focus on trying to understand what motivates your prospects feelings that helps you discover what the dominant buying motive or emotion is. It is those feelings that surface when they give you objections.

The art of master closing is to empower your prospect with the ability to close them self by using all of their information against them and this includes objections. They will give you all the information you need so use it where it will give you the best angle and reprogram it back to them. Only by doing this you can interject your objections and slowly rid them of theirs.

DEALING WITH OBJECTIONS

Whether you have anticipated, uncovered or switched the objections you must know how to deal with them. The terminology may be different (i.e., handing objections or overcoming objections) but both use the same formula for dealing with the reasons that prospects give for not wanting to buy.

Following are five important things to consider before dealing with any objections.

1. Determine the nature of the objection.

    It is imperative that you determine the nature of the objection before you attempt to deal with it. Because objections should never be ignored until you have determined their legitimacy you need to explore the objection by echoing it, appreciating it, agreeing with it or clarifying it. You will find that the majority of objections can be handled by either ignoring or stepping over them. If the objections begin repeating themselves near a closing point then there is perceived value to them and may become a condition of your sale. Remember resistance is an emotion but conditions are logical.

Exceptional salespeople, however, do not listen to the content of the objection, but to the physiology of the prospect when they voice the objection. The physiology—body language, voice, eye contact—their whole personae will tell you whether what they are saying, or objecting to, is really fear or based in something else. By your ignoring a majority of the objections you will find that it is exactly what your prospects will do—ignore their objections.

2. Do not let your prospects objections affect you.

Once you give your prospect an excuse that their objection has had an effect on you they will continue to use it. Remember that every day that you are in sales you will get the same objections and reactions. If, however, you are getting the same results then you are not making any attempt to find or deal with the real objection. It is much like the definition of insanity, "Doing the same thing repeatedly in hopes of achieving different results."

3. Objections invite prospect participation.

When your prospect gives you objections they are participating in the sales process. Earlier we examined how important it was to persuade through involvement and what better way to get your prospect involved by having them object to something. Even if you have already anticipated the objection, let your prospects verbalize it completely. Remember an objection is an expulsion of resistance.

4. Understand the motivation behind the objection.

After you get an objection it is vital that you encourage your prospect to explain what is motivating it. Echo the objection. Listen and sincerely try to understand the objection. Only by your seeking to understand what lies behind the objection will you then earn the right to overcome the objection. By earning the right to solve the objections throughout the sales process you will then have the right to solve the last real objection during the closing process.

5. <u>Listen carefully to each objection</u>.

   Your prospect will categorize their objections. If you listen carefully to each objection you will soon discover that they all are coming from the same source. By understanding this you then can modify your strategy for dealing with each objection until they realize that they are no longer 'fooling' you.

Remember, the formula may be a simple as answering a straight forward buying question to the ever endearing favorite, "We cannot afford it." Whichever strategies you choose to deal with their objections, remember they are **buying signals** and without them you will never make a sale.

FIFTEEN STRATEGIES FOR EFFECTIVELY DEALING WITH OBJECTIONS

1. <u>Do not fear them</u>. As I have repeatedly stated throughout this book, objections are an absolute necessity to the sales process. Without objections you will never make a sale so encourage and welcome them.
2. <u>Positive mental attitude.</u> Should your prospect bombard you with objections do not let them affect you. It will reinforce your prospects fear if you appear upset by the frequency and manner of the objections. Use confident body language, speech, posture, appearance to reinforce your positive mental attitude.
3. <u>Never take objections personally</u>. Selling is an attitude. If you take objections personally you will find yourself continually in a confrontational situation. If you treat all of your prospects with respect, are diplomatic and do not insult or demean them you will earn their respect. Remember, your prospect is always right, in their opinion.
4. <u>Always ask yourself "Why are they saying that?"</u> Unfortunately, human nature tends to encourage people to never say what they

mean. Do not react to your prospects words literally. Watch their physiology and listen carefully to the whole objection and then respond to the complete package rather than the words.

5. Anticipate the objections. You can deal with the objections before they come up if you anticipate when or where in your sales presentation your prospect will object.

6. Convert the objection to a question. Salespeople have a natural tendency to defend themselves when a prospect raises an objection. By mentally converting the objection to a question you are in a better position to deal with it. For example, the statement "Your price is too high," forces a salesperson to defend their price. By mentally changing the statement to the question 'why is your price so high,' allows the salesperson to explain the price. By converting objections to questions you maintain a relationship and avoid confrontation.

7. Use the objection to create value. Ask your prospect questions specifically directed at the objection they have just given you. Working hand in hand with number 6 above you encourage your prospect to explain why they are objecting.

   For example, the objection, "We do not vacation," can be responded to with, "isn't spending quality time with your family important to you?" Their response will usually be, "Yes, but . . ." and another objection will come out.

8. Deny "untrue" objections. If you have a good relationship with your prospect you can smile and say, "Of course, I do not believe that . . . what is the real issue?" This should only be used if the objection is obviously untrue otherwise you will be suckered into trying to logically answer an illogical objection. If you are up front with your prospect you will most likely not meet with this situation.

9. Eliminate objections with good questions. During your discovery process you can gain substantial information that could otherwise become an objection if not verbalized earlier. For example your prospect may tell you in casual conversation that he always makes his decisions so now he cannot use this excuse later as an objection without looking foolish.

10. <u>Agree with your prospect</u>. Let your prospect know that you agree with them on some point before the objection arises. If you agree with their point of view on an 'objectionable' point you then render it unobjectionable. Prospects will not object as much if they believe that you will agree with them on certain points.

11. <u>Ask them why</u>? This strategy is very effective on general objections such as, "Your product or service does not work." By asking them <u>why</u> they think that your product or service does not work will, at the worst, narrow down the objection to something that is more manageable. What happens in most cases is that the prospect will admit that the objection was not really that important after all.

12. <u>Admit to imperfection</u>. This directly relates to the 'too good to be true' idea. If you can admit that what your product or service has its' faults then you are increasing your credibility and eliminating the imperfection as an objection.

13. <u>Put their objection into your words before you respond</u>. Doing this achieves three goals. First, it lets your prospect know that you have been listening. Second, rewording the objection helps to avoid misunderstandings and ensures that you are answering the correct objection. Third, it gives you time to contemplate a response.

14. <u>Directly ask for the real objection</u>. If you believe that your prospect has not given up the real objection at the time of closing, ask them what it is. If you have a good relationship with your prospect they will tell you what it is. Ask them if it is the only reason that they are not buying your product or service. You are looking for a yes response to continue. By answering yes they have now closed themselves and committed to buying.

15. <u>Turn the objection into a reason for buying</u>. This technique boomerangs their objection back to them as a reason to buy. For example their comment, "Your price is too high" can be turned into, "That is exactly the reason you should buy. Cheap is cheap and you really don't want that, do you?"

By incorporating the above strategies in dealing with objections you will soon discover that objections are no longer something to fear, but to be welcomed and expected. It is your ability to consistently uncover the real objections that will separate you from the average salesperson.

OVERCOMING THE MOST COMMON OBJECTIONS

When you are trying to overcome objections you need to be careful. The way in which you deal with the objection must be done in a manner conducive to testing its' validity. Following are some examples for overcoming the most common objections. Each objection can be overcome using any of the six techniques mentioned already. Remember, that these techniques are designed to lead your prospect, not push them.

- Echo
- Feel-Felt-Found
- Boomerang
- Lowest Common Denominator
- Re-directing your Prospects Focus
- Third Party Stories.

TEN MOST COMMON OBJECTIONS

The number one objection, "we need to think about it" is covered at the end of this section. Again, I am using timeshare references, but insert your product or service to understand how to answer the objections.

1. **I (we) do not normally vacation this way (I/We would not use this product or service).**
   a) "I can appreciate that not everyone vacations like this, could you tell me how you vacation?"
   b) "I can appreciate that you feel like that but could you help me understand a little why you do not normally vacation this way?"

2. <u>**Vacations are not a priority (Your product or service will not work for me/us)**</u>.
   a) "I can appreciate that you work very hard, most likely for an unappreciative boss, but if you could find the time to take a vacation, where would it be?"
   b) "I can understand how vacations get lost in the shuffle of working so much, but could you tell me why you think they are not a priority?"

3. <u>**We are saving to put our kids through college**</u>.
   a) "Really, that is great. I am sure that they will appreciate it when the time comes. In the meantime, could you tell me where your family may be going on vacation, before they go to college?"
   b) "Thank you for sharing that with me. Obviously you love your kids, but do not forget that sixty percent of a child's education is at home so spending quality time together is important. If you could have that, and get them through college, would I be looking at a new member today?"

4. <u>**We are saving to buy a house**</u>.
   a) "That is great. Will you go back to vacationing on a regular basis once you have bought your house?" [Yes] "Okay, so it is just a timing issue then?"
   b) "Wow, buying a house is a big commitment. Do you plan to reward yourselves after you buy with a well-deserved and needed vacation?" [Yes] "Okay, you obviously see that owning is better than renting to you are an ideal prospect for our program."

5. <u>**I (we) need to talk to our (my) attorney, accountant, father, banker, brother-in-law, etc.**</u>.
   a) "If you need to talk to someone else before making a choice then I believe that you will need to listen very carefully to what I will be telling you. That way you can be sure to give them all the facts and information. It would not be fair to ask someone's opinion if they are not familiar with this program would it?"

b) "Fair enough but do you mind me asking what advice your (whoever) would give you that would help you in being able to make a decision so that I can provide you with that information?"

6. **I (we) need to shop around**.
   a) "I can understand that you would want to do that but wouldn't it be better to have all the facts before making a choice?"
   b) "I can understand the need to shop around but could you explain to me why shopping around is important to you?"

7. **I want your product or service but my spouse does not**.
   a) "What was it that has you excited about our product or service?"
   b) "Do you mind my asking what the reason is that your spouse feels this product or service is not for him (her)?"

8. **We were just married (I was just divorced)**.
   a) "You have, believe it or not an opportunity that very few couples get. By having and using this product or service, you can experience many years of enjoyment with each other and for your family."
   b) "Congratulations, I wouldn't think of a better wedding present to give each other than years of quality family vacations."

9. **I (we) cannot afford it**.
   a) "I can understand that money may be an issue for you. However without this membership, we have already established that you will spend far more money continuing to vacation the way you are presently, haven't we?"
   b) "Do you feel that your family (or you) deserves a vacation? If so, what would you be able to afford to give them that?"

10. I (WE) NEED TO THINK ABOUT IT.

Fifty percent of all the closing objections you will hear are "we need to think about it" as it is the number one objection offered by prospects. "Think about it" comes in a number of formats:

- We will be back.
- We never make a decision on the spur of the moment.
- We never make impulse decisions.
- We always think about things before we buy anything.

The truth is that "think about it" is not an objection. "Think about it" is camouflage for "we do not trust you, we have no desire, we are totally confused and/or we are (were) not listening to you." It can also mean, "You have been so 'nice' we could not possibly say no so we will lead you along so that we do not offend you."

In most cases once your prospect says that they have to "think about it" the sales presentation is over and you have lost any chance of making a sale. To become a master closer is to understand prospects 'do not think it over.' The instant they leave your presentation the majority have of them have now forgotten you and your product.

The one and only method for overcoming the objection "think about it" is to do a good presentation. There is no magic shtick, just a magic presentation. However for those who could use a little help here are five examples for overcoming "think about it."

1. "You need to think about how you would be able to use your membership next year?" **(Echo)**

2. "I can understand that you feel you need to think about it. Many of our owners who were once sitting where you are now told us that they felt exactly the same way. However, once they began to use the membership they found . . ." **(Feel-Felt-Found)**

"You know that I always feel honored when one of my members tells me that. What it really tells me is that I have made a friend and as such, you do not want to tell me no. Please understand that this is just like buying a pair of shoes. When you put them on, you know, yes or no, whether you are going to buy them. I do understand that it is your prerogative to feel that way but please tell me what part of my presentation (program) it was that you did not like." **(Feel-Felt-Found)**

3. "I have only one concern about your taking the time to think about it is that by waiting too long you will lose that quality vacation time you like to spend with your family." **(Boomerang)**

4. "Since you folks need some time to think about this, do you have any friends or family that might be interested in vacationing this way?" **(Re-directing their focus)**
   "You know I think that you folks are making this very complicated. This is not a decision it is a choice. You are already using the product which even makes more sense to own it, rather than rent it. So let us just fill this out, okay?" **(Re-directing their focus)**

5. "You know people are funny. I have sat and talked with all of my owners about what they were thinking about before joining the club, and they all said . . ." **(Third party story)**

There is one last "think about it" I need to cover and that is giving your prospects a few minutes alone to make their decision. Do not put yourself into a position where you allow a prospect to say to you, "Can you leave us alone for a moment while we talk about it." They are asking you to leave so that they can either think up another objection or they do not trust you enough to tell you what the REAL objection is.

When they ask you to leave the table (or room) for a minute there is normally one little thing that is uncomfortable for them. It is most likely the down payment but you leaving the table or room makes this little thing even more uncomfortable for them. They will start thinking about all the other 'payment' commitments they have and talk themselves out of the sale. Better to stay at the table, directly face them and ask what it is they need to discuss because possibly you could help them resolve the issue. The worst thing that will happen is that they will give you the real objection.

Overcoming objections is very simple. Learn to anticipate objections, acknowledge and clarify them and deal with them appropriately. Unfortunately most of the objections salespeople have a hard time dealing with are because they are not dealing with them correctly in the front end. Avoiding this will only serve to have them come back and haunt you when you begin closing the sale.

Ask yourself these questions before you go for the close. Have you eliminated all the possible objections? Do they really want it? Are there any stones that you have left unturned? Always check with your prospects to determine if the objection has been resolved BEFORE you move forward in the closing process. Ask for the order if your prospects are satisfied that you have responded to their objection. "Now that (state objection) has been resolved, aren't you feeling more confident in becoming a member with us today?" If they say no, ask more questions, uncover more objections and go through the process again until you find the real objection.

Eight five to ninety percent of the objections that you will hear are just smoke screens and are there to dampen your energy level and weigh you down so YOU give up. So, if you are constantly hearing the same objection(s) then you need to re-examine your sales pitch to discover where the objection(s) occurs. Then find a method of eliminating it. Learn from objections you hear because trust me without them you will never make a sale

For you seasoned salespeople, if you get nothing else from this book, **get this**—your sales pitch is your reason for your sales, <u>in your mind</u>. You do not realize that your pitch may also the reason for your inability to make a sale when you hit a slump. If you are talking with a banker, accountant or lawyer and get a 'partner' as an objection, I would hazard a guess that you spent a great deal of time talking about investment, taxes, money or commitment. By doing this you then focused their attention to money matters, hence the objection, "I need to talk to my financial advisor." This also applies when you spend too much time talking about family and show too many pictures to each other. Guess what happens? Then all of a sudden they need to talk to a family member.

So remember this, what you focus the majority of your conversation on during the discovery will usually set your prospects mind on that topic or subject. When commonality and rapport are created around only that one subject, it creates the prominent objection you will hear. Therefore, the biggest objection on your table is what <u>you</u> talk about because that is your only real objection.

Remember deal with all objections in a straight forward, professional and non-argumentative manner . . .

The real secret to mastering overcoming objections is:

> LAUGH. Just laugh when you are in doubt about any objection. If it is a valid objection they will repeat it and if it was a smoke screen they will laugh with you.

Finally there is the one last objection that every salesperson is aiming for, "the price is too high" which was covered in detail in Chapter 9. Now that you have learned how to appreciate objections and use them to your advantage, the next chapter will review more advanced closing techniques to help round out your sales presentation and move you that much closer to becoming a master closer.

16

A Step Above—Master Closing Techniques

Globally we have heard the adages that "he/she can sell snow to an Eskimo" or "sand to an Nomad" but where did they come from? My experience indicates that they rose from regular people, who, through great attitude, determination, perseverance, continual learning, following and understanding the buying curve steps, including repetition to the nth power, honed their skills to be able to "sell snow to an Eskimo" and become exceptional salespeople. But . . . yes there is But involved here! We know that even great sales people cannot close a sale 100% of the time and that there are other salespeople who have done well, but have not reached or realized great success or become exceptional. Why is that?

Well, a large part of writing a sale is using closing techniques effectively. Once you have developed good rapport, communication and discovered all of your prospects dominant buying motives the only thing left is to close the sale. Easier said than done for the majority of salespeople, which is why there are hundreds, if not thousands, of sales books out in the marketplace that list many different types of closes. Some books list "The ten greatest closes," while others have chapters of "The twenty-five greatest closes."

Whichever books you read, including this one, all define variations of the same closes. Let us look at this realistically. Selling and sales have not changed since the first caveman decided to sell his round stone to his neighbor as a means of transportation. The technique of closing a sale is no different now than it was a hundred, or a thousand years ago. It is how you apply those closing techniques that ultimately distinguish you from your peers.

In Chapter 8 we covered the Opinion Orientated; "Yes" Momentum and Involvement Orientated closes as the follow up to doing trial closes. In Chapter 9, I covered the six basic closes: Puppy dog or Adoption; Take Away; Assumptive; Demonstration; Power of Suggestion and Trial. Six additional, intermediate level closes we looked at were: Minor Point, Ascending, Alternate Choice, Hot Button, Third Party and Summary closes. Now, we will look at the closing techniques used by those exceptional and master Closers to achieve those 35% plus closing percentages.

ADVANCED CLOSING TECHNIQUES

1. Approach Close: This is a very strong close that you can use during the pact break or when you meet your prospect. It takes a considerable confidence in your ability to control your prospect when using this close because their sales resistance is at its' maximum. They believe that you are going to sell them and they are determined not to buy anything. This close deflates their resistance and avoids the objections, "Think about it and we need to discuss it with someone."

   For example, say to them, "Jay, Val, let me take a couple of minutes to show you a few of the reasons why so many other people have bought this product, and continue to buy this product. I am not going to try to sell you anything at this time. However, I am going to ask that you look at what I have to show you openly and then determine whether it applies to your particular situation. Then at the end of the presentation you tell me if it applies to you yes or no. Is that fair enough?"

   When you ultimately get to the end of your presentation and are faced with a think about it you can redirect this statement back to them. "Does this apply to your present situation?" If they say yes, then ask, "Well then there must be something that you have not mentioned to me. Could you please tell me what that something might be?" This will usually give you a question or objection.

2. <u>Help me close</u>: This close is very effective if you prospects are not being very cooperative or you cannot seem to find the hidden objection.

    "You know the last people that I toured did not seem very interested in what I was showing them so I went to my manager and ask him what he thought I should do. He told me that I should go through my presentation, bit by bit, then stop and ask you how I was doing. So, the moment that I start to bore you, or you are not interested in what I am saying, please stop me and tell me. If you do this then I will know which part of my presentation needs work. Can you help me?" By asking your prospect to help you will then set up the next close.

3. <u>Changing places close</u>: Find out what they key objection is and change places with them.

    "Okay, put yourself in my place and imagine that you are talking to someone like me, what questions would you want to ask me right now." This will always stimulate them to ask questions about what is important to them and will normally involve credibility, use or money.

    To best handle their response you can counter with, "You know what, those three questions you asked were in the top five [pick any number] that we always get asked. What do you think the other two frequently asked questions are?" This type of close, used effectively will get you not only the objections you are looking for but prospect involvement as well.

4. <u>Ascending close</u>: The ascending close is based on a series of questions, each one leading to the next and each, requiring a yes answer. Similar to a Yes Momentum close this one uses more logic than emotion. The more logical you can make the 'yes' questions then the faster you will close your sale. This is the only instance where logic is used before the sale is completed.

This type of close is used by virtually all encyclopedia sales, life insurance, vacuum cleaner, mutual fund and other sophisticated company salespeople. If you ask enough yes questions the prospect will finally reach a point where they will say, "All right, I will take it."

5. Invitational close: This type of close is an invitation for your prospect to try your product before they buy it. How many times have you heard a salesperson say to you, "Why don't you give it a try?" There are only two ways to go from here. You say "Why not" or you give a reason why you will not.

    Women in sales use this type of close very effectively. Men, on the other hand, are normally more aggressive and this type of close is a little too "warm and fuzzy" for them. Master Closers, however, will never let an opportunity pass without doing an invitational close at the end of their presentation.

6. Feature = Benefit close: The only time you should focus on your products features is when you are showing a comparable benefit. For every feature you mention summarize all the benefits associated with it. Remember to stimulate their desire so that at the end of the presentation they cannot think of anything other than the benefits. Once this happens, assume the close.

7. Summary close: This close lists all the benefits that have value to your prospect, in order of importance, making it a cousin to the previous close. Summarize the benefits to them should they become a member.

8. Ben Franklin close: Similar to a Summary close it is probably the oldest close known to man. You draw a T line on a pad of paper and one side put the heading—Pros (Reasons to do it, Advantages, etc.) and on the other side—Cons (Reasons not to, Disadvantages, etc.) Use whatever type of heading that you think best suits your prospect character.

Under the appropriate heading have your prospect lists all the things that apply to each and then tally them. You will find that you will get twenty good things and only one or two bad things and those will usually apply to money. Then, all you need to do from there is say, "So, apart from the money you folks would be joining our club, yes?" This type of close works very well on Director and Thinker type personalities because they are very detail oriented and to them this is a logical justification to purchase.

I specifically mention the Director and Thinker type personality here but each type of personality can be closed with each type of close. To be a master closer you should have the closes that you use most often designed around each personality type you meet.

9. <u>Sharp Angle Close</u>: This is where you take their objection and turn it around into a closing question and reason to buy. This is very effective when you know that your prospect has run out of resistance <u>and</u> ready to buy.
   a. An example of a sharp angle close would be:
   b. Prospect: "You are crazy I would never pay that interest rate!"
   c. Closer: "So you do not like our interest rate of XX%, is that what you are telling me?"
   d. Prospect: "You bet your ass!"
   e. Closer: "Okay, so if it wasn't for the XX% I would be looking at a new member today?"
   f. Prospect: "Yes"

10. <u>Alternative or Choice close</u>: This close is just as it appears to be because it maneuvers your prospect into a position where they have two or three choices. This type of close takes away your prospects fear of making a decision because no matter what choice they make they have bought the product or service. In simpler terms, any answer they choose will be moving your forward in the sales process.

11. <u>Just Suppose close</u>: This close works very much like the Alternative or Choice close but it has two forms. It does not put pressure on your prospect and allow you to show a benefit or ask another question.

First, in an abbreviated form it can be used if your prospect has made up their mind but is in a "Gee, I am not sure phase." Ask you prospect, "Just suppose you folks were to carry on vacationing after your kids go off to college. Where would you consider going on that vacation?" [This preempts the not vacationing or this is our last vacation objection.]

You could elaborate further by saying to them, "Let us just suppose that you folks were going to do this. I know that you told me you don't think you will be vacationing anymore however I do appreciate your being up front with me about that. Since I have to finish my presentation anyway, let us suppose that you want to go back home and sell this to your friends or family [Referral close], can I show you how it works?" [Demonstration close]

The Just Suppose close allows you to incorporate as many other types of closes as you need to move the presentation forward.

12. <u>Referral close</u>: How many times have you heard from prospects, "You know this does not really sound like it is for us, but my parents, sister . . . could really use something like this."

This is the close where your prospects are trying to avoid you closing them. The best way to use this close is to turn it around using the Power of Suggestion close. "Really, wow, do you really think that your parents would like this? Tell you what, I am going to show you everything about [my product] so that when you get back home you can sell your folks for me, okay?"

They will always agree while at the same time thinking that, "He thinks that we are going to sell it to my folks so we let us pretend we are in the deal." By their assuming this mental position you have empowered them to believe that they are buying on behalf of someone else. Merge this Referral close with an Assumptive close or a Just Suppose close and you will make the sale. Always provide yourself with the opportunity to show your product in an environment that may stimulate <u>their</u> interest.

It is important with the referral close that you are excited about the referral and not let your physiology betray your reaction to their objection. Referrals can be a significant portion of your income if you use this close properly.

13. <u>Boomerang or Reverse Angle close</u>: Take their reason for not buying and toss it back to them, just as you would with an objection.

   a. Prospect: "We do not think that this would be right for us right at this time."
   b. Closer: "That is exactly why you should do something like this."

Every time that you boomerang their response back to them it sounds increasingly ridiculous to the point where they will finally offer up the hidden objection.

14. <u>Walk Away close</u>: This is one of the last types of closes you can use to seal your sale. When you use this close your prospect is into the sale, has the money but still wants to shop around, check prices, see your competition or just knock it around for a while.

There are two ways to handle this. First, if they are a shopper and want to look around some more at this point offer them your First Visit Incentive to make a decision today. Shoppers are normally concerned about money and a First Visit Incentive usually does the trick.

Second, reschedule them for another time if they want to 'knock it around' for a while. Tell them they are done but just before they leave say to them, "Since we are done, what was it that you wanted to knock around until Monday? Is there something that I could help you with? Possibly you need more information or literature perhaps?" Their response will be either they don't know it if is for them or they do not know where the money will come from. Bingo, a new objection will come out and you can start working on another closing angle.

When prospects believe the presentation is over they will give you final objection, which is usually the money. This is why exit and trial programs have been so successful in recent years.

15. <u>Door Knob close</u>: This close, although similar to the walk away close, is the last one you would use. In this instance your prospect obviously will not buy because they are resisting the decision so much they are afraid to offer up the last objection.

The best method to handle this is to say, "Well folks, I appreciate that you have taken the time to listen to me. It is obvious that you are not interested enough to own my product [or service], but before you leave there is just one question I would like to ask you, if I may? [Sure, okay] I have tried to present my product [or service] in the best way that I know. However, I would appreciate it if you would tell me what the real reason was that you did not buy here today?"

Because your prospect believes the presentation to be over and they are no longer under any pressure they will tell you the reason [final objection] why they will not buy. Counter this reasoning with a statement similar to, "You mean I did not really explain that to you properly, this is my fault, let me go over that one more time." Then start closing on the final objection. Again, this is why exit and trial programs are so successful and why there is also that feeling that they received the best deal.

16. <u>Work (or Order) sheet close</u>: This close requires you calling your prospects bluff. This, and the next close, take considerable confidence and should only be used if your prospect is very

compliant and easy to manipulate. This and the Ultimatum close will always stimulate a 'reality' check. Get them real and get a deal.

There are three forms to using this close. The first is very simple. Just fill in the work or order sheet, put it in front of them, ask them to sign it and see what happens. Second, every time that you mention a specific detail or benefit, write it down on the worksheet. By the time you have reached the 'close' they no longer fear the worksheet as they are so used to seeing it will normally sign it. The third is to ask them their pertinent information while completing the work or order sheet by saying something similar to, "What is your exact mailing address so your membership package reaches the right address?" They have made a yes decision if they give you their address.

17. Ultimatum close: Although similar to the worksheet close this one requires, along with filling out the worksheet you do the contracts as well. Once these are done, have them sign them. If they give you no resistance, keep going. You will find that in over ninety percent of the cases your prospect will say to you, "Does this mean we are doing it?" Say yes and congratulate them. If they come back at you with anything other than a signature you still have some work to be done.

The ultimatum close is most often the easiest way to close a deal. You move forward with much energy, excitement, confidence and ASSUME everything. If no objections come out, you made a sale.

18. Intimidation close: This close is designed to embarrass and pressure your prospect into buying. Use this close only if feel you are confident enough to intimidate without creating confrontation—remember that deadly sin mentioned in section 2. For example, say to them, "Look, you folks need this in your life and since I am not taking no for an answer . . . so which one of you has the neatest hand writing?"

19. Origami close: This close involves the art of paper folding and considerable practice before using it on prospect. This is only done at the very end of your presentation when your prospect is firm on not buying anything.

    First, take the worksheet and fold it in half. As you are doing this tell your prospect that all the information that they need to purchase is included on that sheet. If they leave without making a decision they will automatically forget half of what they have heard. Then fold the paper in half again, creating a one-fourth sized piece of paper. Remind them that should they wait until later that day they will only remember one quarter of what you told them. [It is important that you carefully watch their reaction as you fold the paper.] Fold the paper again to make it one-eighth sized and say that if they wait until morning they will retain only one-eighth. After that, fold it into a piece one-sixteenth size. Now, tell them that should they wait a couple of days they will barely remember anything so how can they possibly make a decision on such little information.

    Then, instead of folding it to half that size, unfold it back to its' original size. Ask them if it would not be better to make a decision with all the information in front of them. This simple close works very effectively at showing the prospect that the longer they put off their decision the less they will remember about the benefits. Just remember, practice this one so that you can do it smoothly without taking your eyes off your prospect. It creates a better effect.

20. Einstein close: This is a variation of the Origami close. Einstein once stated that, "Homo-sapiens only retain 40% of what they have heard and seen after twenty-four hours, so how can you possibly make a good decision with only 40% of the information? Wouldn't you rather make a decision knowing 100% of the information?"

21. List the Objections close: This close requires you asking your prospect to write down all of their 'reasons' for not buying and

sign it so that you can present it to your manager. Tell your prospect that you need the information so that management can keep track of the reasons why people do not buy. It makes the prospect see for himself how silly or ridiculous his objections are, especially when he has to sign off on them before he leaves.

You will notice that the prospect will never complete listing all of their 'reasons.' They soon realize they do not want to sign it in front of their family because they were just excuses made up to avoid a decision. In most cases they will tell you that the real objection is the money which you suspected all along.

22. <u>Objection close</u>: Throughout your presentation you should have been closing on objections. Remember there are no sales without objections so your ability to close on objections becomes crucial. The best way to use this close is each time your prospect gives you an objection turn it around into a question.

    Remember, that there will always be one last ditch objection that your prospect will give you. It will probably be nothing more than a smoke screen, so just smile and ask them to sign the worksheet. The real objection will pop out quickly enough.

23. <u>Price close</u>: You will hear your prospect tell you that it is not the right time for them. Well, nobody can ever afford anything the first time it is mentioned or is it ever the right time. At the end of this chapter I will cover this close in more detail.

There are many other types of closes used in sales however I chose not to include them because I have seen these 23 described above work so effectively over the years that I recommend them. As I said earlier, there are thousands of sales books out there if you want more, but mainly they are a repetition of what I have already shown above or are not as effective as they once were. Remember, prospects are no longer naive in the ways of sales, despite the ease in which they appear to be taken in by closing techniques therefore I have included those closes that are the most effective in today's marketplace.

All the above closes, including those previously covered can be used at any point in your presentation. Use the closes that best suit your personality and adapt them to use with the different types of prospect characteristics. Practice them until they become a natural part of your presentation.

CREATIVE SELLING TECHNIQUES

For thousands of years salespeople have been using whatever methods they can dream up to sell people their wares. In more modern times salespeople were then encouraged to 'think on their feet,' but in today's relationship sale, salespeople need to think creatively.

Creative salespeople have a distinct competitive advantage because their fellow salespeople and their competitors do not know what they did. Creativity at the point of sale can never be copied by anyone else because it is intangible. Products are products the world over and it is the ability to be creative that separates the competent salesperson from the master closer.

Creative Selling—Creativity is a natural characteristic in all exceptional salespeople. It is a matter of believing in oneself. Every time that you are trying to convince someone of something you are engaging in a highly creative act. If you believe that you are creative you will be continually coming up with creative solutions to problem situations. Unfortunately, most people do not think that they are particularly creative. You will never be creative if you do not you believe in yourself.

Creativity is stimulated by focused questions, by pressing problems and burning goals. The more intense we are on achieving something the more creative we are. The more focus and specific the questions are the more creative we become in answering them.

There are several areas where creativity is useful.

1. Uncovering buying motive: You have to be very creative when finding out what prompts a prospect to buy. Because they are

2. Get over 'think about it.' In chapter 18 we learned that 'think about it' is not really an objection, but a camouflage for something else. As such, you need creativity to delve under the camouflage and find the real objection.

3. Find new ways to promote your product. Finding new ways to use old products requires considerable creativity.

4. Creating a sale where none previously existed. Every sale you attempt a sale it is an act is pure creativity. You must first create the sale in your mind and then use both your product and your prospects information to put together a business transaction where none existed before.

Remember people buy on emotion not logic. There is no logical reason why people buy your product or service. They buy it because you make them feel good and create a *use or need* where none existed before. You stimulate an emotion using creativity. Later on they and you can justify the sale with logic.

You can sell anything to anybody if you are creative. You do not need tricks to sell anything. The only real trick is for you to become excited and believe in yourself and your product enough to get your prospect enthusiastic enough to buy it. Remember, effective communication is 7% words, 35% voice inflections and 55% physiology or body language.

SMOKE AND MIRRORS (KINKS AND PUFFS)

Are you wondering why I am mentioning "Smoke and Mirrors, Kinks and Puffs" if you do not need tricks to sell? In the old days of sales the only things that salespeople wanted to hear, or wanted to learn was another shtick that they could use. If they could not get a new shtick then they wanted dream up some other trick that they could to get their prospect to buy. In today's relationship sale prospects are too intelligent and educated to the ways of sales that these old 'tricks' can no longer be used.

Granted, there are some salespeople still using these old 'tricks' and looking for that 'magical' shtick to get them a sale. There are also some shticks out there that will turn a sale, but those sales will normally not be very solid and a real pain in the ass to get through the paperwork. Then salespeople spend the 'rescission' period nervous because they think the sale is going to cancel and they will not be paid. Instead of closing the deal solidly on emotion and desire, deception is added because that is what the salesperson thought the prospect wanted to hear.

You should never have to lie or deceive a prospect when trying to sell them because the chances they will find out are not in your favor. If you back door your prospects do not stay in this business. There are two types of people who back door their prospects—one is a burglar, the other is a bad salesperson. Back door salespeople sell on rescission, cancellation or creating the image that they have not bought yet.

A master closer will always let the prospect kink or puff the sale themselves. The secret to kinks or puffs is to **plant seeds**. <u>Let your prospect do the majority of exaggerating the benefits of your product themselves</u>. By using third party stories to plant seeds you can make a prospect think that your product or service does more than they think it can without specifically telling them something that may not true.

You have a responsibility to your specific industry and your prospect. Do not abuse and create unrealistic expectations in your product to obtain the easy sale. All you need to do is just work a little harder and gauge what is acceptable and just.

For example you can create a 'greed' emotion by planting seeds and let your prospects imagination take over for you. In the scenario below the salesperson relayed a third party story about a member who actively rents his membership.

> Salesperson: "Can you think of any way to rent this?"
> Prospect: "Could we . . . rent I mean? . . . Well, we could rent it to our friends because they want to go to South Africa and have said that the hotel wants $300 a

	night. However if we charged them $200 a night instead we could make $1,400."
Salesperson:	"Hey, if you can get $200 a night, not only are the maintenance fees paid for a couple of years but the developer might have to send you a job application. However, please make sure that you do this according to the bylaws"

Your prospect is the one sitting there 'kinking' their own sale. You laid the seed you nurtured it and put sunlight on it. Then your prospect takes over with the "could we do this" or "is it possible to do this" or "is there any restriction on doing this?" Be professional and say no. Remember, No is a very strong closing tool.

This further enhances your prospects credibility in the product because they thought of the solution—you did not sell them on it. As an example you can ask them:

Salesperson:	"Do you own your home?"
Prospect:	"Yes, yes we do."
Salesperson:	"Are you allowed to rent it out if you want to?"
Prospect:	"Of course you can."
Salesperson:	"What would you charge for rent and who determines that?"
Prospect:	"Well, we do. I mean who else but we would know what to charge to rent out our house?"

Once your prospect starts comparing their real life to what they can do with your product or service you can congratulate them on their ability to "get the hang of this stuff." This is the art of allowing your prospect to close themselves. It is important that if you are going to plant seeds for a puff or kink, before you open your mouth, ask yourself "**will this help me write this sale**?"

In many instances telling your prospects the truth or by telling them the real deal, you can empower them with another objection. "No, I am afraid that is not an option with our program." Turn around and use their puff or kink as a take-away. By not lying you will get the objections and resistance that you want. However, if you lie to a prospect and they know that you are lying, you are now providing them with an excuse to not buy. Additionally, if you lie or deceive it does not give you any satisfaction except a bad sale. It also does not give you any longevity in sales or a sense of accomplishment.

No one ever buys anything that is made easy for them because they do not perceive any value in it. You must make your prospects step up and feel as if they are earning the deal you are offering them. So, think, <u>if I use a kink or puff is it going to help me write the sale</u>? Do not lie, puff or kink the sale. If the only thing that a puff or kink would do is keep the reputation of "ripping off their customers or scamming people" in your industry then definitely do not do it.

Remember, if you cannot or do not write the sale, your prospect should leave the presentation with a better understanding and more positive image of you and your industry than they did when they arrived. Do not let them keep their preconceived idea that your business is a rip off or a scam. It is not.

So, lay the seeds have fun, be creative and soon you will have all the angles that you need to close the sale.

TRICKS

Well, now that you are familiar with using 'smoke and mirrors' let us move on to 'tricks and tools.' It is important that you remember that you should have built a solid relationship with your prospect before using any 'tricks and tools' to enhance it. *Do not use any of the techniques in this chapter unless you have built rapport, commonality and trust.* If you have not developed curiosity and desire in your product or service, or they are not asking you any questions, using any of the techniques outlined in this chapter will only hurt you, not help you. You must never allow the decision making process to stop. Never give your prospect an opportunity to change their mind.

You can have double the impact if you use these 'tricks' after you have created curiosity, questions and desire. Your prospect will want to listen and participate and, most importantly, they will retain the information that you are giving them. Once they are listening and participating they will begin to see value and create urgency.

Salespeople may also use 'tricks' in conjunction with 'smoke and mirrors' to prompt a buying decision. In the following pages I will cover the most effective 'tricks' that are currently being used in sales. Successful salespeople know exactly when or where in their presentation that these 'tricks' will provide the most impact on their prospect. Again, there are many salespeople who fail to recognize how effective these 'tricks' can be because they are afraid to use, or try, them.

Twenty-Two Real "Tricks" to Help You Close Your Sale

I will start off with simple 'tricks' and end with more advanced ones that you can use.

1. <u>The Survey Sheet or Questionnaires</u>: In chapter 4 we established that it was important to fill out the survey sheet or questionnaires to gain as much information as we could about our prospects. This trick helps to initiate the discovery process.

   The trick here is to encourage them to complete the survey sheet. Be sincere in telling them that it important <u>and</u> for informational or research reasons only. The survey sheet is a very credible trick to gain information about your prospect if spoken about with conviction.

2. <u>Give them things to do</u>: Again, we did cover this in previous chapters. However by giving them things to do they are actively participating in closing themselves. So give them a calculator, a pen and a pad of paper to make notes. Get them to write down what the highlights of their last vacation were so that you can share it with them and gain more information. The trick here is

that everything will become easier because the prospect feels that they are adding or contributing to the closing process.

3. Credit Applications: The credit application, when used correctly can gain you credibility as you begin the qualification process. The trick here is when they are completing the application they are stepping up in the sales process. By filling out forms your prospects then become used to participating in the presentation and a mode or rhythm is created.

4. Picking three vacation spots: An option to simply flipping through exchange catalogues or magazines is to choose three locations and tell a related third party story to create a mental picture for your prospect. The destinations should reflect where your prospect has vacationed in the past, where they are thinking of going soon and a place that represents their dream vacation. The trick here is that it creates a distinction between their current situation and the one they desire.

5. Use your prospects information against them: At the beginning of your sales presentation you should ask your prospect three questions:
    a) How much do they presently spend, per night, on their vacations?
    b) How many weeks (nights) vacation do they take in a year?
        c) How long they anticipate vacationing? For example: $90/ night x 19 nights = $1,700 x 30 years = $51,000 not including inflation.

    Then use all the information that they provide to show them how inexpensive your product or service would be for them during the same period. The trick here is that they now have an emotional and a logical reason to buy. It does not really matter what the numbers are, just that you are using their numbers and their emotional reasons for vacationing, it appears better if they buy from you.

6. <u>The 1-10 Test</u>: You can use this little trick at any point in your presentation as it is a barometer of your prospects mental state.

"Can I ask you folks something?" [Sure] "On a scale of 1 to 10—10 meaning to join the club today, and one wanting to get the heck out of here, I would like to know where you are at right now based on everything you have heard (or seen) so far? You cannot choose five because it is too ambiguous, it is too much like sitting on a fence."

If they say two, three or four you have not done much work and need create more desire or show more value. Keep building value and telling third party stories until you get a number around eight or uncover more objections or fears. If they say eight, you are at the magic number. If they say nine they are not real and need something to jolt them into reality. If they say ten, you have the "Brady Bunch" sitting in front of you. If you have get the number nine or ten, use more trial closes and tie downs because you have not been asking enough questions that require yes responses. There are instances however where your prospect may offer a nine or ten and mean it. These are 'lay downs' which only need to have a few details sewn up and you have yourself a sale.

7. <u>Show a vested interest in your product or service</u>: If you let your prospect know that you have a vested interest in what you are prompting they will become curious. Your enthusiasm and excitement then become contagious.

For example, you have a Harley Davidson owner in front of you. These folks believe in their club so much that they cannot believe that no one else can see any value or benefit in owning a Harley. Use this sense of ownership and pride to cross the bridge by showing that your product can provide them with the same feeling (benefits).

8. <u>Use your prospects remorse</u>: This 'trick' will usually get you a sale when used properly. If you are not careful, it may backfire

on you. When your prospects come to a presentation they are angry, hostile and negative. Let them be negative with you for as long as it takes for them to release these emotions. When they are done they will feel remorse for venting their anger at you. Depending on the level of remorse your prospect feels you can use it as a closing technique. When people feel remorse they feel guilty and when they feel guilty they buy to appease the guilt.

A good example of this is when a parent yells at a child and sends them to their room because they have misbehaved. Later, when the parent feels guilty for punishing the child they take them out for ice cream to appease their guilt.

9. <u>Use their hot buttons against them</u>: Use their hot buttons to stimulate them to get more information so that when you begin to close you can use them up as a reason to buy. It is important that you do not use all of them at once. Use them only when you feel it is necessary to stimulate a buying emotion and then use a trial close or tie down to seal it.

   For example, say, "Jay, you told me that spending your vacations together as a family was very important to you, what other things does your family do together on vacations?"

10. <u>Little Yes's</u>: In a number of chapters I have covered the importance of having your prospect get into the habit of saying yes. Little yes's are from simple, non-threatening questions that have nothing to do with your presentation but keep your prospects saying yes. For example,
    a) "It is a beautiful day, isn't it?"
    b) "Do you believe that you need more money to do everything you want to do?"
    c) "Do you like . . . ?"

11. <u>Twelve phrases to stimulate concessions:</u> Following are twelve phrases that you can use to offer a concession in return for a concession. If you can memorize half of these you will see a

noticeable difference in your closing percentage and by using all of them your closing ratio will increase dramatically.

a) "**If I could show you a way** that we could get what you really want, would you be willing to let me finish doing my presentation?"

b) "Did you know that . . ."

c) "Would you be interested in . . . ?"

d) "If you could have . . ."

e) "Would you like to see . . . ?"

f) "How would you like to have . . . ?"

g) "Can you imagine yourself . . . ?"

h) "Have you ever seen . . . ?"

i) "Does it surprise you to learn that . . . ?"

j) "Don't you think (or feel) that . . . ?"

k) "May I tell you (or ask you) about . . . ?"

l) "Why is that . . . ?"

12. <u>Compliment and Admonish</u>. The premise here is to compliment your prospect when they say or do something positive and to admonish them when they say something silly or negative. This strategy reinforces positive behavior so that you prospects become inclined to continue giving honest information. Admonishment discourages negative behavior by making it more difficult for them to 'get away' with it.

The trick is to use the admonishment. Do not let the negative comments pass without responding to them. To admonish effectively, roll back your eyes and show an expression of disbelief. Say something akin to, "I cannot believe that you said that, we must be having a communication problem here." Then ask the question reinforcing the positive way to deal with what you are discussing.

Examples of some admonishments are:

a) "Hang on a minute. You point is well taken on the surface. However if I could get you to let me finish with what I was saying, you might appreciate seeing the advantages for yourself."

b) "Wait a minute please. I disagree with that statement. However could you at least give me an opportunity to finish the rest of my presentation, before you decide one way or the other is that fair enough?"

c) "Really, I couldn't disagree with you more . . . ."

d) "Excuse me, maybe I shouldn't say this so bluntly, but seriously . . ."

Say, "Seriously, let me ask you a question . . ." if the behavior warrants a serious admonishment. You can also laugh in your prospects face. Both have the same effect. Later on your prospect will apologize for their rude behavior.

13. <u>Cloverleaf your prospect:</u> This trick here is to take a prospect who is determined in repeatedly interrupting you and returns the conversation to where you were before the interruption. You do this by asking them specific questions.

For example your prospect repeatedly makes one or more of the following statements:

a) "Cut to the chase, what is the price?"

b) "Let's skip all of these pleasantries and get to the sales pitch."

c) "Okay, how much is it?"

You must use discretion and exercise control when you use this technique. Your response should be done in as gently a fashion as possible without creating either a confrontation or interruption.

d) "It is important that you asked that question and I will be glad to answer it for you. However at this time it would be very premature to discuss pricing until we have reached agreement on what type of program would work best for you. So moving along let so let me ask you . . ."

Being able to twist and turn the conversation around just like a cloverleaf can be a very effective closing technique when mastered.

14. <u>Learning when to Agree and Disagree:</u> This trick can be used very persuasively when mastered. It allows the salesperson to direct their prospects experiences into positive feelings regardless of how negative their previous experiences have been.

<u>Agreement</u>: Many prospects attend sales presentations with pre-conceived notions and/or experiences and, as such, salespeople are traditionally stereotyped with the same stamp. To create commonality instead of confrontation agreeing with them can make your prospect re-examine their expectations about you or your product. For example,

a) "You are right, I am a salesperson, however to include me with those experiences you have previously had would be unfair, wouldn't it?"
b) "Exactly, our product (service) did (or does) have some bad times however we have done a number of things to change that image, may I tell you about some of them?"

<u>Disagreement</u>: In other instances it may be important for you to disagree with their notion.

a) "No, I may be a salesperson but I am nothing like those others you have had in the past as you will see if you will let me ask you a couple of questions?"
b) "I am sorry to hear you have had negative experiences in the past, however our product (service) is nothing like what you have described. May I explain to you how our program works . . . ?"

Though this trick may appear simple it is your ability to master it that will create credibility and rapport rather than not using it and having their negative experiences affect your sales presentation.

15. <u>The Domino Theory</u>: Almost everyone is familiar with the Domino theory. Its' premise is that it is never just one thing, but a series of errors, events or problems that all culminate in one negative result. For example, it was not the iceberg that caused the Titanic to sink it was the result of a series of errors.

    The trick to using this theory is to control the dominos. Master Closers have learned that the sales process (result) is not made or lost by only one objection or incident, but a series of things. The power of the domino theory is that not all the objections, trial closes, tie downs, third party stories, etc., be perfect or perfectly handled to work. There is a certain margin for error allowed as it is never one single instance that will make or break your sale.

    When using the Domino theory in sales you must retain control because once you set it in motion it will continually move forward and will not be stoppable. You must know where you are going so that you can deliberately deal with certain elements that could otherwise become the iceberg to your Titanic sales process.

16. <u>Reciprocity:</u> The master closer will give one piece of information, then ask a question. From the answer received they will give another piece of information and ask another question. By doing this throughout your sales presentation you are always getting responses, keeping your prospect alert, interested and involved in the presentation.

17. <u>Creating ownership dissatisfaction</u>: This trick or technique is used when you are working with prospects who already own some form of your product or service. You are looking to create dissatisfaction with what they already own and promote yours as the solution. For example,

<u>Existing owners in your project</u>: You already have a *use* factor so go ahead and congratulate them on being owners. Fifty-five percent of people who buy, buy under their requirements so you must find out what prompted them to buy initially and use that technique. At the same time listen carefully for any negatives and use them to create dissatisfaction with their existing membership. This trick usually results in the owner upgrading or buying additional weeks.

Remember, on initial purchase or in the case of first time buyers, little money = little decision or risk factor. Big money = big decision or risk factor therefore most first time buyers do not buy everything they need and therefore become a potential upgrade prospect.

<u>Owners on exchange to your project</u>: Again you already have a *use* factor so go ahead and congratulate them on being owners. Use the same methodology as with an existing owner in your project.

<u>Package deals or independent travelers</u>. You must find a *use* factor and stimulate it. With these types of prospects you can create a situation where they are being taken advantage of by their travel agents or hotels. Show them the differences between owning and renting. Let them know that in 1983 6% of timeshare prospects owned and now 58% of prospects own. The industry must be doing something right.

18. <u>Taking advantage</u>: A trick you can use to increase the emotional state of your prospect is to tell them that they have been taken advantage of by their travel agent, previous supplier, etc. People hate being taken advantage of. Since they may think of you as the bad guy, turn the tables around and focus on exactly who IS taking advantage of them. People will go on a mission to discover where their excess money is going if they feel that they have been used or taken advantage of.

19. <u>Power of Suggestion</u>: Successful salespeople know that the power of suggestion has a tremendous effect on prospects. By being calm, confident, relaxed, easy going, well groomed and speak with authority you can strongly influence both your prospect and your environment.

    By planting seeds throughout a sales presentation you can affect the subconscious of your prospect. People, including prospects, make decisions based on the stories they hear and word pictures they see. The human brain can hold millions of pictures and stories and that is why successful salespeople always talk in word pictures about their product or service. Use third party stories to influence your prospect.

20. <u>Have fun with your prospects</u>: All people hate being sold, although everyone loves to buy. Talk to your prospect as you would a friend at a party, without boring them and enjoy them. People always buy from people they like and trust.

21. <u>Assume the sale</u>: This is probably the hardest thing for most salespeople to do. Master closers automatically assume that their prospect has bought from them. "When you become a member of our club you will," instead of, "if you become a member . . ."

22. <u>Use, Understanding, Feeling and Affordability</u>: In the last chapter we used these four questions to box money, however you can also use them as a prelude to using your closing 'tools.'

    a) **"Can you really USE this?"** [Pick up the survey sheet and remind them that they do vacation X number of weeks per year and then say, "Yes, you can definitely USE this, can't you!" This is a statement, not a question and is assuming the sale.]

    "Do you fully UNDERSTAND all the benefits of the membership? Do you UNDERSTAND the way our program works?"

"Do you **FEEL** that everything I have shown you here today is totally credible? Do you think that I may be trying to rip you off?" Continue with, "Because if you think that I am trying to rip you off then you will think that my company is going to as well"

Ask them this. Turn this rock over because it is the number one reason why people do not buy. They do not believe that you or your company will stand behind the product or service once the sale has been completed. Tell your prospects that 89% of people will say yes to the first three, then that 89% will say no to the last one. Most people can use it, do understand it and do not think that you are trying to rip them off but the only reason they do not buy is this last question.

"Is this (product or service) **AFFORDABLE** for you?" [No] Then, what they are telling you is that the only reason you would not do this today is the money?" You could also say to them, "So apart from the money I would be looking at a new member here today?"

Learn to master these twenty-two tricks and you will increase your closing percentage dramatically.

TOOLS

The most effective tool used successfully by salespeople to create urgency in their sales is by using **First Visit Incentive's**.

First Visit Incentives were designed to provide your prospect with a better price and create the urgency that is required to motivate your prospect into making a buying decision today. It is important to understand that the First Visit Incentive's alone are not enough to get you a sale. They are only designed to provide a better price and create urgency. If you prospect has no desire for your product or service then any First Visit Incentive's or price that you show them is irrelevant.

Before you show any FIRST VISIT INCENTIVE'S make sure that you have done the following:

- All objections have been overcome with the exception of money;
- You have a firm commitment from your prospect that they like your program;
- You have a firm commitment that they can use it;
- You have a firm money box and verified where they money is coming from;
- You have completed the necessary worksheets showing gross pricing;
- You have asked your prospect for the order at your gross pricing;
- You have explained to them what First Visit Incentives are and how they work.

First Visit Incentive's should be credible and realistic offers to create urgency in your prospect. If they look too good to be true, or look as if you are dropping your price too obviously, you will lose credibility and your sale. You will also hear, "You know what, we need to take some time and think about it."

To help eliminate your possibly entry into the seven deadly sin area, here is a third party story that I have used to help keep my credibility, deal with the "think about it" response and still include the importance of First Visit Incentives. (It can also be used to break the pact)

> Jay, Val I need to share something very important with you before we get started, I give 100% of myself to every client I tour and truly focus my presentation on how to increase the quality of their vacations and hopefully save them thousands of dollars. Now most people I speak to attended the presentation with a mindset of no intention of buying, or even looking at what I have to show, but at the end a large percentage of them are intrigued and seriously consider owning but just can't move forward today and end up walking out without becoming members and I have no problem with that!

However a couple of years ago I was touring a client around the resort and felt a poke in my back, I turned around and a sweet old lady was standing there with a nasty look on her face, "yes, I thought that was you" she said, "do you remember me?" "Vaguely," I repeated. "Well three years ago you were our consultant and showed us around here even though we had only come in for the gift. After your presentation we were very interested in becoming members but my husband just couldn't bring himself to sign up on the day. Therefore we left discussing what we had heard and seriously considering coming back, however while walking down the street we were approached by a young man offering us a rental car for free in return for attending his presentation. It seemed like a good deal, so off we went the next day up in the mountains and met our salesperson whom showed us a similar (or so we thought) program to yours. When he showed us this exchange catalogue we just assumed you guys where part of the same company. Therefore when he assured us that the resort would be built within the next year we believed him. He was a lot more aggressive than you and gave us what we thought was a better deal. Anyway we ended up buying and guess what? They never built it and we lost our money, bottom line if you would have been a bit more assertive and demanded us to say yes or no we would be owners here. Can you help us get our money back?" Well I couldn't help them and thought Wow! If I was a better salesperson they would be happy owners.

So here is the deal guys I never want that to happen again so no matter what the condition, objection or feeling about what I am going to show you today just give me a thumbs up YES or a thumbs down NO and that will never happen to me again Fair Enough ? Shake hands"

If your prospect still does not want your product or service after you have shown First Visit Incentive's then ask them to sign a First Visit Incentive's Release Letter before they leave. First Visit Incentive's Release Letters waive your prospects ability to come back later and take advantage of the price offered. Make sure that you read the First Visit Incentive's Release Letter with your prospect so that there are no misunderstandings about what they are forfeiting. Then have them sign that they are declining the First Visit Incentive's.

As an example, a chain store offers watches on a 50% discount on watches during a sales promotion. The sale covers specific beginning and ending dates. You choose not to buy a watch however a week after the sale ends you change your mind and go back to the store. You ask for the 50% discount but are told you will have to pay full price. Why? Because the sale is over and if they sold you that watch at that 50% discount they would be opening up the 'flood gates.' This is why sale flyers, catalogues and First Visit Incentives or Limited Time Offers are all time specific—it is the law. It is important to understand that First Visit Incentive's will vary from location to location, sales environment to sales environment, company to company and project to project and some companies may not offer them at all.

Remember, products are products the world over BUT it is the ability to be creative and be creative by using Smoke and Mirrors, Tricks and Tools is what separates the competent salesperson from the master closer.

Well, that's about it, I have covered everything that you need for those individuals who sincerely wish to succeed at not only being the best, but becoming an exceptional salesperson or master closer. You must be prepared to acquire a higher level of human interaction. This can only be done by continually learning and studying. Therefore, if you learn the principles or methods that I have outlined in this book you will be successful in sales. Further combine them with the right attitude a strong commitment and an infallible belief in yourself you will become a master closer. The secret to closing a sale is the foundation that you have built in the front end of your sales presentation by learning and understanding your prospects character type and behavior.

In conclusion, if you have learned nothing other than the most effective, bottom line strategy in selling is to keep it simple. Focus on your prospects character type more specifically their dominant buying emotions then ask for the order you will be well on your way to becoming a successful salesperson.

Remember what Emerson said, "If you learn only methods you will forever be tied to your methods . . . but if you learn the principles behind the methods you can develop your own techniques and be successful in any environment."

From this point forward the only thing left is to get paid on your sale. The next section—Coming Full Circle, including understanding how customer service is directly proportional to your commission and will show you how to set and achieve your goals.

SECTION 4

COMING FULL
CIRCLE

- Expanding your
horizons to be
succesfull

17

Customer Satisfaction = Your Commission

Remember back in chapter 9 I stated—when the decision has been made, congratulate them. Stop selling. This is very important. Do not give any more information on top of what you already have given them. It will not only confuse them, but you may inadvertently give them the opportunity of objecting to something new—remember those deadly sins!

Reaffirm their decision to purchase.

> "Congratulations, you are going to love this!"
> "Congratulations, you have made a wise decision."
> "Congratulations, can you do me a favor and send me a postcard from where you go next year."

Any technicality or detail that may arise will go out the window once you have sincerely congratulated them. Help them feel comfortable then seal and solidify the commitment with a handshake.

Traditionally, after people buy something they tend to be excited and enthusiastic. While this enthusiasm is what you have been striving for, you must now calm them down and bring them back to earth. Thus, it becomes very important that once the decision has been made that you totally remove yourself from the decision. Immediately take your conversation back to the warm-up stage. It is this friendly, warm positive conversation that your prospect, now turned client, takes away with them.

AFTER THE SALE

Remember, no matter what the purchase, the bigger the price tags the greater level of post-sale concern. Experienced sales professionals are acutely aware of this phenomenon. Commonly called Buyer's Remorse, exceptional salespeople will take any, and all, steps to minimize its' effects.

It is important that you treat your prospect turned client with just as much respect, courtesy and enthusiasm after the sale as when you greeted them. Make the after sale conversation light and chatty. Go back to your life raft to find something that makes them feel comfortable and safe. You can also use humor as a way to break any remaining tension they may be experiencing by saying something like,

> "Okay, so where are you folks are going to dinner tonight . . . can I make a suggestion . . . maybe you could take me with you . . . relax, I was just kidding!"

If they have a smart phone or camera with them, take their picture. Better yet, have someone take a picture of you and them as a 'family.' This reinforces the belief that you will indeed take care of them and help further eliminate any remaining skepticism.

CONFRONTING BUYER'S REMORSE

Most salespeople can identify with that sinking feeling they get when they think their new client is going to cancel the sale. If, however, you have done everything correctly by creating rapport and commonality, eliminating their objections and stimulating their desire, then chances are your new client will not feel buyer's remorse. If, however, your client still has hidden objections or fears, they will usually bring them to light after the sale and get buyer's remorse.

It is the master closer who will actively confront the possibility of buyer's remorse, rather than ignore it. You can do this in any number of ways—either as a suggestion or as an outright statement. The suggestion, for example, might be "If the product or service does not meet your expectations, it can be changed or modified to accommodate your needs so are there anything I may have perhaps overlooked." An example of an outright statement would be, "Now that you have made the decision to become an owner is there anything that could happen that would cause you to change your mind?"

If you have been up front, honest and sincere in your relationship with them to this point they will appreciate your forthrightness. It takes a strong, confident personality and belief in yourself and your product to actively confront this issue. If your prospect (client) responds with a concern, address it immediately. If, however, they indicate that everything is fine, then tell them, "If you are ever unhappy with me or my product please let me know immediately so that we can take care of it."

A trick that I use to eliminate buyer's remorse is to immediately try to sell them more. When you do this one of two things will happen. First, they will think that you are 'out of your mind' for asking them to buy again (natural reaction). Then they will say something such as, "No, we are happy with what we just bought thank you." Second, they might still think you are 'out of your mind' but will buy more of your product or service. Whichever the response, you have eliminated buyer's remorse.

If your new client wishes to cancel the sale because of buyer's remorse, accept it. Buyer's remorse is a fact of life in sales. Do not be afraid of it and not only learn to live with it, learn from it.

POST-SALE CONCERNS

Chapter 9 covered the importance of buttoning up your sale. Here, I am going to repeat the importance of not only doing some form of follow up and we will also look at maintaining that positive customer satisfaction so that you will be paid your commission. It is your behavior after the sale that will swing the pendulum either to or away from buyer's remorse.

First you should always button up your sale. Make it a point to do something with your prospect turned client after the sale to seal the deal and say thank you. Take them to breakfast, lunch or dinner. Buy them a few drinks or take them golfing, fishing or sightseeing. When you socialize with your clients the odds of turning your business association into a long-term personal friendship are greatly enhanced. Possibly, you are the type of salesperson who buys them a small thank you gift. Whatever method you choose the purpose of buttoning up, or following up on your sale is to reassure your client that they made the right decision in going ahead with the purchase. Start aggressively using these methods to your advantage.

Along with buttoning up you sales you should also make every effort to ensure the balance of their visit or trial period is enjoyable. Provide them with a map highlighting area attractions or shopping areas for her and sport bars for him. Give them a list of restaurants, including your favorites, from inexpensive to higher price for them to choose from. Let them know where they can take tours, play golf, fish and gamble, see the sights or go to that romantic, secluded spot that only you know how to find. Offer them anything that you believe will make their vacation more memorable.

ASKING FOR REFERRALS AND NETWORKING

The only way to get referrals, are to ask for them. Never underestimate the power of commonality and a personal endorsement. New or existing clients are your best source of valuable information on what people buy and use. See every sale that you make as a business transaction and, as such, you should make every effort to expand your business opportunities. In today's competitive world salespeople need every advantage that they can in which to get ahead. Remember it is your creativity in how you approach your prospects and clients that makes you a master closer.

Unfortunately, many salespeople feel uncomfortable asking their 'new' clients for referrals because they feel that they have not yet earned the right to ask until their client is satisfied with their purchase. Remember, that new buyers are on an emotional high <u>and</u> in a positive frame of mind so by asking for a referral you will positively reinforce their decision. It also backs up your confidence in the value of your product or service.

The best prospect for referrals is the client that you have just sold. The second best prospects are the ones referred to you by your new client. The third best is a prospect that has been referred by a friend, family member or a trusted business associate. The endorsement and testimonial of others will make your new prospect much more comfortable about opening up and listening to you.

When you have completed the sale, always ask your new client if they know of someone who might be interested in your product or service. In most cases they will give you at least one person that you can contact. In addition, give them a few of your business cards. One business card for them to keep and the rest to give away to whomever they choose. The more business cards that you give away, the greater the chance of someone calling you to ask about your product or service.

PROBLEMS AND COMPLAINTS

You, like everyone else, would rather hear compliments, however as a rule, people are far more inclined to complain than compliment. Welcome complaints from your clients. If they are complaining to you then they are not complaining to *potential* clients, posting it on Facebook, Tweeting, LinkedIn or IM'ing anyone.

Unfortunately, there are still a large percentage of marketers and companies who fail to appreciate this approach. Ignoring problems and clients may have worked fifty years ago when there was little or no competition however now it becomes a recipe for disaster. You should <u>want</u> to solve your client's problems and complaints. Because, if you try to duck or weave your way around the problem, you are not only taking away an opportunity to solve it, but you are also decreasing the possibility of doing more business. Remember, if you make an effort to solve your client's problem, they will remain your client.

Here is a quote by former IBM Chief Executive Thomas Watson, Jr. that best describes handling client problems or complaints.

> "Solve it. Solve it quickly. Solve it right or wrong. If you solve it wrong, you can solve it right later. Lying dead in the water and doing nothing is a comfortable alternative because it seems without risk. However it is an absolutely fatal way to manage a business."[5]

It is those clients that bring complaints or problems to your attention that deserve thanks and quick, decisive action on those complaints. Remember, you got the sale originally because you created a problem with your prospects previous product or service. If you keep this attitude clearly in your mind then you will reap far more monetary rewards than by ignoring the problem and having your client cancel. Never take for granted that the next salesperson will take advantage of your client's problem or complaint with your product or service.

Therefore, when you approach a new prospect, take a few minutes to determine what level you and your prospects are going to be on before launching into your sales presentation. Work on eliminating problems and complaints from the beginning, especially if you are in an industry that is already suspected. Learn to listen to your prospects and clients because without them you will not survive in sales.

CUSTOMER SERVICE

The first, and only, rule for good customer service, is that you keep in touch with your clients. If you do, then your business and bank account will grow beyond your wildest dreams.

Take the time to send a postcard, short note, birthday or Christmas cards. With today's internet accessibility consider friending them on Facebook, sending an E-mail message or texting them. Find out when

---

[5]   Quoted is excerpted from "The Greatest Capitalist in History" - Fortune Magazine—August 31, 1987

your clients are coming to visit your resort, if you are in the vacation ownership industry. Make the effort to call and take them for drinks or dinner. Every time you keep in touch with your clients provides one less opportunity for your competition to steal them. This advice applies to any sales professional in any industry.

More and more companies are also realizing the importance of communicating with their clients and/or owners. They provide web sites with on-line, interactive customer help, Facebook and Twitter accounts, informational packages and 800 numbers for questions and assistance. Keeping their clients satisfied has become a primary concern. Companies are slowing learning that without good customer service they, and their salespeople, will neither be paid on the sales nor will it change the negative impression of their industry especially with the escalation of marketing and sales cost. It is paramount that your customers and/or clients follow through with the financial commitments realizing that without good customer service this may not happen. Customer satisfaction leads to a more favorable industry impression.

Remember, customer satisfaction equals your commission. Congratulations you have made the sale <u>and</u> a friend in the process.

No sales book would be complete without talking out goal setting so the next chapter will look at how establishing goals can help you expand your horizons to become successful.

18

Goals = Attitude + Motivation

We have all heard the saying, "Mind over matter." Well, it is true. If your attitude is strong then your mind can overcome matter any day because what you think is what you believe and what you believe dictates your actions, aspirations and goals. This chapter will show you how your attitudes fuel motivation that stimulates desire into action which makes goals attainable.

Yes, things do happen in sales that can hinder you, but that is why you are so well paid. If you give up every time an obstacle or tough prospect is put in front of you, consider getting out of sales. However, if you want to write sales, consistently and become a master closer, you have to have some form of motivation or goal.

Overall sales environments are fairly consistent but the difference between an exceptional closer and the average or mediocre salesperson is attitude. Successful salespeople do things a little bit better or with a little more motivation than the others and it adds up to an enormous difference in the long run. The main reason that most salespeople do not reach their goals is that the dominant or self-motivating attitude has been lost. This then creates the action to sell. In chapter 12 we talked about how you need energy and enthusiasm to maintain the right attitude. Well, effort and persistence also work in direct proportion to the amount of self-motivation you possess.

I remember, when I as in school we were graded in two ways, Results and Effort. When my father read my school report and saw a "D" in History under Result, but an "A" for Effort, he would congratulate me. Conversely, if he saw a "B" Result in Mathematics and a "D" for Effort, he would box my ears. There are times when Effort is more important than Results.

WHAT MOTIVATES YOU?

The only way to succeed in life is if you are motivated or stimulated by something. You must have a motivational goal. Later in this chapter we will cover the importance of defining and setting goals, but here we will examine what motivates you.

Self-motivation is probably the most important trait to becoming a 35%+ salesperson. You can read everything in the world about how to <u>be</u> a better salesperson, including this book, but unless you are truly <u>motivated</u> to be a better salesperson, you will never become a master closer. Self-motivation is having a reason to take a specific action to successfully obtain what you ardently desire.

Traditionally there are five main areas of motivation—Wealth; Status; Personal and Professional Accomplishment; Health and Family.

1. Money is the primary goal because it has an impact of everything we do, or hope to do.
2. Status can be materialistic or personal.
3. Personal and professional accomplishment involves being responsible for something specific and important.
4. Being motivated by health tends to come later in life after we have experienced some problems however it can be a motivation to avoid problems later in life. Possibly it is just to feel better about yourself.
5. Family motivation consists of anything and everything to do with you and your family as an entity. Even though you may not be able to set individual member goals, you can set family goals (i.e., vacations, new house, etc.)

So what motivates you? Which of the following areas motivates you to succeed in life? As you read through each one ask yourself the following questions to help you better understand what motivates you? (The blank is for you to insert the appropriate motivation.)

1. Why do I want to be or have?
2. How much do I need to satisfy me?

3.   How much (or how hard) will I have to work to achieve ?
4.   Exactly (specifically) what do I have to do to achieve ?
5.   What are my realistic expectations of achieving ?

Now, go through the following fourteen motivational areas and list the order of priority in your life. Put them into your order of preference, from (1) being the highest to (14) the lowest

☐   ACCOMPLISHMENT: Achieving something important in your life and the need to be successful in all the significant areas and activities of my life. How good do I want to be?

☐   ACKNOWLEDGMENT: Being recognized as successful and gain recognition for all my accomplishments, both personal and professional.

☐   DEVELOPMENT: To have opportunities for personal growth and have the ability to gain more knowledge. What title do I need to be able to identify myself (owner, manager, president)?

☐   EQUILIBRIUM: Gain and sustain a balance between my personal and professional lives.

☐   FULFILLMENT: To experience personal satisfaction and enjoyment from all the activities in which I participate. Do I want to make a significant contribution to society in some manner?

☐   INDEPENDENCE: Freedom both in my personal life and on the job. Have the time to spend with family and friends.

☐   INFLUENCE / POWER: Obtain a position of authority. Be a decision maker over activities of other people and resources.

☐   INTEGRITY: Treat all those I meet without prejudice and in an honest, straightforward, just and fair manner in all aspects of my life. How do I wish to be perceived by those around me?

☐   POSSESSIONS: Do I want a big house? What type of car do I want to drive? What type, and how many "toys" do I want?

☐   RELATIONSHIPS: Have the ability and opportunities to fraternize with corporate leaders, politicians, celebrities, or working with the underprivileged.

☐   RESPECT: I would like to be treated without prejudice and in an honest, straightforward, just and fair manner in all aspects of my life.

☐ SECURITY: Feeling safe, secure and stable in both my personal and professional lives. Experience as few changes and anxieties in my life as possible.

☐ WEALTH: Financial independence. How much money is enough to make me financially independent?

☐ WISDOM: Have common sense, clear judgment and insight when dealing with all aspects of my life.

Now, what priority do these areas take in your motivation? Read through each again carefully and see if they really are in the correct order. In doing this you will discover exactly what areas motivate you the most, or the least, so **you** can prioritize them and make any changes you think you need to make.

Everyone has something that motivates them whether it is wealth, status, personal and professional accomplishment, health or family. The list of motivations is as long as there are people striving to reach their goals. Successful people, including salespeople do not work hard just to make money they work to make money to achieve the goals that they have set for themselves.

DEFINING YOUR GOALS

Goals are dreams with a plan. A goal is something that you really want and it motivates you to perform. Goals must be appropriate to your environment and especially realistic to your sales environment. Goals are also bound by time. Those that are not achieved are replaced by others until we are satisfied we have attained our ultimate goal(s). Goals are designed to motivate you into action. Without a purpose or driving force you would have no reason to get out of bed each morning and face each new day's opportunities and challenges. Make your first goal going to work and to having your manager or colleagues not think badly of you that day. Yes, showing up for work can be goal for some individuals.

Following are six musts for defining your goals:

1. <u>Clearly define your goal(s)</u>. If your goal(s) are confusing and you are not exactly sure what they are, then you do not have a goal. They may be wishes and hopes possibly, but not goals. Goals are very specific.

2. <u>Goals must be believable and realistically achieved</u>. It does not matter that no one else believes in your goal, as long as YOU believe in them. You must also believe that you can realistically achieve them.

3. <u>Goals must be fervently desired</u>. This means that you want something so passionately that it consumes your motivation until you reach it. Goals must also excite and challenge you.

4. <u>Goals must not conflict with each other.</u> Conflicting goals are not achieved, just left behind in frustration.

5. <u>Goals must be visual</u>. If you can see yourself in possession of your goal you are halfway to achieving it. To better visualize your goals here are some suggestions especially if your goal is tangible and material in nature (i.e., car, cruise, house, boat etc.) If your goal is to retire early, use visuals of where you plan to retire, or with whom.

    (a) Cut out pictures and place them everywhere around you so that you may see your goal at all times. Put them on the refrigerator door, bathroom mirror, kitchen cupboards, bedside table, on the backside of the front door or in your car.
    (b) Go to car showrooms, travel agencies, dealerships, marinas, department stores and look at it. Go wherever they sell your goal and mentally buy it. Touch it, feel it, take it for a test drive, ride it, take pictures of it, become used to being around it as often as you can.

6. <u>Goals must be put in writing</u>. By putting your goal(s) down on paper you are making a commitment to achieving it. Goals are not goals if they are not written down. Why is it important to write out your goals?

(a) Writing down your goals to generate excitement, enthusiasm and commitment.

(b) Written goals make it easier for you to stick to them.

(c) Seeing them written down provides a visual stimulus.

(d) Written goals give you a reason to get out of bed every day.

(e) Written goals can be seen by others which will help push you to achieve them.

(f) Written goals also help you get organized.

By defining your goals you are making a conscious effort to work hard to reach them. The next step in the process is to genuinely set goals using the above as guidelines.

SETTING YOUR GOALS

Setting your goals always begins with desire and attitude. You have to believe in the ultimate success and attainment of your goal(s). It is your attitude and desire that work together when you decide to set goals for yourself. One without the other only creates wishes and dreams. Remember, goals are dreams <u>with</u> a plan.

To set your plan in motion you must do all the following seven things:

1. <u>Start with small, reachable goals</u>. Do not set a goal of buying a car unless you realistically know that you will achieve it. Start with something like a new Smartphone or iPad, piece of clothing or dinner in a fancy restaurant. Work up to the big goals. Judge the quality of your goals.

2. <u>Be specific</u>. Don't just set a car as a goal. Make is a cherry red, convertible, high performance roadster. If you are not specific in your goals they become vague, easily changed and not worth pursuing.

3. <u>Set realistic targets and date(s)</u>. This is where the short-term, long-term goal idea diverges. Goals should be something that you can reach realistically. Long-term goals are more valuable providing you can achieve them without giving up in the process.

4. <u>Goals must be put down on paper</u>. Yes, we did cover this under defining your goals, but after you have specifically decided a goal and set a date, write it down as a firm commitment to yourself.
5. <u>Prioritize your goals</u>. Determine which goals you can achieve first, second, third, etc. Trying to achieve them all at the same time will create frustration and you will lose your focus.
6. <u>Visualize your goals</u>. Visualize yourself with, or at, your goal. Savor and enjoy the goal. Look at where you are now and what steps, and effort, you will need to obtain them.
7. <u>Commit to your goal(s)</u>. It still is a dream or a wish if you cannot commit to a goal.

Once you have set your goals you need to pursue whatever means are necessary to maintain and attain them.

MAINTAINING YOUR GOALS

Successful salespeople know how to maintain and stay focused on their goal(s). Following are guidelines to help you maintain and stay focused on yours.

1. Review your goals both mentally and visually at least once a day.
2. Train yourself to visualize the attainment of your goal.
3. Direct and involve all areas of your life in the attainment of your goal.
4. Adjust your goal(s) if it becomes unrealistic or unattainable by your target date.
5. Believe that you will achieve your goal by your target date.
6. Keep a positive mental attitude and pursue your goal(s) with confidence.
7. Tell others you care for about your goals so that they can help you achieve them.

ATTAINING YOUR GOALS

When you reach your goal, immediately go out and present it to yourself. Remember, a deal is a deal and you earned it. If you do not 'pay' yourself quickly then all the hard work that you have done to attain your goal was wasted and will subsequently leave you with no energy to pursue another. Always reward yourself every time you attain a goal. Attaining a goal is easy the hard part comes in setting them.

I have never seen a master closer as excited as when they get a signed worksheet and credit card (their goal) as when the sale liquidates. Congratulate yourself immediately on making the sale, not when you are paid. The payment is your reward for reaching your goal.

SHORT AND LONG TERM GOALS

I have not covered short or long term goals in any detail because what is short term goal to one person is long term one to another and vice versa. Technically short-term goals are goals to be achieved in less than ninety days. Long term goals are anything over that. By setting short-term goals you will have a more positive attitude and exert more energy and enthusiasm to achieve them. Setting short-term goals helps you see results more quickly.

Make long-term goals realistic and attainable. Update your long-term goals as you reach your shorter-term ones. To help you better define a long-term goal imagine what you will be doing, owning or accomplishing in the future. Long-term goals are doable however they will be achieved much faster when done as a series of short-term goals.

So now you understand how **Goals = Attitude + Motivation**. Attitude is the primary factor behind motivation and motivation is the primary factor behind attaining your goals.

Share your goal(s) with another person and your motivation becomes even stronger. Knowing that someone is supporting you and expecting you to achieve your goals compels you to take the needed action. It is a proven fact that when you are motivated by either something or someone you will normally break down barriers you would have otherwise not considered. This is why your friends, family or colleagues motivate you throughout your life, either positively or negatively, to achieve some kind of greatness. Find someone, or something, that motivates you each day. The only way to reach your goal is by totally committing yourself to the process. Remember, if you do not have a goal someone else will have one for you.

To achieve success in sales, or anything else in your life, you must have self-motivation. No one taught me to sell I learned it from the ground up, the hard way. I went out of my way to observe and talk to top salespeople and ask them their secrets. I found out what I needed to know and made it better. I was motivated to become successful because that was my dominant goal.

<u>Motivation is a state of mind, an attitude</u>. There must be some aspiration, aim, dream or goal that arouses, drives, excites, stimulates, stirs and inspires you to be motivated enough to reach it. Push yourself for every sale because attitude and motivation know no bounds. If you are not positively convinced that you can attain your goal(s) you will never get there. It is all in your attitude.

GOALS come from MOTIVATION stimulated by DESIRE fueled by ATTITUDE

19

Sales Pointers, Tips and Reminders

The following information comes from years of experience as a salesperson, later as a manager, then a Sales Director, years of doing training sessions as well as the experiences of many other highly successful salespeople. I discovered years ago that most salespeople would rather read through a quick list of Tips, Do's and Don'ts rather than wade through pages of explanation. As a result these last two chapters consists of a variety of pointers, tips and reminders that could help you in your sales career.

TIPS FOR SUCCESSFUL SALES

1. There is no 'right way' to talk to prospects. Everyone is different. Every problem is different therefore every conversation is different.
2. Prospects do not talk to 'the company' they talk to YOU. You create credibility, dependability and trust first.
3. Create an alliance so that you are speaking on behalf of YOUR prospect to the company. This statement reinforces number 2 above. When your prospect talks to you, you then use that rapport and bond to talk to the company for them.
4. Do not just listen to your prospect learn from them.
5. Prospects never think of themselves as customers they think of themselves as people who need help. Help them.
6. Do not just solve your prospect's problem create the opportunity for a sale.
7. It is not enough to just take care of your prospects you have to care about them.
8. Concentrate single-mindedly on your prospect. Do not be distracted by something that has no sales potential.
9. Let your prospect be the hero. Make them feel important.

10. Learn to compromise. Conversations that are aimed at achieving results create long lasting relationships.
11. There is only one judge of great service and it is your prospect.
12. Great service starts with a great attitude. It is your attitude that makes, or breaks, the sale.

If you are having an attitude problem, hold a mirror up and look at it. That is your problem. Understand it, appreciate it and take an action to correct it. If you cannot get up each day go into work and try, then forget being successful. Come to think of it, forget everything you ever learned about sales and just go out with a great attitude and the sales will come.

It becomes a pointless waste of energy if you keep constantly saying that you are going to improve or manage your attitude and never do. It will become habitual and second nature once you decide to commit to improving or managing your attitude. It will finally reach a point where you have done it and did not even realize it.

Attitude, this whole business is attitude. The common, and most important, element of all successful people is a great positive mental attitude. The other twenty-five are listed below.

Qualities Found in Successful Salespeople

1. They have confidence and competence in both personal and sales situations. They do not have to prove themselves to others.
2. They have integrity and honesty with themselves and others.
3. They are more open about themselves which generates a sense of trust towards their prospects.
4. They can accept complete responsibility for themselves and their life. They are resilient and bounce back quickly from setbacks.
5. They are decisive, eternally optimistic, persistent and self-disciplined.
6. Their confidence is in never to consider failure an alternative.
7. They dedicate themselves to continual personal and professional development.

8. They know everything about their product and when to effectively show it.
9. They dedicate themselves to attaining long-term relationships with their prospects.
10. They associate with those who can assist in their success.
11. They have a reputation for dependability and reliability.
12. They remain secure during stressful or challenging situations.
13. They use time management to achieve the greatest results for time spent.
14. They can quickly establish rapport, trust and credibility with all personality types.
15. They can identify and understand people's needs and desires. Understanding the depth of the prospects needs is critical.
16. They have excellent non-verbal communication skills. They use their physiology and body language to persuade their prospects. Additionally, they pay specific attention to their prospects.
17. They talk less and listen more effectively. Successful sales people listen 80% and talk 20% of the time. High pressure sales people talk 80% and only listen 20%.
18. They can ask first, second and third level questions effectively and skillfully.
19. They show prospect's respect, sincerity, concern, support and reinforcement.
20. They show prospect's value in their product through benefits. They do not 'tell and sell.'
21. They encourage prospects to talk about themselves and participate in the sales presentation.
22. They can put their ego aside to isolate their prospects' concerns or problems that are preventing them from completing the sale.
23. They have earned the right to confidently ask for the order after all concerns and objections have been addressed.
24. They have learned not to take rejection personally as they realize it is a natural part of the human decision making process.
25. All successful salespeople have a goal, vision or dream.

Now let's cover some basic sales Do's and Don'ts:

Do's

1. Listen and learn from your prospect.
2. Listen more than you talk. Remember, two ears and one mouth!
3. Every prospect is a judgment call, the more you know about them the better your judgment will be.
4. Ask questions. It is the only way you will really learn about your prospects.
5. Pay attention to the way your prospect answers your questions both verbally and physiologically.
6. Use their life information to close the sale.
7. Project yourself into the perspective of a teacher or parent.
8. Assume the role as problem solver or consultant.
9. Learn to anticipate problems, objections and buying signals.
10. Develop tolerance, patience and understanding for your prospect.
11. Simplify the decision making process for your prospect.
12. Focus on emotion rather than logic. Battles are won with emotion, not logic.
13. Constantly add value to your prospects perceived benefit of your product.
14. Always be closing your sale.
15. Always wait for your prospect to answer your questions. Do not be afraid of the silence.
16. Welcome your prospect's response to a question, objection or asking for the order.
17. Always be summarizing, highlighting and stimulating the benefits that your prospect would use.
18. Always keep your presentation simple, short and sincere. Too much information will confuse them.
19. Your prospect will ultimately buy from you if treated with respect, sincerity and genuine appreciation.
20. Remember that there are three parts to every sale: Desire, Decision and Money, get the decision first.
21. Close your prospect with confidence.
22. Ask for the sale directly.

23. Always reaffirm their choice or decision to buy. Make them feel comfortable.
24. Always work from Strength.
25. Always be learning and upgrading your skills.
26. Always be prepared to face a prospect in your attitude, appearance and physiology.
27. Always be motivated towards a goal.
28. Have the right sales attitude.
29. Always be enthusiastic, animated, fun and energetic.
30. Always put yourself in the prospect's shoes.
31. Put the needs of your prospect first. Stop selling your product or service if your company cannot provide what your prospect needs. Know the limitations of what you are selling.
32. Ensure that your prospect leaves you with a better impression of you, your company and your industry than when they came in if you cannot make the sale.
33. Always be glad to have a prospect as it is your only opportunity to make a sale.

Don'ts (refer to the 7 Deadly Sins)

1. Never fight or argue with your prospect. You will never win.
2. Never tell your prospect that they are wrong.
3. Talk more than you listen.
4. Never beg a prospect to buy.
5. Never waste time—either yours or your prospects.
6. Never give concessions too early.
7. Never respond quickly to a question or objection. Take the time to think before responding.
8. Never let your ego interfere with the sales process.
9. Never express your opinions to a prospect on personal subject (politics, religion, family, etc.) because you will become involved in a confrontation that leads to nowhere.
10. Never promise anything to close the sale. You will be found out and ultimately lose the sale.
11. You should never bad mouth your competition. Create more value in your product than theirs.
12. Never pre-judge a prospect.

13. Never come across to your prospect as fast talking, glib or insincere.
14. Never make your presentation boring.
15. Never be nervous or afraid to ask questions or the order.
16. Never be vague or obtuse when providing information. Be concise in your words.
17. Never cut your prospect off when they are answering questions or giving objections.
18. Never waste the opportunity to practice on a prospect if you think you will not make the sale.
19. Never let your attitude affect your ability to make a sale.
20. Last, and certainly not the least—Never be afraid to ask for the order.

As we have spoken about so many times in this book—it is all about you, what you do with your prospect and what you don't do with your prospect but what you must accept is that it is all 100% you. What you do or don't do is all about you!!

20

Troubleshooting your Sales Presentation

We have now covered how you can determine if you are in a slump and how to overcome it. We looked at finding your strengths and weaknesses through honest self-evaluation as well as what you should do and shouldn't do. As my last gift to you we will examine some areas that may be causing you problems and how to fix or solve them.

The best way to describe this section is by relating it to the instruction manual you received with your new flat screen plasma TV, DVR or Blue Ray, Stereo, Stove, Refrigerator, computer and, yes, even your smart phone. You know that section at the back of the manual known as *Troubleshooting* or *Tips If Something Isn't Working* or *Quick Fixes*. This section has many names, but all have the same purpose; *If your TV does not come on when you push the ON button; Why? Make sure it is plugged in*to electrical outlet. This may sound ridiculous and very simple, but it is such a common a problem that is has to be included in the troubleshooting section.

It always is the simple things that keep the bigger things from working and this is also true of the sales business. You can be selling up a storm then, from out of nowhere, a tidal wave hits you and you find yourself off floating in a sea of uncertainty and frustration. Never fear, this chapter will give you some quick fixes that will get your feet back on solid ground again.

To simplify this process I have outlined some of the more common problems in the same easy to read format as your TV instruction manual.

The Manual

GREETING & WARM UP STALLED   (Can't Open Box)

- Approach prospect in professional manner, not too aggressive, yet not passive.
- Walk with head up, make eye contact and extend hand for handshake.
- Acknowledge all people in party, engage in light conversational banter.
- Don't interrogate them.
- Aim is to reduce prospects tension, nervousness and make them feel comfortable.
- Use a neutralizing statement to diffuse the tension and bring the concerns of your prospect to a head.

PROSPECT DISPLAYS RUDE, AGGRESSIVE BEHAVIOR   (Manual not in English)

- Acknowledge how prospect feels, sympathize with them and let them expel their anger.
- Without aggravating the situation as if _you_ have offended them in some way.
- Do not start your sales pitch. Let them know it is obvious by their attitude that they will not be buying anything today. Tell them, "So let me just do my job and I will get you out of here as quick as I can, okay?"
- Be polite and cordial. Do not confront the temporary act of aggression. When you feel it depleting, say to them, "Do you feel a little better now," and then shake hands.

INTENT STATEMENT ISN'T EFFECTIVE   (No Picture)

- Repeat the agenda in a different context.
- Ask what they thought was going to happen to them 'today.'
- Say to them that, "Since they are there anyway and whether they have any interest you can take advantage of my knowledge of town, resort, restaurants, etc., fair enough?"

- Tell them that you are explaining the 'tour' so that there is no confusion later on during the presentation.

BREAK THE PACT ISN'T WORKING   (No Power)

- Need to form a relationship before you earn the right for advancing.
- Decisions scare them so change your terminology to CHOICE or alternative way of vacationing.
- A No is cool—but a Yes is Cooooller and you can handle both so get them to relax.
- Take it back and say, "Well, I will take that as a no and that is fair enough, thank you."

PROSPECT WILL NOT OPEN UP   (No Sound, Speakers don't work)

- Find their hot conversational button by doing more discovery or FORM.
- Ask them if they would like to change consultants or salesperson.
- Stop talking and fill in a survey sheet or something else. Silence is your best tool.
- By using a statement of neutrality ask them if you have offended them in some way.
- Think about the character you are portraying and change it to bond with their character more effectively. (It is always you)

PROSPECT NOT PARTICIPATING or LISTENING   (Wrong Channel)

- Tell a third party story about a difficult prospect
- Quit selling features.
- Quit being logical.
- Start stimulating emotional desires by showing benefits.
- You are boring them by talking too much.
- Let them talk.
- Give them something to do. Fill in survey sheet, play with a calculator, ask to see photos.
- Go back to your life raft and do more discovery or FORM."

- "Get 'em real, get a deal"—remember most prospects come for the freebie.

PROSPECT CANNOT SEE ANY VALUE (Cable plugged into wrong outlet)

- Showing too many features and not showing any benefits to them. (Find more dominant buying emotions—do more FORM)
- Pitch more credible or is too confusing.
- You are talking too much and not listening to them.
- You are not using enough trial closing after each value statement. (Get a commitment and tie it down)
- Fear of commitment or hidden objection. (e.g., money, spouse, or need for approval)

UNABLE TO BOX MONEY (Remote Doesn't Work)

- Fear of embarrassment. (Affordability problem)
- Fear of commitment and decision. (Use more trial closes)
- Lack of desire and perceived value. (Show more benefits, build more value)
- Prospect is not sure other members of their party are in the same buying state of mind and are reluctant to give information without their reassurance.
- Money question was posed in to light-hearted a fashion making it easy for them to avoid a money commitment.

NO COMMITMENT (Programming Error)

- Credibility problem (Build more trust using testimonials and third party stories)
- Use a Summary or Ben Franklin close.
- No desire or value (Go back to hot buttons and re-evaluate them and use more benefits, examples and third party stories).
- Prospects have information overload or you have gone past the buying curve (Simplify your pitch and ask more little yes questions)

PROSPECT OBVIOUSLY LYING OR EXAGGERATING   (No Warranty)

- Your credibility is lacking. (They fear you so they will defend themselves)
- Your personality does not stimulate a comfortable conversation or environment.
- Prospect is embarrassed of their social, intellectual or financial position.
- Lack of respect for you. (You need to take more control up front)
- Asking a personal question before you have earned the right.
- Prospect came to the presentation with a strong pact, so you must get them real to get a deal.

THINK ABOUT IT   (No Return Policy)

- People will make decisions, step up and buy things that they are emotionally attracted to, rather than for logical reasons.
- People make actions when they are stimulated emotionally, not logically.
- No desire, No value, No trust (Take the pressure off and relax them and go back to building desire, value and trust)
- You have confused them with too much information (Listen more to their needs and desires and focus your pitch on your prospect, not on your product)
- Agree with them and ask them when they think they will make the choice not really a decision. That way you will get a yes for adopting your product and now you will need to find an alternative stimulus for creating urgency for today.
- Remember think about it is the polite way for them to say no.

PROSPECT CARE   ("Appliance" Care Section)

To ensure that you never have a problem with your prospect make sure to follow these guidelines for prospect care.

- To avoid possible shock hazard be a professional in front of your prospect.

- To maintain a positive attitude with prospect, listen intently and keep smiling.
- Occasionally let prospect vent hostilities to air out bad attitudes and atmosphere and relief pressure.
- When speaking with prospect, take care not to scratch or damage the surface with anything that may cause abrasion. Use a soft, friendly approach maintaining ego stroking of prospect during presentation.
- Never use words that will permanently mar the prospect's attitude towards you.
- Prospect is equipped with protective circuitry that shuts off mind in case of moderate power surges by salesperson. Prospect can be turned back on by gently pressing the Hot Button switch once or twice. This feature is NOT designed to prevent damage due to high pressure surges and is not covered by any warranty.

LEARNING TO HANDLE TRANSITIONS

Transitions are those periods where you go from being the pleasant congenial light hearted "friend" to the salesperson. Some of the ways of handling these transitions we have covered earlier in the book, however if you are in a slump you need to be reminded on how to handle them. Transitions occur in following three areas:

1. During the intent statement:

    Many salespeople do not do an agenda because they believe it is not important to the sales process. To best illustrate this think about the following example;

    If your friend, and manager, said to you, "why don't you come round to my house tonight, I have something I want to show you," what would you do? Most likely your imagination goes wild. You think is he going to cook me dinner, show me a movie or show me his photo albums. Maybe are we going to go out to a party or going to get drunk; worse yet he is going to fire me. The 'what did I do wrong' syndrome starts to take hold and you begin to justify reasons to protect yourself against the negative. You start going all weird just as your prospect does to you.

However if you do an Intent Statement, and you do it clearly, when you finish that you can move along to the next step in the sales process. Doing it without your prospect's fearing what is going to happen next. For example, if that friend said to you, "come round my house tonight for a quick drink and then we will go a show," you will become excited at the prospect, rather than fear it. Clearly explain your intentions.

2. <u>From a point of initial FORM to the sales room or environment where you close deals</u>:

When you are walking your prospects to the sales environment you should remind them of the agenda. This will ensure that you move smoothly from being their "new friend" to their being aware that they are now going to a sales room. First, make sure that you have eliminated the fear of the unknown. Prepare them as you are walking. Have fun with them. Point out something of interest—plants, trees, flowers, waterfalls, etc.—whatever will take their mind off what is waiting for them. Talk about something that is important to them because trust me, they know what is going to happen in the sales room.

You should walk with them if space allows. If there is insufficient space to walk abreast, walk slightly ahead (half a step) but turned sideways to face them. If you are a man, walk next to the man and vice versa. Make sure that you do not walk next to the woman if you are a man as it may make her husband nervous, and vice versa.

When you enter the salesroom, do not let them regain the fear of their environment. Point out something that may be of interest to them—stuffed marlin on wall, oversized pictures of your resort, the lake outside, etc. Let them take in the whole atmosphere without allowing it to bombard them when they walk into the salesroom.

3. <u>Starting the "Sales Presentation"</u>:

This transition reflects all the energy that you created during the discovery process, and carrying it forward into your sales 'presentation.' You can start off this process by making a comment similar to "okay, now comes the boring bit I mentioned earlier." This is another reminder of your Agenda. If this statement is said professionally, with humor you can keep them in their comfort zone as you start into your sales presentation.

If, after a couple of minutes into your presentation, you see that you are losing their attention you can humorously remind them, "You promised me that you would not look bored!" They will usually offer up a minor objection or concern at this point that will help you in deciding which direction to take your presentation.

If you must write something on paper, look up at them every time you put down your sentence or key phrase or word. Sit to their left side if you are left handed, so that when you are writing they can see what you are writing. People like to see what other people are writing it creates curiosity. If you sit on the right side, your arm is in their way and they then try to guess what you are writing. Prospects do not want to guess and will then start to look away and focus on something else. Again another silly little thing, but you would be surprised how easy it is to lose someone's attention. You have to maintain eye contact as often as possible.

All three of these points are called transition stages. Every sales process must go through them. By learning how to handle transitions smoothly you will have no trouble writing a sale.

TECHNIQUES FOR OVERCOMING OBJECTIONS

Each of the previous sections we thoroughly examined objections. We covered how to recognize, stimulate, create and deal with them. However, should you find yourself still having trouble with a specific objection(s) try doing the one last exercise on the next page as often as you may need to make you become an exceptional salesperson.

Remember, when trying to overcome objections you should have several alternatives in your repertoire that can be used on the various personality types you will meet. You always have to be learning. You have to be constantly criticizing yourself, but in a way that stimulates you—wait, that is your manager's job. You may believe that they are there to criticize you, tweak you or abuse you, but they are there to motive, stimulate and initiate you into writing a sale because if you become an exceptional salesperson, they benefit as well!

Sincerity, passion, enthusiasm, confidence all are necessary ingredients in attitude. If you are having trouble with making a sale I will guarantee it is your attitude from the beginning. It is never the back end. Remember, anybody can talk to anybody. Anyone can have fun. Anyone can copy someone's presentation, but it's your attitude that creates curiosity and sincere interest in their taking better vacations or adopting your product or service. Remember always go back to basics if you are having trouble.

Common Objection	ECHO	Feel, Felt, Found	Boomerang	3rd Party Story	Lowest Common Denominator	Redirect Client Focus
Can't Afford It						
Buying a Home or Kids off to College						
Need to talk to Someone						
Do not think would use product or service						
One says Yes, the Other says No						

Just Married or Divorced						
Need to Shop Around						
Product or Service not a Priority						
Do not believe You or in your Product (Credibility)						
Don't Make Decision on Spur of Moment— need to THINK ABOUT IT						

The art of closing is nothing more than enabling your prospect to ultimately close themselves by your using the steps of the buying curve and the other sales techniques I have shared throughout this book.

Thank you for taking the time to "listen" and **GOOD LUCK** in your sales career.

About the Author

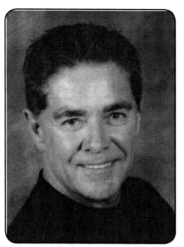

David Fitzgerald is recognized thought the world as the "Real Deal" when it comes to selling Timeshare and Vacation Ownership. He's has grown up (28 years) in an industry that has evolved from a simple fixed week high pressure sales situation in little shady resorts, to its current complicated, multi-faceted product of today, led by stellar group of brand name companies. David started in Europe, dabbled in the US and Caribbean markets and now resides in Mexico and his personal statistics are a 54% net close with a personal volume of over US$65,000,000 and an efficiency of US$8,500. These numbers are unmatched in the timeshare industry, most of which were obtained through the relentless pursuit of the desire to win.

In addition to helping establish on-line sales training sites, he has hired, trained and mentored thousands of sales people over his 28 year career, many of whom are top producers in the industry or have become Project Directors, Sales Directors, Sales Managers and some now even own their own resorts. As a Sales Director, General Manager, Sales Manager, TO and as a salesperson, he has produced close to one billion dollars in sales, truly one of the legends in sales rooms. David continues to reside in Puerto Vallarta, Mexico with his family.

Karen Holden also resides in Puerto Vallarta Mexico, having moved there almost 20 years ago after a successful business career specializing in management, sales, finance and corporate restructuring. She continues to use those business and management skills in working with a number of resort and timeshare properties in Mexico. In 2006 she wrote and published the book Simplifying Timeshare, which was written to help timeshare owners in understanding and learning how to use their timeshare properties successfully. The updated version of her book will be released in 2014.

Lightning Source UK Ltd.
Milton Keynes UK
UKOW05f0706250214

227081UK00001B/85/P